G M

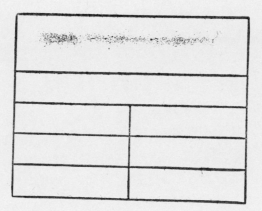

Laura Elliot, writing under her own name June Considine, has written extensively for children and adults.

She has worked as a journalist and magazine editor, and has written scripts for children's television/radio.

She lives in the coastal village of Malahide, in Dublin, Ireland.

The Prodigal Sister is her first novel under the pen name, Laura Elliot.

THE PRODIGAL SISTER

Scared and pregnant, fifteen-year-old Cathy Lambert ran away from her Dublin home. Settled in New Zealand with her new son Conor, she believed the secret she carried would never be revealed . . . When Rebecca Lambert's parents died she took responsibility for her younger sisters. Now, she is still haunted by fears she hoped she'd conquered. And mother of three Julie Chambers is determined to recapture the dreams of her youth. Meanwhile Lauren Moran embarks on a love affair that threatens to destabilise her fragile world . . . Anxious to make peace with her three sisters, Cathy invites them to her wedding. And their journey together through New Zealand, towards their reunion, forces them to confront the past as the secret shared histories of the Lambert sisters are revealed.

LAURA ELLIOT

THE PRODIGAL SISTER

Complete and Unabridged

CHARNWOOD
Leicester

First published in Great Britain in 2009 by
Avon, a division of
HarperCollins*Publishers*, London

First Charnwood Edition
published 2010
by arrangement with
HarperCollins*Publishers*, London

June Considine asserts the moral right to be identified
as the author of this work

This novel is entirely a work of fiction.
The names, characters and incidents portrayed in it
are the work of the author's imagination.
Any resemblance to actual persons, living or dead,
events or localities is entirely coincidental.

British Library CIP Data

Elliot, Laura.
    The prodigal sister.
    1. Sisters- -Fiction
    2. Family reunions- -Fiction
    3. New Zealand- -Fiction.
    4. Large type books.
    I. Title
    823.9'2–dc22

    ISBN 978–1–44480–464–5

Published by
F. A. Thorpe (Publishing)
Anstey, Leicestershire

Set by Words & Graphics Ltd.
Anstey, Leicestershire
Printed and bound in Great Britain by
T. J. International Ltd., Padstow, Cornwall

This book is printed on acid-free paper

In loving memory of my close friend,
Dympna Joyce-O'Byrne.
Her zest for life and her tremendous
courage will always be remembered.

Acknowledgements

I'd like to extend my thanks to the many people who helped me with support and information when I was writing *The Prodigal Sister*.

To my husband, Sean, who accompanied me in a camper van throughout the South Island of New Zealand, where the idea for *The Prodigal Sister* gathered life on numerous scraps of paper.

To my family, Tony, Ciara and Michelle, and my son-in-law, Roddy Flynn. They have given me love, encouragement and support throughout my writing career.

Special thanks to Fran Power for constantly reassuring me that a computer is not a black hole and lost manuscripts are capable of recovery.

To Louise Casey for her willing help and assistance when it is necessary.

To Moya O'Connor whose expert teaching skills guided Cathy through her earlier 'Letters to Nirvana'.

To Barry Considine and Patricia Millis who willingly checked my South Island locations to make sure I wasn't going off course.

To my agent, Faith O'Grady, for her constant support.

To Dr Bill Scoggins. His willingness, at short notice, to manipulate the most stubborn backache and stiff shoulders has kept me pain-free during the most concentrated stages of writing.

Special thanks to the team from Avon/ HarperCollins. To Maxine Hitchcock for her sensitive editing, and to Sammia Rafique, Keshini Naidoo and Yvonne Holland. Their warmth and friendliness made the editing process a pleasure.

I'd like to thank Mary Lee from Cardrona, who broke the sad news to me that the bras on the bra fence, which feature in *The Prodigal Sister*, have been removed. But, as writing is about stretching the imagination, I've used poetic licence and left them in place for the Lambert sisters to enjoy.

I'd like to acknowledge my close extended family who are so important to me. A special acknowledgement to two small ones, my grandchildren, Romy and Ava, who never fail to enchant and delight me.

Thanks also to my friends — those who write and are ready with advice when the Muse goes AWOL — and those with wider horizons, who order me to press Log Off and meet them for a coffee. Writing can become a solitary occupation. The value of such friendships prevents it becoming a lonely one.

Finally, I'd like to remember a dear friend, Scott Rogerson. He lived his life to the full and left us his many songs, and a store of fun-filled memories.

PROLOGUE

21 Heron Cove
Broadmeadow
Dublin
Ireland
Urope
The World
15 April 1985

Dear Mammy,
   This is Cathy. Mrs Mulvaney said to rite you a
letter. Is it stupit to rite to dead people? Mrs Mulvaney said it will stop me being sad. When I sleep
anjels will come and read my letter. Is that true?
Are you a anjel with wings? Is Daddy a anjel to? I
hope you are in heven not hell. I saw a picture
of hell. It is worse than a vulkayno. Is heven far
away? Mrs Mulvaney said it is not. Mr Mulvaney
flys in the window at night to see her when she is
in bed. I dont know what to rite. She said rite the
cat sat on the mat the cat sat on the mat and the
words will come good. Nero dose not chase cats
now. He is fat and old and sleeps with Becks and
puts hairs all over the dubay. It is 3 months since
you and Daddy are dead. Our house is sad like
rain that wont go away. I like Kevins house best.
We play Chuki Egg on his XZ Spectum and Mrs
Mulvaney make us fish fingers and chips. Lauren
is home from hospotal. The doctor cut the plaster
off her legs. All her brooses are gone. She looks

3

nice again. She dont talk to me or Becks or Julie She only talks when shes sleeping and wakes me up. The doctor gave her pills to make her smile but she just stare stare stare at the wall and dont make a face even when Becks komes the notts in her hair. Gramps says Becks is our Mummy and Daddy now. If we are bold the woman with the blak case will take us away. She come lots to our house and rites things down. 2 can play that game Becks said and she has a black book now. She rites when the woman rites and they stare stare stare at each other but not like Lauren. Lauren is just the same as a zombi in a film.

We went to the grave today. Becks gave us seeds to plant. She said stop crying stop crying you are doing my head in. I see you and Daddy all the time. Then I look again and I see red dots that's all.

XXXXXXXXXXXXXXXX to you and Daddy
Cathy

DEPARTURES

1

Havenswalk, New Zealand — October 2008

She will ring her sisters this morning. Now, right now, while the day is still under her control. Right now, Cathy repeats to herself, before Hannah arrives for work. Right now before her son starts demanding, 'Have you done it yet . . . why not . . . why not?'

Once yesterday, and twice the day before, she tried to ring but lost her nerve, hung up before the line connected. Today she will tap out the digits, the correct prefix, wait for the ringtone. But what then? Should she make small talk, apologise, accuse, beg, rant or sob? Should she opt for nonchalance? Whoa there, Rebecca. How's it going, Julie? How do you do, Lauren? Remember me? It's Cathy, your long-lost sister calling from New Zealand . . . yes . . . I know it's over fifteen years since we spoke but time passes . . . and you know how it is . . . what can I say . . . ?

Half-formed sentences and muddled apologies run through her mind as she walks across the lawn towards the grapefruit trees. The grapefruit is ripe and falls easily into her hands. When the basket is full, she lingers for a moment by the shore. She loves this time of morning. The pause

7

between stillness and motion. The mist has cleared and the rising sun is pinned bright as a brooch against the throat of the mountain.

In Ireland, the dark evenings have settled. Leaves are bronze and falling. Children in masks are knocking on doors and dogs are howling.

She remembers the dog, Nero. A squiggle in a sack before Rebecca rescued him from the sludge of a low-tide estuary. When the bangers exploded, Nero heard them seconds before everyone else. A low growling in his throat, followed by a crescendo of petrified barking. Rebecca was the only one who could calm him. Halloween killed him in the end — heart failure — and Rebecca brushed his dead black coat until it gleamed and it was time to bury him at the bottom of the garden. A year later roses were growing there, bold and defiant as a bloodstain. These stingray memories, the sudden darting pain, they undo her.

She shakes herself loose from the past and returns to the kitchen, takes bread from the oven and places the loaves on a wire tray. The smell wafts through the open window, a more potent summons to eat than bells or alarm clocks. No sign of movement from the chalets so far. In the distance she hears the roar of a motorbike. Hannah emerges from a screen of trees and veers around the bend in the avenue, body and bike moulded. She enters the kitchen and shakes her black hair loose from the helmet, sheds her leathers.

On the buffet counter in the restaurant, Cathy arranges serving dishes of muesli, apples, prunes and apricots, nuts, seeds and the fruit, freshly picked. She lays a selection of cheeses on a blue-rimmed platter, stacks yoghurts in triangles, fills jugs with fruit juice and milk, sinks them in a crunch of ice, checks the buffet as keenly as an artist preparing to exhibit: a tweak here, a tweak there. The kitchen is loud with the clang of pots, the clunk of crockery, and Hannah singing one of her Maori songs that makes Cathy feel like swaying as she prepares the terrace for those who wish to eat outside.

'Have you phoned them yet?' Conor joins her on the terrace. His question is petulant, more like an accusation than an enquiry. He knows the answer. With breakfast preparations underway, his mother has a ready-made excuse.

'Later,' Cathy says. 'The guests will be coming in for breakfast soon. I'll do it afterwards.'

'Not yet, they won't.' He opens parasols, arranges chairs around the tables. 'You still have time.'

'No — '

'Yes. Do it now. Stop making excuses. You promised last night — '

'I know what I promised . . . and I will.'

'But if you leave it until later they'll be asleep. What's the sense in making promises if you've no intention of keeping them?'

She is familiar with his lip, the bee-sting pout already in position, the yearning curiosity in his eyes. He follows her to her office, yapping at her heels. She will phone her sisters and he will rake the leaves from the glow-worm trail, a job he has avoided doing for the past two weeks. He is

9

dressed for the task, jeans and boots, a frayed sleeveless T-shirt printed with the face of an obscure rap singer he once admired.

'Think about it,' he says before she enters her office. 'You've got the best end of the deal. I've only procrastinated for a fortnight. You've been doing it for over fifteen years.' He likes to remind her of the time lapse, twist the guilt screw a little tighter. He looks back once, as if to challenge her indecisiveness, then disappears into the forest.

From the window, Cathy watches the first guest emerge from the Kea chalet and head towards the swimming pool. Two women walk across the lawn and sit on the bench that encircles the rata tree. Her hand trembles as she lifts the phone. Rebecca first. Grasp the bull by the horns, the nettle by its sting, the rose by its thorn. Her breath quickens as she dials her sister's number. There should be crackles and clicks, hums, clangs and crossed wires, so many crossed wires, but the connection is instant, a clear double ring answered almost immediately.

★   ★   ★

'Lambert Animal Sanctuary.'
  'Rebecca . . . '
The pause that follows is as startling as a missed heartbeat and, in that instant of recognition, Rebecca discovers that there is nothing, no barriers or soft landings, nothing to prevent the years rushing in and submerging her.
  'Rebecca . . . can you hear me?'
She struggles to answer but her mouth is dry

10

and her heart, racing with relief that the long wait is over, but also with an inexplicable panic, tightens like a fist in her chest. She is filled also with an overwhelming need to weep, but tears will come later when she is alone and able to release this torrent of emotion. For now, she must remain in control. If she frightens Cathy away, there will be no explanations, no apologies, no opportunity for her sister to defend the indefensible.

'Please say something, Rebecca. You've no idea how many times I dialled your number but I always lost my courage at the last moment and . . . oh God! I don't know what to say . . . ' Cathy has acquired a slight New Zealand accent, the vowels compressed, the words precise but pleasant to the ear. She speaks too fast, spilling out excuses and apologies, as if she believes the torrent of words will prevent Rebecca hanging up on her.

'You're not the only one who's stuck for words, Cathy. I can't believe you finally decided to contact us.'

'I've wanted to . . . so often.' Cathy hesitates again then rushes on. 'But, as time went on, it became harder and harder. Try and understand — '

'Understand what? Why you never picked up the phone? Wrote a letter? Paid us a visit?'

'I did keep in touch — '

'Fifteen years! All the time waiting to hear from you. How could you disappear like that? Nothing except postcards . . . Christmas cards that *never* included your address. How can you

11

possibly call that keeping in touch? One of us could have died and you'd never have known.'

'Mel kept me informed about everything.'

'You kept in touch with Melanie Barnes but *not* your own sisters?'

'She was my only support at the time . . . the only person who understood.'

'Understood what, Cathy?'

'Understood why I had to leave. But I don't want to talk about it over the phone.'

'How else do you expect us to communicate?'

'In person, Becks.'

'Becks? You stopped using that name a long time ago.'

'I remember. I remember everything — '

'You said, in person. Does that mean you're coming home?'

'No. Not now, but, hopefully, in the future. I'm getting married in January.'

'Congratulations. I wish you every happiness.'

'Thank you.'

They could be strangers, Rebecca thinks. Word-perfect and skilled in the art of polite conversation. She forces herself to concentrate on what Cathy is saying. Havenswalk, she says, is a relaxation centre where people come from all over New Zealand, and even beyond, to be pampered and massaged. She runs it with a business partner, a woman called Alma.

'It's a wonderful place,' Cathy enthuses. 'And the grounds are beautiful. I'm going to be married there, on the lawn beside the lake. I want my sisters with me, Rebecca. I want us to

12

use the occasion for a reunion and I'm hoping — '

Unable to endure Cathy's enthusiasm, which keeps sliding through her repentant tone, Rebecca's composure finally snaps.

'I thought the prodigal sister was supposed to come home to eat the fatted calf, not the other way round.'

'It doesn't matter where we eat the fatted calf as long as we can be together again,' Cathy retorts.

The wind, gusting through the rain, rattles the stable doors and starts a horse whinnying. Others, hearing, take up the call until it throbs like a wound inside Rebecca's head. Throughout the day she had hoped for rain and it has been lashing against the sanctuary walls for over an hour. With such a deluge coming down, no more horses will be forced to jump the bonfires tonight.

A button on the control panel signals an emergency call.

'Cathy, someone is trying to get through. It's one of our busiest nights. Hold the line a moment.'

Without waiting for her sister to reply, she clicks into the incoming call. Every year Halloween brings them out of the woodwork, the crazies and the cruel, and the sanctuary crew are working round the clock to rescue injured animals. A stray pony has been spotted on wasteland near Naas, burns on its belly, a torn ear, one eye completely closed. The caller — she sounds young, probably a teenager whose night has turned sour — begins to cry. Rebecca asks for details of the location and radios her emergency team with the information. The shock of Cathy's call is beginning to subside, yet it seems unreal, this mature voice with its taut inflections ringing out of the blue.

'Rebecca . . . ?'

Cathy's hesitancy snaps her back to the present. 'I'm listening. You want me to go to your wedding.'

'I'm hoping you will. We need closure, Rebecca.'

'And how do you suggest we achieve closure?' Rebecca clicks her fingers, an audible snap carried across continents. 'Draw a line through the past and pretend it never happened?'

'We can't wipe out the past but we can make peace with it.'

'You really believe it's that easy?'

'Of course I don't think it's easy. But we have to begin somewhere. It's taken me a long time to reach this point. How could I look for forgiveness from anyone else until I had the courage to absolve myself?'

'Is that what you want from me, Cathy? Absolution?' She imagines Cathy squirming away from her questions, as she did so often in the past, settling her face into a hard white mask of defiance.

'Not absolution, Rebecca. I want you to come to Havenswalk to meet my son.'

Can silence echo, Rebecca wonders. Can it crash so heavily that all she hears is the echo . . . son . . . son . . . son . . . reverberating?

14

'Your son?'

'Yes. His name is Conor.'

'Conor?'

'Conor Lambert.'

'What age is he?'

Cathy hesitates, the briefest of pauses, but long enough for Rebecca to know the answer. 'He'll be fifteen in December.'

'Fifteen?' Why on earth does she keep repeating her sister's words?

'You lied to us!'

'At the time I believed . . . it seemed better that way. You wouldn't worry so much — '

'Worry? What do you know about our worries . . . our fears?' Memories of their last encounter press like a claustrophobic band against Rebecca's forehead. She winces and tightens her grip on the receiver. 'Why did you never mention him in your cards?'

'Would you have wanted to know?'

'He's my nephew, Cathy. Of course I would have wanted to know of his existence. You *deliberately* deceived us.'

'I was so confused — '

'Your son?' Rebecca harshly interrupts her. 'Who does he look like?'

'His personality reminds me of Julie.' Cathy swallows, an audible gulp, as if her throat has contracted with nerves, then forces a laugh. 'A bit wild, like all lads his age, and into his music in a big way. He wants to be a vet when he's older so you're there too, Rebecca. I guess he resembles all of you in little ways. Most of all, Conor is uniquely himself. He's anxious to meet his aunts. Please come and visit us. I'll put you up in the chalets so it'll only cost you the plane fare.'

'No . . . I can't. It's nothing to do with the cost. It's just . . . did you really expect it to be that easy?'

'I didn't expect anything. I just hoped — '

'I'm sorry . . . sorry . . . it's too soon. I'm not able to handle this at the moment. I'm sure the others . . . Do you have Julie's number? Lauren's in Spain; I can give you her mobile.'

'I have their numbers. I wanted to speak to you first. Oh, Becks — '

Headlights beam through the darkness: the sanctuary crew, arriving with the latest victims of the night's excesses.

'I have to go, Cathy. Yes, give me your number. I'll ring . . . of course I'll ring. Goodbye . . . goodbye.'

Rebecca hurries to help Lulu May, the sanctuary manager, to calm an injured horse whose hoofs flail dangerously when they lead him down the ramp. Her life has moved on a long way from bobbing apples and dipping for pennies.

The sanctuary is quiet when she finishes her shift; the new arrivals sedated and out of pain. Leaves squelch under her feet as she walks across the field towards her cottage. The dank earth releases the smell of the dying year. She is facing into a grey Irish winter but spring is underway in New Zealand. A time of renewal, Cathy said. A time for closure.

She opens her cottage door. Her legs are

16

leaden, her eyes gritty from tiredness. She switches on her computer. Amazing to think the information she needed about her youngest sister's whereabouts had been only a finger-tap away. All that was missing was the key word — Havenswalk.

Havenswalk does indeed look like a walk in heaven. A cluster of wooden Alpine-style chalets encircle a central two-storey building where guests gather to eat, meditate and practise yoga. Outside, they soak in hot tubs under star-lit skies, relax under umbrellas, loll by a swimming pool that appears to have been hollowed from a rock. Accompanied by the haunting strains of panpipes, Havenswalk promises Serenity, Tranquillity, Spiritual Harmony, Empowerment, Healing Energy, Emotional Balance.

Cathy's photograph smiles from the Home Page. Her eyes are bluer than Rebecca remembers, as blue as a painted icon. No longer wasted behind thick black eyeliner but staring outwards in an open, welcoming gaze. Her crimped Kate Bush hair has been tamed and replaced by a sleek black plait. From Goth to guru in little more than fifteen years. How has such a transformation occurred?

Teabag slithers from underneath an armchair and rubs against her ankles, demanding attention. Rebecca lifts the cat, cradles him against her neck. She stands by the window and watches the sun lift above the fields. Time is a thief, she thinks, gilding sorrow, stealing the intensity of loss and allowing people to move on with their lives. But all it takes is a trigger: a

17

song, a smell, a juggernaut flashing past — or a forgotten voice echoing from another time — and memory becomes a flailing thing, capable of shattering rock.

The rain has ceased. Only tears remain on the sodden branches, glistening like pearls in the milky morning light.

2

Rebecca's Journal — 1985

Name — Mary Green
Occupation — Social worker
Intention — To break up our family
Obstacle to achieving her goal — Me!
Duration of visit — 2 hrs

Mary Green doesn't like it when I make notes but I'm not supposed to object when she does the same. Was she trained to ask questions then wait silently, however long it takes, for me to stumble into her trap? Or did she pick up the trick when she started dealing with 'dysfunctional' families? She makes 'orphans' sound like a disease and 'Care' sound like the Promised Land.

Cathy has nits in her hair ... so what? Everyone in her class has them. It's called an infestation. Julie bunks off school. Her and half of the student population, but when she does it, it's seen like a crisis for the State. Lauren ... well, there's the rub ... I don't have any easy answers but she's not going anywhere and if they try to take her away they'll do so over my dead body. Mary Green says I'm overwrought, hysterical, too young and inexperienced. She forgets to include 'grieving'.

We're drowning in tears. It's awful. Julie is the loudest. She's loudest at everything and her grief is terrible to hear. Crying with her face in the cushions or against Paul's chest, crying over the slightest thing, and I want to scream at her to stop . . . stop . . . stop!! but I can't because it only makes her cry louder and call me a heartless cow.

Cathy cries in corners or behind chairs or under bedclothes. I know by her eyes. They're pools of grief. She's like a shadow behind me, clinging to my presence, afraid I'll disappear if she lets me out of her sight. I don't blame her. I feel myself disappearing all the time, my dreams dissolving one by one. Then I'm furious with myself for being resentful when we have all lost so much. What kind of person thinks about trivial things like college and friends and travel and being able to walk away from it all?

She writes letters to Mammy. She showed me one but I choked up and couldn't finish it. I showed her how to spell 'angel' correctly. Why did I do that? Why didn't I rock her in my arms instead? I would have . . . in the past. I would have held her until her chest stopped heaving and her face was dry. She falls asleep in class. She's slipping behind the main stream. It's all there in Mary Green's little black book.

How am I supposed to manage? I couldn't boil an egg before they died. Julie says my dinners look like Nero's vomit but she eats everything — unlike Lauren, who never says a word, even when she's dumping hers in the bin. Cathy says I'm the best cook ever. She's forever trying to please me but not the way she used to. It's more like she's learning new lines and is unsure of the way forward. After all, I'm the boss now. But I'm only seventeen! I haven't a clue what I'm doing. Little steps, Lydia says, step by little step, anything is possible.

I've accepted the Morans' invitation. A break will do us good. They've a fabulous house, and horses too. Country air will be good for Lauren, put some colour in her cheeks.

Lauren's tears are like icicles. When I hold her, I get nothing but frost burn. I'm afraid if I hold her too tight she'll snap cleanly away from me. I wish she'd cry like Julie, howl and yell and kick the doors. But she's frozen with guilt. I keep telling her it's not her fault. But she doesn't hear me. Even if she did, she'd figure I was lying.

I don't know if I'll ever be able to forgive her.

3

Dublin — January 2009

Lauren Moran awakens to the whirr of freshly ground coffee beans. She hears her husband's step on the stairs and imagines what he will see when he enters their bedroom: her black hair spilling over the pillows, the sultry welcome in her eyes, her voluptuous mouth. Aware that her lips are taut, she clenches her face, holds for a count of ten, then relaxes. A new day is beginning. The day of departure.

Steve hesitates at the door, a light tap, and, without waiting for her response, enters. A tray with coffee and crisp, flaky croissants, lime marmalade and whorls of butter, slender as wood shavings, is placed before her. The centrepiece is a long-stemmed rose in a delicate cut-glass vase. No thorns are visible and the scent is lost behind the aroma of coffee.

'You spoil me.' She smiles at him and lazily rises.

'Always,' he replies. His movements are deft, almost delicate, as he pours coffee for two and butters croissants. The thin straps of her nightdress slip from her shoulders when she leans forward to accept the cup from him. He touches the satiny fabric, lifts one strap back into place and leaves the other resting against her arm. The creamy shade emphasises her tanned skin, draws his eyes to the deep plunge of lace at her breasts.

When breakfast is over, she clips the rose to her hair and clicks her fingers like a Spanish dancer. They feint on the bed, this way and that. He likes games, an initial resistance, which he can masterfully overcome. He is still strong and muscular, his lovemaking as vigorous, if not as regular as in the early years of their marriage. Viagra, Lauren suspects, but, if that is the case, he will never admit it and she will never ask.

Afterwards, she lies quietly by his side while he, his breath slowing back to normal, caresses her cheek. His touch is gentle yet she feels the calluses rasp against her skin as each stroke finishes and begins again. His nails are manicured weekly, his hands nourished with moisturising oils, but the scars he earned from his years on the building sites can never be removed.

'Everything packed?' he asks.

'All organised,' she replies.

'Passport?'

'In my handbag.' Her Gucci handbag rests against the opposite wall, along with her three red leather suitcases and her matching overnight case.

'Tickets, schedule?'

'Stop worrying about me, Steve.' She eases away from him, allows his hand to glide from her cheek to her breasts, then fall into the empty space she leaves behind. Her nightdress ripples as she slides her legs to the floor. Each movement is a slow separation yet she makes it seem like a lingering embrace. She sits at the dressing table and nods towards her luggage.

'Rebecca will go crazy when she sees what I've packed.'

Only one piece of luggage. Rebecca's email had been specific. Anything more will cramp their living conditions. She has studied the dimensions of the camper and knows exactly where everything will fit. The six-berth is her idea, a compromise between backpacking, which is all Julie can afford, and the five-star hotel accommodation Lauren had expected.

Lauren is convinced that Rebecca, even if she were not the first-born of the four Lambert sisters, would automatically have risen in the pecking order and assumed that right. Unable to understand any form of indecisiveness, she makes everything sound effortless — flights, accommodation, itinerary; all the planning and discussion condensed on the email, which Lauren received yesterday and wilfully ignored.

Steve slides her pillow under his cheek and breathes into the indentation where her head rested. The rose lies discarded and crushed on the floor.

'I'm sorry I won't have an opportunity to see you wearing your wardrobe,' he says.

'When I come home, I'll put on a *special* fashion show for you.'

'I'll look forward to it.'

She gathers her hair in both hands and secures it in a topknot. 'We'd better get moving — '

'What's the rush, princess? We won't see each

other for a month.' An astute man, and attuned to her thoughts, he has sensed her impatience.

'You'll be so busy you won't have time to miss me.'

He shakes his head and rises, enters the ensuite. While he showers, she opens one of her suitcases and folds in another dress. A good Girl Guide must be prepared for all eventualities.

After the shock of Cathy's initial phone call subsided, Steve planned a month-long tour of the South Island. He has been to New Zealand before, with his first wife, and knows the sights they should see. Luxury hotels, car hire, lake cruises and helicopter flights were booked in advance. They intended using Havenswalk as their base for the last ten days of the tour, with Cathy's wedding providing the highlight of the trip. But Steve was forced to change his plans when the start-up date for a shopping complex, which he hoped would officially open before Christmas, was postponed until March. Trouble with acquiring new tenants, he explained. Worried about the slow-down in the property market, he phoned Cathy to discuss the situation. Lauren later discovered he suggested that she postpone her wedding until later in the year when he would be free to travel.

'Why are you so angry?' he demanded when Lauren, furious, yet not surprised, at his audacity, challenged him. 'She waited over fifteen years to contact you. What difference will another few months make?'

'He hasn't changed,' said Cathy when Lauren contacted her to apologise. 'Thankfully, I have.

My wedding takes place as arranged. I want you there, Lauren. But if you don't feel capable of travelling without Steve, I understand.'

Stung by Cathy's assumption, Lauren decided to take the trip on her own. Rebecca, then later, Julie, agreed to accompany her. Instead of travelling in luxury, they will do so in a camper van. Rebecca calls it 'a motor home', which makes it sound spacious, almost luxurious. Lauren suspects Steve was closer to the truth when he referred to it as a sardine can.

He used this comparison one night when he invited her sisters out for a meal and offered to pay their hotel costs, car hire and sightseeing trips.

'You girls could do with a little pampering in your lives,' he said, a remark that immediately raised her sisters' hackles. Steve has acquired many skills in his life but handling the Lambert sisters is not among them.

'We girls are quite capable of doing our own pampering,' Rebecca replied, while Julie, whose idea of a manicure was a few strokes with an emery board and a cocktail stick for the cuticles, nodded vigorously in agreement.

'There's nothing wrong with a little luxury now and again,' Steve retorted. 'Wait till you're cooped up like sardines in a tin can, especially in that heat. I've told Lauren to call me immediately if conditions become unbearable.' Even if he had not made the comment, their answer would have been the same. They always resisted his generosity, claimed it patronised them. They had never understood Lauren's reasons for marrying him and those reasons were no longer relevant.

Lauren watches him in the dressing table mirror as he slips on his shirt. Recently, he has gained weight but he is a tall, blocky man and it adds an extra layer of authority to his appearance. He stands behind her and fixes his tie, his hands automatically forming a Windsor knot, his eyes watching.

'You're relieved I can't go with you.' His abrupt tone startles her.

'Stop talking nonsense, Steve. We planned this trip together, remember? I'd no intention of travelling in a camper van. We'll probably end up bored out of our minds and not speaking to each other for most of the trip. I can't think of anything I have in common with my sisters any more.'

'Thankfully, you never had anything in common with them, princess.' His tie is knotted, his suit buttoned. He has a business meeting to attend after he leaves her at the airport. He bends down until his gaze is level with her own. 'What's going on behind those lovely green eyes? Some day I'll figure it out. Then, perhaps, I'll begin to know you.'

'You're such a foolish man.' She turns her head towards him. Her laughter is light and easily silenced with a kiss. He opens his briefcase and removes a small gift-wrapped package.

'A farewell present.'

Jewellery, she thinks, and wonders what has stretched his imagination on this occasion.

'State of the art,' he adds when she lifts out a

27

silver, slimline mobile phone from the wrappings.

'But I already have one — '

'State of the art,' he repeats. 'It will work from anywhere in the world.' He demonstrates its various applications. She smiles as he shows off this latest toy and promises to ring him every day they are apart.

After he leaves the room, she switches on the bath taps and pulls on an exfoliation glove. She sinks into the scented water and scrubs her skin until she tingles all over. On her neck there is an angry weal, a bruise on her breast, red and tender. When does a love bite become a wound, she wonders. A caress become a pain so sharp that she had gasped at his touch? Could what took place between them just now be called 'making love'? She will not sleep by his side for a month yet she went through the familiar choreography of passion without once losing herself in him or responding to his desire, which, she suspects, is fuelled by resentment that she is leaving without him. A month on her own without a safety net to catch her if she falls. She shivers and rises from the bath. The last dress she packed was the wrong one. Too heavy for the summer that is taking place in New Zealand.

Steve is wrong when he says he does not know her. He knows her better than she knows herself. Perhaps that was why he bit so deeply into her neck. Keeping a part of her behind.

4

The house waits for her to leave. Julie Chambers senses its impatience. Perfection is a fine balance and she insists on disturbing it. She buffs the already gleaming kitchen counters, straightens the canisters, clangs her index fingernail off the hanging mugs. Homemade soup and apple crumble have been prepared for her sons' return from school and the hot press is stacked with their freshly ironed clothes. Everything she can do to ensure the smooth running of her home, family and business has been done, and she is anxious to leave before she remembers that she is indispensable.

The taxi is already twenty minutes late and panic is setting in. On a weekend morning the drive from her house to the airport is less than fifteen minutes. On a weekday, it is impossible to calculate. She checks the road. Rain clouds hover over the rooftops and the crows, perched like exclamation marks on the telegraph wires, have a damp, bedraggled appearance. The daffodils will be out when she returns, the cherry blossom coming into bloom.

The taxi driver, arriving ten minutes later, is in no mood for tolerance. 'Make no mistake about it, missus, this *'ucking* city is a bottleneck to hell.' His omission of the letter F is an obvious contribution to the clean-up-language campaign being imposed on taxi drivers, and Julie smiles to

29

show she appreciates his restraint. As she settles into the back seat, he stows her suitcase and her mandolin in the boot. She is cheating slightly by bringing along her mandolin but life without music, as far as Julie is concerned, is not worth living.

The driver grumbles loudly as he bumps over the speed control ramps leading from Baymark Estate. He is a stubby, red-faced man with a tight mouth made for complaining. His querulous voice hardly registers with Julie. Every mile that separates her from home, her demons shout louder for attention. What if Jonathan has another asthmatic attack and the ambulance doesn't make it through the traffic on time? What if Philip is carried from the rugby pitch with a fractured neck? What if Aidan raids the cocktail cabinet and takes to the fields with his friends? Where will she be while all this horror is going on? In a camper van in the Antipodes, playing at being a bush woman.

'Going far?' The driver glances at her through the rearview mirror.

'Far enough,' she replies, hoping to end their conversation and, for a few minutes, he drives in silence through Swords village. The back of his neck turns red as the early morning traffic shudders forward inch by inch.

''*Ucking* traffic,' he mutters. 'They build one 'ucking motorway after another and what do we get? Ulsters! Nothing but 'ucking stomach ulsters. Where'd you say you're going, missus?'

'New Zealand,' Julie replies. 'To my sister's wedding.'

'That's a long way to go for a wedding. You planning on taking in the sights while you're there?'

'That's the idea.'

'Stopping off on the way?'

'Two nights in Bangkok.'

'Sex capital of the world, so I'm told.' He brakes at traffic lights and leans despairingly over the steering wheel. 'If you ask my opinion, this 'ucking country's heading the same way, what with lap-dancing clubs and sex shops springing up like 'ucking mushrooms. The sights I see in this taxi . . . Things have changed for the worst since my young days, I'll tell you that for nothing. As for the 'ucking recession . . . '

She texts Rebecca: 'Hold that plane! I'm at the mercy of a taxi driver in the advanced stages of Tourettes . . . the abbreviated version,' and hopes her sisters will appreciate her attempt at humour.

Paul was supposed to drive her to the airport but an early morning emergency call from the office put paid to that plan. His worried expression and hassled apologies as he hurried towards his car, his mobile phone already ringing, had added to her sense of guilt.

Since Cathy's unexpected phone call, Julie has dithered over her decision to attend the wedding. Paul declared that it was a 'preposterous' decision to make. He used his end-of-this-discussion voice and made it sound as if Julie's being reunited with her long-lost sister was of far less importance than the smooth running of

31

Chambers Software Solutions. Since he established the company from a redundancy package he received during the dot com collapse, Julie has looked after the finances. If she had a business card it would have read 'Financial Controller'. But she has no business card to flash at meetings and her work environment is a laptop on the kitchen table, which competes with the dishwasher for attention.

They argued bitterly over her decision to take time off work. The row lasted a week. In the evenings they hid their anger under a veneer of normality, carrying on conversations at two levels: one audible and polite, so as not to upset their sons, the other inaudible but loaded. Finally, Paul arrived home early from work one evening and presented her with a bunch of flowers and a guidebook called *Traversing New Zealand*.

'I suppose you've made up.' Jonathan, her eldest son, dropped his sports kit in the hall and eyed the flowers she was arranging in a vase.

'Made up what?' she asked, the pleasure of their reconciliation still warm on her skin.

'Give me a break,' her son sighed. 'We could scrape our nails off the atmosphere for the past week. Are you going to the wedding or not?'

'Going.' She plunged the irises into water.

'Good for you,' he replied. 'We'll look after Dad while you're gone. What's for dinner? I'm starving.'

★ ★ ★

32

On reaching the departure terminal, her sisters greet her with relief and hurry her towards the check-in desk. Lauren has ignored Rebecca's instructions about luggage and the expandable lids on her matching suitcases are strained to the limit. Steve looks in danger of a ruptured hernia as he heaves them onto the weighing scales. The excess fee will be exorbitant but he will pay it without a quibble.

'What's with the wardrobe?' Julie demands as they await his return from the excess baggage counter. 'We'll be living in the bush, not the Ritz.'

Lauren is unrepentant. 'I barely managed to fit my knickers into the first suitcase.'

'How come I managed with a rucksack?' Rebecca asks.

'I don't do rucksacks,' replies Lauren, and Julie has to smile at the idea of Lauren bent under the weight of an enormous multi-purpose rucksack.

Steve, returning and overhearing their conversation, says, 'Call me when the going gets rough. My offer still stands.'

'Thank you, Steve.' Julie leads the way towards the departure gate and turns away when he embraces his wife. Spring and autumn conjoined. She has never grown used to their marriage, never will.

'I'll phone as soon as we reach Bangkok.' Lauren hands her boarding pass to the attendant and glides beyond his reach.

An hour later they are airborne. The plane rises from the runway and crosses the Broadmeadow Estuary. Housing estates, surrounded by swatches of green, slant into view. White-capped waves ride towards the viaduct. Yachts and cruisers are moored in the marina, a new addition since their Heron Cove days. Julie strains her neck and is able to pinpoint the house where they spent their childhood. The old chestnut tree still grows in the garden, its bare branches forming a black filigree against the sky. The next house, where Lydia Mulvaney lived until her death, is also briefly visible.

Is Cathy sleeping now, Julie wonders as she settles back in her seat. Or is she lying awake, aware that the day of departure has finally arrived? Is she nervous? She has much to explain and Rebecca will demand answers.

*   *   *

'How come you changed your mind about visiting Cathy?' Julie asked Rebecca one afternoon when she called into the sanctuary to collect her sons, who had been volunteering during their Christmas holidays.

'I want to ask Cathy face to face why she dragged us through hell and back again.' Rebecca, sitting behind her desk, looked and sounded exhausted. Her black hair, tied back in a tight ponytail, accentuated her wide, flat cheek-bones and strong chin. There had been an incident the previous day between her and an alcoholic farmer who had brutalised a donkey. The donkey had been rescued but Julie doubted if the battle with the alcoholic farmer was responsible for the weary slope of Rebecca's shoulders, the smudged hollows under her eyes.

'Don't you think Cathy was in her own personal hell?' Julie demanded. 'You've a short memory span if you've forgotten.'

'I haven't forgotten anything. Including how she misled us afterwards. Her deceit . . . '

Julie saw the familiar anger flare in Rebecca's eyes, her lips compress, as if she was holding back bitter accusations. Their conversation petered out, as it always does when they speak about Cathy. Sitting beside her now, Julie shivers, as if the tension she senses in her older sister has transferred to herself.

The plane lifts higher. Clouds fall like blots over the familiar landscape and Julie is swept into a grey swirl that banishes the world she knows from sight.

5

Rebecca's Journal — 1985

My mother's words are like a song in my head. The kind of song you don't want to hear yet one line keeps repeating and repeating until you long to hit your head off a wall to make it stop.

'Look after Cathy for me,' she said, but I'd other plans that night. Sheila Brogan's parents were on holiday for a week and she was throwing a party. I guess that was the reason my mother — who always seemed to know everything she shouldn't — wanted me to stay at home. That and Jeremy . . .

I glared at her and demanded to know why I was always the one who had to do everything? Why was Lauren, high and mighty Lauren, treated as if she was Ireland's answer to Margot Fonteyn? We'd already been to the opening night of her concert. Why, then, was it necessary for Mammy and Daddy to attend on the closing night?

Oh, I was petulant that evening, sulking and rude and argumentative. I watched her flicking mascara on her eyelashes, spraying perfume on her wrists. She had delicate wrists and long fingers like a pianist. That's what she wanted to be when she was young — a concert pianist

— but she wasn't good enough and she ended up marrying Gerard Lambert and playing marching tunes for us on the piano in the living room. 'Marching Through Georgia', 'Heart of Dixie', 'Anchors Away' — and we marched like little soldiers up and down the floor. She played soft tunes too: 'Where Have All the Flowers Gone? Long Time Passing'. Joan Baez was singing it on the radio the other day. I lunged at it and switched it off before the others heard.

She ordered me to stop arguing. To stop giving cheek and do as I was told for a change. (It's funny — although no one is laughing — how much I sound like her now.)

How could either of us have realised that those words would be the last we'd ever exchange? Angry words that would have been forgotten as easily as they were uttered but now they resonate beyond the grave and chain me to their power.

She dabbed her lips on a tissue and left the room. The next day I found the tissue crumpled on the dressing table. Her lips were imprinted like a bloodstain on the creases.

I didn't look after Cathy that night. As soon as Daddy's car disappeared around the corner, I persuaded Julie to mind her. They were snuggled on the sofa with Kevin Mulvaney when I left, the three of them watching Cagney and Lacey.

I wore my striped tank top to Sheila's party, my best Levi's and my new Adidas trainers. I remember so many things about that night. They come back to me in fragments. How Rory

Jones broke a piece of Mrs Brogan's precious Aynsley china. Sheila cried as she swept up the pieces but no one else cared. I remember how we turned away in disgust, but laughing, when Rick Martin threw up in the kitchen sink. I remember my reflection in the mirror with the gilt-edge frame that hung above the mantelpiece. I danced with Jeremy, cheek-to-cheek, and I could see the back of his head, hear my bangles jangling when I raised my hand and stroked my fingers through his thick blond hair. Our bodies, made for each other, our feet moving to the same step, and he was hard when he pressed against me, so hard it hurt, almost, and that, too, was part of the pleasure. He whispered into my ear, told me he loved me, wanted me, his breath hot on my neck, and I wondered if we dared slip away, slip upstairs to one of the empty bedrooms, and what would happen then, would we . . . could I . . . and he held me tighter still as we danced past the mirror, danced in a slow dark circle, oblivious to what was taking place on the bend of the coast road leading to Heron Cove.

I remember the silence that settled over the party when Sheila came into the living room with a policewoman. The policewoman's mouth seemed full of glass when she tried to explain why a squad car was waiting outside to bring me home. I remember the room swaying. Jeremy tried to catch me before I fell. My head banged off the edge of the table. I don't remember any pain. My new trainers struck out in front of me. Funny thing to remember, my heels clamped together, forcing my toes into a V. I don't remember being lifted to my feet, but someone must have done so because I know I could never have managed to stand on my own. And I remember the whispering that started when the policewoman took my arm and led me away from the party. Jeremy came with me but I don't remember anything he said to me, or if the policewoman spoke to either of us.

Lights were burning in the windows of Heron Cove. Doors were open. Neighbours were clustered in huddles in the hall and the kitchen. I remember their faces, Lydia's tears. Julie's screams as she broke free from Paul's arms and ran towards me. And I remember thinking, as we held each other, that our lives had changed utterly and for ever.

6

Havenswalk — January 2009

The attic in Havenswalk is reached by a spiral staircase. A handy place for dumping broken furniture that has some possibility of being repaired but is inevitably forgotten once the door closes. Next year, Cathy plans to convert the attic into a dance studio but, for now, it is a repository for all the bric-a-brac she and Alma have acquired and abandoned since they moved to New Zealand.

She switches on the light and browses for an hour among boxes and crates, sifts through account ledgers and old books that release the fusty smell of neglected papers. She stops to examine some clothes and toys belonging to Conor, items she decided to save for the memories they evoke. The silence is uneasy. She suspects unseen creatures lurking in the eaves and crannies, but only the spiders ignore her intrusion and continue spinning in gauzy corners.

The edge of the moon shifts from her gaze as she moves the broken frame of an awning to one side. It is heavy and almost topples over. She prevents it falling and waking everyone. Underneath it, she finds a wicker picnic basket. The weave is broken in places. Snapped reeds jut outwards and cobwebs trail like a shiver across her fingers when she snaps open the rusting lock. Her letters to Nirvana. Carefully she lifts them out. They are tied together with an elastic band that breaks with an exhausted snap when she stretches it.

She hesitates, undecided. Does she really want to delve into the past and relive those fragmented years when hormones, confusion and unresolved heartache formed their own convulsive mix? Never look back, Rebecca used to say. Nothing but dust around corners.

The date on the first letters startles her. Was she only eight years old when she wrote it? She always imagined she was older, probably about ten. The early ones were written on notepaper with delicate border drawings, Edwardian ladies with parasols and lacy, ruffled collars. A writing set, she remembers, given to her by Lydia Mulvaney as a starter present. Write to your mother, Lydia said, and when you are sleeping she will read your letters. Angels fly at midnight. Their first stop is home.

Cathy smiles, remembering how the image of hovering angels had comforted her and how, when the fancy notepaper ran out, she wrote on the torn-out pages of copybooks and refill pads, writing by torch light at night when the house was quiet, secret hours under a duvet tent.

If she read the letters before contacting Rebecca her courage would have failed her. Yet the die has been cast by now, Conor at her heels, demanding . . . ring them now now . . .

Her sisters are on their way. She is still amazed that Rebecca changed her mind. Amazed and frightened and relieved in equal measure. She rang her sisters seeking closure but how that closure is to be achieved is impossible to tell. Cathy tries not to panic. Has she made the worst mistake of her life — or is this the beginning of healing, the closing of a wound that has festered for far too long? She sinks to a cast-off settee and begins to read.

7

Letters to Nirvana

Meadow Lark
Wicklow
19 August 1985

Dear Mammy,

How are you and Daddy today? We are having a nice holiday in Meadow Lark with the
Morans. We call them Auntie Olive and
Uncle Steve. They have lots of rooms and no
kids, only horses. Uncle Steve taut us to ride a
pony called Zorbo. Lauren is afrayd to go on
him. When Uncle Steve lift her up she cry
and cry. But she wont fall and brake her legs
again. A pony is not a car. Auntie Olive
brothe her and me to the shops for froks
and socks and nickers and jeans and tops and
shoes. She wont let Nero sleep on the bed
with Becks. No hairs on the dubay or dog
pee smell in her posh house. Becks is cross as
a bare because Nero has to sleep in a shed
and he barks all night. Julie hates it here.
She hates living in the sticks and she hates
the staybell smells and not being with Paul.
Auntie Olive is a teecher. She has big glasses
like a owl eyes. She makes me rite lesons and

43

spell proper. I love Zorbo. I will rite more tomorrow.

XXXXXXXXX to you and Daddy
Cathy

Heron Cove
21 August 1985

Dear Mammy,

We are home again and Becks is cross as a bare. The row was bad. Uncle Steve gave out lots to her about Lauren. No one knew I was outside the door. Auntie Olive said its right he worry. She want to mind Lauren in Meadow Lark and help her kope with being a orpan. Becks said no way ho-say. She told Uncle Steve to shove his opinins up his bum and called Auntie Olive a inturfearing old cow. Auntie Olive keep hugging Lauren at the train station and saying poor pet poor pet and Lauren was like a swan with a hangy neck. She wants to live in Meadow Lark and ware nice froks. Becks said we have to call them Mr and Mrs Moran because they are not real family. Mrs Moran was Mammy's pal when they were little girls but Becks says she is a spy like the woman with the black case. Julie is glad to be home as well. She wants to start the band again but Becks said no way ho-say neybours will talk.

I miss you so much it makes me sick. Tell Daddy I miss him as well as you. I will rite more tomorrow. I love Zorbo.

XXXXXXXXX to you and Daddy
Cathy

26 December 1985

Dear Mammy,

Xmas Day is over. The only thing that made me cry was the Xmas songs at mass and Lauren hating the ballet book I gave her for her present. Kevin gave me sope on a rope and I gave him a Star Wars annual. The Morans called with lots of presents. We have to furgive and furget and they will not take Lauren away only for holidays. I got a pair of jeans. Becks got a really posh food mixer. Julie got a tiket for a rock concert and Lauren got a golden frock with a frill. Gramps gave us money and was drunk. The best the very best present was from Becks. Remember when I told you about finding your hair brush in the dressing table with your hair still in it and how she took it from me because I was doing her head in with crying? She gave me a love heart locket with your hair inside it and photos of you and Daddy. She is the best, the very very best. After dinner we went for a walk. All the waves were white. The wind made my skin sore. We saw the heron. Then we saw Jeremy with Rose More. Rebecca said don't look don't look see if I give a hoot and stuck her nose up in the air when we walk past. Julie called him a bad word. I wont write it down. It begins with W. We fed the swans. The heron flew away. Becks cried when we came home. I thought she was mad about Jeremy not hanging around greef but it was about the food mixer. She kept pointing at it and saying my life has come to

45

this, a f . . . ing food mixer.
My jeans a perfect fit.
Love to you and Daddy
XXXXXXXXXXXXXXXXXXXX
Cathy

Heron Cove
15 Jan 1986

Dear Mammy,
   A year has gone. I keep thinking if I open your
coffins I'll see you laughing like it is a big joke.
We had a mass for your annaversorry. Fr Morris
said your names out loud and made it reel again.
Lauren made a big fuss and ran out of the
church. She said she can not run but she can and
Mr Moran brote her back in his arms. She is still a
zombi but not so much now. Last night she said
F . . . off and mind your bisness when I ask her if
you and Daddy said goodbye. She is spoiled
rotton and she made you dead. We all went to the
balley concert and saw her dancing like a sugar
plum fairy. So why did she make you and Daddy
go 2 times? Why why why? She is a show off
thats why. Becks said I must never never never say
that to Lauren or she will cut out my tung. Me
and Julie sleep in your room now. Lauren sleep on
her own. So do Becks with Nero. It's nice being in
your bed, like I can touch you. Daddy's gitar is
still against the wall. Julie tuned it and we put it
back there again. His jacket is in the wardrobe. I
can't smell him, only mothballs and lether, but I
rub my hands really hard on the lether and that
feels nice. All your books are in the shelfs. There's

46

so many. The Colour Purple has a book mark in it. My favoritt authors are Judy Blume and Enid Blyton. Julie said a year is gone and Maxeemum Volum must be a band again. She is a brill singer. Paul is brill on drums. They sit on the wall and kiss and kiss. Becks said its not on. Neybours will talk. We all had a birthday since you die. Julie is 15 and Lauren 13 and Becks is 18 and I am 9. Gramps comes for our birthdays. He smells bad like the farm is on his skin and he gives Becks money for bread on the table.

Make him stop crying. It makes me cry to and Beck said we have to move on. I don't want to move. I like our house. The red dots are gone. I will rite more tomorrow.

XXXXXXXXX to you and Daddy
Cathy

8

Rebecca's Journal — 1986

Thank goodness for spring. There's green shoots in the ground and the forsythia will soon bud. I thought we'd never get through the year but we did . . . we did. The mass was nice, the church packed and it's good to know people remember them. I felt a hypocrite having the mass when I don't believe in God or any religion that forces us to accept there is a divine plan to anything. But I can't let on. What's the sense in saying there's nothing left except bone and memory when Cathy believes she's writing to an angel and Julie's convinced she'll meet them in heaven?

To lose so much in a year . . . it's too much . . . too much . . . but it's nice to stand in the garden and look at the green shoots. They promise so much. Unlike Jeremy, they'll deliver.

He's still with Rose Moore. Do I care? No way, José. Julie calls him a 'wanker' and Cathy sneaks her hand into mine and squeezes it when his name is mentioned. Their pity unhinges me. Even Lauren came out of her shell for a while after he broke off with me.

Jeremy is not a wanker. He just doesn't know how to deal with it all. I can't blame him.

I don't want to sit in every night either, but I'm too tired to go out and, when I do, I'm worried about Julie being in charge, knowing she's alone with Paul, and Lauren's locked somewhere deep inside herself and Cathy's probably crying or writing those letters, and if I get plastered, like my friends, I won't be able to get up in the morning, and that'll be the very time Mary Green calls and writes her notes and makes me so nervous I want to sit on my hands to keep them from shaking.

On the positive side, my driving is improving. Lydia's a good teacher and doesn't get worried when I can't engage the clutch and the traffic builds up behind us. She's going to help me paint the rooms. But not yet . . . not just yet. Little steps, she says. Everything can be done in little steps. She started art classes after her husband died. She said it started as therapy and became her grand obsession. Her paintings are strange and weird, ruins of abandoned cottages in the middle of nowhere. She calls them 'famine echoes'. If women could work and rear children in such a hostile environment, she says the least she can do is follow their footsteps and record what is left of their existence. Her paintings look similar; crumbling walls almost invisible under ivy, weeds growing like spun sugar from chimney breasts. It's her use of light and shade that makes the difference.

Gramps is beginning to pull himself together. His cheque arrived on time this week. He's promised to stop drinking and come with me and Lydia to the inquest. I dread it . . . and the court case. It's like the anniversary mass. Another stepping stone that walks them further away from us. Life moves on . . . tick tock tick . . . and a year has passed.

9

Letters to Nirvana

13 August 1986

Dear Mammy,
 I have sad news. That is why I did not write for
3 days. Gramps is dead. I cried for ages at his
funral and Im crying writing this. Mrs Mulvaney
said we cry for all sorts of different reasons at fun-
rals. At Gramps funral lots of things came back to
me. I thought I was going to be sick. He is glad to
be dead. He said so to Becks after the court. Do
you think that killed him? He went with her and
Mrs Mulvaney to find out how you and Daddy
died. Why? We know why. A big lorry, that is
why. The lorry driver said he was very sorry. His
family hugged him when the judge said he
wouldn't go to jail because of the rain making the
road slippy. Becks hates his guts. So do I. I don't
want to write any more tonight.
 XXXXXXXXX to you and Daddy
 Cathy

22 September 1986

Dear Mammy,
 Today was nice. We cleaned out Gramp's cottage, what a mess. Whisky bottles everywhere and

mice droppings in the presses. UGG! UGG! Tell him thanks for the money. Becks said it is for our edukayshon. Julie wants to spend it on ecuipment for the band. Maxeemum Volum are going to tour when they are famous and they need a image. She wont do her Leaving exam. Becks said no way ho-say you do it or I'll lock you in your room and throw away the key.

Lauren would'nt help clean Gramps cottage. She sat in the car with her walkman on and told me to F . . . Off when I asked if she wanted to see your bike in the barn. I only asked!! It was covered in cobwebs. I closed my eyes and I could see you riding the road and the wind blowing your dress. Lauren is in a rotten mood again. Remember the last photo Daddy took on the night we all went to her ballet show? Daddy timed the camera so he could get into it too? Well, she broke the glass and screamed at me to stop putting flowers in front of it. I'm never going to speak to her again!!

She didn't want to go to secondderry school because people would laugh at her limp and call her a spa. She has no limp. Only when she's tired and tries to do her ballet. Mrs Moran took her to Arnotts for her new school uniform and they went to a posh hotel for tea.

I have to write to Mrs Moran every week. She sends back my letters with red marks. I hate her. I only want to write to you and tell you all.

I will write again soon.

Love to you and Daddy and Gramps

XXXXXXXXXXXXXXXXXXX

Cathy

15 January 1987

Dear Mammy,

I can't believe you are dead 2 years today. We planted lavender on your grave and put fresh flowers on the spot where you died. Becks wants to put a cross there but the council said it's not on and would be a distracshin for drivers.

The garden is all weeds now. Its Julies job to keep the grass cut but she is a lazy lump and calls Becks a commonist dictater. She told her a fib about playing with Maximum Volume at a concert for cancer. Kevin said it was in a pub where men look up girl's legs and buy kondoms. My lips are zealed. Maximum Volume are my favorite band, next to Adam Ant. Me and Kevin listen to the band when they pratis in the garden shed. Sebby Morris is lead guitar. Do you remember him from around the corner? He is the biggest poser ever and shakes his head when he plays guitar like there are bees in his ears. He keeps pointing his guitar at Julie and making kissing mouths when Paul is not looking.

Love to you and Daddy and Gramps
XXXXXXXXXXXXXXXXXXXXXXXXXXX
Cathy

10 July 1987

Dear Mammy,

Today was nice. We had a picnic in Gramp's river field. It belongs to Becks now. A woman called Lulu May rents it from Becks and keeps horses there. She made us tea in the cottage and brought it out to the picnic and sat with us. The sun was shining. Julie blew the seeds from dandylion clocks and said Seb . . . Paul . . . Seb . . . Paul. All the last seeds said Paul . . . Paul . . . Paul. I'm glad because Sebby Morris keeps talking about going to Austrailya and Julie says she'll go with him. Paul says he's all hot air and gets mad jelous if he even looks at Julie. Please don't let her go away.

Lulu's horses waded across the river to see us. They nussled Beck's cheeks like they loved her too. I'm really glad she didn't sell the field to Mr Moran for his ticky tacky houses.

Please make every day like today.

Love to you and Daddy and Gramps

XXXXXXXXXXXXXXXXXXXXXXXXXXXX

Cathy

25 August 1987

Dear Mammy,

What a week! Julie failed the Leaving. Too much snogging on the sofa with Paul ha ha. Mr Moran says failing was on the cards from the beginning and the same will happen to me and Lauren if Becks doesn't keep a tighter rein on us. The row about the Leaving was bad. I wish Becks would stop bossing us around. I wish Julie would stop driving her nuts. I wish Lauren would smile and talk to me. I don't want to go to the Morans with her. Julie won't go, no way ho-say, and Rebecca says she needs a break so me and Lauren we have to go on our own to Meadow Lark.

Love to you and Daddy and Gramps

Cathy

54

Dear Mammy,

Sad news. All the bangers killed Nero. Becks found him in the kitchen this morning stiff. We had a funeral in the garden and she made a cross for his grave and read a poem about a dog being a woman's best friend. She cried worse than at your funeral.

Love to you, Daddy, Gramps and Nero
XXXXXXXXXXXXXXXXX
Cathy

10

Rebecca's Journal — 1987

They use a language I can't decode. Even Lauren with her lost eyes is part of it. Silent and subtle, implicate in the twist of a lip, the lift of an eyebrow, the flash of their eyes meeting. Even the way they hold their shoulders sends out signals that can change their mood, avert an argument, turn a serious discussion into a joke from which I always feel excluded. I can't remember when I first noticed that it had become Me and Them . . . Us and Her. I know why they resent me. I'm to blame for trying to replace the irreplaceable . . . but what is there to do?

Julie escapes into her music. There's been complaints from the neighbours about the noise from the garden shed but she yawns and sighs and heaves her shoulders when I try and talk to her. I hear my voice, shrill, bad-tempered, bossy, and find it hard to recognise myself. I hate what they've turned me into. Lydia is the only one who understands.

I never thought I'd have anything in common with a woman in her forties but she's been a brick. I talked to her about Jeremy and how he never bothered phoning to tell me he was moving to New York. I had to hear it from Sheila. Rose Moore looked terrible when I saw her in Malahide Village last week. I probably looked the same after he dumped me. I told her it would pass but she took it the wrong way and said she was the one who dumped him and good riddance. She's such a liar.

11

Letters to Nirvana

Dear Mummy,
   It's three years now. Me and Kevin visited
your grave this evening. The gates were closed
but there was a hole in the wall and we could
slide in real easy. We met a Goth there called
Melancholia Barnes. She's two years older than
me and is in First Year with Kevin. Now she's
my friend as well. I thought Goth was all about
sucking blood and pet bats but Melancholia says
it's just about people who want to be different
to the masses. She's actually called Melanie but
she hates her name and thinks Mel is for
bimbos. We went back to my house and had
popcorn and watched The Addams Family on
telly.
   She can talk to the dead. Kevin can't but he
believes you can smell dead people. His father is
dead longer than you so he knows best. Mr Mulvaney had a bad heart and was cramated but Kevin
can not smell ashes only roses, like the ones his
father used to grow in the garden.
   I got a glass from the kitchen and we put our
fingers on the edge of it. Melancholia told us to
close our eyes. She said spirit of the glass speak to

58

us speak to us. We had to press hard on the edge of the glass and it wobbled when it tried to give us a message. I wanted to talk to you and Daddy and Kevin wanted to talk to his father. Becks came into the room when the glass was wobbling and gave out like mad. She believes it's dangerous to meddle with something we don't understand. How can it be wrong to talk to the dead? She is such a pain.

Love to you, Daddy, Gramps Gaynor and Nero,
XXXXXXXXXXXXXX
Cathy

15 May 1988

Dear Mummy,

I have to tell you something. I'm getting little boobs and I've hair down that place. It's scary and I'm afraid to tell Becks in case it's weird. Lauren is four years older and she has no boobs yet. Soon I'll look like Julie. That's scary. She said Cross Your Heart is the best kind of bra. Becks says she's too busy to notice if she's got boobs or not. She has. I saw her standing in front of the mirror in her room one night. She had no clothes on. She thought I was sleeping and was mad as a bear when she saw me at the door. She put on her nightdress and asked me what I was staring at. Who cares?

Paul and Julie are fighting. Not so much snogging on the sofa any more. She is supposed to be studying hard for her Leaving Repeats but all she cares about is the band. Paul says Maximum

Volume can't go touring until he's finished college.

Love to you, Daddy, Gramps Gaynor and Nero.
XXXXX
Cathy

30 October 1988

Dear Mum,Me and Kevin held a séance in Melancholia's house tonight. Did you hear us? Did we
cause a vibration in heaven? Rebecca would go
nuts if she knew. We lit candles and sat in a
circle. Melancholia asked the ouija board to spell
out your name and it did. Rachel. I couldn't
believe it. Kevin accused her of moving the indica-
tor but I know she didn't 'cause I was watching
real close. Then it spelled Jerry. It should have
been Gerry but it was near enough. Kevin asked
the board to spell his father's name and laughed
like mad when it spelled John instead of Kenneth.
But 2 out of 3 is not bad. Do you think the
séance was for real? It must be. I never told Melancholia your names so she couldn't have been
guessing.

Becks thinks she's a bad influence and I should
have friends my own age. I wish she'd stop trying
to run my life for me. Melancholia has tattoos.
One on her butt, one on her breast and two on
her arms. She said it doesn't hurt a bit. Becks
would freak if I dared get one but Leah (that's
Melancholia's mum) didn't mind a bit. It's hard to
believe she's a mother. She looks like Melancholia's older sister except her hair is blonde and she
wears ra-ra skirts with sparkles. She looks younger
than Becks. Julie is still giving out about college.

You'd think she'd be glad she got her Repeat Leaving but she hates computer studies and having to sit in front of a computer when all she wants to do is sing for her fans. Becks says computers are the future and to stop complaining and do what she's told for a change.

Love to Dad and all,
Cathy

12

Letters to Nirvana

Dear Mum,

What a start to the new year. Julie and Paul are all off!! She keeps looking at Sebby Morris like he's a king or something and says she's in love for real. So what was Paul? A dress rehearcell? I feel really sorry for him. I saw him walking in the castle grounds last night and he looked wild with his beard but it's not a proper one, more like he can't be bothered shaving and he doesn't show up much for band practice. Her and Paul have been together yonks and she doesn't give a toss that she's broken his heart. She's such a bitch and I hate sharing with her 'cause all she talks about is going away with Sebby Morris.
    Love to Dad and all,
    Cathy

15 January 1989

Dear Mum,
    I can't believe it's four years. We went to mass and placed a wreath on your grave. We finally got permission to erect the cross in you and Daddy's

memory. Everyone says it's not a distraction on the bend. But they see it and it makes them slow down and that's good. I'm glad the cross is up at last but I hate the reason Becks had to fight to get it there.

Julie's being nice again. She's asleep now with the pillow over her head. She came into the room tonight when I was crying about her going away with Sebby and then she cried too and said going away was all hot air and the far away hills are greener than the garden shed or something like that and she tickled me so much I got the hiccups and so did she and Becks yelled at us to behave and stop doing her head in. I'm glad I didn't tell her about Julie going away because she would have stopped her and had a BIG ROW. This way, Julie made up her mind on her own.

Love to Dad and All,
Cathy

3 February 1989

Dear Mum,
Something happened today. I got my period. I had a pain in my tummy all day and then I saw the blood. Becks said I'm too young. I'm not even a teenager so it must be a mistake. No mistake. She gave me a hot water bottle for my tummy and said the pain will be gone by tomorrow. Julie said I'm now a victim of The Curse and hermoans. She bought me a Curly Wurly bar. I thought you'd like to know. I don't feel any different. Should I?

Lauren says she doesn't care if she never gets

63

her period. She should by now. But you can bleed in other ways. I see cuts on her arms, scabs healing. She makes me sick!! I was going to tell Becks but there'll only be another row so I'm saying nothing for the moment.

I'll write again soon.

Love to you and Daddy and Gramps and Nero,
Cathy.

11 May 1989

Dear Mum,

Major news! I'm going to be an auntie. Talk about trouble. Becks (actually, it's Rebecca now, she says Becks is kid stuff and, as we all claim to be adults, we must call her by her proper name) went ballistic when she heard. Julie is refusing to marry Paul. She says she'll take the baby with her in a sling when she's touring. Small problem. Maximum Volume don't exist any more. Seb's gone to Australia and the new guitarist is useless and Paul's got to do exams to support a wife and child. Wife, my arse, said Julie, are you deaf or what? We're not getting married!!!!!

Lauren's staying in her room as usual and I'm spending all my time with Kevin and Melancholia. I'm glad I have friends. They're so much easier than family. I can't believe I'm actually going to be an auntie!

Love to Dad and all,
Cathy

Dear Mum,

Seconderry school is not as bad as I thought. I cycle with Kevin and Melancholia and I sit beside them in the canteen even though I'm only a First Year and that's insect status as far as the rest of the students are concerned. I'm afraid I didn't make the top stream like Lauren. I'm in a low stream but who cares . . . except Becks and that's just because it reflects badly on her.

Melancholia looks like a Goth even in her school uniform and she couldn't care less what people think about her. When Jobbo Boland makes a pretend cross sign with his arms and calls her Belladonna, she just laughs and calls him a wanker. I never heard the Cure or the Banshees or Bachaus until she played them. I'm never going to listen to Kylie Minogue again.

Julie is getting bigger every day. Paul still wants to marry her. He must be off his head. She has such a temper and if she's not sulking she's bawling her eyes out. She's never ever getting married.

Love to Dad and all,
Cathy

1 November 1989

Dear Mum

Julie's wedding was brilliant. She didn't care about being a whale and kept getting up on the stage to sing with the wedding band. Rebecca walked her up the aisle. It should have been

Daddy but Rebecca said we had to make this a happy day. Lauren looked like a mermaid in her bridesmaid's dress. Mrs Moran eyes slid sideways when Mr Moran was dancing with her and said it's amazing how quickly young people grow up nowadays when there's no proper supervision. I thought Rebecca was going to thump her. I would have! Paul nearly had to carry Julie off the stage so that the band could play Congratulations and send them off on their honeymoon to Galway. We used boxes and boxes of confetti. Julie was so huge she needed it all to cover her tummy! And Jeremy Anderson came!! Home from the Big Apple. Guess he didn't like the taste. He danced with Rebecca and she looked like the happiest woman in the world.

Love to Daddy and all,
Cathy

13

Rebecca's Journal — 1989

Never believe your best friend when she promises not to interfere in your love life. Sheila said it was just the two of us meeting for a meal. We'd seen so little of each other since she got engaged to Brian. I figured she wanted to show off her ring and steeled myself to be enthusiastic when she discussed her wedding plans. But I was wrong. I didn't notice Jeremy at first. Brian blocked him from view until I was almost at the table. Then it was too late to run.

I believed I'd stopped loving him. Convinced myself he meant nothing to me. Believed I hated him for being a coward. Paul stuck by Julie, put up with her moods and her tears and her tantrums and now . . . well, it's not exactly a match made in Heaven but he'll be holding her hand when the baby comes.

Jeremy said he was too young to carry me through the bad times and he ran. It's hard remembering how I felt then . . . when I think back to those years they seem dreamlike, as if we were performing a play on a stage and the world was our audience. I remember people walking to the other side of the street, hoping I hadn't noticed they were avoiding me. I can understand their embarrassment. We were an ordinary family made extraordinary by tragedy. I wouldn't have known what to say either and, sometimes, it's better to keep on going.

Jeremy regrets leaving me, the heartache he caused. I try to remember the heartache but I can't . . . I think my feelings must have been stirred in the greater melting pot of grief.

He's older now and he's back. Little steps. Everything can be done in little steps. He says I can trust him. He's changed, matured, knows what he wants.

VisionFirst have set up an advertising division in Ireland and sent him back from New York to work in it. I'm not surprised. His persuasive powers are good. Julie says I must be off my head to trust him again. The leopard's spots are not for changing. But I have to trust him. He's brought me back to life.

14

Letters to Nirvana

22 November 1989

Dear Mum,

I'm a teenager at last. My birthday party was brilliant. Rebecca gave me a stereo. Melancholia gave me Interview with a Vampire by Anne Rice and Kevin gave me a CD of the Cure. Lauren gave me scented candles. Julie and Paul gave me a gift voucher for Awear. Jonathan gave me a mug with The Coolest Hip Auntie in Town on it. I still can't believe he was born on their honeymoon! Julie said pushing out the Rock of Cashel would have been easier. Mrs Mulvaney gave me a pair of Docs. Mr Moran gave me money and Mrs Moran gave me a dictionary. Bitch! Jeremy gave me Lily of the Valley perfume. I have it on me now and it's gorgeous.

I sleep with Rebecca now. I miss your room but it's Julie and Paul's, and I prefer sharing with Rebecca rather than freaky Lauren. It's strange having a man living in the house. I can't remember Daddy's sounds. Paul sings when he's in the shower and he leaves the toilet seat up and talks to the telly when he's watching football. He's given up college and is working with computers. Jonathan is adorable!

He looks like Daddy. Everyone says so. When I held him for the first time he gripped my thumb so tight I thought my heart would melt with love for him. Lauren was afraid to hold him in case she let him fall. She never wants to have a baby and that's just as well because of the accident and what it did to her insides.

Julie's going to start a new band as soon as she stops breast feeding. Paul can like it or lump it. The only music in her life now is Jonathan crying. At maximum volume!! You and Daddy are grandparents. I hope you know that . . . I really do hope so.

Love to Daddy and all,
Cathy

2 December 1989

Dear Mum,

Lauren cut herself again. Rebecca had to take her to the doctor. She's so beautiful, not like me, what's she trying to do? I'm just an acne dose but she's always going on and on about how ugly she is and staying in her room all the time writing crazy stuff. I hope she means it when she says never again. That's all the news for now.

Love to all,
Cathy

15 January 1990

Dear Mum,

It's five years today. Sometimes it only seems like yesterday but when I think of all that's changed in those years it seems like forever since I knew you and Daddy.

There's strange things happening in your grave-yard. We saw empty cider bottles and burned grass in the old part where no one is buried any more. Someone wrote Boot Boys Rule OK on a tombstone. Rebecca hates me going there but all we do is listen to our music. Leah doesn't go on at Melancholia all the time. Neither does Mrs Mulvaney. She let Kevin paint his room black and stick a luminous skeleton on the ceiling. He had his bottom lip pierced with a tiny dagger. You'd laugh if you saw his hair. He's dyed it jet black and made it straight. He hates fair curls and is sick of being called a blondie pouf! I asked him what it was like kissing girls with a dagger in his lip and he said, do you want to find out? Cheeky.

I still miss you. Do you know it's five years or does that just seem like a little dot in eternity?

Special love to Dad on this memory day,
Cathy

3 March 1990

Dear Mum,

It's so fucking unfair! It was all in the Evening Herald about the gravestones and photos too. Your gravestone was all right. It was the old ones that had the graffiti done on them. Nothing to do with me and Kevin and Melancholia but the woman in the house beside the gate told the guards we hang around there all the time. We don't hang around! We visit your grave if only she'd open her stupid eyes and look. And we

71

don't smash gravestones but no one believes us. The guards came to the house and talked to Rebecca. They asked us questions about the graffiti and the broken angels and devil worship. One of the guards said Rebecca had better keep a closer eye on me in future or there'll be more trouble. He made it sound as if it was all her fault. But it's not. She told me not to go to the graveyard except with her but I like being there with Kevin and Melancholia. Those sick boot boys messed up our rights!!

After the cops left Rebecca slapped my face. She said, that's for running around with sick Goths. What planet is she on? What sick Goths? Just because Kevin dyes his hair, she keeps saying he's like a vampire. It's not fair. I don't cut myself. I don't get pregnant like Julie did. So why am I grounded for a fucking month? Thank God, Jeremy is on my side. He thinks Goth is an expression of individuality. It always sounds pretentious when Melancholia says that but he made it sound true. He was always getting into trouble when he was a teenager. His father said he'd never amount to anything but he did. His ad about the shopping centre won an award for innovation. His photo was in the papers. Rebecca stuck it on the fridge. I see him every time I open the door.

No more ouija board. It's banned from my life. Even if I played snakes and ladders Rebecca would freak! I'd stopped believing in it anyway. I just wanted it to be real because I need to know if you're in Heaven. I'm finding it harder and harder to believe you're there . . . or anywhere except in my head. Maybe you were a dream I dreamed and you and Daddy never existed. Maybe I'm a dream and living in everyone else's dreams. Maybe angels do come at night and read letters. Maybe it's not a con job thought up by Lydia Mulvaney to stop me snivelling over her fish fingers and chips.

X

Cathy

20 Oct 1990

Dear Mum,

I'm back in your room again. Julie and Paul have moved out. They used Gramps' money for a deposit on a house in Swords with wood floors so Jonathan doesn't have to breathe in the dust from our carpets. It makes his asthma worse. Julie gets so scared when he starts to wheeze but the doctor said asthma is not a problem with the right medication and lots of kids grow out of it. Their next new baby will be born in April. Julie calls it 'another mistake' but I know she'll love it just as much as she loves Jonathan. I cycle to Swords with Kevin once a week and we baby-sit so they can go to the pictures.

Sometimes Jeremy stays over in our house. I saw him kissing Rebecca in the hall last night. I didn't mean to spy and was only going downstairs to get a glass of milk. Rebecca's hair was like a rope around his hands and he was pressing her against the wall and whispering, let me stay . . . they won't hear anything . . . I promise . . . promise . . . kissing her all the time. I was afraid to move in case they saw me. She let him stay. He was wrong. I heard. It makes my tummy swoop to think of it and the more I try not to the more I do.

Love to Dad and all,
Cathy

5 Nov 1990

Dear Mum,

Serious news. Lauren's in hospital. We're all in shock. She keeps saying she didn't mean to do it so deep and she's promised Rebecca she'll never do it again. Is she crazy or what? She's in a private room with flowers. Mr Moran said it's only right to look after her properly and he'd pay. He brings her chocolates and fluffy toys. Mrs Moran said if they'd had their way in the beginning, all this could have been avoided. She said it low to Mr Moran so that Rebecca couldn't hear. But I did. The cheek of her. What does she know about anything except being stinking rich and showing off her fancy house in magazines? They'll never be our parents, no matter how hard they try. Watch over Lauren and make her stop hurting herself.

Love you all,
Cathy

15

Rebecca's Journal — 1990

I was searching under her mattress for blades and I found poems instead. Only a few. I suspect she's destroyed most of them or maybe hidden them somewhere else. But I'm not going to pretend I know. She values her privacy too much. I cried when I read this one. I thought it was about gardening when I saw the title but she's obviously still clinging to memories of our mother. At least, in this instance, Lauren has released them in ink, not blood.

Crying is not for the faint-hearted. I thought I'd never stop. Only that Jeremy was calling . . . I don't ever want him to see me in such a state. We've moved on from that time . . . tick tock tick tock tick . . .

I've copied this poem and others into the journal. Some day when she's stronger, I'll persuade her to send them to a publisher.

Deadheading the Red Geraniums

I watch you
Deadheading the red geraniums
The withered petals
Blood-staining your hands

When you snap the head
From its slender stem.

I watch you
Breathe the perfumed air
As sweet peas waltz
On bamboo stilts.
Adrift in pink until the pods
Wither and decay.

I watch you
Gather roses: crimson, cream and
peach.
The prayerful thorns sink
Into your flesh.
Stigmata lifting you
Across the deep abyss.

I watch you
Stroke the birch, the silvery bark.
A family tree, denuded.
A wafer fragment
Falling. Ash to ash . . .
Ash to ash.

16

Letters to Nirvana

26 December 1990

Dear Mum,

Guess what Jeremy gave Rebecca for Christmas. A really flash solitaire. They're getting married in June 1992. Julie and Paul didn't stay long at the engagement party because of Jonathan and the carpet dust. Lauren is good since she came out of hospital. At the party, all the boys wanted to dance with her . . . except Kevin. He thinks she's a real head banger and even though I agree, I hate it when anyone says things like that about her.

Mr Moran proposed a toast to Rebecca and Jeremy and said may all their troubles be little ones. He can talk, said Julie. Where's his little ones? If he had any he wouldn't be so slick with his words. She is afraid Jonathan will have another asthma attack and go to hospital again. Sebby sends her postcards from Australia. She calls them salt in the wound.

XXX

Cathy

15 Jan 1991

Dear Mum,

It's six years today. Rebecca forgot to organise the mass. She can talk about nothing but Jeremy this and Jeremy that and she looks different, like a light is shining inside her. I know you don't mind but she should have done the mass.

XXXX to you and Daddy on this special memory day,
Cathy

12 April 1991

Dear Mum,

I went shopping with Melancholia today. She gave me this amazing jet black cross for a present and showed me where to find fantastic clothes in the George's Street arcade. Black net gloves to my elbows and a long black dress with a scooped neck, perfect with the cross.

Rebecca hates my new clothes. She's always going on about Satanic influences, whatever that's supposed to mean. Well, I know what it means but that's not us. All we do is play our music and read Anne Rice. I don't know how someone as nice as Jeremy can possibly be in love with her. He must be only pretending. He's probably terrified of her. Everyone else is. She keeps going on about me staying out late and how she has responsibility for my welfare. Who does she think she is? You and Daddy were responsible for my welfare, no one else. Julie's too busy to talk since Philip was born. He looks like a troll but she keeps going on at Jeremy about using him for nappy ads. Jeremy is so nice he tries to be polite but he says maternal love is blind as a bat, only not to Julie, of course. Only to me. I was going to say love must be very blind if you're marrying my ugly ageing sister with absolutely no taste in clothes but I didn't.

He thinks I look like Kate Bush. I adore Kate Bush. I love how she sings my name Cat-he-ah . . . Cat-he-ah . . . but what I love most is the way Jeremy says my name. Catriona. I've always been Cathy since I can remember but he says I'm too precious to be an abbreviation. That's what he says. Too precious to be an abbreviation. God! It's time I went to sleep. Rebecca would go nuts if she knew what I was thinking. Thank God we have skin on our skulls to keep our thoughts from escaping.

Love,
Catriona

10 August 1991

Dear Mum,

I need to tell you something. It's not bad or anything but I know Rebecca would be mad if she knew. I met Jeremy outside his office today. It wasn't on purpose. I just wanted to find out where he works. I didn't expect him to come out and see me. He brought me to a café on Baggot Street. It was very crowded yet it seemed like we were the only two people there. I was shaking so much I was sure he'd notice but he just talked about the awful ads he has to make, like the ones for toilet cleaners and constipation. He made a brilliant one about a woman sky-diving on the Curse days. I've seen it loads of times. When she falls from the sky laughing her head off and her arms out like a bird you'd never think she gets tummy cramp or be frightened blood will show on her dress. He said I'm growing into a beautiful young lady. No one ever said that to me before, only to Lauren. He's going to be my brother-in-law. Every time I think about it my eyes sting as if someone blew smoke into them. God! It's time I went to sleep. I hate being like this, my skin shivery every time I imagine them together.

I didn't tell her about meeting him. I was afraid she would get mad and say I was looking for attention again. I wasn't!

I found your copy of Wuthering Heights. It's brilliant and cruel and so sad. I keep thinking about death and how it really messes up life for those still living. I hated and loved Heathcliff. I only loved him because he loved Cathy so much that it made everything else he did seem not so bad . . . almost.

X

Catriona

10 September 1991

Dear Mum,
Rebecca wants her bridesmaids in russet red. Julie thinks polka dots would be very original. Lauren wants us to wear ice-blue. They argue and wave bits of material at each other. My opinion is not sought. Who wants black at a wedding?

He's going to move into our house when they get married. Rebecca's going back to college as a mature student to be a vet like she'd started doing when you died. After she's qualified, she's going to run the animal sanctuary on Gramps' field with Lulu. Her dreams are no longer ash. They're all coming true.

I wish I was her. I can't tell anyone except you. Even Melancholia wouldn't understand.

Catriona

2 December 1991

Dear Mum,

You and Dad would be proud of Lauren. Her first book of poems was launched tonight. It's called Silverfish. She's dedicated her book to you and Dad. Mr Moran made a speech and said she's a new young voice dealing with difficult issues. My throat went really tight when she read the Silverfish poem. It's awful. Sad and weird and very Lauren.

I know what silverfish are. They look like commas and sometimes I see them flicking in the dark. Lauren's wrists have healed up but I still see the marks, like she's drawn little squiggles on her skin.

Jeremy sat next to me. He must have known my thoughts because he said, stop frowning Catriona, you'll ruin your beautiful face. His knee hit mine under the table and his smile went deep into my eyes when he whispered Oops! Sorry, Catriona. I love how he says my name . . . Catriona
. . . Catriona . . . Cat-rio-na . . . like it's a beautiful

sound in a love song.

Afterwards Mr Moran brought us for a meal to the Shelbourne Hotel. He knew everyone and kept introducing Lauren as his poetic protégée. Mrs Moran said she should stop depending on them for everything. But she said it so quiet that only me and Rebecca heard her. She's such a bitch!

Love you,
Catriona

17

Rebecca's Journal — 1991

She couldn't believe I'd collected her poems. I
tried to persuade her to submit them to a
proper publishing house but she refused. Afraid
of failure, afraid of everything. Steve Moran
took over. Vanity publishing. A big launch. What
did it mean in the end? Another crutch.

Silverfish

In the moon skidding hours
I collect silverfish
Somersaulting silverfish
Disco dancing silverfish
Flick flash
Across the ash
And embers dead
Of hearth and home
Sliding in and sliding out
In chink and eave
In weft and weave
Snug in a rug
Smug bugs
In crevices that bleed the night.
Hurry scurry
Playing hide but do not seek us.
Silver scales

Flick flash
Slick slash
Dancing lancing silverfish
Thrashing, slashing twitch-blade runners.

18

Letters to Nirvana

15 January 1992

Mother,
    Seven years . . . did you ever exist??????? Where should I address these pathetic letters? Heaven . . . Paradise . . . Nirvana . . . Cloud Nine? Where are you?
    Cathy

9 June 1992

Dear Mum,
    It's over. He is now my brother-in-law. Rebecca walked up the aisle on Mr Moran's arm. The way she smiled when she said, I Do, made me think about the nice times and how she loved me before you died. I kept remembering and remembering and it made me cry. We wore ice-blue with a shimmer when it caught the light. In every wedding photograph we're smiling fit to burst a gut. Mr Moran made the Father of the Bride speech. Mrs Moran drank too much. Her mouth slid sideways when she was asked to lift her glass in a toast to the bridesmaids and she stayed sitting when everyone else stood up and shouted, To the beautiful bridesmaids.

Jeremy danced with me. His fingers pressed into the small of my back. He said I looked beautiful in blue and that I'd emerged from a chrysalis. I went into the Ladies and stared at myself in the full-length mirror. An ice-blue butterfly emerging from a chrysalis. Flying from a dark place, afraid of my reflection.

X
Catriona

22 August 1992

Dear Mum,

I didn't think I'd ever get used to it but I have. Jeremy eats muesli and croissants for breakfast. He put photographs of his best ads in frames all over the hall. I sleep with cotton wool in my ears and squeeze my eyes tight so that I won't think about them in the next room. But I do . . . I do . . . In the morning I pretend not to notice when they touch every time they pass each other. I pretend not to hear when they giggle over stupid things I don't understand. Rebecca looks so young again. A student now, jeans and a ponytail.

I'm not going to write to you any more. What's the sense in writing to a ghost? I ask myself that question every time I take up my pen. It's stupid to keep looking for a sign that your fingers touched the paper when it's obvious you don't exist!!

X
Catriona

Dear Mum,

Lauren's gone to the University of Westminster to learn to be a proper writer. Mrs Moran organised it, the fees and all. Rebecca is furious. She doesn't want Lauren to leave home but Lauren said it's got nothing to do with her any more. We're all growing up and making our own decisions. I haven't told Rebecca about the night Mrs Moran rang and called me an ungrateful adulterous whore. Her voice was so squeaky and shaky, I didn't know who she was, at first. When I said, you have the wrong number, this is Cathy Lambert, she hung up immediately. Every time I think about that squeaky voice on the phone something twists inside my chest. When I told Lauren, she stared back at me with her haughty expression that shuts everyone out and never said a word. Mrs Moran is mental to think Lauren fancies her geriatric husband. Lauren doesn't fancy anyone but herself.

I wanted to tell Julie but I didn't. I was afraid she'd laugh at Mrs Moran and call her a daft bat. She's in rotten humour since she discovered she's pregnant again. Why don't they take up badminton or marathon running? Sex can't be the only game they know how to play.

It'll be easier in the house without Lauren. Not quieter, she never made a sound, but calm like we can open doors without being afraid.

Love you all,
Catriona

Dear Mum,

I'm in deep shit. Grounded for ever, as far as Rebecca is concerned. Remember I told you about Melancholia's idea for the Halloween Goth party? My date with disaster, as it turned out!! Rebecca thought I was sleeping over at Melancholia's house and had even checked with Leah, who pretended I was.

We held the party in a warehouse down on the docks. It used to belong to Melancholia's uncle. All the buildings around are empty too so it was creepy and perfect. We made a papier-mâché coffin and a tombstone and put black netting over the walls. We only invited Goths so it was hush-hush. Or so we believed. Melancholia sneaked vodka from Leah's cocktail cabinet. Two bottles. Sharon had wine and Kevin brought beer. I drank vodka for the first time. It was like a volcano inside my chest. One of the Goths kept giggling 'cause you're not supposed to drink it neat. It was easier going down with the orange juice
. . . smooth and easy . . . easy and slow.

More people came, gatecrashers, not Goths. We all danced together but not touching. Goths don't touch or invade private space. The gatecrashers didn't care. Jobbo Boland called me a vampire bitch and begged me to bite his neck. They started a fight and broke bottles against the wall and carried the coffin on their shoulders like it was a real funeral. When there was no drink left they went on to the next party. Most of the Goths went as well.

My head felt fuzzy and my eyes were whirling around. Everything was dark and awful until I saw you. Yes, you, angel Mother, dancing on your own. You were as clear as a star in a jet-black sky. The music was so beautiful. I wanted to dance with you for ever. Kevin shouted at me to stop dancing with shadows but I couldn't. I twirled around and around, and you twirled with me. The music played louder and louder until it seemed as if my head would explode. Then your face went spinning towards the moon outside the window. You were going away again. I wouldn't let you. Not this time.

I screamed and my fist went through the window. I don't remember the glass breaking. Just the moon turning silver and your face vanishing into the night. I woke up in hospital with bandages on my hands. Not a good idea, said the doctor when he came to see me. Don't do that again, young lady, unless you're into blood sports.

When I got home from the hospital Rebecca made me look at myself in the mirror. Black panda eyes and black smeared lipstick. I wanted to die. Black . . . black . . . black. She kept shouting and flinging my clothes on the bed. She looked at Daddy's guitar and your perfume bottle shaped like a pyramid, still half-full, and my silver locket with your hair inside. She said my room is nothing but a shrine and it's time I started living in the real world. She tore my posters of Bauhaus and the Banshees and The Cure from the wall and crumpled them in a ball. Tomorrow I have to paint your room. Primrose yellow or rose-petal pink, I have two choices.

Alcoholic poisoning is what I had. My stomach was pumped. I'm going to stop writing to you for definite this time. Angels don't read letters. They don't even exist. Death is a black and bottomless sleep. I'm grounded for 6 weeks. Shit!

Catriona

6 November 1992

Dear Mum,

Your room is painted primrose yellow. I have kitten posters on the walls. Jeremy painted the ceiling and I did the walls. When he did his Michael Jackson moonwalk across the floor, we laughed so much Rebecca came in to see what the joke was about. When I told him I was never going to drink again, he said alcohol is only disgusting when it's handled recklessly. I was too young. I broke rules. I was heedless of my own welfare. I have to look upon this experience as a baptism of fire. He asked me why I did such a crazy thing. It's dangerous and corrosive to keep bottling up your feelings, Catriona, he said.

I began to giggle, a high awful giggle that I couldn't stop. Take it easy . . . it's all right . . . take it easy. His voice was sharp, then soft, like he was coaxing me over a dangerous place and I stopped as suddenly as I started. Goose bumps ran all along my arms when we sat on the bed and he leaned close to me. You should laugh more often, Catriona, he said. But not like that . . . not like that.

X

Catriona

Dear Mum,

Lauren rang today. Eight years, she said. Who'd have believed it. She lives in one of Mr Moran's apartments. Real plush, she says, with a view of St James's Park. He brings her out for posh meals when he's in London on business. I bet Mrs Moran doesn't know! I asked who held his zimmer frame when they kissed and she said I was way off the mark on that one. He's a father figure, kind and decent and nothing more. You're forgetting rich, I said, and married to the teacher bitch. The teacher bitch has nothing to worry about, Lauren said. Her husband can obsess all he likes but I'm not interested.

I wonder if she's telling the truth. The boys in school used to call her The Ice Queen and put bets on who could get her to go out with them. They never won. She has lots of boyfriends now but their names keep changing: Louie, François, Colm, Toby, Saul.

She's OK again after falling off her bike. Rebecca flew over to make sure and said she's living like royalty.

Look after her and keep her away from blades.

Love you all,

XX

Catriona

Dear Mum

I have to write about this. Forgive me . . . forgive me. I never meant it to happen. This evening I met Jeremy by accident on Merrion Square. At first he didn't recognise me in my Goth make-up. Goth coat and dress, lace over my face, my black cross.

When I said hello he stopped like he'd run into a wall and said, Good God, Catriona, is that really you? You look amazing.

He gave me a lift home. The rain started when we were leaving the city and was pouring down by the time we reached Broadmeadow Estuary. There's a storm coming, Jeremy said. Even as he spoke, we saw lightning flashing across the viaduct. We parked by the shore. The waves raced under the arches and the ducks flapped their wings into the wind. We saw the heron standing as still as ever. Then the thunder rolled over the estuary and lit up the swans like ghosts on water. Jeremy put his arm around my shoulder and said it was nature at her proudest, showing off for all the world to see. Like Goths, he said. Showing off her darker side.

I began to cry. Don't ask me why. He lifted the lace from my face and laid it over my hair. He took off my net gloves and stroked my fingers. Nothing else. Just stroked and stroked until my whole body was shivering. My sweet innocent Catriona, he said. Are you a child playing adult games or a woman caught in a child's mind? Why does such anger radiate from you? He talked about the accident. No one ever does but he asked questions and it was like drawing splinters out of my skin.

Sometimes I wake from a dream and hear Julie screaming. I jump out of bed and crash into the wall because your room is different to the room I slept in then. Rebecca should have been minding me but she'd sneaked off to Sheila's party. Jeremy explained how she feels guilty about disobeying you and not being at home when the police called to the house to tell us about the accident. He said that's why she tries so hard to do what's right.

I wish she'd stop trying. She can't make it different, no matter how hard we pretend. Then I told Jeremy the most dreadful thing of all. How my anger sometimes makes me hate you for being dead. It's not true. It's me. I hate myself for thinking such awful thoughts but they go like a skewer through my brain.

He said the line between love and hate is as fine as a wire vibrating. I don't understand what he means but it sounds right. He understands how things can happen in a part of your mind you never knew existed.

He kissed the tears on my cheeks and on my eyelids. When he kissed the tears on my lips he opened his mouth and pulled me closer. Then he was kissing me for real, tongue touching tongue, and even though I was frightened, I didn't want to pull away, ever. I thought about Rebecca and all her dreams coming true. The wind nearly blew me over when I opened the door of his car. He said, Don't be silly, Catriona. Get back in! I'll drive you to the house. He feels as if he's playing with fire

when we're alone. It would be the end of everything if Rebecca found out about his moment of
weakness. She won't . . . she won't find out.

Don't warn me against him. Don't remind me of
his age, of Rebecca, a whole life I'm too young to
understand. I'm in love with him. The age difference doesn't matter. That's nothing where love is
concerned. I'll dream about him tonight. And
tomorrow I'll daydream through the waking hours.
His eyes are so piercing they can see right into my
soul. Even now, when he's not with me, I feel him
beside me, feel his touch on my skin, his fingers
stroking mine, and the thunder enfolding us. Is
that how it was with you and Daddy? Tell me
what to do!!
Catriona

10 Feb 1993

Dear Mother,
Kevin's bedroom is now painted white. The
skeleton has gone from the ceiling. Ask me how I
know. I'm not supposed to be there. Off limits,
isn't it? Go on, ask! I'm going to tell you anyway.
I lay on his bed and listened to The Cure but it
was different to before, like he could stop being
my friend and be something else. He took the tiny
little dagger from his lip and put it under the
pillow. When we kissed I closed my eyes. I kept
seeing Jeremy's face. The way he combs his
wheat-yellow hair straight back from his forehead
yet there's always a bit hanging down. I could see
his eyes, blue like the sky, and his voice soft when
he said, Catriona . . . Catriona . . . Catriona.

I lifted my black dress above my ankles so that Kevin could see my net stockings and my shoes with the silver buckles. He parted the lace at my throat. He opened the buttons on my dress. So many buttons down the front but he didn't mind struggling, one button after the other, stopping to kiss me in case I was bored it was taking so long. Then I saw his blond roots where he's growing out the black and I had this terrible feeling that I was ruining our friendship by allowing him to open buttons and kiss my neck, his tongue licking the hollow in my throat, making shivers on my skin while all the time I was thinking about someone else.

Then the buttons were open and he was able to take off my bra. My heart gave a skippy kind of jump when he touched my nipples. He pressed me deeper into the bed. His face was hard, a stranger's face. I didn't know him any more. I wanted to hug my breasts away from his eyes and be safe in my room with you in the kitchen making dinner and Daddy's key in the front door, and the way he used to shout, 'Hey, you parcel of beauties, I'm home.'

I shouted at him to let me go. He didn't hear me. My dress was down around my waist and he kept whispering my name . . . I love you Cathy . . . Cathy . . . Not Catriona. I hit his face with my fist and he jerked back, his eyes opening wide. Then he slumped beside me, breathing fast, as if he'd been in a race that went on too long.

Nothing happened, Cathy, stop crying . . . calm down . . . calm down . . . His words came from far away but eventually I heard him. He kept apologising, said he'd misread the signals, thought I felt the same, nothing happened, nothing to stop us continuing to be friends as before. But I knew he lied. That he, like me, could see our friendship dissolving with every promise we made.

I can't think of anything else to tell you tonight. Watch over me. I'm in a dangerous place.
Catriona

16 March 1993

Dear Mum,

Jeremy's kiss is like a dream. Perhaps it was. I don't ever want to think about it again. I saw Kevin this evening when I was walking along the estuary. The dagger's gone from his lip. We haven't talked much since that night. A girl was with him. She has swinging fair hair like a shampoo advertisement. I was afraid he'd told her about the time in his bedroom and could feel the shivers coming just thinking about it. Her name is Andrea and I just know she hates The Cure.

Tomorrow is St Patrick's Day. Remember the parades and the sleet and us dancing on floats in our Irish dancing costumes? Blue knees? The parade has changed a lot since your day. I'm going to watch it with Melancholia and her friends.

I've kept the worst news until last. Rebecca flew out this morning to see Lauren. How does she always know? She's determined to bring her home and make her better again.

X
Catriona

19

Rebecca's Journal — 1993

I never should have allowed Olive Moran to send Lauren away but, truthfully, I was secretly relieved she was leaving us. I wanted nothing to come between Jeremy and our happiness. I convinced myself it was a good idea to let her handle life on her own. I've enough on my hands with Cathy and her Goth friends.

It could have worked out. She sent me sections of her novel. It was raw and revelatory, and was, I suspected, giving her an opportunity to release her feelings. I read her tutor's critiques, his belief that it would be recognised as a serious work of fiction. If only she hadn't been knocked from her bike. It happened so easily — a driver opening the door of his car without looking. She went flying and the second car had to swerve to avoid her. The squeal of brakes brought it all back. She was still screaming when the ambulance arrived. They sedated her in hospital, then discharged her.

She swore she was OK. I believed her because I wanted to. Is it like drugs, I wonder, the sweet swooning oblivion that comes over her when the drip drip drip becomes a flow? There were men; I met some of them when I was there. They brought her flowers and chocolates, and fluffy animals with love notes embroidered on their fur. They make her forget. Why then does she send them away and reach for the only relief that gives her comfort?

I knew as soon as the poem arrived. Just a verse but it's all there. Her cry for help.

Rage river rage
Rage towards the night ocean
Where the tide waits
To crest you towards distant
Reefs of coral
Sharp as the lover's blade
When it sinks into the flesh of a barren moon.

20

Letters to Nirvana

18 March 1993

Oh Mum . . . Mum!

I need to tell you what happened. I can't tell
anyone else, never, ever until the day I die.
Rebecca will kill me stone dead . . . what have I
done?

We watched the parade going through
O'Connell Street then met Melancholia's friends at
the bank on Dame Street. Do you remember the
one that's shaped like a square mushroom? That's
where we sat on the steps and watched everyone
walking by. It felt good, being part of a group and
everyone looking at us, but pretending they
weren't. Then we went up Grafton Street. Buskers
were playing guitars and there were jugglers and
fire-eaters and a man who stood like a statue and
had a frozen face like Lauren, except when he
winked. Melancholia's boyfriend, Chaos, and his
friends bought cans of lager in the off-licence and
we sat on the grass in Stephen's Green drinking
them.

Wrong brew, said Jobbo Boland when he came
by. It should be blood. He called me Vampira. I
hate him!

We told him to get lost but he kept hanging

around. I felt so good with the muzzy far-off feeling inside my head. Jobbo kept shaking his head
like music was switched on in his brain. We went
to McDonald's for burgers. A woman shouted
something about devil worshipers and we chanted
We are Goths . . . We are Goths . . . We are Goths
. . . back at her. We passed the acrobats turning
cartwheels, passed the buskers and the traveller
children with their mouth organs, the pavement
artists with the Virgin Mary pictures. I saw myself
in a shop window. Eyeliner streaked like soot, my
hair all over my face. Vampira Lambert on her day
out.

It was hot and crowded in McDonald's. The
tables were full of families, children with painted
tiger faces, bobbing balloons. Jobbo sat opposite
me and Melancholia went to the counter for chips
and Big Macs.

You look out of it, Vampira, Jobbo said. Are you
not used to drinking blood or what? His piggy
pink eyes kept darting all over the place and his
head was shaved except for a wispy bit at the
back. He told me to relax for a change instead of
always looking like I was going to cut my wrists. I
nearly said, wrong sister, but I didn't. Have some
fun for a change, he said, you'll be in your coffin
long enough. Then he gave it to me. Maybe, if he
hadn't mentioned coffins, I wouldn't have done it.
Maybe I would . . . I don't know anything any
more.

The tiny square of paper had a clown's face
painted on it. Who's that, I asked him, Ronald
McDonald?

He laughed like I'd said the funniest thing in

the world. Believe me, Vampira, it'll blow all those negatives out of your mind. You'll float like a bird.

In the Ladies I licked the tab and wondered if angels would cry because I swore to Rebecca I'd never touch drugs. An oath taken at your grave-side one Sunday afternoon when we were pulling weeds. I couldn't eat the Big Mac or the chips. Melancholia called me an ungrateful cow and dumped them in the bin.

We ran down to College Green where a band called Ovida Jones was playing. The lead singer had long red hair. He was so casual, smoking and joking with the guitarist, ignoring thousands of people watching him. The drummer hit a cymbal. The amplified boom almost lifted me off my feet. Everyone jumped then roared laughing. Where did our laughter go, all our throaty laughter floating up into the dark mysterious night? Did it reach Nirvana before it faded away? Jobbo said I'd float like a bird. Like an eagle. No one to touch me when I'm on top of the world.

The musicians began to play and the thoomb-ing noise crashed from my heart to my head. The singer grabbed the microphone and the crowd screamed. The noise was incredible, a thoomb . . . thoomb beat like a great pounding beast. The singer shoved the microphone towards us and we sang the chorus. 'Under the clock clock . . . clock . . . under the clock. Holding my heart in hock for you under the clock . . . clock . . . clock!'

Again and again we sang the words and I was screaming with them, only there was no sound coming from my mouth because it was frozen in a huge O, tears pouring down my face, and all the fans were crazy wild. Melancholia was sitting on Chaos's shoulders but there were loads of people between us, all strangers. I tried to push my way back to her but I'd lost her in the crowd.

I couldn't stand the thoom in my chest. I had to scream before it choked me. Someone kept shouting, Get her out of here . . . bring her home.

Kevin and his girlfriend stood in front of me. They had their arms around each other. She whispered something behind her hand when she saw me. Kevin pulled my face around.

Jesus! What did you give her? he shouted and hit Jobbo with his fists. He knocked him into the crowd. His girlfriend screamed when Jobbo hit him back. Security men in yellow coats pulled them apart. The fans shook their heads, Jumping crazy, and swayed back as Kevin was dragged away.

I heard Jobbo calling me. Vampira . . . Vampira! Over here. His legs dangled over the plinth of a statue. He hauled me up beside him. I gripped the legs of the statue. Long smooth legs that I must climb if I was to reach beyond the clouds. People kept yelling and pointing as I stretched beyond Jobbo's grip, bracing my knees. Gratton, an Irish patriot, a brave man. It was easy to climb his body, crevices in the elbow, the collar of his coat. I clung to his neck and kissed his face.

Smoke billowed around the magic musicians as they dipped and swayed on the silver stage. When I looked up, the sky was full of silver birds flying in formation. I was among them, an eagle flying forever towards Nirvana.

The wind grew cold. It would blow me from the patriot's neck. Far below I saw a dark hole opening

and I screamed because I knew I was going to fall into it. A man lifted me down. I ran away and pushed through the crowd until I was free. I slid to the ground inside a phone box. It was warm and dark like a coffin. The music seemed far away. I was laughing so much no one could understand and I was calling her name . . . Rebecca
. . . Rebecca . . . Rebecca.

Boys were waiting outside. One of them opened the door and blew smoke in at me. Don't hog the effin' phone all night, he said, and then I remembered that Rebecca was in London with Lauren and Jeremy kept saying, where the hell are you? Tell me immediately.

I waited by the railings of Trinity College. Remember . . . it's where you and Daddy met? I saw ghosts at the gates. Ghosts behind the windows, waving, pale ghosts drowning in silver dust.

His face melted like candle wax and came together again. He called me . . . Catriona
. . . Catriona, come to me. Be safe . . . come into my arms. He took my hand and led me away from the noise. His car surged through the night. We left the city behind.

It was dark on the estuary. Music played on the radio. The swans were sleeping. A bed of white feathers rising. The water sparkled when a train passed over the viaduct. He held me to him and I was carried through ribbons of light. I love you . . . love you . . . kissing him, I repeated the words over and over again. I knew it was going to happen. My fingers sank through his flesh. I watched them disappear into his spine . . . shimmering . . . his hair sparking when I stroked it, filling him with radiance. There were stars above us and the thooming music was still inside me. His voice whispered, husky commands. You're safe. Safe in my arms, my beautiful Catriona.

I saw Rebecca's sweater lying on the back seat, two of her books about animals and her Eurythmics CD. I couldn't stop crying but he kept saying, it's all right . . . it's all right . . . stay still . . . it's all right. I wanted to shout stop stop stop but his hand was over my mouth and I heard him sigh, as if there was a great pain within him that must be relieved by reaching into that place . . . that private place that belongs only to me.

Stars fell from the sky and faded. His face was anxious, frowning when he told me to hurry. We could be seen. But only the heron kept watch on the estuary. He never meant it to happen. I'm jail bait, he said, a dark torment. He fastened the buttons on my dress, not fumbling like Kevin, but sure, as if he had done it so often to Rebecca he knew exactly how to slide them into the buttonholes. Oh God oh God, I can't believe what I'm writing to you . . .

I'd made him angry. His mouth was a hard straight line. He parked at the high wall on the edge of Heron Cove and dried my eyes. Don't break Rebecca's heart. You owe her everything. I placed my hands across my face. I no longer wanted to fly. Only to be alone. There was nothing inside me, not even the sound of music thooming.

I feel so sick this morning but there's nothing left in my stomach to throw up. I've lost my silver locket with your hair inside it. I don't remember getting into bed but I must have shoved my clothes underneath it. They smell of smoke and perspiration and beer. My black dress is covered in dirt, my panties crumpled inside them. The dark rust stain against the white cotton was so shocking I rushed to the basin to rinse it out, scrubbing and scrubbing until the water ran clear. Until then, I thought it was a dream!

His car has gone. There's no one in the house but me. Please hold me . . . hold me . . . hold me!!!

Cathy

24 March 1993

Dear Mum,

Kevin called to the house tonight. The security men roughed him up, blackened his eye. When he gave back cheek they called the guards. Poor Mrs Mulvaney had to collect him from the garda station. His girlfriend dumped him afterwards. He asked me to come over to his place some night and listen to his new Cure album. I said yes, and the heavy feeling lifted from me for a little while.

Lauren is still in hospital. I understand her a little bit better now. She knows about fear and how it can wreck the mind. I'm walking on eggshells. Love and hate, it's a fine wire vibrating. I think of Jeremy's kisses, and the way he tosses his head when he laughs and I'm sick all over again with love for him. What a mess I've turned out to be. What a pathetic mess!

Love you all,
Cathy

Dear Mum,

I'm a waitress. In other words, I'm an invisible species with a tray. Leah's boyfriend gave me and Melancholia summer jobs in Chilli Factor. It's the best Mexican restaurant in Dublin and there's sparks on my heels when I run run run. No time to think about anything except burritos, enchiladas, tostadas, salsas, tacos and sizzling chillies. But the real reason why I haven't written for ages is because I'm anaemic. My eye sockets look really pale pink. Last week I was dizzy in work. Melancholia said it's the slave galley conditions. I keep thinking anaemia or a rare blood cancer . . . anything other than what I really suspect. Oh God, I'm so scared.

Every time I go to the loo I check. Nothing. I think about it first thing in the morning. Last thing at night I pray, please please, God, let it happen tomorrow. If I go to a doctor I'll know for sure. I keep intending to go but suddenly it's a week later and I'm still doing the normal things that everyone else is doing. I stare at people, wondering what's going on behind their faces. Are they pretending too?

In the Pro-cathedral I light a candle. The Virgin stares down on me. She is sad and compassionate but she hasn't answered my prayers. Holy Mary, please listen to me. Let it happen soon because if it doesn't I'll soon be three months late. Officially.
Desperate,
Cathy

Dear Mum,

The cat sat on the mat the cat sat on the mat
the cat . . . oh God, I don't know what to do . . . I
don't know what to do. I threw up in work today.
All the spices and the smell of garlic was so
strong, I couldn't help it.

Melancholia sounded far away when she told
me to open the toilet door. She'd seen me running
to the loo twice and heard me being sick. She
asked if I'd missed a period. I told her three. She
looked so shocked I wanted to grab back the
words. I'd made it real by saying it out loud.

I'm going to her house after we finish our shift
tomorrow. She's buying a pregnancy test kit. She
knows a girl who used one when she was late. As
soon as she discovered the test was negative her
periods came back. It's worrying that causes the
problem.

So many times I've leaned into the silence of
empty rooms to hear you whisper my name. You
have only offered me silence in return. Help me
now. Tell me I'm going to be all right!! I'm begging you . . . please help me.

Cathy

6 July 1993

Dear Mum,

The rain is coming down. Sheets of it turning
the graveyard into a mud river, soaking your bones
and stirring the dead clay. I feel it soaking through
the cracks of your shining walnut coffin with the

brass handles and the white lace framing your face. I wish I was dead. Dead as you and Dad. Shadows, not substance. Shadows flit. Substance suffers.

As soon as I came home from work, I knew Rebecca knew. But not everything. Thank God she does not know everything. Melancholia is the only one who shares my secret and she has sworn an oath on the blood pricked from our fingers that she will never tell.

I'm not the only one who's pregnant. Sheila Brogan, who is now Mrs O'Sullivan, was at the Rotunda Hospital today. I didn't see her but she saw me. At first she thought I was with Melancholia but then she heard the nurse call out my name. She's Rebecca's best friend so needless to say she felt it her duty to ring my sister and tell her. Bitch, bitch, interfering bitch. What am I going to do?

Rebecca demanded to know everything. I told her I didn't know the father's name. Liar, liar, she said. It's Kevin Mulvaney, isn't it? She kept saying his name over and over again. I didn't nod. I know I didn't nod but she shouted that it was bad enough with Julie, but now I was going the same way and Kevin would know all about it, oh, yes, he would, she'd see to it that he did the right thing . . . I put my hands over my ears and ran out of the house. I could smell the rain on the estuary but it was still only a cloud and I sat on the jetty until it was dark. When I came home Rebecca had gone to Kevin's house to have it out with Lydia.

Oh God, oh God, I can't bear it . . . I've tried to

talk to Kevin on the phone but he hung up on me. What am I going to do? TELL ME. Stop sitting on your Cloud Nine and do something useful, for a change. TELL ME WHAT TO DO!!!!!
Cathy

15 July 1993

Dear Mum,

Do you agree with Rebecca? A man should know that he is to become a father? It sounded strong and proper when she said it but I don't know anything any more. I went to his office. VisionFirst is engraved on a brass plate outside the front door. There was a bell to ring and a receptionist to pass before I was brought in to him. A nerve twitched in his cheek when I said he was the father.

Delusions . . . delusions . . . this is not his baby. He stated this fact with conviction, repeated it twice, as if the force of his words would make it true. Everything sounded different when he repeated it back to me, like echoes bouncing off the wrong walls. I must stop lying. How could we have been together when I was out of my head on drugs that night? Drugs that make the mind crazy. Hallucinations and paranoia. He never did anything to me. He knows for a fact I was screwing around with Kevin Mulvaney, no matter how often Kevin denies it. He grabbed my arm, hurting me, and demanded to know if I'd told this ridiculous lie to Rebecca.

I began to cry, knowing I could never tell her and he, knowing this also, locked me into his secret. I must have the baby adopted, he said. His voice was soft, consoling, as it used to be when I poured my heart out to him. He would talk to Rebecca, convince her it was the right decision. She might even consider adopting it because she always has my best interests at heart. It's my baby, I said. Yours and mine.

I sensed his fear, a clammy, sick fear that made him speak too fast. He called me wild and wilful, a liar intent on destroying my sister who had given up everything to look after us.

When I began to cry he ordered a taxi to bring me home. He tried to give me money for the fare. I ripped the notes up and flung the pieces back at him. I ran past the receptionist and the hanging plants and the gleaming brass plate at the entrance.

Beyond the railing of Merrion Square I saw beds of white flowers shaped like stars. I recognised his car parked by the railings. I removed the black cross from my neck and dug it deep into the wing of his fancy Saab. The gouging scraping noise made my teeth water. I wondered if our baby cringed from the sound. I pushed harder, moving the cross backwards and forwards until it fell from my grasp. I slumped against the door and tried to catch my breath. The alarm went off. The sound whirred around my head. I turned and saw Rebecca. She stared at his car, then back at me. The clamouring alarm drowned her voice. I ran past her outstretched arms and into the traffic. I got the bus to Heron Cove and rang Kevin. Mrs Mulvaney said he was out but I knew she was lying 'cause I could hear The Cure playing in the background. I begged her to get him and he came on the line and said to stop bothering him and to never speak to him again.

I packed a bag. I took my letters and my family photograph of the ballet concert. I stole money from Rebecca's purse and left a note on the table. I went back to the city but I didn't know where to hide. Then I remembered the warehouse on the quays where we had our Goth party. I forced the door open. It was easy. I lay on the floor. I must have slept. It was dark when I woke up.

I walked along the quays. A truck stopped when I lifted my arm. The cabin was warm. A heater blasted air on my legs. Slogans were stuck on the dashboard. Robbie calls his truck 'Ramblin' Rosie'. He has a beer belly, a wife named Doris, two daughters and a son. Their photos were pinned above the window. His eldest daughter is my age. He'd take a stick to her backside if she dared hitch a lift from a trucker. It's asking for trouble, he said, and there's enough of that about without seeking it out.

I told him I had to go to my grandmother, who was seriously ill. He travels on the night ferry, delivering fresh fish to restaurants. He played music, country music tapes, Emmylou Harris, and sang along with her. We stopped at a roadside takeaway van. Truckers stood around, talking and eating chips. They muttered something to Robbie, slapped his shoulder.

You're lucky it's me picked you up, he said. Some of them truckers would teach you a few tricks if they got their hands on a pretty little thing like yourself. He asked what was wrong with

111

my grandmother and frowned when I said cancer of the heart. He's never heard of that kind of cancer. We passed through sleeping villages in Wicklow, then Wexford. He braked when he reached the terminal in Rosslaire and turned on the overhead light. He didn't believe my grand-mother story and, because he has a daughter, Anna-Marie, my age, he decided to lecture me. Running away from home never solved anything. Child, he said, if you're in some kind of trouble go to the police or a priest. The road's not the place to sort it out. He sounded like a father . . . I think. I've forgotten what Daddy was like. I told him about the baby.

Tell your mother, he said. Mothers understand about these things more than you realise.

I've told her already, I said. She understands but there's nothing she can do to help.

He went very quiet when he heard about the accident. He asked me my second name. He knew the driver who caused it. A prickly feeling ran all over me, like someone had walked on my grave. They used to travel over on the ferry together. The driver doesn't drive any more. He's got something that brings flash-back memories. All the time we were talking, Robbie was moving towards the ramp with the other truckers. Ro-ro, he called it. Roll on, roll off. He didn't ask me to get out of his truck. On the ferry he shared his sandwiches and bought me soup. He has a sister in London called Alma. I have her address in my pocket.

The engine is like a drum beat under my feet. I'm at sea, in every way. I keep thinking about Rebecca. Her eyes watching me. The shock on her

face, like I'd punched her hard. I can't go back
. . . I can't. I left a note. They won't worry.

There's two seagulls flying with the ferry.
Where are all the others? They always fly in
flocks. Maybe it's you and Dad. Anything is possible . . . anything. Always stay with me, wherever
I go.

Love and kisses for ever,
Cathy

15 November 1993

Dear Mum,

Looking back, I don't remember much about
getting to London, just a long road and Emmylou
singing. A furry disc hung from the window of
Robbie's cab, nodding and bobbing in front of my
face. I think I slept a lot, even when he put me on
the train with a map showing me how to reach
Alma. He gave me money. I think you sent him
from heaven. Alma laughs when I say that. She
says he's the grouchiest old bastard this side of
the Alleghenies but angels come in many forms.

Last night she waved a gold ring over my stomach and said I'm going to have a boy. I'll have to
go back to the name book if I do because I think
it's a girl. You had four girls. Why should I be
different? I've no space in my tummy for swooping
feelings or lonely thoughts or pining for my sisters. It's full of my baby. I waddle like a duck
when I walk. If Melancholia could see me she'd
howl laughing and call me Donald. So would
Kevin, if he would forgive me. But I don't want to
think about them any more.

113

I help Alma in her shop. It's health food and vitamins and crystals. Her name means fostering and loving. Nadine means hope. That's what Alma called her little baby, but Nadine was adopted so she doesn't know if that's still her name. It was a long time ago. Things change, she said, and look at me now. In London with my own little business. I can call my baby Nadine if it's a girl. Alma would like that. Nadine . . . when I whisper her name I can see my way through the next day and all the days to follow.

Love you all,

Cathy

21

Rebecca's Journal — 1993

If only the police had taken me seriously in the beginning. But they knew best. Sisters fight and Cathy would come back home as soon as she had cooled her heels. They refused to start a search until all the obvious possibilities had been checked out. I knew better. Her note was stark.

'I'm running away and starting a new life. Don't bother searching for me. I'm just Trouble. Goodbye. Cathy XXX'

I kept rereading it, as if, somehow, I could decode a clue she had planted. Lauren is good at leaving a trail but Cathy has not given anything away. By the time an official search was launched she was well gone, and the first postcard arrived from London a few days later.

'I'm fine. I'm with a good friend and have found a place to stay. Don't worry about me. Cathy XXX'

What friend? She had no friends in London and the ones at home hadn't, or claimed they hadn't, a clue where she was staying. I believed Kevin, but not Melanie Barnes. She put on her usual Gothic mask of inscrutability when I asked. I wanted to shake the truth from her. Her gaze unnerves me. She's hiding something but I suspect nothing will persuade her to talk.

I'd already decided to go to London and search for her when the second card arrived and informed us that she had had an abortion.

I've been here for two months now. There's an underground map on the wall in front of me. Seven more stations before I reach Heathrow and the last leg of a fruitless journey. Jeremy was right. He said she didn't want to be found, but at least I tried. How I tried . . .

The bedsit in Kilburn was a dump but it was cheap and all I did was sleep there. I've searched the city, the side streets and squats, the shops and the cafes where I hoped she would be working. I wrote letters to the newspapers, stuck posters on walls, handed fliers to people rushing through the underground. I've even been on radio programmes begging her to contact me. Only once did I believe I'd struck gold.

On the King's Road I looked through a shop window and saw a girl in baggy dungarees with an olive-green T-shirt. She was pregnant, which didn't fit my picture of Cathy. But the frizz of black hair spilling over her shoulders sent such a wave of joy through me that I ran blindly into the shop and called her name.

The shop smelled of jasmine and cedarwood oils, and that weedy smell of herbal teas. The girl had disappeared and there was only a woman with red hair standing behind the counter.

'Need any help, love?' she said. Her accent

was obvious, Dublin inner city, born and bred. She was polite but definite that the girl I saw was her daughter. Nadine, she called her. I didn't want to believe her. I kept walking up and down the aisles. Her skirt swept the floor when she walked to a shelf and stacked it with blocks of soap. The scent of lavender was so strong it was in my nostrils for ages afterwards. She called her daughter a brazen hussy for dodging off work. I gave her the leaflet with Cathy's picture and she pinned it to a notice board, alongside the advertisements for reflexology and yoga. I told her how desperate I was. Something about her made me suspicious. The way she kept fussing around me, like she was afraid to let me out of her sight. Maybe she thought I was a shoplifter, though what there was to steal was hard to know.

I pretended to examine the labels on vitamin jars and herbal shampoos. The narrow door leading into the interior of the shop remained closed.

'Take care, love,' she called out when I was leaving. 'If I were you, I'd try and not worry your head too much. Young people have a way of surviving and you never — ' The chimes drowned her last words. I didn't go back. I'm sick of listening to platitudes.

I spent hours watching her shop. She didn't see me when she came out to close up for the night and secure the window with a steel grid. Lights were switched on upstairs. I recognised her at the window, her embroidered smock and distinctive hair. No one left the premises. I came back the following day but no matter how often I walked past, or how many customers entered and left, I only ever saw her inside. I finally accepted it was a false trail and moved the search to Islington. Another blank. I hate it here. How can she do this to me? I loved her so much and now I've lost her. How did I let that happen?

Jeremy will meet me at the airport. He'll hold me close and comfort me. We'll lie together. Our bodies are made for each other. But my mother's words will continue to echo in the emptiness Cathy has left behind.

22

Letters to Nirvana

15 January 1994

Dear Mum,

Today I visited Highgate Cemetery with Melancholia. It's where all the Victorians are buried. Lots of amazing headstones and vaults, really Gothic designs and statues of lions and Karl Marx and Egyptian columns and mausoleums as big as houses. But I didn't want to be there. I didn't want to be in the shadow of dead people when I have given life. But it's nine years since you left and I wanted to be in your space for a little while.

I held Conor up towards the statue of a stone angel so you could see my baby. Melancholia wants me to come home. She said Rebecca won't notice the resemblance but I knew by her voice that she was lying. Even now, even at this early stage when Conor's gaze is still milky, we both see it, the wheat-blond hair and sky-blue eyes. So she didn't insist. She just hugged me and said shit happens. Then held me until I stopped crying.

Rebecca called to the shop one day before Conor was born. I saw her through the window. I thought I was hallucinating at first. My heart thumped so bad I was afraid it would burst right out of my chest or I'd have a heart attack and die like Gramps Gaynor. I hid in the staff room. I heard her talking to Alma. I had to hold myself down in the chair to stop myself running to her. I was frightened Alma would feel sorry for her and tell her the truth. But she didn't let on. She knows all I want is for Rebecca to be happy. I did a terrible thing and this is my punishment.

I don't get much time to write any more. So don't worry if you don't hear from me. I'll never be far away.

Love you all,
Cathy

THE JOURNEY

23

Havenswalk

Conor strikes out towards the centre of the lake. His supple body parts the water with knife-like thrusts. He is used to the temperature, the shock of ice on his skin. The lake is small by the standards of others on the South Island and does not even register as a blue dot on a map. Its size makes it even more special, like a secret shared with a few close friends who, like him, are familiar with its moods and personality. This morning the mood is buoyant, frisky. His mother prefers the lake in the evening. She comes here in the gathering dusk when she needs to be still, but he uses the lake as a punch bag, hammering his energy into early morning swims, water-skiing and windsurfing, kayaking, fishing, sailing.

He turns and floats on his back. Clouds, pink and streaky as fish bones, trail across the sky. His aunts have started their journey. In twenty days' time they will be in Havenswalk. Real flesh and blood aunts instead of the virtual-reality figures he Googles on the internet. His mother calls the internet a spy hole on the world. As descriptions go, it's apt. He has found them all. Lauren, his slinky aunt, at some posh function with her elderly husband, who looks like he owns a large chunk of the world. Julie looks like she was born

123

to hug people and solve all their problems. She has three sons, Jonathan, Philip and Aidan. After his mother made contact Conor started emailing Aidan, who is his own age, and shares his taste in music, rugby, and girls.

In the distance, he hears Hannah's motorbike. Ruthie has already arrived to cook breakfast and Lyle is at work in the garden. Conor strikes out again, swims underwater until his lungs can no longer take the strain. The sun dazzles his eyelashes as he surfaces and heads for shore.

The site that interests him most is the Lambert Animal Sanctuary. He's read everything Rebecca has on it: animal abuse, recovery programmes, pleas for funding, advice to kids who keep horses in housing estates. He's looking forward to meeting her most of all. He has been unable to find her photograph on the website, only images of horses and donkeys grazing in a field.

He has to rely on the family photo his mother kept hidden in the attic. Once the past opened up, she had it enlarged and reframed. It now hangs in the restaurant and the guests always ask about it. Lauren is dressed like a fairy and Julie is cool, a rock diva, eighties style. His mother, eight years old and skinny as a stick, looks like Rebecca. Admittedly, Rebecca is much older, with curly hair to her shoulders, while his mother has two pigtails jutting out on either side of her head — and Rebecca is smiling like a sexy model, unlike his mother, whose first teeth are missing — yet the more Conor examines the photo, the more he sees the resemblance.

He's spoken on the phone to Julie and Lauren. Julie's voice choked up, like she was trying not to cry. She sounds exactly as his mother described, crying and laughing in the same breath. She wants him to come to Ireland as soon as possible to meet his cousins. He likes the sound of Lauren's low sexy voice but she never seems to know what to say to him, and that makes him sound just as stilted. He hasn't spoken to Rebecca yet. Julie jokes that she's too busy counselling dysfunctional donkeys to bother with phone calls. Conor knows it's connected to his mother running away from home. The Unspoken Subject.

She is busy serving breakfast when he enters the kitchen.

'Good swim?' she asks, between orders.

He nods. 'Any word from the aunts?'

'Give them a break, Conor. They're in the air at the moment.' She takes a jug of milk from the fridge and closes the door with her hip.

'I wish they were coming here first, instead of touring.'

'It's the way it worked out. And Rebecca needs to be home in March for some conference she's organised. By the time they arrive, I'll have finished working and Havenswalk will be ready for them.'

'Are you scared?' he asks.

'What do you think?'

'I'd be scared shitless but then I'd never ignore my family for fifteen years.'

'Don't start, Conor,' she warns.

'I'm not starting anything. I just said — '

125

She's gone, hurrying towards the restaurant. He watches the door swing back and forth. He still can't believe it. A year ago, it was just the two of them. Now he has three aunts, two uncles, three cousins — and a father.

Hannah sings and slices bread. From the window Conor watches his father's Jeep disappear around the bend in the avenue. The kitchen is warm, yet he shivers, the chill of the lake still on his skin. The school bus will arrive soon. He lingers a moment longer, hoping his mother will return to the kitchen and he can say something, not exactly an apology, but something neutral to dispel the tension between them. She's tense as a bent reed these days. Tense as she was on the evening Conor's father arrived at Havenswalk to claim his rightful place in their lives.

24

Bangkok

In a ladies' restroom at Bangkok airport, Lauren slips out of the comfortable top and trousers she had worn on the flight and unpacks a sundress from her overnight bag. She wriggles her feet into a pair of matching sling-back high heels. Her discarded clothes are carefully folded into the bag. She is a seasoned traveller, used to different time zones, different climates. The shrill tone on her new mobile phone startles her. It is a loud, demanding summons. She keeps intending to change the ringtone but forgets until Steve's next call reminds her. She smooths a streak of blusher into her cheeks before answering. Steve is rushing between meetings, anxious to know if she landed safely. He phoned when they were awaiting their connection at Heathrow and then, as now, she assures him their flight was uneventful.

At the baggage carousel, their luggage slides into view. Rebecca claims her rucksack and Julie anxiously inspects her mandolin. Neither of her sisters make any attempt to help her remove her suitcases. The nail on her index finger breaks when she lifts them onto a trolley. The break is low down, a snapped acrylic fracture that will need immediate attention. The hotel is bound to have a nail bar and will be her first port of call.

They head towards the arrivals terminal where a slight, middle-aged man holds aloft a sign marked 'LAMABERT'. He shakes hands and introduces himself as Kasem. 'May I be the first to welcome you to my wonderful City of Smiles. This is your home away from home.' His smile washes over them like a blessing, his gaze lingering on Lauren for an instant longer than necessary. She is used to such flickering glances and, as they step into the humid breath of a Bangkok evening, it registers just long enough to be noticed and forgotten.

Julie fans her face with a travel brochure. In her crumpled linen trouser suit, she has the wilted appearance of a long-haul traveller. Rebecca, in jeans and a denim jacket that should have been left behind in the stables, is equally unprepared for the cloying heat.

Kasem stows their luggage into a compartment at the side of the coach and begs leave to be excused. He must collect another traveller whose plane has just landed. Their driver lounges against the coach, smoking and chatting to another driver. People surge past, preoccupied with their own internal journeys. A couple hurry towards the terminal building. Their two children, riding a trolley on top of the luggage, shriek with excitement. They remind Lauren of the once-familiar anticipation of family holidays, their father at the wheel of his Ford Anglia, Julie leading off the singsong. 'Ten Green Bottles,' 'Two Little Boys,' 'Lily the Pink,' 'Ob-La-Di, Ob-La-Do' . . .

The courier and his passenger emerge from the airport. The passenger inclines his head towards the women and smiles as he enters the coach. Dressed casually in a navy linen suit with a white open-neck cotton shirt, his black hair cut short and flecked with grey, he is already working on his laptop when the coach moves off. Unlike Julie, he wears his creases elegantly.

'Tomorrow I will be honoured to show you the sights of my bewitching City of Smiles.' Kasem's tourist patter increases in persuasiveness as they journey towards their hotel.

'No getting away from the 'ucking traffic.' Julie gestures towards the slow-moving lines of taxis, buses and cars stretched along the dual carriageway. 'Taxi-speak,' she adds, and giggles. She still giggles like a teenager and is the only woman Lauren knows who can get away with it.

Rebecca glowers at the familiar yellow double arches set into a block of shops. 'I didn't expect to be that close to a Big Mac in the City of Smiles.'

'Globalisation.' Kasem shrugs apologetically and assures her that beyond the trappings of modernity, Bangkok is a city of magnificent temples, universities, palaces, museums, galleries and religious festivals. As for food . . . he kisses his fingers in an elaborate salute to Thai cuisine. 'Let me recommend the perfect restaurant for tonight.'

An elephant lumbers past in a parallel traffic lane, the animal's enormous bulk reducing the cars to toy size. When the traffic lights turn red, it stops obediently and waits for them to change.

'I don't believe it.' Horrified, Rebecca stares at Kasem. 'What's an elephant doing on a dual carriageway?'

'Ah, yes, indeed.' Kasem nods in the direction of the animal, who appears remarkably composed amidst the chaotic honking of horns and squealing brakes. 'Our Thai elephant is a most intelligent — '

'It's the most outrageous sight I've ever seen. Are you telling me it's allowed?'

'With regret, madam, this is an unfortunate example of our changing times.' Kasem accepts her indignation with a patient smile. 'This elephant would once have worked in the logging camps and came with its owners to the city in search of employment. I agree with your sentiments. It's sad to see them reduced to such menial tasks.'

'Menial! It's cruel and degrading.' She glares at Julie, who is taking a photograph with her mobile phone. 'Stop that, Julie. You're only encouraging this appalling animal abuse.'

'But I want to send it to the boys.' Julie, ignoring her sister's command, leans precariously out the window for a better shot.

'Our mahouts are riders of great skill.' Kasem raises his voice against the roar of traffic. 'Once they led our great elephants into battle — '

'They're still leading them into battle.' Rebecca looks as if she wants to lunge from the coach and escort the elephant to the nearest animal sanctuary. Lauren sighs and examines her broken nail. How could she have forgotten Rebecca's obsession with animal rights? The

130

man sitting opposite them opens his briefcase and plugs a pair of earphones into his ears. A sensible idea. Lauren catches his eye and smiles, but he seems too absorbed in his own thoughts to notice her. The lights change and the traffic eases forward. Suddenly, the coach driver shouts something in Thai. From the vehemence of his tone, Lauren figures it has to be a curse, especially as the elephant shows signs of veering into their traffic lane. The driver brakes abruptly and she lurches forward, almost sliding from her seat. The man opposite her tries to steady himself but his briefcase slips to the floor before he can catch it. With a muttered exclamation, not unlike the word used by the driver, he pulls out his earphones and bends to pick up the contents that have fluttered free. As far as Lauren can see, they are mainly handwritten sheets of music, except for a photograph that lands near her feet. She picks it up but has only time for a quick glimpse before he reaches forward to take it from her. It has the glossy sheen of a publicity shot and features an orchestra grouped around a female violinist, who is dressed in an elaborate Thai ceremonial costume.

'A beautiful woman.' Their fingers touch for an instant as she hands it back to him.

'Thank you.' He returns the contents to his briefcase and snaps the locks. No lingering, flickering, telltale glance, but Lauren knows he is aware of her. His nationality is difficult to define. Lauren is usually good at recognising features and attributing them to a particular country. His

131

skin reminds her of a dark, rich honey but his face lacks the refinement she associates with the Thai population. His nose has been broken and badly reset, the crude bend on its high bridge disturbing the symmetry of his features.

She wants to ask him about the photograph but he begins to work again. Is he part of the orchestra, she wonders, watching his slim fingers race rhythmically over the keyboard. Unlike Rebecca, he is unfazed by the antics of the elephant as it comes to a halt under a flyover and is immediately surrounded by tourists with cameras.

They reach the hotel shortly afterwards and register; walk together to the elevator. Anxious to shower off the effects of long-haul travel, Lauren is conscious of his nearness when they move closer to make space for more guests. She steals a discreet glance at her reflection in the elevator mirror and is satisfied with what she sees. The cool peppermint shade of her dress enhances her cat-green eyes and hugs her teenage skinniness like a second skin.

'How long are you staying in Bangkok?' he asks as the elevator glides upwards.

'Two nights,' Julie replies.

'Like myself. A short stopover. Bangkok is an enchanting city. I hope you have a pleasant trip, ladies.'

'Isn't he divine?' Julie sighs as they walk towards their room. 'His eyes remind me of dark melting chocolate.'

'Steady on, Mamma Mia,' Lauren warns. 'You may have escaped from your husband's reins but you're still a respectable married woman.'

'So what? All I'm doing is looking at the menu. As long as I don't order . . . '

Julie never orders. No time in her busy schedule to follow up on the aftermath of a lingering glance.

★ ★ ★

The suite they will share during their two-day stopover is spacious and airy, booked courtesy of Steve, who had argued that his original bookings for Bangkok and the first night in Christchurch remain in place. The suite contains three double beds, a plasma television screen, luxurious sofas and a black massage chair that looks, Julie declares, like an electric chair, but promises gently to soothe all traces of long-haul stress from the body. She is equally impressed by the mini bar and ice-making machine, the bowl of fruit and ice bucket of champagne in the centre of the table. Her phone camera clicks busily as she wanders from the bathroom to the bedroom to the balcony. Ignoring her sisters' laughter, she photographs the contents of the mini bar and asks Lauren to photograph her in the massage chair where she sticks out her tongue and pretends she is being executed.

'I could get used to this lifestyle very quickly.' She flings herself onto the bed and stares at the ceiling. 'It sure as hell beats nursing a parcel of brats through measles and mouth ulcers in a caravan when it's raining.' With this statement she dissolves into tears. 'It's my trouser suit,' she sobs. 'Look at the creases. Four hundred euros for a rag that I'll use for cleaning windows when I go home.'

'Withdrawal symptoms.' Rebecca opens the bathroom door. 'There's only one antidote.'

Julie sobs passionately into the pillows while Rebecca runs a bubble bath for her and Lauren searches in her cosmetic bag for a tube of eye gel that promises almost as much relief as the massage chair.

★ ★ ★

An hour later, showered and refreshed, they leave the hotel. The street noise hits them like an avalanche, sweeps them past ice-cream barrows and mounds of glazed sweets, past stalls fluttering with silk paintings and T-shirts. In a quiet side street, they locate the restaurant Kasem recommended. Seated on the rooftop, they sample each other's dishes and allow the waiter to replenish their wine glasses. The food is as wonderful as Kasem promised, and the view over Bangkok dazzles with neon. Bars and internet cafés are still open when they leave the restaurant. The exuberance of the earlier traders has quietened. Most of them are packing up for the night and it is easier to move through the streets. A different trade is now being plied. They pass massage parlours with heavily curtained windows and discreet doorways. Others show an open face, scrubbed clean with large 'No Sex' signs at the entrance.

Young women in short skirts and glittering stretch tops lounge indolently against shop fronts and call out to passing tourists. Incense seeps from a shop where a teenage girl sleeps, her head resting on a counter lit with flickering Buddha shrines.

'They're so young,' Julie mutters. 'I can't believe they're all on the game.'

'Well, they're certainly not saying their prayers,' Lauren replies.

Julie stops and stares into a shop window, amazed at the price of bespoke tailored suits on display. She photographs the row of mannequins. She will order two suits for Paul and text to find out his exact leg measurements.

'Tut-tut,' says Lauren. 'Twenty years married and she doesn't know the length of her husband's legs.'

'Nineteen,' says Julie. 'But who's counting? I wonder if Paul's awake? What's the time difference again, Becks?'

Rebecca presses her hand to her forehead and yawns. 'Seven hours ahead. They're still sleeping, Julie. Let them go. Make up your mind about the suits tomorrow.'

The street they enter is wider, more traffic. Another elephant, or maybe the same one, poses for photographs under a flyover. They watch as a group of Japanese tourists stand before the elephant. Cameras flash like fireworks and the passing traffic adds to the illuminated chaos. Before her sisters can restrain her, Rebecca rushes forward and forces her way through the photographers towards the elephant.

'*Excuse* me!' she shouts up at the mahout with all the authority gained from her years in the sanctuary. 'Do you realise the damage you're doing to this unfortunate elephant?'

The mahout grins and yells down at her. 'Ah, lady, tell me now? You want to ride or feed elephant?'

'No! No! Not feed . . . save from pain. It's cruel . . . very cruel.' She clutches her throat, makes gasping noises. 'Carbon monoxide.'

'Ah, you feed . . . you feed! You buy food.' He rummages in a satchel and flings down a bunch of bananas, which are caught by another man, who appears suddenly from behind her.

'Seventy baht! You pay me. Seventy baht. No? Tell me what you pay?' The second man pushes the bananas towards her, speaking rapidly in English. 'You give me dollars, lady? Right now, you give me dollars. Two, three dollars? Yes?'

The elephant, noticing the bananas, swings its trunk from side to side and forces Rebecca to duck in case she is caught in mid-swipe.

'Oh! For heaven's sake! When will she ever get sense.' Julie runs towards Rebecca, who is pinned between the flyover and the animal. Before the second man can recover, she pushes Rebecca away from the tourists, who have turned their cameras in her direction.

'Leave her alone!' she shouts. 'She doesn't want to feed the elephant. Bad mistake . . . she's a crazy woman. Crazy, *crazy* woman!' She grabs Rebecca's arm and pulls her back to the pavement.

'Are you mad or just totally insane?' Julie gestures towards a one-legged beggar propped against a wall. His dog lies patiently in front of him, a tin can balanced between its paws. 'If you want to protest about something, look around you. Human beings also exist on this planet. Even St Francis took a breather now and again.' Julie sounds as if she is ticking off one of her sons. When she drops coins into the can, the dog barks but the beggar, his eyes half-moon slits, ignores the gesture.

'Well done, Becks.' Lauren pats Rebecca's shoulder when her sisters return to the pavement. 'The elephant population will be relieved to know it has such an excellent trade union representative.'

'Very funny.' Rebecca's expression veers between rebellion and mortification. 'If you saw the sights — '

'Yeah, yeah, we know. Man's inhumanity to animals.' Julie casts a last glance at the bespoke suits and walks on. A group of women, dressed in long black skirts, their shawls and hats glittering with silver discs, flounce towards them. Their trays of jewellery attract Lauren's atten- tion. She picks up a tortoise-shell comb from one of the trays. The woman, sensing a sale, moves closer and produces a mirror from a pocket of her voluminous skirt. Another woman jangles earrings at her.

Rebecca shakes her head and follows Julie. 'Are you coming?' She gestures at Lauren to follow. She is recovering her composure and, with it, her authority. 'I've seen enough of this city for one night. We've an early start in the morning.'

'I'll see you back at the hotel.' Lauren, studying her reflection, allows the woman to twist her hair in an upwards knot and stab the comb into position. Her mobile phone rings. Steve again. She lifts it from her handbag and switches it off. This is his fourth attempt to ring her since she left, and she has lost count of the number of texts. Her sisters, moving ahead, are lost from sight when they turn the corner.

★ ★ ★

Their hotel is in the centre of a small square slung with coloured lanterns. High steps, swing doors, a porter standing outside. Lauren can visualise everything except its name. The road she enters is narrow, darker. She passes overcrowded bars, the winking signs of strip joints and clubs, the murmuring promises of young prostitutes, their jutting hips reminding her of awkward children mincing across a school stage.

Once, when she was a child, she strayed from her mother's side during a shopping trip. She has never forgotten the panic, the crowds, the sense of being abandoned. The same panicked feeling comes over her again when she fails to find the hotel. Why did she dally and allow the women to flatter and cajole her? To flash pendants and dangle earrings, sweep her hair upwards with their tiny, busy hands.

Two middle-aged men walk towards her,

accompanied by a woman, sleek as a caterpillar in a green satin dress. She links their arms, her hips swaying as she leads them into a doorway. Light glints behind the broken slit of a Venetian blind. Streetlights glaze the shadows. A door opens and they disappear inside.

Lauren turns another corner, then another. The streets look identical. She keeps on walking, hoping to see the familiar high steps but recognises, instead, the beggar and his dog. The elephant has disappeared and the beggar, a moon-faced man with one trouser leg pinned above his knee, reaches out as she passes and grasps her ankle. She frees herself and begins to run, almost crashing into a tiny, hunched woman pushing marigolds in a wheelbarrow.

A man wearing a backpack approaches. Walking faster, almost running, he holds his head high and wards off the advances from a line of prostitutes.

'No, thanks! No, *thanks*. Sorry . . . not interested,' he mutters.

'Excuse me, can you help me?' Lauren tries to detain him but he shies away.

'Fuck off! I'm not interested.' His beard, ginger and spiky as an armchair tuft, vibrates with nervousness.

Too panicked to be indignant, Lauren suddenly remembers a boutique called Style Focus. She noticed it when she was leaving the hotel and hopes to browse through it tomorrow. She approaches a prostitute who calls out to the passing pedestrians in English.

'Excuse me. I'm lost — '

'You sex seek?' The prostitute's voice is soft, almost sibilant.

Lauren shakes her head. She should have heeded Rebecca's advice and bought a phrase book. 'I'm looking for a boutique called Style Focus.'

'You seek sex? Good time, yes?'

'Style Focus.' Lauren raises her voice. 'Can you tell me where it is?'

Perspiration trickles under her arms. The moon is a washed-out quarter, almost invisible above the hazed neon. The humid night air, trapped between the narrow streets, is redolent with incense and the sweet scent of tiger lilies.

'You fucky fuck lady.' There is an alertness about the woman as her gaze shifts beyond Lauren. 'Go way to hell. Go way.' She shrieks in Thai, her arms flailing. The shrill intensity of her voice drives Lauren backwards.

'Can I help you, madam?' A man stands in front of her. 'If you want the services of my girls, then you deal only with me.' A luminous yellow shirt strains across his stomach. His pallid features and acquisitive gaze belong to the night.

'I wasn't looking for anything except directions to my hotel.' Dry-mouthed, Lauren swallows and forces the words towards him.

'The name of your hotel?'

'I don't . . . I can't remember — '

'Where is it located?' Perspiration beads his upper lip. Thinning blond hair hangs lankly to his shoulders.

She cringes, as if she has made contact with

140

his skin. 'I was with people. I didn't take down the details — '

'Voyeuristic bitch.' In a movement so swift she is unable to brace herself, he shoves her against the wall. 'For my girls you pay like everyone else. Or would you prefer one of my boys to stretch your cunt?' His cold dispassionate stare is more brutal than his words.

She wants to reach out with her nails, tear the skin from his face, but something about his eyes warns her to stay silent. She will collapse if he does not release his grip. For an instant longer he increases the pressure until she is unable to breathe. Then, almost playfully, he opens his arms wide and allows her to escape.

'Go back to your hotel, slut,' he shouts. 'And don't waste my girls' time.'

She begins to run. Voices clash. Musicians play in cafés. Neon lights spin. She is overwhelmed by the familiar terror of tumbling through the night. She kicks off her shoes and leaves them behind. In the babble of voices, one sound emerges. A male voice, close and urgent, calling on her to stop. She is deaf to the sound but his footsteps gain on her, his arm forces her to a standstill.

'You ran before I could reach you.' The passenger from the coach breathes heavily as he holds out her shoes. He has changed from his casual linen suit into a formal tuxedo. A white silk scarf hangs around his neck.

'There's no need to be afraid.' He places her shoes on the ground. 'We're almost at the hotel.'

He holds her when she collapses against him. Her feet are grazed but she is unaware of pain as

141

she slips on her shoes. They walk towards the high revolving doors.

Julie rushes forward when they enter the hotel and hugs her. Rebecca turns from the reception desk where she had been discussing the possibility of informing the police about Lauren's disappearance. Her sisters look quizzingly at her but Lauren has no desire to discuss her experience. The pimp and his sordid power games are behind her. She is safe now, anxious to move on to the next stage. Her companion offers to buy her sisters a nightcap. They refuse, claiming exhaustion. They wait to be introduced but Lauren makes no effort to do so. Names are not important. He is a ship briefly passing through her night. The moment matters, nothing more.

25

Her sisters are sleeping when she returns to the suite. She enters the ensuite and turns on the light above the mirror. Her bottom lip is swollen and the two tortoiseshell combs she bought hold her hair upwards in a style that emphasises her long neck with its delicate wishbone tendons. Her dress is ripped beneath one arm, the frayed material as unsightly as a weal against her tanned skin. The air conditioning hums softly as she walks through the bedroom towards the glass doors. She stands on the balcony, watches the dawn rise and break above the high conical roofs of temples and pagodas. On the dressing table, her mobile phone vibrates silently, flashing a warning light.

In the small intimate hotel bar, he ordered a bottle of Evian with a twist of lemon. Reluctant to drink any more wine, she also sipped a glass of iced water. She tries to remember what they talked about. Their childhoods, mostly. His was spent on the island of Phuket where his parents ran a beach restaurant. His father is a New Zealander with Scottish roots; his mother, now dead, was originally from Bangkok. In his teens, he divided his time between his father's old boarding school, Christ's College in Canterbury, and the coral beaches where he was equally at home in sea or on land. Bare feet and freedom, striped blazers and routine. Lauren imagines his boyhood, the contrasting traditions and cultures as he journeyed between Thailand and New Zealand.

He is a composer, he told her. His latest composition had been performed earlier in the Thailand Cultural Centre. He was returning from the concert when he saw her running and recognised her.

'Your music, what inspires you?' she asked.

'Life,' he replied. 'And you, in your poetry? What is your inspiration?'

'Destruction,' she answered. She had told him she was a poet, regretting the words as soon as she uttered them. She can barely remember the poems she wrote during that brief flowering, and it is many years since she has had any inclination to write. She spoke about her own childhood, that special time when life was a prism dazzling with possibilities. Nothing in her demeanour, or in her tone, suggested that the prism had been smashed beyond repair, and that her life, from then on, was defined by the splinters.

The barman dimmed the lights, except for the lamp shining above their table, and left the bar. As the hotel settled into the quiet hours, the stained-glass lampshade shadowed their faces with jewelled hues. She pressed her fingers against his lips when he asked her name, refused to allow him to divulge his own. He stood and offered her his hand. She arose without hesitation and accompanied him to his room.

Lauren is not a faithful wife. There have been other men in her life, daytime lovers, faceless, eager men from whom she demands nothing

144

except discretion and the ability to be gone from her life before the affair grows stale. She is always careful — no telltale clues, no whispering, inopportune phone calls, no gifts, no secrets exchanged or experiences shared. She does not want their baggage and they are discouraged from peering into her past. Occasionally, she confides in Julie, who might moralise but will never betray a confidence.

'Why take such risks?' she asked Lauren once, unable to understand how it feels to balance on the edge of a blade.

Lauren moves restlessly across the room and opens the fridge, pours orange juice into a glass. Julie's faint snore is comparable to bees droning above lavender, and will, Lauren suspects, drive her and Rebecca crazy before the holiday is over. She lifts her mobile phone and reads the text from Steve. He misses her and hopes she is thinking about him. She sends back a response that she knows will please him, and returns to bed. She is married to a man who adores her. An obsessive man who cherishes her and keeps her from falling. As his beloved, she holds all the aces. This affair, she warns herself as she tosses sleeplessly, must not stray beyond the brief hours they have spent together.

★ ★ ★

Kasem guides them through the heat-filled day. Temples, pagodas, palaces and flower markets. Lauren's head spins with a kaleidoscope of impressions. She is intrigued by the ferocity of warrior statues, comparing their war-like expressions with the passive smiles of the saints she worshipped as a child, lighting candles before St Joseph, bargaining over lost items with the ever-obliging St Anthony. Julie, spotting a statue with a human face and elephant tusks, orders Rebecca to stand in front of it. She will send it to her boys and caption it 'The Day We Discovered Rebecca's Perfect Man'.

Barefoot, they enter the temple of the Emerald Buddha and kneel, as instructed, their feet pointing away from the Buddha. A woman, oblivious to the tourists thronging the temple, kneels before the tiny bejewelled Buddha on top of the high conical altar. She carries flowers, which she lays before her, and bows her forehead to the floor. Lauren envies the woman's belief in a promised reincarnation — the expectation of a second chance.

She has passed the day in a fever, her eyes seeking him out in the hotel breakfast room, in the foyer before Kasem collected them, on the coach, hoping he too would have decided to partake in the tour. As they journeyed through the crowded streets and viewed the shimmering temples, she grew more anxious but now, she tenses, draws her breath slowly inwards when a movement to her right alerts her. She glances sideways and watches as he moves through the crowd and kneels beside her. Rebecca's expression is remote but Lauren knows she is aware and watching.

After a few moments, Lauren arises and walks towards the temple door. A light, almost translucent scarf covers her bare shoulders. An ivory skirt floats above her ankles. She moves with the nonchalance of a woman alone and unobserved in a crowd but every fibre of her being knows that he follows a pace behind her.

The courtyard is thronged, the shoe racks overflowing. He bends and lifts her sandals from the top shelf and lays them before her. On this occasion he does not have to hold her steady when she slips them on. She pulls her sunglasses from her hair to her eyes and nods, an almost imperceptible gesture of thanks, before she walks away.

At the temple gates, Kasem steers them past the vendors who descend like a scattering of crows, waving postcards and joss sticks in their faces. Inside the hospitality coach, Lauren watches him hail a taxi and disappear into the traffic.

'Who does he think you are?' Julie demands. 'Cinderella?'

'Prince or pauper, he's of no interest to me,' Lauren replies, and is suddenly transported back to her childhood when she and Cathy used to analyse the gravity of lies. A little white lie, a fib, a falsehood, a whopper.

'Oh, really?' Julie raises her eyebrows. 'I believe you . . . thousands wouldn't.'

'Cinderella was home before midnight,' says Rebecca. 'So Lauren doesn't qualify.'

'What time did you get in?' Julie looks curiously at her.

'Late,' said Rebecca. 'Do you want to tell us what's going on, Lauren?'

'Nothing is going on, Rebecca.'

'But — ' says Julie.

'Julie *please*, I don't want to discuss this.'

'Suit yourself.' Julie, sounding distinctly huffy, takes out her mobile phone and texts her sons.

This time Lauren will not talk. Words will bring him to life, put shape on her experience, give meaning to a physical encounter that is nothing more than a one-off holiday fling.

The buttons on Kasem's blazer sparkle like newly minted coins as he coughs apologetically to attract their attention. They will now see his City of Smiles from the Chao Phraya river.

* * *

Tired from the day's excursion, they decide to eat in the hotel restaurant. Lauren plays with her food, spears a prawn and lifts it to her mouth. She resists the urge to spit out the rubbery substance and swallows. Outside the temple he touched her feet. His fingers stroked the inside of her ankle and she was gripped by a delirium that will give her no rest until they lie together again.

'Come to me tonight,' he whispered. She shook her head, knowing that to do so is not only foolish but reckless. His black eyes told her she lied. When the music is over, he will be waiting in the bar for her.

The restaurant door swings open. An elderly man and a young woman enter. A waiter immediately approaches and escorts them to a nearby table. The tall, silver-haired man is at least forty years older than his companion. She knows the waiter. Lauren notices the glance they exchange and his immediate return with a daiquiri. Her companion is Australian, a businessman with a twanging accent that carries across the restaurant each time he speaks on his mobile phone. Without consulting the woman, or even glancing in her direction, he orders steaks for two. She spins the daiquiri glass by its delicate green stem and makes no attempt to eat her meal when it is placed before her. He takes out a calculator and declares figures. His brain is a spreadsheet, projecting, planning ahead. She removes a phone from her evening bag. Rings, heavy with cheap stones, glint as she begins to text. He frowns and reaches across the table. She pouts but does not protest when he takes the phone from her and places it firmly beside his plate. Lauren's skin crawls, remembering the visceral hatred the pimp stirred in her, stronger even than her fear.

'Creep!' Rebecca, glancing across the restaurant towards the Australian, speaks too loudly for comfort. 'Sex tourists like him are a boil on the arse of humanity.'

'Lower your voice, Rebecca.' Julie coughs warningly into her hand. 'For all we know, she could be his wife.'

'Hardly likely. Those stones are fake. A trophy wife wears the real thing.' Rebecca's gaze skitters towards Lauren's rings and away again. Unable to hide her embarrassment, she adds, 'Yeah, maybe she is his wife. What do I know about jewellery?'

Lauren stands up. Her leg jolts against the table. The wine glasses wobble, red wine sloshes on the white cloth.

'Excuse me. I need some fresh air.' If she does not walk away, she will smack Rebecca across her smug, self-righteous face.

In the ladies, she smudges foundation over her flushed cheeks, moans inwardly when the door opens and Rebecca enters.

'I'm sorry . . . did I say something to upset you?' Rebecca turns on the taps and washes her hands.

'What on earth gave you that idea?'

'I wasn't suggesting . . . I'm really sorry if I offended — '

'Forget it, Rebecca. It's not the first time you've called me a trophy wife.'

'I didn't call you — '

'I know what you think about my marriage.'

'No, you don't — '

'Let's just leave it, shall we?' Lauren removes the combs from her hair and brushes it. Fifty strokes a night, her mother used to say. Lauren brushes and brushes until the black strands spring outwards, as if touched by electricity.

Rebecca shakes moisture from her hands and holds them under the dryer. She applies hand cream and vigorously rubs her hands together. She is dressed in a pair of chain-store jeans. Her cotton top has the print of a seal's face on the front and was obviously designed for some animal protest march against the culling of seal cubs. Her only concession to glamour is the red silk scarf Lauren gave her for Christmas, which is casually draped over her shoulders. But Rebecca has the height to wear jeans and make them look elegant, the erect shoulders to turn a scarf into a statement. Lauren has the same height but not the effortless style that Rebecca can achieve without trying or caring how the end result looks.

'Are you coming back to the table?' she says. 'Your meal will be cold and you've hardly touched your food.'

'Listen, Becks — ' Lauren stops, bites her lip. She can't remember the last time she used Rebecca's nickname. 'Go ahead, Rebecca. I'll be with you in a few minutes.' She piles her hair upwards and stabs the combs back into position.

'Whatever you say.' Rebecca turns and almost collides with the young Thai woman, who moves aside with a polite apology. The door swings closed on Rebecca's heels.

The Thai woman stands before the mirror and settles her eyes on Lauren. Her glance is swift and appraising. A delicately drawn sunflower is tattooed on her arm, childish and cute, as is the face lurking beneath the sultry make-up. She is young enough to be Lauren's daughter. The pain that comes with this realisation is almost sweet in its familiarity. Lauren dabs perfume behind her ears. The smell of cheap perfume wafts upwards as the young woman sprays it on her cleavage. Lauren removes a tube of lipstick from her bag. The other woman rummages in her bag then pouts and strokes her lips until they glisten like over-ripe plums. Aware that they are mirroring each other's actions, Lauren quickly closes her handbag and hears the same snap from the prostitute's stone-studded clasp bag.

Steve rings. Lauren moves from the mirror, turns her back on the young woman and assures her husband that she is missing him as much as he is missing her. She married him during a Caribbean cruise. Sand in her toes, a woman minister presiding. No one except the captain of the liner and his first mate to witness the occasion. Why, her sisters demanded Why? Why? What they failed to understand was that there was freedom in defeat. Everything calm, passive, icy.

The prostitute has left when she turns around again. Her perfume remains in Lauren's nostrils. She stands motionless in front of the mirror. Slowly she lifts her hands, splays her fingers before her reflection. Ten perfect acrylic nails and genuine jewels.

★　★　★

Red triangles of material flutter like butterflies from her shoulders as she walks from the restaurant towards the bar. Chairs are grouped intimately together in alcoves. Her heels click against the marble tiles. The composer rises to greet her.

★　★　★

In his bedroom, she kisses his eyes, the bridge of his nose, his demanding mouth. A vein throbs in his forehead. She lightly traces it with her lips and the delicate pulse shivers against her tongue. Her palm presses against his heartbeat and she lifts his hand, rests it above her breast so that he too can experience the same hurrying rhythm. He moves downwards, his breath playing over her belly, her thighs, and she trembles, moans softly when she feels the pressure of his tongue probe and glide along the arteries of pleasure. She is overwhelmed with the need to give and to receive, aroused to the brink of surrender, then slowly calming the moment until they are able to continue their slow exploration. His dark eyes burn, then grow opaque as he lays his lean hard body over her and she opens to receive him. Sweat gleams on his chest, a smear of honey on his dark skin. She echoes his cry, torn savagely from him, as they move together into a swooping, pulsating release.

Dawn is breaking when she gathers the strength to rise from his bed. They shower together, the musky odour of spent passion vanishing from their bodies. She yearns to smooth his wet, spiky hair, kiss the lacquered sheen of his shoulders, to ask what happened to his nose. She yearns, also, to whip the white towel from his hips and lie beside him again. Far better than to allow another need, a demanding, more intrusive need, to possess her. She wonders if the taste of him will ever leave her lips.

26

Christchurch

They are flying in a timeless zone, movie channels switched off, seats tilted back. Julie sleeps and Lauren, on the opposite aisle, also appears to have dozed off. Rebecca is restless, unable to concentrate on her book. She has already watched one movie and has no interest in viewing another. She walks along the aisle towards the end of the plane. Lauren's companion from Bangkok is on the same flight. A pinpoint of light shines on the book he is reading. He does not look up when she walks past.

In an open area by the kitchen, she bends forward and stretches, then raises her arms and arches into a back stretch. He is standing in front of her when she straightens. Startled, she moves aside to let him pass. He has the tired, ruffled look of a long-haul traveller, dark stubble on his chin, shadows under his brown eyes. Instead of walking past Rebecca, he smiles and stops, leans against the wall to steady himself.

'You too are unable to sleep?' He speaks English flawlessly but with a slight hesitancy that suggests it is not his first language.

'Yes.' She nods, wiggles her fingers. 'I might as well try to avoid a thrombosis?'

'Lauren told me you are travelling towards a family reunion.'

'She's obviously filled you in on our family history,' Rebecca replies. 'But I'm at a slight disadvantage. I know nothing about you. Not even your name.'

'Niran Gordon.' He has a firm handshake. The warmth of his flesh makes her think about the intimacy he shared with her sister. A telltale flush rises on her throat.

'Are you holidaying in New Zealand?' she asks.

'No. I will stay there for the summer and work. As I do every year.' If he senses her thoughts, he gives no indication as he describes his holiday home. It sounds remote and basic, and is located on a headland on the western side of the South Island.

'Near the glaciers?' Rebecca asks.

'Closer to Haast,' he replies. 'It's on the way to Jackson Bay.'

'The West Coast is on our itinerary, but not Jackson Bay.' Rebecca has studied maps of the South Island and knows the general area he is describing.

Suddenly his expression, open and friendly while they were talking, becomes inscrutable, emphasising the Asian cast of his features. The shift of his attention from Rebecca to someone over her shoulder is so obvious that she turns and sees, as she expects, Lauren approaching. The atmosphere changes, becomes charged with an indefinable emotion that instantly excludes her.

'Excuse me. I'd better go back to my seat.' She stops when she reaches her sister and whispers, 'I worry about you.'

She had forgotten Lauren's stare. Haughty and withdrawn, defying anyone to challenge her. 'It's my life, Rebecca,' she whispers back. 'Step off it.'

★ ★ ★

After the clamour of Bangkok, Christchurch, with its drifting green willows and wide ordered streets, is a tranquil oasis. Not an elephant in sight, declares Julie, as they journey towards the hotel. They will collect the motor home tomorrow morning when they have recovered from the flight.

Lauren does not join them for dinner. As soon as she has showered and dried her hair, she leaves the hotel. She advises her sisters to eat without her. She is meeting Niran Gordon for a farewell meal and will be late returning.

'What's she playing at?' Julie asks when the door closes behind her.

'It's called a dangerous game,' Rebecca replies.

'No fool like an old fool,' says Julie.

Steve Moran is no fool. He waited a long time for Lauren to reach for the trinkets he offered. Trinkets for the bird in the gilded cage: ladders, mirrors, spinning wheels, dainty delicacies.

Rebecca is still awake when Lauren quietly opens the door and moves through the room, a fleeting shape, barely visible, but she feigns sleep, unwilling to endure her sister's spicy breath whispering secrets into her ear. Not that that is likely. She has never been Lauren's confidante and whatever happened tonight will not be discussed in breathless, confessional asides.

Her thoughts turn to Bangkok. She is glad to be away from the City of Smiles, with its glittering history and the ugly underbelly she had glimpsed. She thinks about the elephant, its nobility thrashed beyond repair amidst stinking petrol fumes. Elephants belong in the wild. They belong in herds, mother trunks linking baby trunks, shaking the freedom of the earth with their thundering hoofs.

She is still shocked by her impulsive action. Unplanned deeds and misguided sympathy achieve nothing except confusion. 'Well known Animal Activist Dies in Failed Elephant Rescue Bid' — despite her agitation, Rebecca smiles as she imagines the headlines had she been trampled to death by the elephant. But it was a crazy thing to do.

From the bed on the other side of the room, she hears a sigh, as heavy as a wave collapsing, and, later, Lauren's breathing deepening. What is it like to break vows without compunction, Rebecca wonders as she stares into the darkness. Bodies tossed on a maelstrom of passion? She curls her fingers around the duvet and draws it tightly against her chin.

On more than one occasion, Julie has accused her of having a Miss Havisham complex. She believes Rebecca is halfway to becoming an eccentric spinster, and the episode with the elephant will have reinforced this conviction.

Spinster is a scratchy word; eccentric somewhat softer. Put them together and Rebecca can see her future stretching before her. Already, she has acquired the trappings. A cottage in the country, a cat called Teabag, and a tendency to talk to herself when darkness settles. Sometimes, she plays the bongos to alleviate the silence of a Wicklow night but this hobby could become an obsession, and Teabag will be followed by other cats, countless cats crawling over her furniture and comforting her when she is menopausal or crazy, whichever comes first. And, strictly speaking, she is not a spinster. She was married once and loved her husband with a passion that seemed invincible.

27

The white, streamlined vehicle glistens from a recent wash. All traces of its previous occupants have been bleached and polished from existence.

'You must be joking!' Lauren climbs aboard the home she will occupy for the next twenty days and collapses into the nearest seat. 'This tank was designed with hobbits in mind.'

'What did you expect?' Rebecca slings her rucksack onto the table and laughs at her sister's horrified expression. 'A luxury liner?'

'I didn't expect a set from *The Lord of the Rings*.'

'Stop being so dramatic,' Julie chides her. 'It's more than adequate for our needs.' She examines the presses with an experienced eye, snaps the doors open and closed. 'It's got a neat kitchen. We'll stop at the first supermarket and buy our supplies. An army can't be expected to march on an empty stomach.'

Lauren has no intention of marching anywhere. 'Steve was right when he called this 'a sardine can'. You told us there were six beds, Rebecca. I can't see *one*, let alone six.'

'They're up on top. The table also converts into a bed at night. You take that bunk.' Rebecca points upwards to a space above the driving cabin.

Cautiously, Lauren climbs a ladder to inspect her sleeping quarters. 'Why didn't you tell me

I'd be sleeping on a luggage rack?' She peers back down at Rebecca. 'The time has come to bring Steve to the rescue.'

'No, you don't,' Julie replies. 'He's sleeping in his king-size bed at this very moment. Different times, remember? Why do you think your phone is silent?'

'We'll sort the beds out later.' Lauren is overdoing the wilting maiden act but Rebecca is also startled at the smallness of the camper. She waits until Lauren has hauled her three suitcases on board then, ignoring Lauren's complaints that she has broken one of her fingernails, she climbs into the driver seat and turns on the ignition. 'It's time to hit the road.'

Accompanied by cheers of encouragement from Julie, she eases the camper from the forecourt. It is a Saturday morning and traffic is sparse. She drives with ease through the streets, noting road signs: Oxford Street, Hereford, Chester, Bath, Gloucester. Hard to believe they are on the other side of the world.

'Don't forget the Irish.' Julie flicks the pages of *Traversing New Zealand*. 'There's Tuam Street and Armagh Street and Cashel — '

'Can we skip the geography lecture?' Lauren presses her fingers to her forehead. 'We all know there isn't anywhere in the world that hasn't seen the crack of an Irish builder's arse.'

'Being married to one, you should know.' Julie grins and snaps her guidebook closed. 'And, as we're on our holidays, I'd rather you didn't mention your husband's arse in my presence.'

160

She removes her mandolin from its case and begins to tune it.

'Oh *my* God, not only have we turned into hobbits but now we're expected to have a karaoke.' Lauren closes her eyes and leans her head back against the headrest. 'Did you pack any Panadol, Rebecca? I've a vicious headache.'

'It's probably caused by sleep deprivation.' Rebecca jerks her thumb over her shoulder. 'You'll find them in my rucksack.'

'Thanks.' Lauren opens the rucksack and removes a small first-aid box. She swallows two tablets with bottled water and replaces the rucksack behind the seat.

'You were *very* late coming back to the hotel again last night.' Rebecca focuses on the traffic. She tries to remove the disapproval from her voice, but the words have their own force and she senses, rather than sees, Lauren's shoulders stiffen, her gaze freeze.

'Is that a statement or a question, Rebecca?'

'It's a fact.'

'Now that we've established that fact, can we change the subject or do you want to continue discussing my business?'

'That's up to you, Lauren.'

'Shut up, you two. I'm going to sing for peace.' Julie begins to play. The tune is familiar. Something from Abba. She used to hate Abba, parody their songs in the glory days of Maximum Volume, so confident that the big record companies would discover their unique talent.

Lauren studies a road map. She calls out

161

directions to Rebecca as they make their way towards their first sight-seeing destination on the road to Havenswalk.

★ ★ ★

The Christchurch gondola cranks and clunks its way to the summit from where they will view the vast sprawl of the Canterbury Plain as it rolls across the miles of farmland and forests, stretching outwards towards the snowy shoulders of the Southern Alps. Julie moves around the gondola and positions herself for the best possible shots. Rebecca has lost count of the number of photos and texts she has sent to her family since she left home. Her phone seems like an extension of her personality. Whenever Rebecca visits, its bleeping is a constant summons for Julie to collect her sons from their numerous activities. Rebecca has advised her to burn, bury or drown it, but Julie is a slave to its dictates and unable to function without its tyranny.

When they reach the summit, they turn in different directions and agree to meet up in the Summit Café in an hour for coffee. Rebecca makes straight for the observation deck. She leans her elbows on the rail and stares at the dizzying vista below her and beyond towards the distant Kaikoura Peninsula where she will swim with the dolphins. This is the land where Cathy made her new life. Where she cast off her past like an old skin, then rang out of the blue looking for 'closure'. Such a glib concept. Rebecca hates

162

the word, its neat explicitness, its comforting cosiness, as if its very utterance grants some unique form of amnesia, an instant delivery from grief. She does not want to talk about Cathy until the journey is over. The others have agreed. Time enough for retrospection when they are all together.

Her thoughts are disturbed by a group of youths in rugby team tracksuits who enter the observation deck. Just as well Julie is not around. One glance at their gelled hair and downy chins would have her reaching for her handkerchief. The boys are accompanied by a heavily built, bearded man with cameras slung around his neck. They jostle each other, shout and lean precariously over the railing until the photographer, displaying the patience of a sheepdog, herds them into a tidy formation. He photographs them against the mountainous backdrop. When he is finished, they race each other towards the Summit Café. Rebecca relaxes into the silence they leave behind.

'Please . . . just stay in that position.' Before she can turn round, the photographer's quiet voice holds her still. He raises his camera and clicks. 'Do you mind?' He steps to her right-hand side, then clicks again. 'I never pass up the chance of an atmospheric shot.' He smiles and stands beside her. 'You with the mountains in the background. You look so content, so tranquil.'

'I can assure you, I feel anything but tranquil.'

'Never mind. Perception is everything. This will be a good one. Do you mind if I use it?'

'For a newspaper?'

'Or a magazine? I'm a freelance photographer. Willing to sell my soul to the highest bidder.'

'Then I hope I'm of assistance in the sale.'

'Tim Dawson's the name.' He has a vigorous handshake. 'You here on holiday?'

'I just arrived today. I'm Rebecca Lambert.'

'Welcome to New Zealand, Rebecca Lambert. What do you think of the South Island so far? Or is it too soon to form an opinion?'

Mid-forties, Rebecca reckons, with a ruddy, out-of-doors complexion that suggests he spends as little time as possible behind a desk.

'I'm sure I'm going to love it. My sister certainly does. She lives here.'

'Travelling on your own?'

'No. I'm with my two other sisters. We've hired a motor home.'

'What route are you taking?'

He nods in approval when she describes their itinerary. 'You'll see some magnificent scenery along the way.'

A second man with the blocky shoulders of a prop forward enters the viewing deck and beckons to him.

'Duty calls. He's the team manager.' Tim rummages in his pocket and produces a notebook. 'Do you have an email address? I can send you on the photo.'

She tells it to him. 'I'll be checking my mail along the route. Thanks, Tim.'

'Nice talking to you, Rebecca.'

She strolls from the deck and heads towards the souvenir shop. Julie and Lauren have disappeared and are probably waiting for her in the café. A row of nature books on a shelf catches her attention. She selects one with a scaly frog-like creature on the cover and purchases it.

'I thought you'd fallen off the viewing deck,' says Lauren when Rebecca enters the café. 'What kept you?'

'The view. It's magnificent. You two should check it out.'

'Will do.' Julie rises. 'What would you like? Cappuccino, a muffin?'

'Just a cappuccino, thanks. Stay where you are. I'll get it.'

The team jostle each other at the counter. As Rebecca is returning to the table with a loaded tray, one boy, pursued by another, runs past and jogs her elbow. She struggles to regain her balance and gasps when hot coffee splashes over her fingers.

'Get back into line, you braying hoons.' Tim Dawson's roar startles the team into a temporary stillness. 'You're not on the bloody rugby pitch now.' He takes the tray from Rebecca and carries it back to the counter. Ignoring her protests, he insists on replacing the order, adding an espresso and a meat pie for himself.

'Where are you sitting?' he asks.

She gestures towards her sisters and follows him to the table.

'Mind if I join you?' Without waiting for a reply he pulls out a chair. 'I need some civilised company after those little hoons. I've been following them with my camera all day. The sooner I see their bloody arses disappearing into the bus the better.'

'Hoons?' asks Rebecca.

Tim grins. 'Yobs to everyone except their mothers.'

'They appear to have quietened down a bit,' says Julie, whose hearing, Rebecca suspects, has been permanently impaired by prolonged exposure to her sons' music.

'A temporary aberration, I assure you.' He lifts Rebecca's hand, checks her fingers. 'No damage done. You'll survive to tell the tale.'

The book she bought in the souvenir shop catches his attention. He points towards the creature on the cover.

'Hochstetter's.'

'Sorry?' She glances down at the bulbous eye sockets and alarmingly long toes.

'That's a Hochstetter's frog. Check the caption inside.'

Rebecca does as she is instructed. 'You're right. How did you guess?'

'I know my frogs, Rebecca. I've photographed enough of them in my day, including this little blighter.'

'I thought you were gainfully employed photographing hoons,' says Lauren.

'Hoons put bread on my table. My real interest is photographing endangered species.'

'What an extraordinary coincidence.' Rebecca, turning the pages, admires the clarity of the photographs. She sees his name among the credits. 'Did you do all the photography for this book?'

'It was a collaboration between a group of us.'

'You'll have to autograph it for Rebecca,' says Lauren.

'She has this amazing sanctuary. Tell him about the horses you rescue.'

'I'm sure Tim's not remotely interested — ' Rebecca aims a kick at Lauren's ankle.

'She occasionally attempts to rescue elephants,' says Julie.

'Give over, Julie.' Her sister's ability to carry a joke beyond its sell-by date is well known, and Julie has sung the chorus of 'Nellie the Elephant' on at least three occasions since they left Bangkok. As she delivers a blow-by-blow account of the elephant encounter, his laughter is contagious and Rebecca finds herself laughing with him.

'How long are you staying in Christchurch?' He cuts into his meat pie and chews vigorously, flicks crumbs from his beard.

'Only tonight,' she replies.

'I'll be happy to give you all a whistle-stop tour of the city. We could have a meal together, take in some music.'

'Thanks for the offer, Tim.' She smiles apologetically but firmly across the table. 'We're heading off first thing tomorrow to Lake Tekapo.'

'We don't have to,' says Julie. 'I wouldn't mind another night in Christchurch.'

'Neither would I,' says Lauren.

Her sisters steadfastly return her gaze. Miss Havisham, they are thinking. With her dusty veil and moribund memories.

'I'm afraid the answer is still no.' Rebecca

167

smiles and holds out her hand in farewell. 'It was a pleasure meeting you, Tim.'

'A mutual pleasure, Rebecca.' He produces his notebook again and tears out a page. 'I can't promise you an elephant but you'll have to visit some of our sanctuaries while you're here.' He sketches a rough map and hands it to her. 'If you're passing through Twizel it's worth stopping to see the black stilt. I've written down directions. While I have my pen out I might as well sign this as well.' He picks up the book and writes on the flyleaf, 'Welcome to the South Island, Rebecca. Enjoy your trip. Tim Dawson.'

'Safe travelling.' He shakes their hands. 'Don't forget to check your email along the route, Rebecca.'

'What do you think of him?' Julie asks when he leaves the café.

'Apart from using his beard as a bird table, I didn't form an opinion either way. You'll have to stop trying to fob me off on every man we meet, Julie. It's getting ridiculous.'

'Didn't you like him?'

'Just because we share a common interest in Hochstetter's frogs doesn't make us soul mates.'

'Why does he want you to check your emails?' Lauren asks.

'He took my photograph on the viewing deck. I'm a study in tranquillity.'

'You don't look very tranquil to me,' says Julie.

'It's all about perception. So Tim believes.'

'Then check this out,' says Julie. 'It's time you started having fun again. You can't mourn Jeremy for ever.'

168

'I'm not ... this has nothing to do with Jeremy.'

'Then what was the big deal about having a meal with the mountainy man?' demands Lauren.

'It's my life, Lauren,' Rebecca replies. 'Step off it, please.'

'*Touché*.' Lauren smiles, shrugs.

Julie casts a longing look at the adolescent boys. She blinks rapidly and follows her sisters from the café.

28

Lake Tekapo

On the turn of every corkscrew bend there is a gorge to admire, the fluted bowl of a valley sinking into the afternoon haze, a river tumbling over rocks. They reach Lake Tekapo in the late afternoon and spill from the camper, anxious to feel fresh air on their faces. A motorboat, trailing children in a water-raft, is the only fissure on the stained-glass surface.

Julie, a veteran of camping holidays, shows her sisters how to connect the utilities to the camper.

'Better get used to it,' she warns when Lauren breaks another nail. 'Everyone has to pull their weight on a camping holiday.'

'I've *every* intention of pulling my weight.'

'I hope you still sound so enthusiastic when it's your turn to visit the dump station.'

'Which is . . . what?'

'Emptying the toilet cassette.' Julie tries not to sound too gleeful. 'Don't look like that. It's a simple job. You'll only have to do it when it's your turn.'

'But that's Stone Age nonsense,' Lauren shrieks when Julie explains the procedure to her. 'I'm sorry, folks, I'll do anything else you ask but there's no way I'm doing that. I signed up for a holiday, not an apprenticeship in a septic tank.'

Rebecca ends the argument by rummaging in her rucksack for a swimsuit. She shoves a pair of goggles into her hair and slings a towel over her shoulders. 'I've been looking forward to this all day.'

'Way to go,' yells Julie as Rebecca runs towards the lake and disappears down an embankment. 'It's glacier meltdown water,' she explains to Lauren. 'I read about it in *Traversing New Zealand*. Rebecca is actually going to swim in an ice cube but she'll dive straight in, wait and see.'

Rebecca reappears and dives without hesitation into the water. She plunges underwater and reappears, her arm slicing like a scimitar through the turquoise shimmer.

'Told you so.' Julie returns to the camper and surveys the kitchen. It's nothing more than a cooking galley and will strain her resources to the limit. In Geraldine, where they stopped to shop, her sisters had to lead her forcibly from the supermarket. Food, she believes, is the perfect antidote to life's tensions. She works deftly in the narrow space, banishing blandness with cumin and ginger, adding flavour to the chicken with thyme and oregano, making a gravy from the juices. Julie's vegetable paella is flavoured with saffron, garlic and paprika. Roast potatoes are crisp to the knife and mouth-watering when opened. They sit outside the camper to eat. Her sisters raise their glasses to their cordon bleu cook, who even managed to produce an apple crumble for dessert. The flame of a candle flutters in the night breeze, a solitary light in the gathering gloom.

'Amazing to think you couldn't boil a kettle when you married Paul,' says Rebecca.

'Needs must.' Julie holds her hand over her glass and shakes her head when Lauren offers her a refill.

On the steps of a neighbouring camper, two little girls play with dolls and a tea set. When their mother calls them for bed, they beg for a few minutes' more playtime. Above the twitter of their voices, as clear as the chimes of a bell, Julie hears her mother calling out the same words and receiving the same response. Suddenly, she is gripped by a sorrow so intense it forces her forward, her hands instinctively clutching her stomach. She straightens and reaches for her mandolin and begins to sing softly. The children draw nearer. Encouraged by her smile, they move into the ring of light and sit crossed-legged, their chins cupped in their hands, until their parents, smiling politely but not disturbing the singing, carry them off to bed.

'Time for a nightcap.' Rebecca pours brandy liqueur into glasses.

Julie lays her mandolin down and accepts the drink. Perhaps it is the close proximity of the children that causes their conversation to drift effortlessly towards childhood, half-remembered episodes finding shape in their collective memories. The back garden in Heron Cove, wild at the bottom and entered through an arch of forsythia that was always first to bloom in spring. Their mother gardened in the top half, growing loganberries, raspberries and blackcurrants, creating a bower where she could sit in the evening to catch the sun. But in the other half, dandelions and thistles grew tall, and the untamed bushes had tunnels running crookedly into hidden dens. In the labyrinth of bushes, Cathy and Kevin Mulvaney played hide-and-seek, and Rebecca kept her rabbit hutches and bird tables, the cats that came to breed and give birth in the long grass. Julie practised with her band in the garden shed and Lauren pirouetted on the flat roof. The crimson evenings in the Before time: the Before and After time. Like a knife through butter, their existence severed into two distinct periods that could, on a moment such as this, create an atmosphere taut with emotion and sink the flippant, carefree remarks of a few minutes earlier into a weighted space that no words can fill.

'Where did the years go?' Lauren breaks the silence.

'We blinked,' replies Rebecca.

'I'm going to cry my way through this holiday.' Julie holds her napkin to her face. Tears seep into the soft tissue.

'Then I'm taking the next plane home,' Rebecca warns.

They laugh with relief and rise from their seats. The cicadas fall silent. It is time to bring their first day on the road to a close.

29

'Such early risers. I hope it's not contagious,' Lauren moans from the depths of her bunk and raises her hands above her head. '*Fuck*. There goes another nail.'

'Get your arse down here,' Julie orders. 'Breakfast is served.'

'We've a busy day ahead of us.' Rebecca carries coffee and a croissant to the table and opens a map. 'Should we visit the black stilt hide before doing the trek or the other way around? What do you think, Julie?'

'We should trek in the late afternoon when it's cooler,' advises Julie. 'I'll rustle up some leftovers from last night and make a picnic — '

'What's all this talk about a trek?' Lauren demands. 'I never agreed to go on any trek.'

'Yes, you did.' Rebecca spreads honey over her croissant and pours a second cup of coffee. 'Check the itinerary. I pinned it next to the fridge. It says, 'Three-hour trek.' '

'*Three hours?*' Lauren sounds as if she is being asked to walk slowly and bare-footed over burning stones.

'Three hours is nothing,' says Rebecca. 'Some treks take four days to complete. You agreed last night we'd do the walk.'

Lauren seizes on the word 'walk' and shakes it like a terrier with a bird between its teeth. A walk could mean a trip to the nearest restaurant, bar or shopping centre. It certainly could not be defined as a three-hour ordeal over mountainous terrain swarming with mosquitoes and other undesirable wildlife best viewed behind glass cases in museums. She swings herself down from her bunk and disappears into the shower.

Ten minutes later the door of the shower cubicle opens, releasing a cloud of steam, and Lauren, swaddled in a white bathrobe. She hunkers down in front of a suitcase and rummages through her clothes. Unable to find what she needs, and flushed from the heat in the camper, she flings off her bathrobe and hauls a second suitcase out from under the table.

Julie averts her gaze from the small firm breasts, the childlike rosy-pink nipples. Size eight, she reckons, which is a ridiculous size for a woman of thirty-six.

'This is crazy!' Lauren bangs her elbow off the table leg and sits back on her heels, defeated. 'There's no space to find anything.'

'Then I suggest you dump your luggage in the next charity shop we reach,' suggests Rebecca. 'From where I'm sitting, you seem to manage quite well without any clothes on.'

'She's right about your suitcases,' complains Julie. 'I've tripped over them twice already this morning. Look at my shins. They're black and blue.'

Having found what she wanted, Lauren fastens a wisp of yellow lace across her breasts and wriggles into a pair of matching briefs. 'What's this about a brown sulk — '

175

'Black *stilt*.' Rebecca is struggling to remain calm.

'Remember?' says Julie. 'Tim recommended it.'

'Ah, Tim,' says Lauren. 'The mountainy man.'

'If you mention his name one more time — '

'OK . . . OK.' Lauren finds a dress that pleases her and slips it over her head.

'Anyway, this has nothing to do with Tim Dawson.' Rebecca bends over her South Island map and calculates the time it will take to reach Twizel. 'I'd already listed the visit on the itinerary. The black stilt is one of the world's rarest wading birds. Twizel is where it's being preserved from extinction.'

'Bully for Twizel,' says Lauren. 'But you're not seriously expecting me to crouch in a smelly bird hide. I could get bird flu.' She switches on a hairdryer. Crumbs rise and scurry like insects across Rebecca's plate.

'Would you mind doing that somewhere else?' Rebecca shouts.

'Where would you suggest?' Lauren shouts back. 'On the *fucking* roof, for instance.'

'Black stilts in their little nests agree,' chants Julie.

'Bird hides and *trekking*.' Lauren wails above the hum of the hairdryer. 'If you want to see the scenery that much, what's wrong with taking a helicopter ride?'

'We're taking a helicopter when we visit the glaciers.' Rebecca pulls the itinerary from the wall and stabs her finger at the various dates. 'You can sit here and repair your nails for as long as you like but I'm going to visit this bird hide and I'm going trekking and that's *that*.'

Julie wipes down the draining board and flaps tea towels. To think of the money she spent travelling so far when she could have stayed at home and listened to her sons squabbling. 'Let's have some Abba.' She smiles brightly as she plugs in the CD player.

'Not bloody Abba.' Lauren switches off the hairdryer and empties the container of CDs over the table. 'You used to hate them.'

'They weren't relevant to my life then.'

'Relevant? How can 'Bang-A-Boomerang' be relevant to anyone's life?'

'It's actually 'Money, Money, Money' that turns me on, closely followed by 'Mamma Mia'.'

'While appreciating their sociological significance, can I respectfully suggest you bin them and play U2 instead?' Lauren throws the Abba compilation into the litter bin.

'It's too early for rock,' says Rebecca. 'What about Tom Waits?'

'Not Tom Waits,' wails Julie. ' 'Martha' always makes me cry.'

Rebecca presses her hands to her ears. 'You're driving me crazy, the pair of you. I'd forgotten what it was like living with two-legged animals.'

'Bow wow wow.' Lauren sticks out her tongue and pants. Julie whinnies and gallops on the spot.

'I can't take any more of this.' Rebecca runs from the camper and slams the door behind her.

'We're driving Becks crazy again.' Julie watches her sister head towards the forest at the perimeter of the camper park and disappear between the pines.

'Nothing changes.' Lauren kneels and folds her clothes back into her suitcase. 'I don't think I'll be able to hack the outdoor life. Look at my nails.' She holds out her hands. Three nails down, seven to go.

'Stop going on about your nails! You'd swear your fingers had been amputated, the way you're carrying on. Tell me about Niran Gordon.' Julie has waited expectantly to hear the details of Lauren's brief liaison but, so far, no information has been forthcoming.

'I've already told you, I don't want to discuss him.' Lauren's giddiness instantly disappears. Her aloof expression warns Julie off.

'He's different, isn't he?' Julie rescues Abba from the litter bin and tidies the CDs into a neat stack. 'Moondance' by Van Morrison looks like a choice that will please everyone. She places the CD into the stereo. 'You can't vanish this affair so easily.'

'Julie, did you hear what I said? Drop the subject.'

'Why? Just because it suits you? It didn't bother you on those other occasions when you used me as your wailing wall.'

'Are we going to have an argument?'

'You don't argue, Lauren. You just retreat.'

Julie stands at the camper door and gazes across the holiday park. Campers, similar to their own, are already departing and the sites are acquiring a dusty, deserted appearance. Her anger simmers. Dutiful Julie, always ready with

178

the cup of tea and sympathy. She has never sought Lauren's secrets. Often, she feels uneasy when family occasions draw them together and she sits across the dining table from Steve Moran. Can he be so oblivious of his wife's infidelities — or does he accept them as the price he must pay to possess her? After all, he makes his money by investing in high-risk property.

Light footsteps sound behind her. Lauren's arms slide around her waist.

'Don't be cross, Julie.' Her sister's voice is subdued. 'If I talk about him, I'll fall apart. Try to understand.'

'I'll never understand you, Lauren.' Julie's anger evaporates as suddenly as it ignited. She knows, if she turns to face her sister, that Lauren's eyes will be bleak and tearless. 'But that doesn't matter. I'm here to listen if you need me.'

★ ★ ★

The sun flashes between the pines as Julie walks along the narrow forest trail. Rebecca has been missing for an hour and it is time to leave the holiday park. The ferns are dense and shoulder-high, the trees entwined with creepers that brush against her face as she ventures deeper into the forest. She enters a loamy clearing and discovers Rebecca sitting on the trunk of a felled tree. Unaware of Julie's presence, she is sobbing unrestrainedly. Julie hovers, undecided. Rebecca would hate to be discovered in such distress. Perhaps last night . . . all that talk about the past

179

. . . it must have stirred so many memories. A scaly creature darts through the ferns and disappears. Julie, unable to prevent a shriek, jumps to one side. Rebecca turns around. Too late for pretence, she buries her face in her hands.

'Poor Becks.' Julie kneels beside her. 'We're driving you mad again.'

'No . . . it's not . . . ' She swallows, unable to continue.

'It was only a silly argument, not worth upsetting yourself over.'

Rebecca wipes her eyes, blows her nose and stuffs the hankie back into her shorts. 'It's nothing to do with the row.'

'Then what?'

'It's just . . . why is everyone calling me Becks?'

'We're not.'

'Yes, you are.'

'It's Cathy, isn't it? She's the reason you're so uptight.'

'Absolutely not.' Her voice wobbles.

'Rebecca, we all have our opinions about what Cathy did. But this is our opportunity to put the past behind us.'

'Is that what you really believe?'

'Dust around corners, Rebecca.'

'What?'

'That's what you used to tell us. Don't look behind. There's nothing but dust around corners.' Julie stretches out her hand and helps Rebecca to her feet. 'I spoke to Cathy last night. She's as nervous as you are about this reunion.'

'I told you, I'm *not* nervous.'

'Conor seems nice.'

Rebecca breaks off a frond from one of the ferns and waves it over her cheeks. 'I wouldn't know.'

'He asks about you every time we talk on the phone. Why won't you speak to him?'

'I'll meet him soon enough.'

The breeze stirs the forest and the ferns sway like ballerinas. Another scaly creature crouches against a stone. Almost indistinguishable, apart from a pair of beady eyes, it watches them unblinkingly.

Julie clutches Rebecca's arm as they walk past it. There are probably hundreds of them, invisible eyes observing the strange antics of humans. Rebecca is staunch. Unlike Julie, she does not find relief in tears. Or maybe she only cries when she is alone and unobserved. In a sudden rush of sympathy, Julie tightens her grip on Rebecca's arm. 'Let's go find Cinderella.'

Lauren is sitting on the steps of the camper. 'I thought you'd abandoned me.' She holds up a CD of Kiri Te Kanawa. 'No more arguments about music. This is the perfect choice for today.'

For once there is unanimous agreement. With the New Zealand diva singing *La Traviata*, they head for the home of the black stilt.

30

Cromwell

Days begin to blur. They take turns driving through the heat, stopping to picnic or visit wineries, to seek shade and relax under the parasols of pavement cafés. The scenery becomes more rugged, the ghosts of a gold-mining past visible in the shaly brown hills and decaying mining sites. Julie keeps up a running commentary. Since the trip began, she has appointed herself as their official guide and *Traversing New Zealand* has acquired the authority of a Bible.

On their fifth day they arrive in Cromwell. Rebecca books the motor home into a holiday park. Somehow, without realising it was happening, they have formed into a well-organised team that moves into action as soon as they arrive at a new destination, connecting electricity, checking out internet cafés, bathroom and kitchen facilities, and anything else necessary for survival. While Julie busies herself in the kitchen and Lauren applies sunscreen lotion, Rebecca enters the internet café.

Lulu's email assures her that all is going smoothly in her absence. Sheila's email is filled with details of her children's latest achievements. She notices an email from Tim Dawson.

The tranquillity photograph is attached. She opens the attachment and stares in amazement at the photograph. Tim has captured the sky and the sea in a harmonious movement and linked her in their frame. Her expression is pensive as she stares across the breadth of a city and its surrounding plains. Tendrils of black hair blown by the breeze curve back from her forehead and reveal its broad plane. Her nose is slightly on the large side but is balanced by her wide mouth, which is curved in a half-smile. The photograph covers half a page and is captioned 'South Island Reflections. Rebecca Lambert visits the Christchurch Gondola.'

She clicks into his email.

Hi Rebecca,

Hope the trip is going smoothly. Where are you now? You mentioned that you hoped to cruise Milford Sound and you'll be staying overnight in Te Anau. Will you be there on Friday? I'd like to meet up with you again. I'm doing a photo shoot at a conservation centre in the Fiordland National Park. As you're interested in our endangered species, you might like to see a takahē breeding centre. The bird was believed to be extinct . . . never mind . . . I'll tell you about it when I see you. Your photo is attached. It's beautiful. You've become the Southern Eye pin-up girl. Looking forward, hopefully, to meeting you again.

Tim Dawson

Rebecca has never seen herself as beautiful yet Tim has captured something, redefined her features in a subtle way that gives her lips a crushed, kissed look that is rather arresting, even, dare she think it, sexy. Before she can change her mind, she taps out a reply.

Hi Tim,
Thank you for the photograph. We're really enjoying the trip and will be in Te Anau by Friday. Hope to see you then.
Rebecca

★ ★ ★

Cromwell, once famous for its gold mining, is now famous for its fruit orchards. Above the high orchard walls, the leafy branches of fruit trees offer a welcome shade from the sun. Street stands and shops, piled with pyramids of fruit, are doing a lively business. Drawn by the promise of homemade ice cream, they approach a café and find an empty table on the veranda.

Intrigued by the name of the town, Julie checks *Traversing New Zealand* and announces that it was called Cromwell by a group of English gold-mining surveyors who wanted to annoy the immigrant Irish miners.

'That would have done the trick all right.' Julie stabs her ice cream and speaks in the passionate voice of one who has endured eight hundred years of oppression.

'To hell or to Connaught,' says Rebecca.

'If he was alive today he'd be charged at The

Hague for war crimes,' declares Julie.

'Not to mention ethnic cleansing,' agrees Rebecca.

'Every beast has some evil properties but Cromwell had the properties of *all* evil beasts,' says Julie. 'That's a quote — '

'Give me a break!' sighs Lauren. 'I want to enjoy my smoothie in peace.'

'By some archbishop,' says Julie. 'I remember reading it in school.'

'Archbishop John Williams,' says Rebecca.

'Now, can we change the subject?' Lauren tilts her sunhat over her eyes and flicks the pages of a magazine. Rebecca dips her spoon into blueberry ice cream and listens as Julie explains how the first fruit trees to grow in Cromwell were planted by hungry miners, who supplemented their meagre rations with fresh fruit. Today, Cromwell is at the heart of the South Island's fruit belt while most of the town's gold-mining history is buried under the Lake Dunstun reservoir.

Dust around corners. Had she really said that to her sisters? Never look behind? Yes, Rebecca nods. She probably did. She can see the lake from where they are sitting on the veranda. The past is buried yet it still lives. Beneath the façade of this friendly town with its gold-mining roots and leafy orchards, under the calm surface of the sparkling reservoir with its swag of gold, lie the broken dreams, the back-breaking drudgery of hungry, immigrant miners, the exploitation and the greed; all dead now, the gold and the dreams. Only the seeds remain. Rooted deep in the earth, they link the past to the present in a bountiful harvest.

She rises, moves briskly towards the cash desk to pay the bill. At Lake Tekapo she had buckled. Alone in the forest, the past crept up on her and she had sunk to the ground under its weight. This loss of control must not be repeated.

The temperature is high. She feels it dragging at her footsteps as they return to the motor home, their arms laden with punnets of fruit, chilli oils and sauces, marmalades and jams. A herd of deer run through a nearby field, swaying as they turn in a fluid sweep of flank and hoof.

31

Rebecca's Journal — 1994

I keep waking in the small hours. No matter how tired I am, or how late I go to bed, it makes no difference. Everything seems so much bleaker then. And the questions start. Insidious questions. Cathy has robbed me of serenity. She has destroyed my dreams. Yet I miss her so much I ache all over.

I keep thinking about how it used to be before they died. How she used to watch out for me when I was due home from school, her plump little legs pumping as she ran down the driveway to greet me, her plump little lips full of kisses. She hung on to my every word, rode my back like a koala bear. We were the eldest and the youngest, bonded in love. How could things change so much?

The gouging scrape of a black metal cross on the wing of Jeremy's car. It's a more accusing sound than the one-time echo of my mother's dead voice. Even when the Saab was repaired I imagined the scratches, deep as an open wound. Why? Cathy was rebellious and argumentative, but never vindictive. I loved the car. I loved its comfort and style. But, mostly, I loved it because it was our escape hatch before we married. I was always conscious of my sisters in the other rooms, hushing Jeremy, afraid they'd hear. We parked in dark places along the estuary. The radio played late night music and we were greedy for each other. Jeremy talks about selling it. I wish he would. I don't like driving it any more. My heart palpitates in the small hours and I must rise, go downstairs, heat some milk, which is supposed to help one to sleep, but nothing works. I can't read a book or listen to music.

We have the house to ourselves now. Lauren's back in London, back writing her novel. She claims it's coming together in a most satisfactory manner. She has the look of a poet, rather than a novelist. Novelists can be anyone. Poets are more rarefied, slender and nervy, possibly with suicidal urges, constantly struggling to express their lives in the deeper veins of language. OK, so it's a caricature but then . . . what's life?

Jeremy had the grace not to say, 'I told you so,' when I returned from London without Cathy. He'd warned me I was on an impossible quest. I wouldn't listen but I'd no idea London was so vast. A city with so many faces, colours, creeds, cultures. She could have been anywhere. On the other side of the street. She has broken my heart.

'Hearts mend,' says Jeremy. He holds me tightly when he awakens and finds me sleepless. 'Your parents would want you to be happy. Cathy has done nothing but make your life a misery. Let her go, Rebecca. She doesn't want to be found.'

How does he know? How can he be so sure?

Lydia Mulvaney doesn't speak to me any more. I passed her in the city last week. Her paintings were hanging on the railings in Merrion Square. If she saw me, she gave no indication. I can't believe someone who was such a radical in the seventies would blindly support her son against all the evidence. Where is the bra-burning feminist who worked with single mothers and rape victims, and lobbied for equal rights for women? What does she think Cathy and her son were doing all those times in his room? Studying the Bible? Playing Monopoly? Doing crossword puzzles?

Work helps a little. I miss college but I blew Gramps' legacy on a hopeless search and I was lucky John Carmody took me on. He's a good vet, compassionate, and, even though I'm only the receptionist, he's noticed that I'm good around animals. Funny that, being so good with animals and hopeless with people.

I want a baby.

Jeremy says we're not ready yet. We are . . . we are . . . we are . . .

32

Havenswalk

Conor's paddle whips the lake in short, sharp thrusts, but Lyle is already ahead. For a man in his sixties, Lyle is fit and strong, and never patronises Conor by letting him win. To be constantly beaten by an old man is disheartening but the training schedule is building up Conor's strength. Next year he will run, kayak and cycle across the South Island in the Coast to Coast Triathlon. He accelerates through the water. The wind frisks his face. His head sings with the energy of being young and fit.

Yesterday, Julie sent him a photo from her mobile phone. It was taken in a café in Cromwell and, for the first time, he saw Rebecca as an older woman. She was still recognisable as the younger Rebecca in the family photograph — and the resemblance between her and his mother has grown rather than diminished since their separation. His aunts are holding glasses of ice cream towards the camera and smiling, like they are all saying cheese together.

He has plans for Rebecca. Horse trekking and a visit to Abel Tasman Park to see the llamas. He wonders if she rescues horses from apartment blocks. Having seen *The Commitments*, he knows that horses live in apartment complexes and tiny urban gardens, but he is unable to imagine any green space that does not stretch beyond his horizon.

London, where he was born, is a vague memory. He remembers cars at night, a dark staircase leading from Alma's shop to her flat upstairs, and the smell of aromatic oils. He still lives with the smell of oils. They ooze from the corridors of Havenswalk and are as much a part of his life as the sight of people doing shoulder stands or releasing the yoga breath of life.

His childhood memories are mainly of the South Island and Havenswalk — not the Havenswalk of today, with its restaurant and veranda and swimming pool and meditation rooms, but a rackety old house with holes in the roof and a stone floor where rats scurried and the cobwebs seemed thick enough to use as hammocks. He lived with his mother and Alma in the nearby farmhouse while the old building was repaired and the chalets built. Workmen carried him on their shoulders, sent him to the foreman with an order to bring back a glass hammer, and sang ballads about gold mines and sugar cane fields, and driving seven hours to reach the nearest pub. When they went home at night, he walked by the lake with his mother and listened to her talking about a centre where people could come and be serene. He asked her what 'serene' meant. Not to have thoughts clambering around in your head and regrets bowing you down to the ground, she explained. She called the lake 'Heron Cove'. The workmen had another name for it, a proper name that once belonged to a Maori princess, yet his mother's nickname stuck.

When Havenswalk opened, Ruthie and Hannah arrived to work in the kitchens. Others came and went, yoga instructors who stood like arrows before the lake, and tai-chi practitioners moving their arms in slow motion replays. Then, four years ago, Lyle knocked on the door and asked his mother if there were any spare jobs she could give him.

Conor paddles faster and catches up on Lyle, who has stopped paddling and is relaxing back in his cockpit, drinking water. Conor draws alongside and rests his blades, watches a fish glide under the kayak. Through a gap in the trees, Lyle's house, looking as dilapidated as usual, is visible. It is little more than a shack with a corrugated iron roof hanging low over mottled walls. Uninvited callers are not welcome but Conor calls any time he likes. Lyle is the nearest thing to a father he knew until his real father came on the scene. It amazes Conor how seemingly unrelated events can create momentous happenings. If his mother had refused to look beyond Lyle's shabby clothes and bony face, his shoulders so stooped he seemed to be clasping secrets inside a shell, they would not have a garden filled with vegetables, fruit and herbs, no rose arbour or glow-worm grotto, no lawn sloping to the lake where the marquee for her wedding will soon be erected. And Conor would never have met his father.

33

Queenstown

Lauren's nightmare is familiar. The landscape, even the characters, can change but the face remains the same. It appears at the window. Eyes stare in at her, illuminate the interior of the camper but Lauren remains frozen, unable to move or call out a warning, as the camper begins to move. She screams but the sound is a whimper, barely audible and her sisters sleep on, unable to hear her, unaware that the camper is gaining speed, and they are plummeting downwards through a forest where branches bend and buckle, and claw against the walls. Her mother, dressed in her old gardening clothes, reaches out her arms to stop it. Her grip is weak, a ghost flitting by. As they hurtle past, Lauren sees a young girl standing by her mother's side. She recognises the prostitute from the restaurant in Bangkok, her slinky black trousers and red satin blouse, her figure moulded by a glittering silver belt. When the camper crashes into a tree, the older woman shields her from the sight. Lauren, trapped in her own nightmare, is unable to escape the grinding screech of steel turning on its side. The sound is too terrible to endure and Lauren, knowing she is the only person in the world who can handle this chaotic terror, screams once again and jerks herself awake.

The hushed night remained undisturbed. Where there was turbulence there is now silence, apart from a faint droning snore from Julie. Lauren hopes her dreams are gentle. Afraid of disturbing her sisters, she climbs down from her bunk and makes her way towards the fridge. Magazines and brochures are scattered over the table. Underwear hangs from rails and the backs of chairs. Her sunglasses lie on the floor beside her beach bag. She pours cranberry juice into a glass and drinks deeply. There are moments when the experience of being alive is a strumming, quivering relief. Her mother looked so real. Warm enough to hug. The familiar slacks with the baggy knees. The old leather boots, clay moulded into the soles. Etchings of a life ended too soon.

Wide awake and with all the signs of insomnia in place, she feels the atmosphere in the camper thickening. Moving as silently as possible, she pulls on a pair of trousers and a jacket, locates her mobile phone and a torch.

'What's wrong?' Julie whispers, her arm dangling over the edge of her bunk.

'It's suffocating in here. I'm going outside for some air.'

'Be careful. Take your gloves . . . it's cold . . . '

The residue of the nightmare still clings to Lauren as she leaves the holiday park and walks towards the lake shore. She finds a sheltered bench underneath a tree and sits down, waits for the phone to ring.

'Where are you now?' Steve asks.

'Queenstown. We arrived this afternoon. I'm sitting in the moonlight beside a lake.'

'On your own?'

'I could be the only person left alive on this island.'

'No toy boy.'

She remains silent. Lately, his jokes have a cutting edge, as if he wants to diminish the age gap between them with remarks about anti-ageing creams and toy boys.

'I'm only joking, Lauren. Where's your sense of humour?' He chuckles indulgently. She imagines him at his desk, his spiky iron-grey hair and tough, forceful chin. He must be drinking coffee; she hears him sip and swallow. He drinks it black and strong, without sugar.

'Have your sisters thrown in the towel yet?' he asks when she makes no reply.

'They're thriving on the outdoor life, especially Rebecca.'

'And you?'

'I'm coping.'

'Trekking through the wilderness is not exactly your style, princess. Another two days and you'll be begging for room service.'

'I'm not exactly made of cotton wool, Steve.'

'Pure Dresden, princess, and streamlined for luxury. I'm sorry I'm not sitting in the moonlight beside you but things are a bit difficult at the moment.'

She forces herself to concentrate on what he is saying. Something about the Wallslowe deal and an argument with an investor.

'Is there a problem?' she asks.

'One or two glitches that I need to keep an eye on. Apart from that — '

'What kind of glitches?' Alarm clutches her voice, raises it into an anxious question. Boom to gloom, riches to rags; the media's coverage of the global economic downturn was unrelenting before she left. She is glad to be away from the constant reports, the grim predictions, the closures, the anger, the political wrangling and bitter accusations.

'Nothing for you to worry your pretty little head over.'

He calms her fear. Of course there will be glitches. No property deal worth millions will flow without problems surfacing at some point. But Steve is canny and experienced, tough in negotiations, hard-headed when challenged, and, ultimately, always successful in acquiring what he desires. He will come through this recession, just as he did during the difficult eighties when they met for the first time.

Lauren has no recollection of their meeting which took place at her parents' funeral. How could she, a child of twelve, remember a man in his forties? But, in time, she came to visualise the scene he described and — honed from his own memories of the occasion — she took them as her own, allowing them to replace the blank space in her mind whenever she tries to recall that day. What a huddle the Lambert sisters must have made, mud on their shoes, black berets glistening with rain. She was in a wheelchair, briefly allowed out of hospital, eyes bruised, the taste of nettles still in her mouth. Steve said she looked beautiful even then. He wanted to hold her safe. To banish for ever the terror in her eyes.

After his phone call ends, she stays in the same position, reluctant to return to the cloying heat of the camper. Shot through with silver, Lake Wakatipu traps the moon's reflection and eddies it gently along the surface. The wind, blowing stronger, keens between the mountain clefts but she has moved far beyond this mountainous landscape and is kneeling barefoot in a crowded temple, the scent of joss sticks in her nostrils. His presence strumming towards her across the curious, the worshipping, the oblivious crowds. She should have known it would be impossible to fly close to the flame and not singe her wings.

She whispers his name. Niran. In Thai, he told her, it means Eternal. She behaved like a whore in his arms. No, she corrects herself. A whore would feel no pleasure in such brief stolen encounters. Her body clenches in the grip of remembered pleasure. When they met again in Christchurch, he told her about his holiday home. He called it 'his crib'. He is there now, composing his music. Outside his window, the waves roll like thunder over driftwood sands, froth and foam and spinning force.

He drew a map with directions that she should follow.

'I can't,' she said when he handed it to her. 'It's impossible.' But she took it from him, determined to tear it up as soon as she was alone.

She reaches into the pocket of her trousers and touches the folded paper. Too dark to see the marked directions but she does not need light to see the curving bends and distinctive X. She has checked Rebecca's itinerary. They will travel along the West Coast. Jackson Bay is not included.

34

Queenstown is a brash and bold, adrenalin-pumping city that challenges the fibre of a person's courage. Rebecca's itinerary includes a lake cruise, a *Lord of the Rings* tour, white-water rafting and bungee jumping, which they will do today from the Kawarau Gorge. This experience, according to Rebecca, who has bungee jumped in Colorado and Chile, will be the highlight of their trip.

On reaching the gorge, she strides towards the jump station with the confidence of one who had fallen into a void and survived to tell the tale. Julie, never one to shirk an adrenalin rush, looks equally self-assured as she jokes with Rick, their instructor. Tall and muscular, in denim shorts and a red bandana, Rick projects the brisk authority of a kindergarten teacher welcoming his latest batch of terrified toddlers.

'OK, you guys,' Rick says. 'Ready for action?'

Lauren's legs begin to tremble when she looks down on the thin line of the Kawarau River rushing blue and dangerously between the rocks. Rebecca is the first to venture forward.

'Latex,' Rick grins, when she enquires about the strength of the bungee cord. 'It's strong enough to keep the condom industry in profit and the global population under control.'

'Absolute rubbish,' Julie quips. 'How the hell

do you think Jonathan came on the scene? We've never trusted — '

'Shut up!' her sisters shriek in unison.

Lashed in Velcro, dangling on latex, Rebecca drops like a brick over the edge.

'Goodbye, cruel world,' she screeches, the sound torn silent by wind and speed.

Julie and Lauren move to the edge of the platform. Far below, the river is an inaudible roar. Lauren imagines its power slamming against her chest, her body, randomly tossed on the raging current.

'One, two, three . . . ' Rick begins the countdown. Hesitating increases the risk of dropping out, he advises Lauren when she takes a step backwards.

She sinks to her knees, her green eyes sludgy with terror.

'I was just as terrified the first time I did it.' Rick, no longer teasing, kneels beside her. 'It's perfectly safe and the sensation is absolutely fantastic. You'll be on a high for days afterwards.'

Lauren is unable to look away from the glaciated gorge. The face . . . how can he not see the face? She watches the tortured features from her nightmare emerge. The chiselled eyebrows and bulbous eyes ready to blind her with their terrifying stare. She blinks her long dark eyelashes but still the face remains, and the river, no longer inaudible, roars with pent-up violence in her ears. Her chest tightens. She rocks backwards and forwards and presses her hands to her eyes. Rick, realising that her fear is as deep as the gorge below, persuades her to her feet. He opens the Velcro fastenings. She sways when she hears the abrasive texture separating. He holds her upright as her knees give way again.

'It happens.' He shrugs, grins good-naturedly. 'Perhaps, another day.'

'I'm sorry . . . sorry . . . ' Her voice trails away.

Down below, Rebecca has been taken aboard an inflatable raft. Lauren whimpers as another body hurtles into a swan dive and disappears.

'You go,' she says to Julie. 'I'll be all right.'

'I'll bring you back to the camper first. Come on, hold on to my arm.'

Lauren fixes her gaze firmly to the front as Julie helps her, step by careful step, across the suspension bridge. When they reach the camper Lauren collapses into a chair.

'New Zealand is not exactly the best country to discover you have a problem with vertigo,' Julie says.

'I thought . . . I thought I'd just keep falling.' Her cheeks are clammy. Perspiration trickles along her spine.

Julie takes bottled water from the fridge and hands her a glass. 'How are you feeling now?'

'Better.' Lauren walks to the open door, gulps in deep breaths of air. Rebecca returns, hyper with excitement, and shows them the photograph that was taken when she went over the edge, bulging eyes, her mouth wide open in a whipped-away scream. She fits into this landscape, is thriving on the hurtling, adrenalin-pumping activities it offers. The sense of space overpowers Lauren. She is used to city noises, coffee-bar conversations, the swish of carrier bags, the confines of tall secure buildings. Here there is no containment. Nothing to break the isolation that will descend on her if she falters for an instant. She steps outside. The air is cool on her cheeks. She stares beyond the clumps of thyme and scabweed, the tussocks of wild grass and jutting boulders, the dead trees, silver-flamed and jutting like arrows above the bracken.

35

On their third day in Queenstown, Julie and Lauren rebel and demand a day off. Julie wants to do nothing more demanding than turning the pages of a book. Lauren is in dire need of a facial and a manicure. Rebecca sticks to her itinerary and heads off on her own to explore Arrowtown's gold-mining past.

After her sisters depart, Julie heaves a sigh of relief. Before she can relax, she restores order to the camper. Despite her best efforts to keep it tidy, underwear dries on lines slung across the shower cubicle, make-up, shower gel, tampons, magazines, towels, swimsuits, road maps, empty wine bottles and Lauren's overflowing ashtray seem to manifest themselves over every available space. She works quickly and efficiently. Soon, shining surfaces and neatly made-up bunks have replaced the chaos her sisters left in their wake.

She showers and changes into fresh shorts and a short-sleeved shirt. She sits on the steps of the camper with her book and a glass of wine. A camper van reverses into the empty bay beside her. Teenage boys erupt from the open door. Their raucous laughter sounds like a familiar melody. A heavy-set man emerges and begins to connect electricity.

'How's the trip going?' he calls across to her.

'Wonderful so far,' she replies. 'How about you?'

He scratches his arm, grins. She recognises his Belfast accent. 'Apart from the sand flies. The wee fuckers have bitten me to bits.' His buttocks loom alarmingly from his shorts every time he bends over to connect the water and electricity, and his legs are ringed with bite blotches. Paul has kept his lean figure. Apart from a slight thinning of hair on his crown and deeper lines around his eyes and mouth, she can still see the man she married. She places her wine on the step and closes the book. Time that once had wings has slowed to a snail's pace and she does not know what to do with it. The longing to ring her sons, to send a text, over-whelms her. They are sleeping on the other side of the world. The rain is probably falling, the broken garden shed door slapping to and fro. The time difference adds to her sense of separation. They can not even think about her at the same time as she is thinking about them.

Paul rings each night and makes her absence sound like an accusation. Why is he having difficulty accessing essential files on her system? Where has she left the VAT returns? What about the pay roll? How can he get Aidan to study without holding a gun to his head? Why are his sons intent on breaking the sound barrier when all he has the energy to do is sink into a coma when he comes home from work?

Julie stands up and checks the camper. Spotless. She checks the food supply. Milk and fresh bread are needed. The supermarket is only a short walking distance from the camper park. She browses among the shelves, examines the blue fish, asks questions about how it should be cooked, then moves on to the vegetable counter, pauses to survey a mound of sweet potatoes. They call them kumaras in New Zealand. She picks up a publicity recipe for kumara and mussel chowder. She debates trying it tonight . . . but all those greenlipped mussels, so much bigger than the ones at home, not to mention debearding them . . . maybe some other occasion. She stops at the fruit section, checks the juiciness of mangoes and grapes, tests the pliability of avocados, compares the prices to those in her local supermarket.

A teenager walks past. Despite the heat, she wears a military jacket with medals and numerous quirky badges adorning the front. Her skirt trails the floor and her hair, dyed a luminous green, is as spiked as an iguana's spine. She is every mother's nightmare, thinks Julie, and every individualist's dream. Tears well in her eyes and roll down her cheeks.

'Dear me.' An elderly woman with pink candyfloss hair pauses. 'Are you all right, child?'

Julie pulls her sunglasses over her eyes and nods. 'I'm fine. It's just . . . happiness.' She pushes her trolley onwards, sobbing to the vacuous strains of tranquillity music. Outside, the sun is shining. Birds are singing. People are paragliding, white-water rafting, hacking through glaciers, hanging above a gorge by their ankles. That's a definition of happiness, not wandering through the aisles of a supermarket. What has happened to her? What has she become? She searches for a tissue in the pocket of her shorts.

Unable to find one, she grabs a plastic bag from a roll and rubs her eyes. The candyfloss woman catches up with her at the bread counter. 'Pray to the Good Lord, child. He will not turn his eyes from you.'

'Thank you.' Without looking right or left, apart from the herbal counter where she flings a bottle of St John's Wort into the trolley — excellent for depression, according to a health magazine she read — Julie heads for the checkout.

Her footsteps drag as she climbs the hilly road back to the holiday park. Gondolas, journeying to the summit of Bob's Peak, hover like bees above the beech forests. She stops under the trees, her head bent as if searching for pennies among the weeping willows.

A Jeep is parked outside the camper. Tim Dawson lounges in a deck chair. He waves when he sees her and rises.

'We meet again.' He is a big man, hulky, and his beard is bushy enough to hide nesting birds.

'How are you?' he asks.

She holds up a bag of groceries. 'Apart from the occasional cathartic experience, I'm fine. Rebecca's not here, I'm afraid.'

'Oh.' His smiles fades.

'She's panning for gold in Arrowtown. I'm expecting her back soon. Would you like a drink?'

'I could skull a beer.' He sits down again and accepts a bottle, cold from the fridge. 'Choice.' He takes a long swig. 'This'll wash out the dust of the road.'

Julie pours a glass of wine and sits beside him. 'I thought we were to meet you in Te Anau?'

'I decided to take off early.'

'Did you now?' She grins at him. 'We bought six copies of the *Southern Eye*. Nice photo.'

'Nice subject.'

'She thinks your book is a mine of useful information.'

'What else does she say about me?'

'Not a lot, to be honest . . . apart from the frog.'

'The Hochstetter's.'

'That's the one. She's been trying to recognise one. No luck so far.'

'Is she married?'

'Was.'

'Divorced?'

'Widowed. What about you?' Julie studies the man lolling beside her, his sturdy brown ankles crossed, a pair of shabby boots that look as if they have trampled across many miles of wild terrain.

'Divorced. Six years since I last eyeballed my ex-wife.'

'I'm sorry.'

'No need. She preferred the city. I like open spaces. Irreconcilable differences.'

'My husband and I have never had a chance to find out if we have irreconcilable differences.'

'You're lucky.'

'No. Just too busy.'

'Children?'

'Three boys. The eldest is nineteen. We call him the honeymoon baby.'

'You were a child bride.' His attempt at flattery pleases her.

'Nineteen and very pregnant.'

'Ah.' He tilts his head back and finishes the bottle.

She hands him a second bottle, tops up her own glass. 'A year later we had another son and then Aidan, the youngest, came along.'

'You've been a busy lady.'

She nods, warns herself to stop talking. One glass of wine and she turns into Mrs Motor Mouth. 'I miss my family like crazy yet I couldn't wait to get away from them. Perhaps that's an irreconcilable contradiction. Does your wife still live in Christchurch?'

'She moved to the North Island and married again. Two toddlers now. We've become friends.'

'Is it difficult, recovering from a divorce and becoming friends?'

'We earned our friendship the hard way,' he admits. 'It wasn't easy at first. Now, if we meet occasionally at a friend's wedding or party, I try to remember what it was like lying beside her at night. All that passion . . . Now she reminds me of my sister when we hug.'

'I can't imagine being friends with my husband if our marriage ended.'

'What then? Being enemies sure uses up a lot of negative energy.'

A flock of birds rise above the lake. Suffused in gold, they spin in a spiralling loop and glaze the sun's reflection. So much gold everywhere: lost gold, forgotten gold, fool's gold. She touches her wedding ring. Impossible nowadays to remove, except with hand cream.

'Are you happier since you split up?' Julie is amazed to hear herself asking such personal questions. Yet she is easy in his company and the afternoon has taken on a lazy, relaxed feel. For the first time since leaving home, she is not gripped by an urge to fill the vacuum.

'Not happier. Content. It's a worthwhile compromise.'

'Rebecca would agree. She likes her own company, if you disregard the horses.'

'How did her husband die?'

'An accident. She doesn't talk much about it. In fact, Rebecca seldom talks about anything personal.'

'Sounds like she's been hurt.'

'Who hasn't?'

He nods, squints his eyes when a taxi pulls up. Rebecca climbs out and pauses when she notices him. The rush of colour to her cheeks could be attributed to the sun. Julie hopes it has another source.

'Hey, Tim?' She taps his arm. 'Why don't I put your name into the cooking pot tonight?'

'Thanks for the offer but I've other plans.' Tim speaks softly, his gaze fastened on Rebecca. 'What are my chances?'

'A whinny should give you a good head start,' Julie advises. 'Failing that, talk about the frog.'

★ ★ ★

'So, how was it last night?' Julie asks as she clears away the breakfast remains. 'Did Tim show you his takahē?' She giggles.

Rebecca grins and flaps a tea towel at her. 'Think about the zoo as a career choice, Julie. I hear there's a vacancy in the hyena quarters.'

Lauren lowers herself from her bunk and growls through a mane of tousled hair. 'What on earth is the sense of being on holiday if we have to rise before the dawn?'

'It's eight o'clock and we've a long journey ahead of us,' says Rebecca.

'Haven't we always?'

'We've been here for three days. It's time to move on.'

'I'm trying to find out about Tim's takahē.' Julie is unable to resist pushing the joke a little further, perhaps by flapping her arms and singing 'The Birdy Song'. Maybe another time.

Lauren pulls on a tracksuit and sits staring into a cup of coffee. 'This is hard labour,' she declares.

'And it's going to get even harder,' says Rebecca. 'You'd better visit the dump station before we leave.'

'I beg your pardon?'

'The shite site,' says Julie. Lauren's laziness is seriously beginning to annoy her.

'No way!'

'Time to climb down from your ivory tower,' warns Rebecca. 'We've all taken our turn at the sewage front. Why should you be any different?'

'You use the loo as much as the rest of us.' Julie, having already performed the task twice, is not prepared to be merciful. 'All you need to do is unlock the toilet compartment, remove the cassette and empty it into the dump station. It's as easy as falling off a log.'

Eventually, still protesting and holding the cassette as gingerly as a primed grenade, Lauren departs for the dump station.

Her sisters give her a round of applause when she returns. 'Happy now?' she demands. 'If so, I request permission to *vomit*.'

She grabs her toiletry bag and heads towards the public shower facilities. Thirty minutes later, fully restored to her normal sleekness, she returns. Just as Rebecca is about to disconnect the utilities, she bolts towards the small claustrophobic bathroom they share. The retching sounds she makes are audible but when she emerges, whey-faced and holding the side of the table for support, she brushes aside her sisters' concern.

'I was not born to empty shite down a drain,' she announces.

'Who was?' demands Julie. 'I don't know why you're making such a fuss. It's processed shite, sanitised.'

'I've been shovelling so much shite all my life I can handle the dump station with my eyes closed,' Rebecca agrees. 'You should see what the horses leave behind — '

'The nappies I had to change . . . ' Julie shudders at the memory.

'Can we skip the details, please?' Lauren's voice warns them to quieten down. 'Listen to me for once. We've done our stint in the camper and I, for one, am sick and tired of living in cramped conditions.'

'I feel the same way every time I knock my shins on your suitcases,' Julie snaps.

'Leave it out, Julie. We've done my suitcases to death. Why not leave the camper here, order a taxi and book into the nearest hotel?'

'What a brilliant idea,' drawls Rebecca. 'We just abandon our motor home and walk away. Maybe we should set fire to it first, prevent it being traced back to us.'

'No need for sarcasm or dramatics,' Lauren replies. 'We can contact the hire company, tell them to send someone to pick it up.'

'But we paid for it,' Julie protests. 'I can't afford to stay in hotels.'

'Steve will pay. This is just short change to him. Why not travel in comfort when we have the opportunity? You could at least consider the idea.'

'Let's vote on it then,' says Rebecca. 'All those in favour of Lauren's proposal, put up their right hand.'

Julie folds her arms and nods. 'Two against one. I guess that's the end of the matter.'

'For the moment,' mutters Lauren, and on that sour note they depart Queenstown.

36

Milford Sound

Everywhere they look, it seems as if a divine hand has hacked deep into the mountains, releasing waterfalls that crash boldly over rocks or glint slyly between chasms. They are lucky, their captain announces, as they sail from Milford Harbour. The prevailing winds from the Tasman Sea usually blow moistly over Milford Sound and visitors can only experience its grandeur through a haze of mist or rain. This morning, apart from a few bobtail clouds, it seems as if the fjord and the sky have conspired to turn the morning blue.

On deck with her sisters, Lauren leans into the breeze. Boats and cruisers, dwarfed by the sheer scale of the Mitre Peak, bob like a flotilla of bath toys. The sea planes, gliding around the barren pinnacle, look as defenceless as a scattering of storm-tossed birds. Beech, rata and red fern soar above them in a dense green collage. The captain explains the ecosystem of this fragile rain forest. The trees are rooted, he explains, on nothing more substantial than a dense foundation of moss. This, in turn, clings tenaciously to a cliff face. The constant rainfall creates a shifting instability within this sodden structure. Occasionally, when the rain is particularly heavy, the moss loosens its grip and the emerald forests slide into the fjord.

Lauren imagines the seeping undergrowth collapsing. The suckling roots, suddenly rootless, and the trees with their high proud branches tumbling, pell-mell and helter-skelter into the icy reaches. How does it sound, this collapsing forest? Creaking, cracking, moaning, high buckling screams?

Rebecca shouts and points towards the cliff path where she has glimpsed a chamois fleeting past. Tim Dawson leans forward over the rail and adjusts his camera. He manages a number of shots before the elusive creature disappears. Lauren swallows, fights to control a sudden wave of seasickness. Damn Julie and the pancakes she insisted on making for breakfast. Her diet since she came away is shot to hell. Black coffee and a cigarette. A salad for lunch, steamed fish and vegetables in the evening. Impossible to maintain in the face of Julie's cooking. No more, she vows as the cruiser passes through the thunderous roar of the Fairy Falls.

Passengers brave enough to venture under the cascading waterfall hold out containers to catch the spray.

'Come on, let's do it.' Julie holds out a cup and leans forward, demands to be photographed. Within seconds she is drenched, her hair flattened like a skullcap, her nipples puckering under her soaked T-shirt. Oblivious to her appearance, she grins into the camera and holds the half-filled cup triumphantly over her head. Lauren has lost count of the number of

214

photographs Julie has sent to her family. What Paul will make of this latest image remains to be seen but Lauren knows exactly what Steve would think if she sent him a photograph of herself in such a state. Julie, suddenly aware that her top is as transparent as a seventh veil, and that a group of bikers are staring at her with undisguised enthusiasm, clasps her hands across her chest and runs off in search of her jacket.

On the rock islands, seals bask in sunshine or slide sleekly into the fjord. Reef formations blend with the trees and reflect in the mirrored floe of ice. The panic attack comes with such unexpected ferocity that Lauren grips the cruiser rail until her knuckles whiten. She sees the indentations on the side of the Mitre Peak. The contorted features emerging — mouth, nose, dazzling eyes bearing down on her. She leans over the rail and vomits into the churning water before stumbling below deck to the bathroom.

She splashes cold water over her face. Carefully, she applies make-up, lipliner, lipstick. Her expression wavers in the mirror. Her face is an abstract alignment of features, lacking depth and character. As Steve fears, the cracks are beginning to show.

★ ★ ★

On the journey back to Te Anau the road twists and plunges. Pockets of snow glint in the gorges and in the serried mountain slopes. Locked into her own thoughts, Lauren closes her eyes. Sensory overload, she thinks. What is the sense of admiring a thundering waterfall when they will pass another equally stunning one shortly afterwards? The high peaks intimidate and reduce her to an insignificant dot moving across a foreboding landscape. Julie checks the rear-view mirror.

'Ringwraiths!' she announces. During their tour of *The Lord of the Rings* film locations, she so impressed the guide with her knowledge of Middle Earth that he asked if she had majored in the works of Tolkien.

'No,' Julie replied, 'I just bred three hobbits.'

Lauren glances down at the bikers. From the insignia on the back of their leather jackets, she recognises them from the cruise. With the sun flashing off their reflective shades and splintering the handlebars of their bikes, it is easy to imagine an army of Black Riders charging into battle. They divide and ride escort-style on either side of the camper, raise their gauntlets in salute before effortlessly reforming and gliding around a bend on the road. Julie, slowing as she approaches the corner, realises that it leads into a series of corkscrew turns. Suddenly she is face to face with an oncoming camper van.

Distracted by the bikers, the elderly driver has swerved too far towards her side of the road. She sees his startled face, his eyes widening when he realises what has happened. He wrenches the steering wheel and the woman sitting beside him raises her hands to her eyes. Julie pulls her own steering wheel as the two campers dance an indecisive waltz. Gravel spits beneath the wheels. She veers towards a screen of trees. Branches whip the windows like demented wipers until she manages to bring the camper to a halt. They are engulfed in a dappling green canopy of leaves that rustle above a grassy embankment. The embankment slopes steeply downwards to a river. Rapids spin around rocks, a white-capped frenzy swirling branches on its crest. Lauren staggers from the camper, clutches her stomach. Her screams streak upwards like a bird soaring from the thicket of her chest and wing uncontrollably through the branches.

'We're OK . . . we're safe. Calm down . . . we're safe.' Julie's efforts to pacify her only increase her terror. She continues to scream until Rebecca grasps her firmly by her shoulders and slaps her cheek. Stunned into silence, she collapses into Rebecca's arms, a child again, seeking protection from nightmares.

★ ★ ★

A juggernaut is defined as a relentlessly destroying force. After the funeral, Lauren looked up the word in her dictionary.

Words were important. On the night of the accident, it had not rained for a fortnight. When the rain eventually fell, it was a light drizzle that oiled the surface of the road. For the driver of the juggernaut, sleep-deprived from a long-haul journey, it was too late to stop the relentless skid that carried him sideways into the oncoming car where Rachel and Gerry Lambert were travelling with their twelve-year-old daughter. Lauren, drowsy and warm, still hearing the tinkling

217

music and the applause of the audience, had too much stardust in her eyes to witness what was about to happen. But her mother, sitting beside her in the back seat, had seen everything in that split second as the juggernaut skidded from its path and veered towards them. Did Rachel Lambert have time to balance the pros and cons of survival before she opened the car door and thrust her child forward into the luminous night? Or had she spontaneously obeyed the same primal urge that gave birth to her daughter, all her daughters, before the roots of her life were ripped loose and there was no other sound except the screech of the night collapsing?

At his trial, Lauren examined the driver's features, striving to transpose them over the gargoyle face of her nightmares. But he was indistinguishable from any man she would pass on the street: middle-aged and of medium height, a blocky figure, his stomach beginning to protrude, bushy eyebrows. He complained about nightmares, post-traumatic stress. He escaped with a fractured arm, broken ribs and a five-year driving ban.

★   ★   ★

'You sound exhausted.' Steve rings as she is about to climb into her bunk. Lauren takes the phone outside and sits down on a picnic bench. The holiday park is in darkness, the travellers intent on an early start.

'I'm not tired.' She keeps her voice light. 'I'm coping perfectly well. But it's been a long day

218

and I'm about to sleep on a luggage rack.'

'Chuck it in, princess. The last thing I want is my beautiful wife coming back to me looking like an old bag woman.'

'I don't think there's much danger of that, Steve.'

She thinks about their last morning together, how she danced like a marionette before him. How he stroked her hair, stroking and stroking until the desire to scream ran like a blade through her.

37

Te Anau

Her sisters refuse to allow Rebecca to go on another date wearing a T-shirt with a badger's face and a slogan about the cruelty of badger-baiting printed on it. Julie turns to Lauren, who is stretched out on the cushioned bench. 'Have a root in your case, Lauren. You're sure to have something glamorous she can borrow.'

'You don't wear something glamorous to a smelly bird hide,' Lauren retorts, but she rouses herself and rummages in her cases. She bullies Rebecca into an Armani top and jacket, and a tight-fitting pair of Gucci jeans.

Rebecca buttons the jacket and surveys her midriff in the small mirror Lauren holds before her. The jacket feels as if it has been waiting all its life to caress her skin. 'I could probably buy a new stable for what this little lot cost you,' she says.

'Two,' Lauren replies, and returns to the bench.

'I'd be very wary of a man who wants to show me his takahē,' Julie warns when Tim draws up in his Jeep. 'Just make sure it doesn't bite.'

Rebecca moans and runs from the camper. When she looks back, her sisters are standing in the doorway, flapping their arms and singing 'The Birdy Song.'

* * *

The breeding centre is closed to the public and Rebecca is delighted at the opportunity to visit it. The takahē, a bird not unlike a turkey except for its hooked red beak and the blue-green sheen of feathers, was thought to be extinct until it was rediscovered in the late 1940s. Tim proves to be an informative guide. As he prepares for the photo shoot, he explains that although the female is capable of laying three eggs in the wild, stoats and other predators prevent her from hatching them. Usually only one survives, and to encourage the survival of all her eggs, the breeding centre has devised a method of rearing the young takahē before releasing them into their natural environment. Rebecca watches the baby birds being fed by hand-puppets resembling the mother bird.

'Surrogate parenting,' she says, after they leave the centre. 'A puppet would probably have made a better fist of it than I did.'

'That comment deserves some attention.' Tim switches on the ignition. 'I know the perfect restaurant where it can be analysed.'

* * *

She is reticent about discussing her family and Tim refrains from asking direct questions. She regales him instead with stories about animal

221

rights demonstrations and protests, and he has his own stories to tell. They are the last diners to leave the restaurant. Te Anau is the gateway to the fjords and travellers retire early. They stroll along the shore road and sit on a wall overlooking the lake. A ferry moves slowly towards land, its lights drawing circles on the dark water.

'Julie told me your husband died. What happened to him?' Tim asks the question quietly and Rebecca hugs her chest, shivers despite the balmy air. He is reaching for an intimacy he has not, until now, tried to establish.

'Is that an intrusive question?' he asks when she does not reply.

'It's difficult, Tim. I don't find it easy to talk about Jeremy.'

'Then don't. I'm sorry I asked — '

'There's not a lot to tell. He died five years ago. I've moved on with my life since then.'

Passengers, disembarking from the ferry, create a brief babble of noise as they mount the steps and disperse in different directions. The captain switches off the engine and secures his vessel. He too mounts the steps and bids them good night. His boat is in darkness, the shore road quiet. With the departure of the ferry passengers, they seem to be the only people abroad.

'Do you have children?' Tim asks.

'No.'

'Neither had we. When the crunch came it made it easier.'

'It's always easier without children.' If she says

it often enough she might begin to believe it. 'We tried for a baby but I never managed to conceive. The doctor said there was no reason but it simply didn't happen.' She shrugs, smiles. 'Time is the healer, isn't that what they say? Time to move on. Time for closure. I hate platitudes.'

She leans against his shoulder and remains silent for a moment. When she speaks, he listens, nods occasionally, waits without interrupting when she hesitates. She is conscious that the information she relays is factual, clinical.

'We'd fallen out of love long before then, of course.' She bangs her heels off the side of the wall, barely conscious that she is doing so until Tim places his hand on her knees and stills her agitation. 'I've no memory of when that happened. You'd imagine it'd be etched on your soul, wouldn't you? The moment when something so fundamental to your happiness no longer exists. But love simply seeped through the pores of our marriage and left nothing behind.'

'Nothing?' he asks

'Nothing,' she repeats. 'Except memories and regrets, too many regrets.'

He strokes her arm, his fingers gentle on her skin. For such a burly man, he seems to have an innate sensitivity. She trusts him, had done so from the first time they met, and knows he will not demand more than she is prepared to give.

'Are those regrets behind you now?' he asks. 'As you said, you've moved on with your life.'

'Yes.' She nods, knowing she lies. She lifts his hand and presses it against her lips. 'Thanks for listening, Tim. I bet you didn't expect to comfort

223

this endangered species from Ireland tonight.'

'If anyone's endangered, it's me,' he replies. 'You're seriously affecting my heart.'

'Don't make me responsible for a cardiac arrest.' She keeps her tone light. It is so long since she has been drawn into the warmth of a man's gaze. She finds it as disturbing as dust lifting on old times.

'You could be, if we don't meet again.'

'I'm surprised you want to see me again.'

'Why is it so surprising? I meet a wonderful woman who happens to feel as passionately as I do about animals. She makes me laugh, holds my attention every time she speaks, intrigues me because I feel as if I'm barely touching the surface of her personality. Truthfully, this woman has come between me and my sleep.'

'Tim, I'm only here for a short while. Why complicate matters — '

'What's wrong with complications?'

'I avoid them wherever possible.'

'By living in your sanctuary?'

'I'm not a nun, Tim. My sanctuary is for injured animals.' Her breath quickens when his fingers rest against her bottom lip, touch the moist inner curve.

'Is it?' He cups the back of her neck and draws her to him. His beard hides a soft mouth and his warm, exploratory kiss demands nothing from her except an acknowledgement of the time they have spent together. He eases away from her, his hand still resting against her neck, the slight pressure holding her close. She can break it easily if she chooses. She is adept at defusing such tensions but she makes no effort to resist when he kisses her again.

'Why don't you come to the wedding with me?' she asks when they return to his Jeep. The question, impulsively asked, is immediately regretted. She has no need for a man at her elbow when Cathy walks up the aisle. He nods, reaches for her hand.

'I'd like that very much.'

'So would I.' Surprised by her response, she feels her throat swell, her eyes fill with a sudden stinging need to cry. She blinks away the threatening tears. She needs to get a grip on her emotions or she will turn into Julie. She rests her head on his shoulder as he drives her back to her sisters.

38

Rebecca's Journal — 1996

The For Sale sign is down at last. Heron Cove is sold. Cathy should be pleased with her share. Our parents' will stated it be divided equally between the four of us but we couldn't sell until we heard from her. I guess moving to New Zealand helped make her mind up. The solicitor representing her was unable, or unwilling, to give me any information on her whereabouts. Client confidentiality. Well, she has her share now, along with her legacy from Gramps Gaynor. A tidy sum with interest. Amazing that she never touched it while she was in London. How did she survive? She stole money from me. A pittance. It wouldn't have lasted more than a day.

Her solicitor was a portly man with an inbred superiority . . . or, perhaps, I just hate him because he has access to information denied to me. According to Sheila, Melanie Barnes is studying law. No doubt she will find it a satisfying experience to indulge her obsession with the macabre by embracing the legal profession, with its wigs and gowns fetishes. I don't contact her any more. I can't force information from her and there's something in her eyes, a dangerous knowledge that glitters hard as a diamond. It frightens me. She knows the answer to the question I'm afraid to ask. Or so I believe when I lie awake in the small hours.

I don't belong in our new apartment. It's close to Jeremy's office. At night the city lights blaze below us. They seem to sway like waves on a retreating tide. In the morning, my dark suspicions fade and there is only space for the reality of my life; for what I can see, touch, smell, embrace, and try, once again, to make a baby. Each month adds to my anguish. Jeremy too. But he is busy with work. I suspect his disappointment is tempered with the pressure of his newest ad campaign. Our gynaecologist advises us to relax. There's absolutely no reason why a healthy couple like ourselves can't conceive a child. We must find something else to occupy our minds. Jeremy wants me to invest the money from Heron Cove in stocks and shares. No way, José. I know exactly what I'll do with it. I'm going back to college and investing the rest in the sanctuary.

Heron Cove is in new hands. Already, the owners are making changes. I walked past last week. There's a new front door and the front garden has been cobble-locked. Lydia Mulvaney was about to climb into her car. She hesitated when she saw me, then came forward and spoke to me for the first time since I accused her son. She figured I must have heard from Cathy when the For Sale sign went up. We were formal with each other. I told her the truth. I know nothing. She asked me if I still believed Kevin was responsible. I wanted to shout, 'Yes! Yes! A thousand times, yes!' but the words stuck in my throat and I could only reply, 'I simply don't know what to believe.'

Kevin is studying engineering in Cork. Is she lonely without him? She has plenty of friends, artists like herself with paint under their fingernails — and the old masters they discuss are not their husbands. She looks older, her features more hawkish, her cropped hair has turned grey. I wish she was still my friend.

39

Havenswalk

Conor lands the first trout and quickly dispatches it with the cosh. The proper term for the cosh is a 'priest' but ever since the time Conor landed a massive blue fish and yelled, 'Where did I leave that fucking priest?' and Lyle doubled-over laughing before admitting he used to be a priest, Conor leaves the word out of his fishing vocabulary. Another trout hits the deck, then another. Once the catch is sufficient for tonight's menu — Ruthie plans to serve stuffed trout — he is content to let the boat drift. The afternoon stretches before him.

His aunts have done the fjords and are heading back to Queenstown. Mel Barnes arrives this evening. She plans a week of yoga and meditation with the other guests before chilling out for the wedding.

The first time Mel visited Havenswalk, Conor, who was nine at the time, thought she had stepped straight from a vampire's coffin. He is older now. Last year she stayed for a month. By the time she left, he was in love with her. Just looking at her sent electric shocks through him. Ridiculous, considering she was even older than his mother. But age made no difference to his feelings. All that black lace, skinny leather boots and eyeliner, her coal-black hair with the fringe hiding the dark mystery of her eyes. It's impossible to imagine his mother looking like a Goth, whereas Mel looks as if she started playing with bats in her carry-cot.

Mel used to be called Melancholia. In bed, in secret, he whispers, 'Melancholia . . . Melancholia . . . Melancholia . . . his hand moving faster and faster until he gasps into his pillow and becomes calm again. If anyone knew . . . just thinking about being discovered brings him out in goose bumps. His father might understand, man-to-man talk, except that Conor finds it impossible to talk to anyone, even Lyle, about his feelings for Mel.

'When did my mother become a Goth?' he asked her when she stayed with them last year.

'She was never really into the scene,' Mel replied. 'Behind all the drama, Cathy was a sweet young girl whom everybody loved.'

Everybody still loves her. All the guests and staff, and her friends who come to visit, tell him he is lucky to have such a thoughtful, understanding mother. Yet she wanted nothing to do with her family for more than fifteen years. He knows she was up the duff but that was the nineties, not the Dark Ages. Had she considered aborting him? His expression hardens as he squints into the sun. Birds glide over the lake, claws for surf boards and giddy from the morning heat. To have missed all this. He toes a dead trout out of his way, suddenly unnerved by the frozen eyes staring at him.

Born into the lives of two women and living in

the relative isolation of Havenswalk, it had taken time to sort out the difference between his own life and that of his friend Oliver, whose father trained the youth rugby team. On Saturdays he took Oliver and Conor to matches where the fathers standing on the sidelines seemed to have only one function: to roar at their sons, the referee, and the opposing team. By the age of eight Conor understood enough about sex to realise that fathers did not pop from Christmas stockings or come gift-wrapped on birthdays. He questioned his mother about his own father and she replied, 'This is not the time, Conor,' or 'When you're older, we'll talk.'

He sometimes wondered what would have happened if she had not become ill. He was ten years old at the time and the sound of her coughing in the next room, a hoarse, barking sound, scared him. She was never sick, not that he could remember. Usually she was the one cooling him down, nursing him back to health. It unnerved him to see her lying so listlessly in bed, as if a natural order had turned upside down.

On the morning she named his father, he entered her bedroom and found her staring at the ceiling. Her cheeks were red, her skin hot. He sat by her side, inarticulate and uncomfortable. What if she died? He was filled with fear. She always said that mates become family when you lived abroad but Alma and Hannah and the others were not family, no matter how hard she tried to pretend.

He seized the opportunity to ask again about his father. When she evaded his question, he grew angry. She fucked someone once and he was the result. Oliver had stated this fact when they were discussing fathers in the school yard, but it sounded different then. Speaking it out loud seemed to shrink her into the bed. Fat, slack tears trickled down her cheeks and neck. He was ashamed yet a sullen insistence kept him silent, waiting for her reply.

'Your father's name is Kevin Mulvaney,' she said. He listened, almost afraid to breathe in case she stopped talking, as she explained how, being only fifteen when she discovered she was pregnant, and Kevin two years older, they were too young to become parents. She was frightened over what they had done and ran away. She shook her head when Conor asked if she could contact his father. Kevin was working as a volunteer engineer, sinking wells in Africa. That was all Mel had been able to tell her. Lydia, his mother, had died and he had no plans to return home to Ireland.

It was the only time his mother mentioned his name. After she recovered, it was as if their conversation never took place.

'Our secret,' she said. 'Don't tell anyone.'

Knowing his father's name made it even worse. He composed an essay about volunteer work in Africa and was asked to read it out in class. He wrote a letter to his father and signed it Conor Mulvaney but never posted it. Then, last year, just when he believed nothing would ever change, his father entered their lives and nothing has been the same since.

40

Queenstown

The sound of music draws them into the Bindwood. Tim recommended the pub, the place to go if they want to hear good music. The small floor is crowded with dancers, the air loud with conversation. While Lauren finds space, Julie pushes her way to the counter and orders drinks. She studies her reflection in the mirror behind the bar. Her hair, twisted upwards and secured with two geisha pins, makes her neck look longer, slimmer, her chin more elfin. She is Lauren's creation. Before leaving the camper, her sister took out her cosmetic tray and transformed Julie from a domestic goddess into a *femme fatale*. Astonishing, Julie thinks, as she reluctantly turns her attention from her reflection to the barman, what can be achieved with a few tubes and colour palettes.

After a brief pause to allow the dancers time to recover their breath, the music begins again. The fiddle player holds an electric fiddle against his chin and dances the bow across the strings. An ageing rocker in Buddy Holly glasses grabs the microphone and launches into a version of 'Tequila Sunrise'. A group of bikers, menacing in black leather, enter. The Ringwraiths are obviously following the same route as the

Lambert sisters. The bikers approach Rebecca with a tattered copy of the *Southern Eye*. She looks mortified as she autographs it for them and is then whisked onto the floor by a rock-chinned biker. Another biker looks as shocked as a small boy when Julie informs him of the near-accident that resulted from their reckless driving. He insists on ordering a round of drinks as an apology.

More people crowd into the bar. The heat grows overpowering.

'Time to boogie, Mamma Mia. On your feet this instant.' Lauren's fingers drum against the table, her feet vibrate to the music.

'Check out the guitarist,' Julie shouts as she follows her onto the floor. 'Does he remind you of anyone?'

Lauren glances at the guitarist, who chews gum, a laconic expression on his long, narrow face, his brown hair drawn back in a sleek ponytail. She shrugs, shakes her head. 'He looks vaguely familiar. Don't ask me why.'

As if aware that he is under scrutiny, the guitarist glances towards them. His eyebrows lift when he smiles and Julie, embarrassed to have created such a response, looks away. Her head is beginning to buzz, a danger sign she has learned at her peril to ignore. The door to the beer garden is open, the tables empty. She leaves the pub and sits down beside a narrow stream, banked by white bell-headed flowers. The rippling flow is soothing, a change from the crashing water-falls and rivers that have marked their journey so far. The noise from the bar fades to a faint throb and the breeze, floating from the stream, cools her cheeks.

'Excuse me. Can I speak to you for a moment?'

Unaware that the music has stopped, Julie is surprised to see the guitarist standing in front of her.

'Are you . . . you have to be Julie Lambert? I recognised you as soon as you came in.'

He smiles again and the surge of memory forces her to her feet.

'Sebby! Oh *my* God! Sebby Morris.' She flings her arms around him. 'I can't believe I didn't recognise you. You haven't changed in the slightest.'

'You haven't either. How long is it? Nineteen? Twenty years?'

'Say that softly.' She covers her ears in mock-horror when he sits down opposite her. Impossible to believe she had not recognised him at first glance. 'I can't believe it's *really* Sebby Morris . . . '

'Actually, it's Seb now.'

'Mmm . . . Seb. OK, Seb it is.' His eyes are more hooded than she remembers, his features sharpened with age, but still attractive enough to send shock waves through her. 'I thought you were in Australia.'

'Australia, Japan, the States — you name it, I've been there. I came here a few years ago. So far the scene's been good. What about you? Still joined at the hip to Paul?'

'Still a hip joint.'

'God, I fancied the pants off you.' He laughs

and slaps his hands off his knees. 'Not that I ever had a chance. That jealous bastard made damn sure I never got within an ass's roar of you.' He reaches across the table and holds both her hands. 'What are *you* doing on the South Island?'

'Touring with my sisters. We're meeting Cathy. She also lives here.'

'Cathy? Is she the Goth?'

'Was. She's into the holistic lifestyle now and has a yoga centre near Nelson.'

'I must check her out next time I'm up that direction. What's the name of the centre?'

'Havenswalk. It's on the web.'

'So, update me on the family?'

'Jonathan, my eldest, is nineteen now.'

'Jesus, you can't have a son that old!'

'We had a head start, remember?'

'I heard.' He grins. 'I wasn't surprised. The two of you were hot. Do you still sing?'

'Of course not. It was just a kid's thing.'

'You don't lose a gift like that.'

'You know what they say? If you don't use it, you lose it.'

'Rubbish! Maximum Volume could have been bigger than U2, and we had the advantage of having a brilliant female vocalist.' His eyes, slate-grey and warm with memory, embrace her.

He is talking about a stranger whose skin she once occupied, someone she glimpses occasionally when she has time to pause and remember. The Glam Rock image. All those bows and pirate hats and embroidered jackets, shaking her shaggy hair as she strutted across a stage in knee-high boots, her energy exploding in song and music. A different image today. Her blonde hair clipped short, easy to blow-dry, and the face of a woman who knows exactly what the end of each day will bring.

'Stop it, Seb, or I'll start crying.' She is determined not to ruin her extravagantly curling eyelashes. 'Tell me about yourself. At least, you're still playing guitar. Paul hasn't played the drums since we married.'

'Well, I play for bread but I'm still hoping to make it as a song-writer.'

They laugh and reminisce until the fiddle player emerges from the pub, a bottle of beer in his hand.

'Hey, Seb, I wondered where you'd gone.' He stares quizzingly at Julie. 'How about an introduction?'

'Certainly.' Seb flaps his hand from one to the other. 'Jake Vale, allow me to introduce Julie Lambert, the famous Irish diva.'

'I am *not*,' Julie giggles, and instantly wants to murder the sound.

'Why don't you sing a number with us?' Jake asks.

'No way . . . It's years since . . . I couldn't . . . absolutely no way.'

'I'll try and change her mind.' Seb kisses her forehead and follows Jake back to the bar. 'See you inside.'

Julie returns to the table. The bikers are back at the bar but have sent over another round of drinks. 'You'll never guess who the guitarist is?' she shouts above the music. 'Seb Morris.'

Rebecca looks puzzled for an instant before nodding. 'I remember Sebastian Morris. Didn't his family have a red setter called Briar Rose?'

'That's right,' says Julie. 'Remember the time Nero tried to jump her bones and Seb's mother had to throw a bucket of water over them?'

'Please, Julie.' Lauren shudders. 'If you must discuss the sexual predilections of the canine population, do so when I'm not around.'

Julie sips a vodka and watches the dancers take to the floor again.

'Hey, folks, listen up.' The fiddle player smiles over at her. 'We're honoured tonight to have a guest singer in our midst. She's come all the way from Ireland! Give a big Kiwi welcome, folks, to Julie Lambert!'

Horrified, Julie's gaze flickers from the musicians to her sisters. 'I can't . . . I can't!'

'Yes, you can.' Rebecca begins to clap. 'You're a brilliant singer.'

'No . . . no . . .'

The dancers form a passage towards the stage as Lauren, ignoring her sister's protests, pulls her to her feet. The singer hands over the microphone with the jaded air of one who has performed the same concession to amateurs once too often.

Julie stares out at the packed floor and wonders how long it will take before her legs collapse.

'Sing 'Dancing Queen',' Lauren stands on a chair and yells through cupped hands.

' 'Dancing Queen' . . . 'Dancing Queen',' chant the bikers and raise their glasses. The musicians gather around her. Jake raises his fiddle. Seb pops a fresh stick of gum into his mouth. They begin to play. Julie's voice shakes then scoops the notes, carries them on the arch of music towards the dancers. Terror gives way to elation when she notices the polite expressions on the musicians' faces change to ones of surprise. Their playing becomes more purposeful.

She encores with 'Rainy Night in Georgia', relaxed now, her body swaying, Paul's favourite song, and the dancers pause, cease moving, the loneliness of the melody dropping like tears over their upturned faces. Julie knows she has them then, such a sweet, glorious feeling. An instant of silence follows the last note before the applause starts. The sensation, once familiar, is bittersweet. She ignores Seb's entreaties that she sing again and returns to her seat, the applause ringing in her ears. She wants to sing all night but it is important to quit while she is still ahead.

'You old sly puss cat.' Lauren hugs her. 'I didn't think you still had it in you.'

'Excellent.' Rebecca pats her hand. 'Sneaking out the window behind my back served some purpose after all.'

A tray of drinks, courtesy of the owner, is placed on their table. Seb jumps down from the stage and rushes over to Julie to hug her.

'Fantastic! You sure as hell never lost it and never will.' He shakes hands with her sisters, then waves at the barman to bring another round of drinks. 'I live in Kaikoura. Why don't you drive there tomorrow and stay a few days at my place? You can park practically beside the ocean.'

'We'll be in Kaikoura towards the end of our journey but, unfortunately, we're heading in the opposite direction tomorrow,' says Rebecca. 'Our itinerary's really tight — '

'I've gotta get back to the band.' Seb pulls Julie to her feet and hugs her again. 'Try and change her mind. God!' He sighs and holds her tighter. 'A taste of home and old times. You've made my night.'

'Why can't we go to his place?' Julie demands. 'We're not booked in anywhere.'

She studies her glass, surprised that the level had dropped so fast. 'What's the big deal about keeping to your itinerary? You'd swear it was carved on tablets of stone the way you keep going on about it.'

'We've planned a long journey,' Rebecca replies. 'What's the sense in having an itinerary if you keep demanding that I change it?'

'I'm not demanding. I just asked — '

'And I'm just telling you, it's out of the question.'

Seb grins over at her, ruefully lifts his eyebrows. Sebastian, Sebby, Seb, the abbreviated man. A Rory Gallagher fan who now plays easy-listening songs in a New Zealand pub. Julie shudders as more vodka burns its way down her throat. The band plays 'Lucille'. Loose wheel . . . loose wheel. They mocked that song once, the great Maximum Volume, arrogant in their youth, confident that they would send a seismic shock through the music industry. She lifts another glass, studies the colourless liquid before tossing it back. The earlier buzzing has returned, only now it sounds as if bees are entangled in her hair.

'Go easy,' advises Rebecca. 'Just because someone buys you a drink doesn't mean you have to swallow it in one gulp.'

Lauren sinks into a chair and dabs her forehead. 'Those Kiwis run up and down too many mountains. I can't keep up with them.' She glances at her sisters. 'What's going on here?'

'Julie's drinking too much.' Rebecca stands up and slings a cardigan over her arm. 'I'm settling the tab and then we're leaving.'

Julie directs a Nazi salute at her back.

'How dare Becks accuse me of been shrunk?' She leans confidingly towards Lauren. 'She's a boil on the arshe of humanity.' She takes a deep breath. 'I could've been a sharr. Why you laughin', Lauren? Don't you think I coulda been a sharr?'

'You are a star, babe. That was some performance you gave up there tonight.'

Lauren's face blurs before her, then comes into focus again. 'I wanna sleep with Shebby . . . Sheb . . .'

'Not a good idea, Julie.'

'I shont love him 'ny more.'

'That was a short-lived affair.'

'No. *My hushband.* I shont love him 'ny more.'

'Of course you do. You're just tired and emotional. And *way* over your limit.'

Rebecca returns to the table and stares resignedly at Lauren. 'What's she going on about now?'

'I'm shrunk, Becks. Shrunk as a *skunk.*'

241

Julie takes a step forward before realising that the floor has moved with her. 'I coulda been a sharr.' Holding on to a chair for support, she slumps down and starts to weep.

'She's turned on the waterworks again,' Lauren groans. 'We'd better get some strong coffee into her before we all drown.'

Julie has no idea whether she is laughing or crying. Do tear ducts know the difference? Is there a special spigot that decides which tears should be released for the appropriate occasion?

'Try and get a grip, Julie,' says Rebecca. 'You're making a show of yourself.'

Julie hiccups, giggles, weeps. ''Scuse me.' She presses her fingers to her lips and hiccups again. 'I wanna talk about Cathee . . . Cathee . . . likkle Cathee . . . Becks . . . do you know . . . ?' She stops and places her hand over her mouth. Rebecca's face swims before her. Such a stern, familiar expression. Don't touch, don't reach, don't break. Julie's head is clear. She could talk all night. Talk for Ireland. She giggles, unable to stop, and the words disappear.

'Let's get her into the ladies.' Rebecca puts her arms under Julie's shoulders and helps her to her feet. 'She's going to throw up. Hold her arm, Lauren.'

'I'm not shick . . . ' Julie struggles to her feet. 'I'm a sharr . . . a shining sharr . . . '

Seb waves and plays a sympathetic riff to accompany their departure.

Julie is still unsure whether she is laughing or crying when her sisters lay her down in her bunk and switch off the light.

Nemesis arrives in the morning when she awakes to the thud of horses' hoofs drumming across her forehead. Rebecca orders her to vacate her bunk. It is after ten o'clock. Ample time has been allowed for the recovery of a self-induced hangover.

'I warned you about the dangers of binge drinking, but you wouldn't listen.'

'Fuck . . . off.'

'No need to take that attitude. We can't possibly leave until you're strapped into the passenger seat.' Rebecca bullies her down from her bunk, then holds her upright under the cold shower — an act of sadism that will, Julie vows, create eternal enmity between them. Unaware that an impending death threat has been issued against her, Rebecca towels her dry and dresses her with as much compassion as she would show to a vivisectionist.

Strapped into her seat, Julie hangs her head out the window and breathes deeply into the fresh air.

'Make everything ready for departure,' Lauren shouts.

Julie quivers as Rebecca slams the press doors closed and does a final check to ensure that the safety catches are on.

'Roger. Over and out,' she shouts.

Lauren switches on the engine. 'Cabin crew, take your seats.' She glances across at Julie. 'Everything OK in the sick bay?'

'I want to die,' Julie whines.

'I take that as an affirmative.'

Julie bends her face into the bowl that Rebecca places beside her and utters a silent prayer that when the time comes, her sisters will bury her with dignity and full honours in the glacial depths of Lake Wanaka.

41

Cardrona Valley

Rebecca shields her eyes against the sun's glare. Is it her imagination or is there a line of bras fluttering along the length of a high wire fence? Julie, drifting in and out of recovery, shows slight signs of animation.

'Looks like the Sisterhood have abandoned their bras again,' she says. 'Let's take a look at their vital statistics.'

Lauren indicates and crosses the road. A small converted van with psychedelic flowers and butterflies painted along the sides is already parked by the fence. The women descend from the camper and inspect the collections of bras that are tied to the fence and range from serious foundation designs to frivolous scraps of satin. The various colours add a rainbow gaiety to the collection. Two Australian women, picnicking on the steps of their van, have already added their contributions from Brisbane, if the shapes under their skimpy belly tops are any indication. The fence began as a joke, they tell the sisters, and has now become a tourist attraction. Regularly, women passing by add to the display.

'Don't forget, the jet boat's booked for two o'clock.' Rebecca returns to the camper, but for all the attention her sisters pay she might as well whistle into the wind.

'This is the United Nations Bra Fence!' declares Julie. The sight of the Bra Fence appears to have completed her recovery. 'I'll send a photo to Paul. Brighten his day, if possible.'

'We should make our own contribution.' Lauren flings her T-shirt over her head and reveals a cream splash of lace across her tanned breasts. 'In Rome . . . as they say.'

'Rome?' Rebecca had settled into the driver's seat. She blasts the horn and leans out the window. 'Check it out, Lauren. No centurions or chariots. We're in Kiwi territory here. Put your clothes back on, you shameless hussy.'

'Who's next?' Lauren ignores her sister and grabs Julie around her waist. 'Come on, Mamma Mia, fly the tricolour for your country.'

Julie, giggling, takes off her shirt and waves it like a matador's cape. Her bust, she often complains, drags her down from a great height when all she wants from life is a perky uplift. She unbuttons her bra and swings it over her head.

'Oh, my God! I can't believe I'm doing this!' she shrieks as she ties her bra to the fence. 'I've just surrendered my greatest support. Drivers passing by will think it's a parachute.'

Her eyes have a dangerous sparkle as she approaches the camper. 'Come on, Rebecca. One for all and all for one. Pretend you're Lady Godiva.'

'Get dressed this instant and let's get moving.' Rebecca's voice rises authoritatively. 'This nonsense has gone on long enough.'

'Shame on you,' yells Lauren. 'What kind of an

ambassador are you for your country?'

'Silly me,' Rebecca shouts back. 'I planned for all eventualities but forgot to include a dance pole. If you two want to behave like a pair of slappers, that's your problem but if you're not dressed and in this camper within the next two minutes I'm driving off without you.'

'Ready, steady, go!' Julie shouts, and charges the camper. 'Let's go get her.'

Her sisters grab Rebecca before she has time to lock the door. Ignoring her protests, they hold one arm each and pull her down the steps.

'This is sexual harassment,' Rebecca yells.

'No, Rebecca,' Julie yells back. 'It's sibling harassment.'

The door slams behind them. Accompanied by cheers from the Australians, Rebecca surrenders to her fate and ties her bra on the fence. Her breasts swing freely as she moves backwards. The sudden liberating sensation of sun on her bare skin is sensual, exciting, liberating. Did the bra burners of the sixties experience the same kind of giddy hysteria as the pyre burned higher, she wonders.

'Enough of this frivolity.' Julie claps her hands and demands silence. 'It's time to salute our Republic.'

She sings a chorus of 'The Soldier's Song'. The Australians stand to attention throughout the Irish National Anthem, then follow with a verse of 'Advance Australia Fair'. All five gravely salute the United Nations Bra Fence. They shake hands, exchange addresses, promise to look each other up if the opportunity ever arises. The Australians drive off, flapping their arms in farewell from the open windows. The bras flutter lightly in the breeze.

'Oh-my-God! The Ringwraiths are back.' Julie's laughter turns to a shriek as the distant roar of motorbikes penetrates the horizon. With one accord the sisters dash towards the camper, only to discover that the door is locked from inside.

'Now look what you've done,' Rebecca wails as she tries in vain to turn the handle. 'Have you got the spare key, Julie?'

'Hardly.' Julie scurries behind the camper and shields her breasts as the bikers draw nearer. Lauren flings herself to her knees beside her. Rebecca is the last to sink out of sight. The bikes pass in a rush of noise and speed.

'We could try breaking the window,' suggests Julie.

'We could begin by putting our bras back on.' Rebecca moves from cover and heads towards the fence.

To her horror, she hears the bikes returning.

'Oh God . . . oh God . . . oh God.' Julie moans into her hands.

Rebecca grabs the bra closest to her and skids back behind the camper. It barely covers her breasts and is a hideous shade of pink with nipple tassels. So many bras and she has to pick the one left behind by a pole dancer. She stretches out her hand to pick up her T-shirt but it is just out of reach.

The bikers brake and approach the fence.

They guffaw loudly as they inspect the collection.

'Tell them to go away, Becks,' whispers Lauren. 'You're the only respectable one among us.'

Rebecca, hitching the boned and wired cups into place, hisses back. 'You call *this* respectable?'

'It's a lovely bra,' Julie whispers encouragingly. 'Red always looks brilliant on you.'

'It's cerise,' says Lauren.

'Looks like red to me.'

'Shut up!' Rebecca allows Julie to hook the fasteners into place. 'I swear, I'll swing for the pair of you before this trip is over.'

'Go on, Becks,' Julie nudges her furiously. 'They'll see us naked if they come any nearer.'

'Anyone at home?' A biker knocks on the camper door.

'Yes, I'm home.' Rebecca emerges from hiding. Walk tall, her father always advised her. No matter what the circumstances, hold your head high.

'Some display.' His eyes sweep boldly over her tassels. 'We thought we were hallucinating and came back for a closer look.' He grins and points to the fluttering fence. 'If that's a hallucination I hope they never find a cure.'

'I've a slight problem.' Rebecca primly folds her arms over her breasts. 'I've locked myself out of my motor home. Are you any good at picking locks?'

'I'm an accountant. Not much opportunity to pick too many locks in my profession.'

Rebecca bends down and reclaims her T-shirt. She shoots a warning glance at Julie, who looks as if she is suffering from a convulsion, and Lauren, crouching beside her, is equally helpless with laughter. She has a fleeting thought about Steve Moran. What would he think if he could see them now?

'I need to get inside.' Rebecca returns her attention to the current problem. 'Can any of your friends help?'

'Dave's a repo agent.' The accountant, who introduces himself as Kenny, gestures towards the tallest biker. 'He's picked a few locks in his day.'

Dave reluctantly leaves the Bra Fence and saunters across to the camper. He has the pugnacious expression of someone totally at home repossessing homes and cars.

'No problem.' He checks the lock, then removes some wire and a flat screwdriver from his pannier. His movements are precise and confident as he works on the lock. The bikers, fascinated by his speed and delicacy, gather around to watch and support his efforts. They clap him on his back and cheer when the door finally clicks open.

Rebecca enters the camper and glances through the back window. Her sisters make pleading gestures at her to send the bikers on their way. Their unrepentant shoulders are still heaving.

'I don't know how to thank you.' Rebecca stands on the steps and loudly addresses the bikers.

'A beer wouldn't go amiss,' says Dave.

'With pleasure.' They crowd into the camper. Rebecca opens the fridge and hands out cans. They belong to a biker club in Wellington, burly men heading into middle age on their Harley-Davidsons, and having fun along the way.

'Coffee, anyone?' She switches on the kettle, opens a packet of biscuits.

They leave an hour later. By then she is able to distinguish one from the other: Dave, Andy, Kenny, Ollie and Edge, the latter a dedicated U2 fan with the name Edgar on his birth cert.

When they finally disappear over the horizon, Julie and Lauren emerge from their hiding place.

'Don't ever ask for forgiveness,' warns Lauren. 'Even on your deathbed.'

'They've eaten all the biscuits,' Julie wails.

'Guess you'll have to bake some more.' Rebecca returns the tasselled bra to its rightful place and drives contentedly towards Wanaka.

42

Wanaka

Julie adds nectarines and kiwi fruit to a salad, sprinkles parmesan cheese over pasta. She removes a tray of bluefish with a herb and mustard crust from the oven, slides in the almond tart she will serve for dessert.

Paul rings as she is about to serve the meal. Rain is falling in Dublin and there are problems in the office. As if to emphasise his business, a printer, lively as a foot-tapping chorus line, clatters in the background. He sounds so fed up that Julie has a momentary urge to take the next flight home. She decides not to tell him about the day's activities: an exhilarating powerboat trip on Lake Wanaka and a leisurely tour through a winery.

'Did you pick up the email I sent?' he asks.

'Not yet. Why?'

He tries without success to sound calm. 'You *promised* to check every day.'

'I do. Almost. What's the problem?' Her sympathy ebbs with every word they exchange.

A second phone rings but remains unanswered as he launches into the latest catastrophe to occur since Julie left home.

'Gavin's having some difficulty accessing your data — '

'Gavin?'

'Gavin O'Neill. He's giving us a hand until you come back. He started yesterday but he's says there's a glitch — '

'There shouldn't be any *glitches* if he knows what he's doing.'

'Afraid that's not the case. He's trying to sort out the spreadsheets . . . it's chaotic — '

'Is he being paid to create chaos?'

'Not funny, Julie.'

'Just answer yes or no.'

'He's a graduate with a degree in business studies. I can hardly expect him to work for nothing.'

'Of course not. A labourer is worthy of his hire, especially when he has a *degree*.' She can just imagine this Gavin, with his white teeth and insufferable forehead bulging with knowledge. 'Tell him to check his email in ten minutes. I'll explain to him *exactly* how my system works. And stop giving me grief. I'm supposed to be on holiday.'

'Lucky for some.'

'You go abroad all the time,' she retorts. 'You were in Germany *twice* last year.' Lately, Julie noticed, they have started emphasising their words like bullet points.

'How can you possibly consider my attendance at a computer trade fair to be a *pleasure* trip?' His indignation quivers down the line.

She clicks out of the call and flings her phone into the centre of the table.

'He's insecure without you,' says Lauren.

'He's not insecure, he's resentful,' Julie snaps.

'And he's paying some creepy graduate for *all* the work I do for nothing.'

'You've both made financial sacrifices — '

'*Nothing*,' Julie repeats. 'That's all I get for slaving night and day. A husband who takes me for granted and who only cared about how *he* was going to manage when I told him I was going away.'

'Oh, come on, Julie, as husbands go, he's not the worst in the world.' Rebecca sounds as if she is consoling one of her sick donkeys.

'He can be a real dote at times,' agrees Lauren.

'I've the most boring marriage in the world and I'm the most boring part of it,' Julie cries.

Her sisters rush to reassure her. She is loving, kind, a great listener, sympathetic, the best cook, the nicest person they know. Nice! Boy bands in white suits are nice. So is jelly and ice cream. Julie sinks her face into her hands and chants, 'Boring . . . boring . . . boring.'

In the internet café, she accesses the problem and solves it. She is about to sign out when she notices an email from Seb Morris.

Hi Julie,

Hope the hangover didn't give you too much grief. Seeing you was a real blast from the past. Why don't we meet up again when you stop off in Kaikoura? I can book a table for the four of us. But, personally, I'd prefer it if we could have a one-to-one about old times. Why not come to my place for a home-cooked meal and a catch-up on all the gossip? I'd love your opinion on my demo CD.

    Let me know what suits.

    Your auld pal,

    Seb

On the next computer, a young Maori with tumbling black hair and a moko on his forehead races his fingers over the keyboard.

'You OK, girl?' He glances across at her.

'The night is so warm.' Julie flaps her hand before her face. 'I'm not used to it.'

He nods, turns his attention back to his computer. The moko on his forehead, a fan-like swirl of delicate lines, is related to family. She read about it in *Traversing New Zealand*. A moko adorning the face refers to the genealogy of both parents, mother on right side, father on the left. She received a coat-of-arms as a wedding present from the Morans, a wooden plaque bearing both their names. It used to hang in the hall. Lambert/Chambers. She wonders where it is now. Probably in her attic, gathering dust.

Hi Seb,

    A home-cooked meal sounds good. I'd be very interested in hearing your CD. My hangover was momentous but worth it. See you soon.

    Julie

    PS. Will I bring my mandolin?

A text arrives from Paul as she is returning to the table: 'Received info. Tks 4 solving prob. Sorry for being such a grouch. Everything falling apart since u left. I miss u tons. C't wait to have u home again. X'

Julie sighs and deletes it. Lauren lights citronella candles on the table outside. The night is warm and heavy, the mosquitoes gathering to bite.

43

Haast

For miles, they have not passed a car or a camper van that they can salute in recognition. The landscape is primeval, etched in solitude. Julie drives past forests of bent, windswept trees. The Tasman Sea, glimpsed occasionally between rocky outcrops, flails with a wild green energy that is both exhilarating and awesome to watch.

They locate a camper park outside Haast Village and prepare lunch. The sea roars beyond the sandy confines of the camper park. The sound is distant, melodic, restful. Julie relaxes in a deck chair and closes her eyes.

'On your feet,' says Rebecca as soon as they have finished eating. 'It's time to swim.' She grabs towels from the camper and throws one over Julie's upturned face. 'I've sussed out the route. It's only a short walk from here.'

'Get lost!' Julie throws the towel back at her. 'Can't we just spend one afternoon relaxing?'

Rebecca refuses to listen. 'Plenty of time to wind down when we reach Havenswalk. Shift your lazy butt. We can't come to New Zealand and not swim in the Tasman Sea.'

'Why?' Julie demands. 'We'll have ample opportunity to get wet tomorrow on the river safari.'

'That's river wet,' Rebecca explains. 'This is sea wet.'

'Oh, silly me not to have realised there is a *difference*.' Julie grumbles as she gathers her sunglasses and sunscreen from the table.

Following a sign to the beach, they climb over a stile and continue along a grassy path lined with reeds on either side. Rebecca draws ahead, briskly swishing the reeds with a branch she has fashioned into a staff.

'You'd think she was trying to break the world record for strenuous activities,' grumbles Julie as Rebecca stops at a V junction to get her bearings, then veers to the left. She gestures at her sisters to follow and pushes onwards. The path narrows and the reeds, reaching to their waists, form an unbroken swathe before them. The turning tide carries the smell of seaweed. It mingles with the fetid scent of rotting vegetation that rises whenever their feet sink into the swampy undergrowth.

'I can hear the sea,' Rebecca shouts back. 'It's just beyond this ridge.'

'No, it's not,' Julie replies. 'We're supposed to be heading to a public beach. No one with children would choose this route.'

'It'll open out in a minute.' Rebecca refuses to stop. 'Trust me.'

All traces of the path have now disappeared. Lauren and Julie stumble over fallen branches, grab on to each other to keep their balance.

'You're bringing us through a jungle,' Julie shrieks. 'Who do you think you are? Captain Bloody Cook?'

'No need for sarcasm.' Rebecca waits until they catch up with her. 'We're almost there.' She moves confidently through the spiky bush. The dull roar of the sea is audible now. Something wriggles underfoot. Julie screams and clings to Lauren.

'Are you all right?' Lauren steadies her. 'You look like you want to strangle Rebecca.'

'I would, if I could keep up with her. *Why* won't she listen? We're lost in a fucking jungle and she makes it look like a stroll in the park. *Bitch.* Why does she always have to be in control?'

Her temper rises as she slides on the slimy trunk of a fallen tree, trips over tangling vines. 'She forced me to marry Paul. All that shit about disgracing Mum and Dad's memory. They would have wanted me to be happy but all she cared about was her bloody reputation.'

'Whoa! Hold it right there, Julie.' Lauren sounds shocked by her outburst. 'No one forced you to marry Paul. You loved him, remember?'

'But I was just starting my life.'

'We're almost there,' Rebecca shouts triumphantly. 'Keep going, you slackers.'

'Remember Seb?' Julie ducks to avoid the spikes of a gigantic yucca.

'Yes.' Lauren lifts an eyebrow.

'He's been emailing me.'

'Dare I ask what he wants?'

'He suggested meeting up when we reach Kaikoura.'

'Good idea. We'll be ready for some fresh

company . . . that's if we haven't murdered each other by then.'

'Actually, it's more along the lines of a one-to-one meet-up.'

'I see.'

Julie shrugs. 'He wants to talk about old times.'

'A likely story.'

The colour deepens in Julie's face. 'Don't start moralising, Lauren. You're on swampy enough ground as it is.'

Without replying, Lauren quickens her pace.

'I've reached the sea.' Rebecca's triumphant shout prevents the conversation taking a dangerous turn. When they catch up with her she is standing on a stretch of whey-coloured sand cluttered with moss-green seaweed and chunky driftwood. 'There, I told you we were on the right track!'

'This is not the beach.' Julie runs towards a scattering of gulls wheeling above the breakers and sinks to her knees. 'Why can't you admit you're wrong for once in your life?'

'Maybe it's not the proper beach, but it's magnificent.' Rebecca drops her backpack on the sand and pulls off her T-shirt, kicks off her trainers, stamps out of her shorts. Her muscular body glistens with sweat. 'This is exactly what we need to cool off.'

'You're not going to swim in those waves.' Lauren points towards the breakers as they crash ashore, hazing the air with spray and spume.

'Of course I am. Why do you think we came here?'

'We didn't come here,' Julie screams. 'You dragged us here.'

'Oh, get over it, Julie! We have this fantastic beach to ourselves and all you can do is moan.'

'I assure you, Rebecca, moaning is safer than strangulation.'

Rebecca laughs and flings out her arms, spins in a circle, kicking sand. 'We might even see some penguins while we're here. Tim says they nest among the rocks. Come on, Lauren. Get your knickers off. Last one into the water is a chicken's neck.'

'You must be off your head if you expect me to swim in those waves.'

'Why not?' Rebecca gives a whoop and runs towards the sea.

'I can't believe you're going to follow her.' Lauren's voice rises as Julie fastens the catch on her bikini.

'I feel like doing battle.'

'Just don't expect me to mount a rescue operation if you get into difficulties.' Lauren sits down on one of the stranded logs. 'I'm washing my hands of both of you.'

Julie shrieks as a wave washes over her, the sound almost indistinguishable from the cry of gulls.

Unable to sit still, Lauren pulls on her bikini and follows.

Hand in hand they emerge from the foam and tumble like rag dolls towards the gleaming sand.

44

Jackson Bay

Today, as they struggled to find the beach, Lauren recognised the giddy excitement in Julie's eyes when she mentioned Seb Morris. She wanted to fold a protective cloak around her sister's marriage but Julie had ignored her words of warning. Look to the mote in your own eye, she had snapped, and Lauren had no answer. She turns in her narrow bunk and tries to sleep. Tomorrow they will embark on a river safari, then head for the glaciers.

They have travelled hundreds of miles across an ever-changing terrain. Days have blurred, places have faded from memory. Rebecca's itinerary is dog-eared and ringed with coffee stains. The most distant memory of all is Bangkok. Her phone is silent, her text messages unread.

She has seen the road sign for Jackson Bay. Niran Gordon's map carries the imprint of her hand. Straightforward directions that she must ignore. It is miles off their route, a finger jutting towards the sea, a road leading nowhere.

★ ★ ★

The morning mist wreathes the mountain slopes, and strange windswept trees, their branches coiled tight as broccoli, flit in and out of the milky haze. Occasionally, through the bush, Lauren catches a glimpse of the high-kicking surf collapsing over the sand. The scenery grows more isolated. She drives past occasional homesteads, red roofs visible beyond wooden fences. Sheep graze in rugged pastures and a road construction crew wave as she passes.

'I'm not going on the river safari.' She made her announcement at breakfast, calmly facing down her sisters' questions, their suspicions, their disapproval. 'I need some time on my own. I'll drop you off at the embarkation point and collect you when it's over.'

Before reaching Jackson Bay, she slows and checks the map. An X marks a turn-off point. She indicates right onto a narrow road that soon peters out into a sandy trail. She keeps driving, following dusty tyre tracks until a screen of trees blocks her passage. A patch of gravel serves as a car park. She parks the camper and walks between the trees, emerging from the gloom into a clearing. A few planks nailed roughly together form a bridge over a river. His home is little more than a shack, wooden walls and a corrugated iron roof. Fishing tackle and the battered remains of a propeller lie outside. A mountain bike is propped against the wall.

She knocks but receives no reply, knocks harder, then moves along a narrow veranda towards the back. His home is as she imagined: windows without curtains, no frills or bric-a-brac, some paintings on the walls, and a long veranda to catch the evening light. Wooden floors and easy chairs are visible in a spacious living area. A piano, its lid upraised, stands in the centre of the room, sheet music in place. She peers into a kitchen, which is furnished with an old-fashioned dresser, a long wooden table with sturdy matching chairs. Breakfast dishes rest on a zinc draining board. Life has been stripped to its essentials and the owner is not at home.

The back door opens easily. She hesitates, then steps over the threshold. Heedless of the cautionary voice ordering her to leave, she enters his living room. She touches the piano, his laptop, riffles through sheets of scribbled notations. Some musical symbols are recognisable from childhood piano lessons — crotchets and quavers, treble clefs; the language almost forgotten, as are the sounds of the scales she once practised daily, determined to conquer stiff fingers and play as skilfully as her mother.

Two framed photographs stand on a shelf. The first one is familiar. It fluttered to her feet and she picked it up, their fingers touching for the first time. Lauren stares at the violinist, her ornate ceremonial costume. Haloed in a spotlight, she stands in the centre of a stage, her bow raised, the violin tucked under her chin. The orchestra, grouped behind her, form a dark collage of indistinguishable shapes that focus attention back to her radiating presence. Such vitality in her expression, her blackbird swing of hair and sharply defined profile, her slender hands raising her bow.

A second photograph shows the same woman in a white T-shirt and jeans, standing with Niran on the veranda of a straw-roofed bungalow. Their arms are around each other, faces close together. His nose is perfect, nothing to suggest the break that distorts its high, slender bridge.

Lauren replaces the photograph, carefully settling it back into the precise position she found it. Her hands are moist. Sunlight streams through the wide windows. What is she doing here? What madness has persuaded her to enter another person's private space? She lifts a cushion, presses it to her face, then lets it fall to the floor.

In the doorway, she listens to the swooshing waves, the shriek of herring gulls. The sounds come from beyond a barrier of rock. She finds a cleft between the boulders and enters a dense tangle of bush, similar to yesterday's terrain. A beach stretches beyond the bush. Running across the sand, she stops beside a lagoon filled with small circling fish. Alerted by her shadow, they dart out of sight. Beyond the lagoon, the sand rises then steeps sharply towards the flailing waves. Except for her own footprints, the sand remains smooth.

★ ★ ★

Clouds whip across the sun. A flurry of sand stings her eyes. Sky and sea merge, smoky grey and threatening. The song of petrels and shearwaters falls silent as the first drops of rain since Lauren's arrival in New Zealand marl the seashore. She shivers, hugs her arms across her chest as she retraces her steps. The path she travelled is no longer visible. She faces a wall of tree trunks, tight as a palisade. Gulls and shags reel into the approaching storm, sweeping the air with the powerful beat of their wings. She plunges under the leaves, wanders in a circle before arriving back to the beach. She continues searching, the rain soaking through her T-shirt and skirt. Again, she tries to penetrate a gap between the trees, remembering how easily they lost their way the previous day.

The air is heavy, humid. Steam rises from the earth, releases the stench of things long dead. As the ground turns swampy, she forces herself to stay calm. Mud sucks at her sandals, soaks her ankles. How could she have been so stupid as to ignore the safe parameters she placed around her life?

Lightning flashes, followed by a roll of thunder. Hands over her ears, she stumbles against the trees. Their bent weathered shapes remind her of old women bowed with osteoporosis. She slips, crashes to the ground. Her sunglasses disappear into a thicket of moss. She too will disappear into the undergrowth. No one could possibly find her in this wilderness. The night in Bangkok, running from the pimp — the same terror surfaces. It was the start of everything. This will be its end.

Rain splatters through the leaves. Above her is a canopy of green, the last thing she will see before she closes her eyes. The fear when it comes is sharp as a blade. Who was this stranger who had mesmerised her with his bold black eyes? Had she really expected to sit and drink tea with him? Make small talk about the trip or the weather or share secret intimacies of their past lives? This passion that drew them together . . . what has it left in its place? A thought, barely conceived? Something that propels her blindly through the shivering green gloom, past the spiky yukkas, the windswept trees and monstrous ferns. Suddenly, a path opens in front of her. A bird darts from the undergrowth, its tail almost fanning her face.

In the camper she leans her head against the headrest until her breathing steadies. Her hair straggles across her forehead, drips into her eyes. Saliva fills her mouth. She swallows, shudders against the taste of bile. Unable to prevent the hot gush rising, she opens the door and stumbles towards a tussock of grass. She wipes her mouth with the end of her wet T-shirt and hunkers behind the camper until she feels strong enough to stand.

The rain stops as suddenly as it started. High in the sky, the sun forms a metallic disc and the rainforests, hunched against the glaciers, emerge from the haze, their luminous branches steaming. Everything is washed clean, raindrops glinting on each blade of grass. Back in the camper, she switches on the ignition and does a three-point turn. She emerges onto the main road and turns for Haast. From her rear-view mirror she sees a 4×4 approach and indicate to turn into the lane. She sees his arm resting on the open window, honey brown and taut. She presses her foot against the accelerator and sets her sights on the road ahead.

45

Rebecca's Journal — 1998

Olive Moran called to the sanctuary before she left for India. I never liked her — all those rows over Lauren and Cathy when they were young, particularly Lauren, but I admire her now. She looks younger, lighter somehow, as if she has freed herself from mind games. Backpacking through India, she said. Feel the land under my feet.

She wanted a daughter, not a replacement. She refused to believe that Lauren and her husband were not having an affair — or, perhaps, she understood that obsession is a more dangerous enemy than infidelity.

There are more ways of sinning than in the flesh,' she said to me when she finally decided to end her marriage. 'She runs like a fever through his blood and what am I to do . . . what am I to do?' She stepped back from the edge of insanity and took to the open road.

I wanted to tell her that I too am adrift in suspicion. Phone calls that have no voice at the other end, only someone breathing softly, hoping a different hand had lifted the receiver. But there is always an excuse to explain it away, and it could be a wrong number. The woman from his office who got drunk at the annual Christmas party and slapped his face when she knew I was looking . . . but she was drunk and, later, I watched her friends support her from the hotel. The faint hint of perfume on his shirt . . . but it could be aftershave. Nowadays, men are peacocks, they groom and moisturise. The receipt for drinks in the Horseshoe Bar, Guinness and Margaritas, on a night when he was working late — that one is difficult to explain but I could easily have mixed up my dates. There are always ways to ease my suspicion and I have no idea why I cling so tenaciously, so fiercely, to them.

Steve Moran is playing with the big boys now. Serious property development. A Celtic tiger on the prowl. He sold Meadow Lark and lives on Howth Head, right at the very top. Exactly where Lauren wants to be. Different horses for different courses. She insists she played no part in the break-up of their marriage. Is she pretending or simply delusional?

My sanctuary is everything to me. Lulu was glad to hand over the responsibility and stay on as my manager. The horses that come to us are victims. There's nothing proud and highbred about them. They come with broken limbs and missing eyes. We give them shelter. There's so many of them, adrift on waste ground, in cramped sheds, tied to stakes in barren fields, wandering blindly into oncoming cars. We give them shelter and healing. At the end of the day, isn't that what we all crave?

46

Fox Glacier Village

Ancient Maori history is buried in the roots of Te Wahipounamu, their guide explains as they travel through the Haast River Valley. Translated it means 'the place of green-stone'. Rebecca leans forward as they pass ancient rainforests, hoping to catch a glimpse of dolphins and seals. Julie takes photographs and wonders what her sons would think if she became a biker.

They sprawl opposite her, the Ringwraiths, escapees like herself, families and mortgages, tidy front gardens; their swagger caused by too-tight leathers rather than menace. She imagines herself on a Harley, the wind in her hair. Easy rider on Route 66.

When the rain falls, they shelter under the canopy. The bikers' plans are similar to their own. They will spend the night in Fox Glacier Village and explore the glaciers in the morning. They invite the sisters to their cabin for a barbecue in the evening.

'Come around seven,' says Edge. 'We'll provide the steaks.'

'I'm a vegetarian,' says Rebecca.

'Veggie burgers,' he says. 'No problem.'

'Where's your sister?' asks Dave, the lock-picker.

'She vants to vee alone,' Julie replies. She leans into Rebecca's ear and whispers, 'I think he wants to pick the lock on Lauren's chastity belt.'

'He's too late.' Rebecca trains her binoculars on a colony of penguins strutting like short, fat waiters along the shoreline.

'Do you think she's with him?'

'I don't think so,' Rebecca replies. 'I know so.'

'Have you tried talking to her?'

Rebecca shrugs. 'She's not my concern, not any more. If she wants to play with fire, that's her business.'

'I'm worried about her.'

'Then you talk to her.'

Julie tries to concentrate on the guide but she finds it impossible to follow the history of earthquakes and glacial meltdown. What is Lauren doing? Staring at trees, climbing rocks, admiring a river? Hard to imagine — in fact, quite impossible. She is not waiting for them at the disembarkation point. The bikers lounge against their bikes, smoking and joking about mounting a search party. Julie, holding his helmet like a decapitated head under her arm, poses on Kenny's bike and demands to be photographed. He calls her his 'pillion bitch' as he revs the engine and orders her to hold on tight. The wind whips her breath away as he increases speed. The trees blur and the sun dazzles the handlebars. She recognises the camper. Lauren is driving so fast she does not notice Julie waving.

'Better go back,' she screams at Kenny. 'Cinderella has returned from the ball.'

The camper vibrates with tension. Bedraggled and pale, her legs scratched and covered in bites, Lauren endures her sisters' complaints with uncharacteristic humility. Their mood has not improved by the time they reach the camper park. The brief spell of rain had added to, rather than dispelled, the heat. Rebecca's shoulders radiate from sunburn.

'I'm going to cry off the barbecue,' she declares when Julie begins preparing a platter of seafood to take with them. 'I've a splitting headache. It's probably sunstroke.'

'Take something for it,' Lauren suggests. 'I'll rub in after-sun to cool you down. You'll be fine once you get a glass of wine inside you.'

But Rebecca refuses to be coaxed from the camper. 'I feel sick to my stomach at the thought of smelling roasted animal flesh.' She shudders and winces when Lauren rubs after-sun into her shoulders.

'Give us a break.' Lauren snaps the lid on the lotion and flings it on the table. 'I've had it up to here with your fucking animals.'

'Don't start a row.' Julie slices lemons, mixes a salad dressing.

'Why not?' Rebecca demands. 'I'm suffering from sunstroke because *she* left us out in the scorching sunshine for hours on end.'

'She was only thirty minutes late. Perhaps we should stay with you — '

Tiny blisters glisten on Rebecca's shoulders. 'Just go, Julie. And try to be quiet when you return. I don't want a repeat of your Bindwood experience.'

Julie's sympathy disappears in an instant. 'I bet she doesn't speak like that to her horses,' she fumes as she walks with Lauren towards the bikers' cabin. 'I can't imagine why a nice guy like Tim Dawson keeps texting her.'

'We should congratulate him on overcoming the disadvantage of having only two legs,' agrees Lauren.

'Did you know she's asked him to Cathy's wedding?'

'He's not just a one-night stand then?'

'Apart from looking at his takahē Rebecca doesn't *do* one-night stands.' Julie flicks a prawn back into position between the slices of lemon. 'Which begs the delicate question . . . where were you this morning?'

'Communing with nature.' Lauren grabs her arm. 'Come on, girl. Let's go bag ourselves a Ringwraith.'

With their bikes lined like steeds outside a cabin, the bikers are easy to find. Beer and wine sit in a sink of crushed ice. Tina Turner blares from the stereo on the windowledge. The barbecue pit is flaming and Edge is in charge of the steaks. Lauren adds wine to the fridge and Julie hands over the seafood platter, which the bikers devour in an instant.

Darkness links the campers and cabins in a ring of light. When the first sighting of a sandfly is reported, chairs are gathered up and carried inside. More wine is uncorked, beer cans snapped. Kenny talks about Wellington. Julie talks about Dublin. They compare photographs of their families. He slaps his head when he realises he was drinking beer with Rebecca while she and Lauren were hiding topless behind the camper. His gaze admires what he missed and sends a pleasant tingle along her spine. He rolls a joint and passes it to her. She inhales deeply. Lauren rejects it with a slight hand gesture.

Edge cranks up the music and accompanies Lynyrd Skynyrd on air guitar. At home, Julie would have yelled at her sons to turn down the volume. If they could see her now. The thought makes her laugh so loudly that Lauren leans over and asks, 'What's with the spliff, sis?'

'Old times.'

'Mamma Mia, what's happening to you? Are you becoming a bold girl again?'

Julie inhales, closes her eyes. 'Absolutely.'

Edge abandons his air guitar and dances with Lauren. She glides like a moth, her white dress flaring when he twirls her under the light. Her brittle laughter adds to Julie's uneasiness. Her sister is walking a tightrope. A step either way, a tautening, a slackening, and Lauren will fall.

The music is so loud it takes a moment to realise someone is banging on the door. Dave opens it and is brushed aside by a small, sturdy woman in knee-length tartan shorts. 'Turn that noise off immediately.' Her English accent is clipped and authoritative. 'I don't mean turned down, do you understand? I mean off. If you fail to do so there will be immediate repercussions.'

She surveys the empty cans and bottles, the plates and bowls littering the room. 'If I hear another squeak from your cabin, I'm going straight to management to report this appalling breach of regulations. My husband and I booked into a holiday park, not a drunken nightclub.'

Dave bows with exaggerated courtesy. 'Have a drink, lady, and join the party. Ice? Lemon? We're all mates here.'

'We certainly are not mates.' Silhouetted against the light from the open door, her body vibrates with indignation. 'As you are obviously incapable of telling the time, let me remind you. It's now after ten o'clock and this holiday park is supposed to be silent. People expect peace and quiet, and the opportunity to sleep without having to endure an infernal racket. You have been warned.' She turns on her heel and slams the door behind her.

'We'd better turn down the volume.' Julie moves towards the stereo but Dave reaches it before her.

'No Pom with a tartan arse is going to spoil my fun.' His eyes glint with anger as he lurches towards Lauren and swings her roughly in a circle. She laughs, struggles to free herself. He spins her again, almost lifting her off her feet. A chair crashes to the ground. He loses his balance and brings her down with him in a sprawl of arms and legs.

'Stupid fuck.' Edge pushes him to one side and helps Lauren to her feet.

'Who're you calling a stupid fuck?' Hauling himself upright, Dave leans against the table. It tilts to one side. Bottles and glasses crash to the floor.

Without knocking, the manager enters the cabin, closely followed by the Englishwoman.

'You know the rules.' He points to a notice pinned on the door. 'No noise after ten p.m. We expect our residents to have consideration for their neighbours.' He pauses, sniffs, his expression hardening. 'If you're not off my property within the next ten minutes, I'll call the police and have you arrested for bringing drugs onto the premises.' He points to Julie, who signed them in at Reception. 'The same rule applies to those of you staying in a motor home bay.'

'But there's no noise coming from our bay,' Julie protests. 'The camper is rented in our sister's name, Rebecca Lambert. She wasn't at the party. Why should she be evicted?'

'Vehicles don't make noise. It's people who cause problems. Don't ask me to repeat my warning or you'll discover I don't make idle threats.'

'Rebecca's going to murder us.' Lauren leans heavily on Julie's arm as they make their way back to the camper.

'Murder's too easy,' Julie whispers. 'She'll hang, draw and quarter us, then dance on our bones. God! Did you ever see anything like those tartan shorts?'

'Scotland the brave,' whispers Lauren.

'Brave arse,' Julie giggles.

'Tartan Pom.' Lauren, forgetting her injury, raises her arms above her head and mimics a Highland fling.

'Be serious.' Julie stops outside the camper.

'You've danced enough for one night. Where are we going to go?'

'To hell or to Connaught,' says Lauren.

Julie splutters, laughter erupting inside her. The same hysterical laughter that gripped her at the Bra Fence, gripped her throughout her teen years, gripped her hardest when Rebecca ordered her to behave, and she, recognising the signs — nerves, guilt and something indefinable, perhaps the desire not to cry — clutches her stomach in a vain effort to control it.

'How considerate of you to return.' Rebecca raises herself from her bunk. Her shoulders flare angrily under the light.

'You told us to go,' Julie protests. 'You insisted we leave you alone.'

Lauren limps towards the nearest chair and bends to examine her ankle.

'I took a bad fall, Rebecca. I think I've a broken ankle. Julie had to support me all the way back to the camper.'

'What do you expect when you're obviously incapable of walking in a straight line?'

Julie removes a frozen packet of peas from the freezer and applies it to Lauren's ankle. 'Actually, Becks — '

'Stop calling — '

'Actually, Rebecca . . . ' Julie coughs loudly before continuing, 'we've been ordered to leave the site. I told the manager you weren't responsible. He wouldn't listen. I'm really sorry but he's insisting we leave this instant.'

'I'm not in the mood for jokes, Julie. In case

you haven't noticed, I'm suffering severe sunstroke.'

'It's true.' Lauren grimaces as the icy peas bite into her skin. 'This is really sore, Rebecca.'

'Then limp out of here to the nearest hotel and take your sister with you. You're supposed to be adults, for goodness' sake, not a bunch of drunken teenagers. For your information, I've no intention of moving anywhere so no one had better make me.'

'I beg to differ.' Unnoticed, the manager enters. 'I said ten minutes. It's now fifteen. If you're not off this site in five I'm calling the police and reporting you for causing a disturbance and smoking dope on my premises.'

'Dope!' Rebecca stares at her sisters, her eyes resting longest on Julie. 'We'll be out of here in five minutes.' She turns to the manager. 'I'm sorry they caused so much trouble.'

'Five minutes or I take immediate action.'

After the manager departs, she places her head in her hands. 'Smoking dope! I can't believe this — '

'I shared a joint with Kenny, that's all.' Julie's defiance is straight from her Maximum Volume days. 'You'd swear we were sniffing coke, the fuss he's making.'

'We need to ring Steve and get him — '

'Steve's got nothing to do with this.' Impatiently, Rebecca interrupts Lauren. 'This mess needs to be cleared by you and Julie.'

Lauren lifts a spoon, taps it against the table. She seems unaware that the sound is growing faster and faster until Julie leans over and snatches it from her.

'Why is everyone so allergic to a little luxury?' she demands. 'Think warm baths. Room service, hairdressers. A big double bed instead of a coffin. That's what it's like up there.' She jerks her hand upwards. 'Sleeping in a fucking coffin.'

'So what do you want?' demands Rebecca. 'A big double bed like the one you didn't sleep in when we were in Bangkok?'

The silence that follows rasps the atmosphere. 'I'm not a fool, Lauren.' Rebecca's voice cuts across any pretence. 'Nor am I blind to what goes on in your so-called marriage.'

'Rebecca, if you want to lecture anyone about the hallowed state of matrimony, look in the mirror and start talking to yourself.'

'How dare you bring my marriage into this conversation?'

'You don't appear to have any problems throwing mine in my face. In case it's escaped your attention, what I do with my life has nothing whatsoever to do with you.'

'I agree. What you do behind your husband's back is absolutely no concern of mine. But when you ask me to accept his charity, it does become a matter of some significance.'

Lauren's face remains impassive. Even her eyelids seem suspended in midair. 'You're such a sanctimonious bitch, Rebecca Lambert.'

'And you're a married woman who's deceiv-ing — '

'Cut it out, you two,' Julie warns. 'We have to leave here or the manager — '

'Ahem . . . Do I duck or is it safe to enter?'

279

Kenny answers his own question by entering the camper. 'The lads aren't in a fit state to drive anywhere. I asked my cos, Akona, to pick us up. Follow the ute and park the camper in the garden.'

'An ute! What the hell is he talking about?' Rebecca demands after he leaves.

'I think it's a pick-up truck,' says Julie. 'We'd better get ready to leave.'

Rebecca shakes off her assistance. She disconnects the electricity and water. A short while later a pick-up truck appears. Some of the bikers wheel their bikes up the ramp. The rest will be collected on the second run. Kenny gets into the passenger seat and slaps the driver's shoulder. The driver, wearing a wide-brimmed hat, leans from the window and gestures at Rebecca to follow. Without exchanging a word with her sisters, she drives from the slumbering holiday park.

47

Evicted from a motor home park. What a joke. What a story to tell over the dinner table. Julie will dine out on it for years to come. The hazard lights on the pick-up truck in front flash warningly as the driver turns sharply down a side road and plunges through a tunnel of trees. Ferns loom large and ominously from the edge of the road. According to Tim, the Maoris used to plant them as sign-posts for their people. In which direction are they leading them tonight? *Mysterious Disappearance of Lambert Sisters Remains Unsolved.* Yes, it will make an interesting headline, nothing more. Rebecca is too tired and hungry to care.

Julie cleared the fridge of food when she made her seafood platter. A hardened chunk of cheese and a withered pear were all she left for Rebecca to eat. Tears of self-pity sting her eyes. Furiously, she brushes them aside. The driver takes another turn, a narrower road this time, little more than a track. The trees are dense, the trunks congested with vines. Parasitical vines, clinging and tenacious like her sisters. Branches whip the camper. Swathes of bush have been ravaged by summer fires. The silvery ash flares the darkness, reminds her of banshees' tresses sweeping the sky.

Julie, obviously still stoned, switches on an iPod and clicks her fingers to an inaudible

281

melody. Lauren appears to be asleep. Her sprained ankle looks remarkably slim and the frozen peas are mulching into a watery mess under the passenger seat.

Rebecca brakes in front of a one-storey house with a wooden veranda. The wheels crunch on gravel, judder over a pothole. The pick-up driver dismounts and directs her to the side of the building.

'Any idea where we are?' Lauren opens her eyes after Rebecca has parked.

'Could be on the lip of a volcano, for all I care,' she retorts.

Julie rummages in a press and removes a gas lantern. 'We obviously can't expect laid-on facilities.' She lights the lantern and places it on the table, stretches her arms above her head. 'That's enough excitement for one night.'

'Time for this whore's beauty sleep.' Lauren prepares to climb into her bunk.

'I never called you a whore.' Every time Rebecca moves, she feels as if her skin is under attack from burrowing, sharp-clawed insects. She has no desire to argue any further with her sister. All she wants is sleep. The heat is unendurable. She flings open the door and steps outside. If she does not escape she will shatter the windows with a scream.

She hears laughter coming from the house, the sound of a guitar striking up. The bikers, having unloaded their bikes from the truck, are still determined to party.

'You settled in OK?' The driver leans on the veranda rail and calls out to her. 'Take water from my house if you need it.' To Rebecca's surprise, the voice, although deep and gruff, belongs to a woman.

She walks towards the driver, who straightens and holds out her hand. Under the porch light her face is visible: brown leathery skin and a frizz of white hair under the wide-brimmed hat.

'You're welcome to my house.' Her grip is welcoming. 'My name is Akona.'

'I'm Rebecca.' She tries not to stare at the startling tattoo fanning across the woman's chin. The intricacy of the design fascinates her. She remembers Cathy's tattoo, the raven's head needled on her shoulder, and the row that followed. 'I'm sorry we caused you so much trouble.'

'Not at all. Kenny's friends are my friends.'

They listen to Edge — it has to be Edge — singing 'I Still Haven't Found What I'm Looking For'.

Rebecca smiles, nods towards the open window. 'You have a house full of them tonight.'

'A house full of bold boys.' Akona's cheeks are a network of wrinkles but her dark eyes flash with energy. 'I live alone so a little company now and again is nice, no matter what shape it comes in.'

'Have you always lived here?'

'I'm from the North Island. Rotorua. I bought this land when I retired from teaching. Now I fish and farm a little. And you? What brings you to New Zealand?'

Rebecca grips the veranda rail. Humming black insects float before her eyes. She is aware that the ground is rising to meet her but she can do nothing except sink into the moist, spinning darkness.

'Sunstroke,' says Akona, when Rebecca opens her eyes. 'Dehydration.'

'I'm fine . . . it's nothing.' Rebecca licks her lips and tries to struggle upright. Her legs have turned to jelly. It is easier to close her eyes again. She shivers as Akona's cool hands touch her forehead.

'Come with me to my house.' Her voice sounds far away. 'We need to treat your sunburn immediately. When did you last drink water?'

'Earlier . . . I forget.' Rebecca sways as she is helped to her feet.

Akona holds her in a firm grip and guides her across the veranda. She opens the door of the room where the bikers are singing and calls for silence. To Rebecca's astonishment, this order is instantly obeyed. Once a teacher always a teacher, she thinks as she slowly walks with Akona to the end of a long hall.

They enter a wide, airy room. A throw, embroidered with ethnic symbols, not unlike the moko markings on Akona's chin, covers a bed. Akona folds it back and gestures at Rebecca to lie down. The sheets are cold against her skin. She shivers at the contrast and moans through dry lips. The scent of lavender rises from the pillows. The smell grows stronger when Akona returns to the room with a jar of cream and gently massages it into Rebecca's skin. She works along Rebecca's shoulder blades, the back of her neck, her touch light and soothing.

'It's my own ointment,' Akona says. 'My grandmother gave me the recipe. It will work quickly to ease the burn. I'll fetch some water. You must drink regularly and rehydrate.'

Rebecca sips slowly and forces herself to concentrate. 'My sisters . . . can you tell them where I am?' Her eyelids begin to droop. 'We're exploring the glaciers tomorrow and we've an early start.' Another early start. How often has she uttered those words since the trip began?

'Tomorrow you will stay away from the sun,' says Akona. 'And from the ice.'

'But we have to move on. I've booked in advance. Our schedule is very tight. We can't afford to lose a day.' Rebecca's voice, muffled by the pillows, lacks decisiveness. 'We're going to my sister's wedding.'

'The glaciers have been here since the ice age,' says Akona. 'They will still be here when the time is right for you to visit them. But tomorrow you must rest, not only in body but also in your spirit. The day after tomorrow you'll be a different person and the distance won't seem so long.'

'Thank you.' It feels deliriously wonderful to hand over all her control to a stranger.

'This wedding? A joyous occasion, eh?'

Rebecca shakes her head. 'We haven't seen Cathy since she ran away over fifteen years ago.'

'Many of my people go missing too.' Akona sighs and wipes her hands on a muslin cloth. 'It breaks the heart of a family. But now you have time to make peace with each other.'

'Peace?' Rebecca whispers. 'Somehow, I don't

285

think so. I still don't understand why I made the decision to come here.'

'The reason will be clear to you before your journey is over. Now I will leave you to rest.'

Rebecca's eyes close. She is sleeping by the time Akona leaves the room.

48

Rebecca's Journal — 2002

Lydia Mulvaney is dead. Cancer, corrosive, terminal. She was dead within a month of diagnosis. I visited her in the hospice. She wore a bandana with sequins and turned her ward into a studio. Her friends were there, the same lively bunch, but she sent them away when I arrived. She seemed genuinely glad to see me.

She had an album of old photographs, all of them dated, named. We sat together on top of the bedclothes and lost ourselves in the past, image after image reminding us that time is a stealthy thief. I saw Julie in a Superman cape and Cathy in her pram and Kenneth Mulvaney, her long-dead husband, playing basketball with his son, and Lauren winning medals for running and high jumps in the school sports. Funny, I'd forgotten her lithe ballerina strength. I asked about Kevin. He was on his way home from Australia where he's been living for the last year. Burnout from Africa.

Lydia gave me a painting when I was leaving the hospice: a cluster of cottages clinging to the edge of a mountain, a rock standing like a sentinel above them. Open windows, and gaping doorway, the roofs collapsed under the weight of rain and wind. Hidden figures within the ruins but, perhaps, I'm imagining those mother ghosts who have never left the shadows.

She was dying but she was the one to offer me solace. There was pity in her eyes when we said goodbye.

So many people came to her funeral. I shook Kevin's hand. We only had time to exchange a few words. He was such an intense teenager, always trying to pull aside the veil and demand answers from the underworld. I remembered his pallid face and the grim jet-black hair, but he is an open-faced man with untidy blond locks that would need sheep shears to control. Like his mother, he has a direct gaze and he looked me straight in the eye. He would never have betrayed Cathy. I guess I've always known that . . . so what then . . . what is the truth?

Jeremy rang from New York tonight. VisionFirst have landed an amazing account. I told him the line crackled so much I was unable to hear him.

49

Havenswalk

Conor dismounts from his mountain bike and removes his helmet. Three hours on the road have left him sweaty and itchy. He wants a bath and a long cool drink. He climbs the stairs and passes his parents' bedroom. The door is open. A dress lies on the floor, a crumpled pair of trousers beside it. He shies away from the mental picture it conveys, clothes abandoned where they fell. Difficult grappling with the thought of his mother and sex. Stupid to be jealous. Oedipus complex and all that rot. He confided in Lyle, who assured him it was not jealousy, at least not in that weird sense, but is based on the fact that the man his mother is about to marry has access to the history denied Conor and would still be denied him if it was not for the Coast to Coast Triathlon.

Since he was eleven years old, Conor and his mother have accompanied Lyle to the starting point on Kumara Beach. They have ferried his bike and kayak across the island and along each stage of the competition until the finish on Summer Beach. The sight of the competitors lining up and the roar from the spectators fuels Conor's determination to take part as soon as he is old enough. Lyle always ends up somewhere in the middle but Conor's ambition is to win.

Last year, his mother was too busy to take time off. Alma offered to do the driving and, after the competition, they stayed overnight in Christchurch with a woman who regularly visited Havenswalk to meditate and step off the treadmill of life. That was what she told Conor as she drove them to a beach party. Lyle came with them. His decision was made at the last moment because, earlier, he had said he was too exhausted. And that decision changed Conor's life.

As the night wore on, the crowd gathered closer to the flames of a driftwood fire. A woman played guitar and Alma accompanied her on the spoons, rattling them off her knees, her arm, even off Conor's head. The crowd laughed and applauded her. A group of Australians added to the music with a harmonica and bongos. People began to sing. Lyle put on his glasses and stared across the fire at a man sitting underneath an Australian flag. The flag, suspended between two poles, had been planted in the hard sand and the man, in frayed denim shorts and a black Guinness T-shirt, played the bongos with more enthusiasm than talent. After the singing ended, he grinned and bowed to the applause.

'Dowser,' said Lyle in a soft voice. 'Dowser,' he repeated, this time shouting the word across the flames.

The man heard. He stopped grinning and looked puzzled.

Lyle stood up and held out his arms. 'Hey, Dowser,' he shouted. 'Over here.'

'I don't believe it!' the bongo player shouted and clenched his fist, flung his arms in the air. 'If it isn't the holy man himself.'

He seemed to leap across the flames and then he was beside them, him and Lyle bear-hugging and thumping each other on the back and shouting about coincidences and what the hell were they both doing in this neck of the woods?

When the excitement died down, Dowser sat beside them. The two men talked about Africa. They asked questions about old friends and each other's lives since they had last met. Lyle introduced him and Conor moved closer to the stranger, who sounded uncannily like his mother. He could listen to his accent all night.

When the singing started again, Dowser fetched the bongos and handed them to Conor. 'Want to try and rap a tune?'

'No, thanks,' Conor replied. 'I'd murder them.'

'Can't be any worse than the punishment I've inflicted on them.' Dowser lifted his beer and said, '*Slainte mhath*,' which, Conor knew from his mother, meant 'Good health' in Irish.

'You've settled in Cairns then?' Lyle asked.

'As much as I can settle anywhere,' Dowser replied, and Lyle nodded, like he understood that kind of restlessness.

'Are you from Ireland?' Conor asked.

'Born and bred.'

'My mother is Irish. So is Alma.'

'Are they now? And what county do they hail from?'

'Dublin.' He looked around for Alma but

could not see her anywhere.

'Dublin jackeens like myself,' said Dowser.

'Do you miss Ireland?'

'What's there to miss?' Dowser shrugged and laughed. 'Unless you want to grab a Celtic tiger by its tail.'

'I've never been there. My mother lived in a place called Heron Cove.'

'Where?' Dowser sounded astonished.

'Heron Cove. It's beside an estuary — '

'Yes . . . I know it well. What's your mother's name?'

'Cathy.'

Dowser knocked over his stubby. The beer trickled down his leg and disappeared into the sand. He kept staring at Conor and then he said, 'Cathy *Lambert*?' although Conor had not mentioned her second name.

'Yes. Do you know her?'

'My God! Cathy. Yes . . . yes. I used to know her.'

'I work for Cathy.' Lyle sounded astonished. 'Havenswalk is the longest place I've stayed since I left the priesthood.'

But Dowser did not seem to hear him. 'Your mother and I go back a long way.' He held Conor's hand in a tight grip. 'I never knew she had a son.'

'Do you know my father?' Excitement splintered his chest. His past was so close he could almost touch it. Heron Cove was small, his mother said. It was shaped like a horseshoe and everyone knew everyone else. 'His name is Kevin Mulvaney.'

Someone flung more driftwood onto the bonfire. The flames spluttered and shot upwards, flickered across Dowser's shocked expression. He released Conor's hand and bowed his head, pressed his fingers against his forehead. Lyle's face seemed frozen, his mouth open. The silence that followed was unbearable. Conor tapped the bongos. Just a gentle rhythmic tap but it startled Dowser into looking at him again.

'What did Cathy say about your father?' He spoke so quietly, Conor had to strain forward to hear.

'Nothing much. Just his name and stuff.'

'What stuff?'

'About him and her being too young to have a baby.'

Lyle pressed Conor's hand and stopped him tapping. 'Conor, don't — '

'It's OK, Lyle,' Dowser interrupted him. He peered at Conor as if he wanted to see him more clearly. 'Dowser's just a nickname — '

'You find wells?' Conor tried to swallow but his throat felt scratchy, sore. He had read about dowsers, people with a gift, twigs in their hands, snapping downwards. When he gasped, the sound tore from his chest but he was still unable to speak. Scenes like this happened in books and films. They were played out in his dreams. He wanted to pinch himself to see if he was still awake but he was afraid to move, to make any gesture that would disturb the reality of this unbelievable coincidence.

'You're my father.' His voice had been slipping up and down the scale but when it broke on this

293

occasion he knew it was permanent. 'Aren't you?' he demanded.

Fear pushed through Conor's eyes. Why did he have to blurt it out? He should have waited, left it to his mother to tell him, given his father time to adjust to the idea. Instead, if the dazed expression on Kevin Mulvaney's face was any indication, Conor had ruined everything.

For an instant his father did not speak. Then he nodded, just once, a movement almost imagined in the shadowy flames. Then he heaved a deep, shuddery sigh before stretching out his hand. 'I'm very pleased to make your acquaintance, Conor.'

When he stood up, he was smaller than Conor expected. Not that Kevin Mulvaney was small. He was just a little under six feet tall, Conor guessed, but in his imagination his father had always towered.

The following day his mother was working in her office when he entered Havenswalk.

'Welcome home.' She turned from her computer and held out her arms. 'How did it go? I suppose Lyle ended up in the usual muddled middle?'

'I've brought someone to meet you.' The pressure in Conor's chest was painful. 'He's waiting at reception.'

'Who is he?'

'You'll know when you see him.'

Her office window gave her a view of the reception area. 'Oh, Jesus Christ!' She pressed her hands against her chest and sighed, a wheezy noise that alarmed Conor until she coughed and cleared her throat.

'He's looking for you,' Conor said. 'I told him you were here.'

'What else did you tell him?' For an instant, he thought she was going to faint. Even her lips looked white.

'The truth. He knows who I am.'

'Oh, Conor . . . ' She placed her arms on the desk and pushed her face into them. 'I'm sorry . . . I'm so sorry.' Her voice was muffled but he could hear the dread in every word.

'Why? I thought you'd be pleased he's here.' He wanted her to look at him, assure him he had done the right thing, instead of sounding as if he had stabbed her heart.

She straightened and shoved herself upright. 'Wait here, Conor,' she said. 'Stay here until I call you.'

'But — '

'Do as I say,' she repeated.

Through the office window he watched his parents greet each other. They shook hands and stood staring. His mother must have cried because his father took out a handkerchief and passed it to her. She shook her head, pushed it away, and said something that made his father turn to leave. Conor fought back the urge to rush from the office and push them together. His father stopped at the door, as if he had heard Conor's involuntary cry. He turned and it seemed as if he looked directly into Conor's eyes, impossible with a wall separating them but Conor knew, in that instant, that everything was going to be all right. His father walked back to his mother and pulled her into his arms. They stood like that. Two pieces of a jigsaw linked so perfectly it was impossible to find the raw edges that once separated them.

Six months after his parents were reunited, his father moved to New Zealand. He worked with an engineering firm in Nelson now. His arrival seemed to open a window in his mother's head and blow fresh air through it. She told Conor about Heron Cove and the Broadmeadow Estuary where she used to fish with Kevin for crabs. They played in the marshes, riding their bikes over the bumps: wheelies, bunny hops, ledge drops. Kevin had photographs of Malahide village with the high church spire and the trains running across the viaduct, the estuary seething under the arches before sweeping onwards to the sea. And other photographs of Goths, his mother unrecognisable with her mask-white face and crimped black hair, metal studs in her ears, long black clothes that made her look like Dracula's bride, sexy and bold. His father frowned into the camera like it was his enemy. His hair was black, sleek like Dracula, and he had his arms folded, except when he was hugging Conor's mother.

★ ★ ★

Conor enters his bedroom and opens the window. His mother is standing by the lake, gazing across the water. She is too far away for him to see her face but he knows she is staring beyond the lake, her thoughts gathered so tightly

296

into herself that nothing else exists except the place she visits in her mind. Kevin is the only person who can snap through her tension and make her smile. At night Conor hears them laughing. The sound comes through the wall . . . and other sounds also. Muffled moans that stop abruptly, as if a hand has been placed over lips to stifle something intimate and private. Conor is on the outside, looking in on a love affair that belongs only to Kevin and his mother.

His father keeps trying to make up for the lost years. They go to rugby matches together and kayak on Nelson Swamp. But no matter how hard Conor tries, he finds it difficult to call him 'Father' or 'Dad'. The words sound false, like out-of-tune notes. He likes Kevin an awful lot but it is much the same feeling as he has for Lyle and Alma.

His friend Oliver hates his father, or so he says: They fight all the time and his father often beats him with his belt. Conor has seen the bruises, yet, once, when another pupil called Oliver's father 'a drunken hori', which was an insult no self-respecting Maori could tolerate, Oliver hit him so hard it took three teachers to pull him off. Conor would be angry if someone insulted Kevin but he could not imagine fighting so fiercely, the tears pumping from his eyes. Maybe that kind of love is formed at birth and all that comes afterwards, no matter how bad, can never wipe it out.

50

Akona's Place

Steam rises from the earthen oven studded with hot stones. Julie hunkers beside Akona, fascinated by the preparations involved in a traditional hangi. They will dine on the veranda. The table is set with a white linen cloth and cut-glass crystal. Lauren recognises the pattern. Olive Moran was a keen collector of Galway Crystal. When her marriage broke up, she smashed each piece against the wall of her drawing room then walked away, leaving Steve to clear up the shattered fragments. As a symbolic gesture, it was worthy of respect.

Akona prepares a jambalaya with rice, tiny potatoes and seafood. The aroma whets their appetites as they sip a pre-dinner drink. Peace has broken out in the camper. Akona's presence has been a benign influence and they have spent the day relaxing beside the lake.

Akona puts on a CD of Clannad. The haunting voice of Marie Brennan singing 'Trail of Tears' washes over them. The Irish and the Maori have close links through marriage, she tells them. Her own family tree has an ancestor from the City of the Tribes. Sean Mooney was an immigrant gold miner who married her great-great-grandmother. Akona is in regular email

298

contact with his descendants in Galway, hence the glassware and her collection of Irish music.

After the hangi ends, they move indoors. She switches on a CD of Maori music, a harmonious blend of female voices with war-like whooping males adding urgency and excitement to the gentler swaying melodies. Akona's life seems so isolated — no houses nearby, only a rusting pick-up truck to keep her in touch with civilisation. She fishes and works her vegetable patch, keeps some sheep. She also writes poetry: the ultimate hippy dream.

'Lauren used to write poetry,' says Julie.

'It never amounted to anything much.' Lauren is embarrassed by the enthusiasm in Julie's voice. 'Too self-indulgent, I was told.'

'By whom?' asks Akona.

'Her husband,' says Rebecca.

'It wasn't just . . . Steve was right. I had to move on. He published that first collection. Do you really think anyone else would have bothered with it?'

'You took the easy option and never tried to find out,' says Rebecca. 'You got good reviews. I still have them.'

'You do?'

Her surprise must have shown because Rebecca says, 'Of course. I was very proud of you.'

One of the reviewers described her work as a tentative and emerging voice. It seemed an inadequate way to describe the struggle between destruction and creativity played out in the stillness of her room. Stray words flicker . . . *In the moon skidding hours* . . . something about silverfish . . . *Somersaulting silverfish* . . . she tries to remember the lines but she forgot them a long time ago.

'Let's have more music.' Akona reaches towards the CD rack and removes a disc. 'This is a composition by one of our composers. No, not Maori,' she shakes her head in answer to Rebecca's question. 'He's *päkehä*. Our Maori name for foreigners, those outside our tribes. He spends his summers here. A reclusive man when he is composing.'

'Niran Gordon.' Julie takes the cover from Akona and speaks his name softly before handing the disc to Lauren. 'Yes, we've heard of him.'

'This piece commemorates the victims of that terrible tsunami.' Akona slides the disc into the CD player.

Before the music begins, Lauren rises to her feet. Neither of her sisters glances in her direction. She mutters an apology to Akona. She is expecting a phone call from her husband. Outside, in the darkness, she follows the low swash of the lake. The island is gouged with the glacial sheen of lakes and rivers, and she has no idea what this lake is called.

From the house, she hears his music, listens to the flautists, their lush notes fluttering into birdsong, the lively urgency of a new day. Each note plays like mercury over her skin until she loses herself in the medley of sound that carries in its background the repetitive beat of a snare drum, ebbing and flowing through the babbling

300

chorus of voices. A tidal flow ripples over the sand, the sensation so visceral that Lauren can see the golden beaches, the sea birds wheeling through the spray, children scampering in the shallows. The drumbeat persists but it is different now, growing more powerful yet still soft, almost hypnotic until it is overlaid by the dull distant rumble of a tuba. Slowly, inexorably, it gains momentum. The sudden trill of a violin screams a warning that no one, not one of those joyous voices on shore, can hear.

Always, when Lauren viewed images of the tsunami on television, she was presented with a sanitised version of unspeakable horror. Now she listens to the violin quiver a note so high it will shatter glass, wood, the brittle beach umbrellas, the solid verandas where people are breakfasting, unaware that they will never again feel the sun on their faces. Thousands of stories ending and thousands more beginning in the instant the wave looms and the scream becomes audible. She awaits the aching reverberations that will follow when the wave crests the shore and hears them in the requiem wail of strings, the crash of gongs, cymbals, note after note rearing and collapsing, electronic sounds she is unable to decipher, the thunderous bellow of an organ, and drums, ferocious in their palpitating measure before the music slows to a final heart-stopping silence.

When Steve rings, her body jerks so sharply she almost drops the phone. Dully, she listens as he describes the weather in Dublin, showery and overcast with a promise of sun in the afternoon.

She tells him about the barbecue, a witty condensed version she believes he will enjoy. His tone warns her she has misjudged his mood.

'Where are you now?' he asks.

'Somewhere on the edge of the world.'

'Bush country?'

'I'm fine, Steve. I've just participated in a hangi.'

'What the hell is that?'

'A Maori feast.'

'You're with Maoris?'

'One Maori. Akona. She's been very hospitable to us.'

'You'll be doing the fucking haka next. This holiday is not only turning into a farce, it's becoming dangerous.'

'I'm not going to break that easily, Steve.'

'Dresden breaks, princess. And you were not born to live like a knacker.'

She grips the wooden slats to steady herself. When did Dresden become a euphemism for unpredictable, irrational behaviour, slipping, somehow, into his vocabulary, weighing it with coded nuances?

'I'm not living . . . it's quite a comfortable camper.'

'I want to speak to Rebecca right now.'

'She's busy, Steve.'

'Right now.'

'I told you, she's busy. I've no intention of disturbing her.'

'You even sound different. I should never have allowed you to go off on your own.'

'Allowed? You allowed me to go — '

'You know as well as I do how unstable your behaviour can be when you don't take care of yourself. Are those leathernecks still with you?'

'No, they left for the glaciers this morning. It's just Akona and us. She's part Irish.'

'Pull the other one.' His disbelief jars against her ear. 'Next thing we know, you'll be inviting her home to céilí.'

Lauren leans back and flings her phone into the lake. She pulls her pashmina around her shoulders, gathers her knees to her chin, hums softly between her teeth.

She sees a figure poised under the porch light. Rebecca, she guesses, ready to probe. She remains silent and her sister, after hesitating, makes her way to the camper. Lauren twists grass around her fingers. The rasping texture strings her palm, draws a faint line of blood along her index finger. She tugs harder before releasing the blades of grass and stares intently at her hands.

★ ★ ★

Lauren awakens, filled with an energy verging on elation. She no longer feels cramped in the camper or dreads the long drives from one location to the next.

'No bleeps,' says Julie. 'Has Steve lost the power of his fingers?'

'I mislaid my phone last night.'

'Will I ring it for you?'

'You can try. But I doubt you'll hear it.'

Julie tries, shakes her head. 'No signal. Nothing.'

'I guess I'll just have to manage without it. You should try to do the same, Julie. It's a liberating feeling.'

'Maybe some day . . . like when I'm coffined.' Julie laughs and whisks the breakfast dishes into a basin. 'Do you want us to organise a search party for your phone?'

'No, thanks. Some things deserve to stay lost.'

Akona knocks on the camper door. '*Ka kite ano* . . . until I see you again.' She leans forward and touches Lauren's nose in a hongi then hands her a signed book of her poetry.

'From one poet to another. When your next book is published, you will send it to me, eh?'

Lauren wants to say, 'Don't hold your breath,' but she smiles and thanks Akona, holds the book to her chest.

★ ★ ★

Swaddled in anoraks, fleeces and jogging pants, they descend from the helicopter and crunch across the frozen snow. They hack splinters with their crampons, their breath heaving in a vaporous sun salute. Sculptured billows of ice rest like a somnolent path of lava between the brows of Fox Glacier. Lauren allows her sisters to move ahead. She stops to photograph an ice cave, domed and magnificent. Nature's chisel is evident everywhere she looks but Fox Glacier, for all its sturdy grandeur, is a moving force that is slowly melting.

The glittering sculptures remind her of a business function she attended with Steve shortly before she left for New Zealand. The lunch buffet was lavish and an ice-sculptured swan created a centrepiece on the table. Lauren had admired the ice-blue shimmer and exquisite feather detail, the fragile elegant neck. By the time the guests departed, the swan had started to melt. As the glistening translucence thawed back to its natural order, Lauren had experienced the same ephemeral weightlessness, the sensation that she too would soon seep, erode, disappear . . . like the glacier she stands on now, the slow, erosive trickle from its cut-glass veins swelling the slate-grey river at its base.

Distracted by her thoughts, she skids and falls. Another nail cracks. She is ashamed of her own nails, which she started to bite after the accident. Rebecca used to dip her fingers in lemon juice to discourage the habit but Lauren was never able to fight the compulsive urge. Nowadays, regular manicures and the hard sheen of acrylic hides their brittleness yet they have continued to break throughout this arduous journey.

She bites against the acrylic and spits it out. Brittle blood-red slivers scar the ice. She bites harder. Sweat gathers on her forehead, on the back of her neck. She fights down a wave of nausea, remembering stories about animals caught in traps, chewing off their limbs to be free. Suddenly, the energy that had gripped her earlier is depleted. But her own nails have emerged, soft as jelly, pale, insignificant, stubby.

51

Kaikoura

A lethargy descends over the camper when they leave the West Coast and drive across Arthur's Pass. They have no desire to linger in the mountainous passes, and move at a faster pace, aware that their journey is nearing completion. Julie's enthusiasm for cooking under gruelling conditions fades. So does any inclination to keep the camper tidy. Paul's last phone call revealed a stark truth.

'You're indispensable,' he said. 'We're falling apart without you.'

This realisation fills her with dismay. Soon the trip will be over. Cathy will be married and, hopefully, old scars healed. Julie herself will return home, Mamma Mia, to wither away, stale yet indispensable. Freedom. Such a small demand. Its power seduces her.

Yellow cliffs rise like magnificent organ pipes as they emerge from Arthur's Pass and drive towards Kaikoura where there is an ocean to explore. Tomorrow, they will swim with dolphins.

★ ★ ★

Seb's house overlooks the Pacific. High wooden steps lead to the front door. From the fold-up table and canvas chairs, the basic shelves and the galley kitchen, his house has been designed for the minimum amount of indoor living. Four guitars hang on one wall. Another wall is entirely filled with shelves of CDs, tape cassettes and a collection of vinyl records. Julie remembers when he started collecting the vinyls. The hours they spent together in second-hand shops going through crates of dusty, discarded records. Collecting music he would never find time to play because Seb Morris was always restless, his feet dancing him over the next green hill.

She perches on a high stool and watches as he cooks dinner, pasta and prawns with a lemon sauce. His bedroom is separated from the living area by an aquarium of tropical fish. King-sized and placed on solid wooden legs, his bed looks like the only sturdy piece of furniture in the house. She admires the fish, the vibrant flick of fin and tail providing a boundary between sanity and sin. What are his intentions? Her demons begin to chant. What are yours? Does he practise safe sex, keep an up-to-date supply of condoms? What if he sees you naked and your stretch marks cause him to suffer erectile dysfunction for the first time in his life? What if Paul rings when you are in the middle of an orgasm?

As her thoughts roam hysterically from one crisis to the next, she discreetly switches off her mobile phone. Perhaps Lauren is right about that liberating feeling.

'You seem nervous.' Seb pours her another glass of wine.

'Not at all.' She forces herself to sip, not gulp.

'It's good to meet up again and talk about old times.'

'You didn't bring your mandolin.'

She shakes her head. 'It needs tuning.'

'Tuning is essential.' He holds her hand, traces his finger across her wedding ring. 'Have you been happy?'

'Highs and lows.'

'You've told me very little about your life.'

What can she tell him? He will yawn if she describes school runs, company accounts, shopping excursions, family holidays. Paul is a good man, she wants to say, reliable, hard-working, dependable. But how boring that will sound? She only has to look at the framed posters hanging on the walls to realise the different paths their lives have taken. Posters of travelling troubadours, bearded and brooding musicians posed against different backdrops, in different countries. There are women too, sexy singers, guitarists and drummers, tough-talking and hard-drinking, unafraid to experience the extremes life can offer. Julie could be in those posters, chic and waif-like, even bisexual, and no stranger to rehabilitation. She could be every tabloid journalist's dream, every teenage boy's fantasy, if only she had had the courage to go with him.

Seb talks about his ex-wives, two marriages, but Julie is unable to see any wedding photographs. He walks to the other side of the aquarium and through his bedroom, flings open slatted doors leading onto a balcony. The vibrations cause the fish to dart and dive within their coral caves. He carries food and a bottle of wine, places them on a circular table and pulls out chairs, lights candles. The flames barely move in the breeze. After they have finished eating, he switches on his stereo and plays a CD of his songs. He has sent it out to play stations. A little bit of luck and some airtime should not be too much to expect. Julie hears the undertow of doubt in his voice. When does reality set in, she wonders. When is it no longer advisable to dream?

'We could have made it in Australia.' As his voice sings in the background, he stares across the table at her. 'Your voice, my songs. I've thought about you many times.'

'I've thought about you too, Seb. I treated you badly.'

'We were young. It's allowed.'

'The odds were stacked against us. When it came to the crunch . . . I couldn't leave them.'

'Them?'

'My sisters.'

'And Paul?'

'I went back with him after you left but we probably would have drifted apart in time. Like you said, it's hard to get through the young years without hurting others. Then I became pregnant . . . ' She shrugs. 'He was there, determined to do the *right* thing. What's the right thing? And who benefits by it? Becks saw it as a personal betrayal. Paul saw it as a responsibility. I saw it as an unbelievable bloody awful mistake.'

Sand glints on his jeans. Earlier they had walked the beach and left their footprints behind. She pulls her hand free and brushes his knees, watches the grains scatter and disappear. 'No one ever warned me condoms could burst.'

'Ah . . . I wondered.' He leaves the balcony and returns a few minutes later with a framed poster, hands it to her. 'My favourite,' he says.

Julie stares at Maximum Volume. The photograph was taken on top of the garden shed in Heron Cove. It lacks the sleek confidence of the other posters but she is struck by their youth and exuberance. Her sons, particularly Aidan, display the same cocky assurance and she wonders, sometimes, as she encourages them in their latest ventures, if she is seeking wish fulfilment through their own dreams.

Seb glances sideways at her, studies her expression before he asks the question on both their minds. 'Are the odds still stacked as high?'

He offers her a carefree passion and she, on the other side of the world, freed from familiar constraints, is filled with a heady excitement. She can meet his gaze, hold it for an instant longer than necessary, the instant of acquiescence, and, afterwards, everything will be different. She will carry a secret. A memory she made without thinking about anything other than her own desire.

'The odds are balanced on a pinhead at the moment, Seb.' She stands and walks to the balcony rail. Crimson clouds drift above the distant peninsula. Earlier, from a headland, they had watched a whale rise, humped and hulking as a barren island, before its tail splashed off the waves and it sank again into the deep.

He stands beside her, takes her into his arms. Everything about him is unfamiliar, the pressure of his lips, the confident stroke of his hands on the small of her back, his whispered endearments. The poster lies abandoned on the table, along with the remains of their meal, their empty wine glasses. She sees Paul sitting behind his drums, drumsticks raised, his face split in an infectious grin. A week after the photograph was taken, her parents were dead. At their funeral he held her grimly. She felt him trembling and pressed her face harder into his denim jacket. He was her rock then, the two of them suddenly made mature by tragedy.

She thinks about the row they had over her decision to come here. The evening he returned home early from work with flowers, the passion and tender aftermath, and how, when they rested in the familiar hollow of their bed, he gave her *Traversing New Zealand*, the dog-eared copy she has kept close to her throughout the trip.

She sways back from Seb, knowing that the same courage that made her stay behind when he left will carry her through this moment.

'It's not going to happen, is it?' He leans against the balcony rail.

She shakes her head and breathes deeply into the briny air.

'Paul Chambers is one lucky bastard.' He grins ruefully. 'He told me once he'd wrap my guitar strings around my neck if I didn't leave you alone. But he needn't have worried. You've always been able to make up your own mind.'

He leads her through his bedroom and on to

311

the living room where his guitars and his posters cover the walls. Earlier, her eyes riveted on the different bands, she had not noticed Maximum Volume hanging in the centre. He hangs the poster back in its customary position.

'Want to try the guitars?' he asks.

'Absolutely.'

Julie plays until her fingers are sore. The light is beginning to seep from the ocean. Only the ruffled trim of waves is visible as the tide rides across the beach to shift their foot-steps from the shore and obliterate their presence in a single surge.

★ ★ ★

She takes a taxi back to the holiday park where her sisters, awake and ready to attack, demand to know where she has been until two in the morning. Even Lauren has the nerve to stare accusingly at her. Why does her marriage matter so much to everyone? Do they see it as the rock in the chaos of their own lives?

Julie collapses into the nearest seat and kicks off her sandals. 'I was making music with Seb Morris.'

'What kind of music?' Rebecca demands.

'The best kind,' says Julie. 'Now, give me a break and let me get some sleep. I'm exhausted from my musical activities.'

'Better contact your husband first,' advises Lauren. 'He's been ringing Rebecca regularly since midnight. The least you could have done was leave your mobile on and let us get some sleep.'

'What did you tell him?' Julie sits up straight and clutches her hair.

'What were we supposed to tell him?' demands Lauren. 'You left no instructions on how we should lie with conviction.'

'But we did our best.' Rebecca flops back on her bunk and yawns. 'We told him you were suffering, yet again, from alcoholic poisoning and had been transferred to a local rehabilitation centre.'

'You bitch! You did not?' Julie grabs a pillow and beats it against Rebecca's head.

'It's a better excuse than telling him you were making music with Seb Morris.' Rebecca swings her legs over the side and grabs her own pillow, launching a counterattack. The shrill of Rebecca's mobile is almost inaudible as they shriek and chase each other around the camper.

'Oh, holy Jesus! What am I going to tell him?' Julie grabs the phone from Rebecca and leaves the camper.

'I've been trying to contact you for hours, Julie.' Paul's anger instantly ignites her own.

'I heard.' She hurries towards a deserted sun terrace and sits down. 'Is everything all right at home?'

'We're doing fine. Where were you until now?'

'I was with Seb Morris.'

'Seb Morris is in Australia.'

'Not the last time I looked. He told me you once threatened to garrotte him with cat gut.'

313

'Too bloody right I did. What were you doing with him?'

'Talking about old times.'

'Old times?'

'Yes. Dreams and how they become trapped by reality.'

'Is that how you see our marriage . . . a trap?'

She has hurt him. She can always tell by the way his voice sinks. Her anger ebbs away. She holds the phone a little tighter, as if, somehow, this can lessen the distance between them.

'Yes, it was a trap, Paul. How could it have been otherwise? I wasn't ready for babies, neither were you. But, until tonight, I never realised that the door was always open. There are no locks in a marriage, or walls that can hold it together if someone wants to escape. I could have escaped tonight, even for a brief while. I chose not to.'

He is silent at the other end.

'You can decide whether or not you believe me.'

'Come back to me soon, Julie.' He clears his throat but is unable to steady his voice. 'The heart has gone from our home since you left.'

52

A grey sky broods over the Pacific. Aboard the boat, swimmers shuffle awkwardly in their flippers, snorkels ready to be clamped into position. At their indoctrination course, no guarantee was given that the dolphins would appear. They are wild and independent. Jumping through hoops or bareback displays are beneath their contempt. If the dolphins do appear, each swimmer is advised to make the most of this unique encounter and enter the water quietly.

For a while it seems as if the overcast weather has dampened the dolphins' enthusiasm. Then, a triumphant shout from a woman causes the passengers to surge to one side of the boat. Julie aims her camera as the dolphin leaps upwards and turns a cartwheel. Other dolphins, determined not to be upstaged, arise from the water, their synchronised movements drawing gasps of admiration from the onlookers.

Lauren moves closer to Rebecca, nervous now that the moment has arrived. Gillian, the young woman in charge of the trip, herds them into position at the stern. She is a jolly bronzed girl with sandy hair, completely at ease in her ocean environment.

Lauren gasps as her body adjusts to the cold but the thrill of being surrounded by somersaulting dolphins soon outweighs her discomfort. They spin and cavort among the waves until, as if responding to an inaudible command, they dive under the waves and depart as swiftly as they arrived. Lauren hears the whistle from the boat and prepares to follow the swimmers back on board. As she turns in the water she realises that one dolphin has remained behind and is swimming in increasingly close circles around her. She has been warned not to touch the dolphins but the urge to reach out and touch the sleek flesh almost overwhelms her. She stares into its eyes and the dolphin, as if sensing her thoughts, noses against her, a gentle flip, almost imagined. It glides under her, a buffeting motion that should alarm her but has a dreamlike choreography where fear and anxiety and loss, all the emotions she understands and carries within her, fall away until there is only weightlessness. The dolphin lifts her on its back and carries her through the water with a sensuous swishing motion before ploughing a final circle and diving deep into its subterranean world.

Lauren climbs back on board and faces Gillian's stern reprimand. As the skipper turns and follows the dolphins, the swimmers again take their positions on the stern.

'Ready for action,' Gillian shouts as the dolphins rise from the water and begin another acrobatic display. The swimmers plunge overboard once more. Lauren walks to the centre of the boat and takes off her snorkel. Her chest expands, the sensation so powerful she understands why happiness is such a potent emotion, only given in doses small enough to hold the heart steady.

'But you must.' Gillian is adamant when Lauren shakes her head. 'This is a unique opportunity to swim with dolphins. Just obey my signals and you'll be fine. No need to be afraid. I've been watching you. You're a strong swimmer.'

'I'm not afraid.' Lauren smiles and removes her flippers. 'I don't want to go back in again. Anything else will be an anticlimax.'

Above her a small plane dips like a dragonfly before scooping the air and disappearing beyond the cloud-wreathed mountains. The dolphins leap, as if they too want to see beyond the distant peaks.

★ ★ ★

Rebecca's phone rings and startles them awake.

'Yes, she's here.' Her voice croaks with tiredness. 'No cracks last time I noticed. OK! Keep your hair on, Steve. I'll see if I can waken her.' She hands the phone to Lauren.

'At last we're in communication again.' Steve makes no effort to disguise his annoyance. 'Why can't I get through on your mobile?'

'I left it behind in Akona's place.'

'Left it behind? Bloody hell, princess, it's state of the art. And what's to stop you purchasing a phone card? You know I worry if I can't contact you.'

'Why on earth should you worry? I've never felt better.'

'Not from what I've heard.'

'Meaning?'

317

'I had to speak to Paul Chambers to hear about the accident.'

'What accident?'

'Julie emailed him about your reaction to the crash.'

'There was no crash. We got a fright but no one was hurt. Not a scratch, even on the camper.'

'I'm not talking physical injuries. The shock alone would be sufficient to trigger . . . '

He is difficult to hear above the staccato blast of a Tannoy system speaker. Must be an airport. Lauren tries to remember if he mentioned his travel plans in a previous call.

'I won't stay long on the phone,' he says. 'I'm at the airport rushing to make a connection. The deal's done on Wallslowe, princess. Ts crossed, Is dotted. Just in time too.'

'Congratulations,' she replies. 'That was fast work.'

'Fast and fucking furious.'

'Are you drunk?'

'Just celebrating. The property bubble hasn't just burst, it's in total freefall. Lucky I saw it coming and made my plans. You don't have to worry about cutting up your credit card, princess.'

'I wasn't worried — '

'I'll keep this short,' he interrupts. 'I've one business stopover to make in Singapore and, assuming there are no delays with my connections, I'll be at Havenswalk to greet you.'

'What are you talking about?'

'I'm on my way over. I'll be glad to escape the

weather. It's hailstones here. What's it like at your end?'

'You're coming *here*?'

'Got it in one.'

'But it's crazy to travel so far — '

'I assumed you'd be pleased.'

'Of course I'm pleased . . . delighted.'

'I'd better go. They've called my flight. And organise that phone tomorrow.'

'Steve . . . wait. Let's discuss this — '

He hangs up in midsentence, in transit, out of contact.

⋆　⋆　⋆

Moving quietly, Lauren locks the door of the ensuite and removes a blade from the lining of her cosmetic bag. She draws the edge lightly along one finger and presses the wound against her palm. She shudders when she sees the patina of blood on her skin.

'Are you all right?' Rebecca taps the door, a bloodhound on the scent.

'I'm fine.' Lauren slides the blade back into its hiding place and opens the door.

'Want to walk?' Rebecca has pulled on her jeans and a sweater.

'Might as well. I won't sleep after Steve's call.'

Julie remains sleeping and Lauren wriggles into a dress and quietly opens the camper door.

They walk along a tree-lined path. Tiny silver lights shine on the branches but, otherwise, the holiday park is in darkness.

'Is he coming to the wedding?' Rebecca is the

first to break the silence.

'He'll be in Havenswalk before us.'

'I see.'

'Why do you dislike him so much?'

'I don't dislike . . . oh, what does it matter what I think? If I thought you were happy — '

'I am *happy*. How can you believe otherwise when you know what I was like before . . . you remember?'

'You didn't have to marry him. There were other ways — '

'Pills and psychoanalysis. I'm familiar with the routine. It wasn't for me.'

'Niran Gordon — '

'Is inconsequential. I'm not going to break up my marriage. I owe Steve so much.'

'You owe him *nothing*.'

'Except my sanity.'

'Sanity is not your problem, Lauren. It's fear of trusting your sanity that's keeping you trapped.'

'Rebecca, why don't you say it out straight?'

'What?'

'Trophy wife. Pampered doll. Take your pick.'

'I wanted you to be free, Lauren. To be courageous and find your own happiness.'

'Did love serve you well?'

'At least I wasn't afraid to experience it.'

'But at what cost? I don't want that kind of baggage in my life.'

'Or children? I often think about the accident — '

'Don't!'

'We never do. I never gave you permission to

talk about them — '

'*Don't* . . . ' Even now, all those years later, their memory still has the power to strangle her vocabulary.

Lauren draws away from her sister and turns towards the camper. 'Let them rest in peace. It's easier that way.'

53

Rebecca's Journal — 2003

It's OK to shed tears when the old year passes into the new. This year, I'm not going to make any resolutions. I never keep them. Last year I promised myself I'd find a reasonable excuse and refuse Lauren's invitation to her New Year's Eve drinks party. Failed again. I was there last night, raising my glass of champagne and kissing strangers.

I searched her face for signs of stress but she appears happy, fulfilled. She has perfected the art of air kissing and is a confident hostess. Julie looked lovely. Six months at Weight-Watchers has done the trick. Paul, too, looked well. They kissed each other so passionately at twelve o'clock I almost said, 'Behave yourselves. I don't want the neighbours talking.'

That's when I started to cry. Stupid carry-on! Thankfully, in the New Year euphoria, no one noticed and I hid in one of Lauren's bathrooms until I was in control again. Then I ordered a taxi and slipped away. Back to the horses, their quiet breathing, their nuzzling gentle loving.

Six months since Jeremy died. Six months! Unbelievable. I still don't know how I feel. Lulu wants me to go for bereavement counselling. I suspect she's afraid I'll wander off into the woods and go crazy among the hollies and elderberry. What good will counselling do? Perhaps it might help me define my emotions . . . name the numbness. Is it grief, anger, betrayal . . . relief?

Unlike my parents, Jeremy never knew what hit him. His death was due to a cerebral oedema, his brain swelling so quickly he died almost immediately. The cause of death was a lunch box falling from the sky — or, to be more accurate, a skyscraper scaffolding. Before I was escorted to the morgue, the doctor at the hospital relayed the details — academic information that I was unable to absorb — but the scene that greeted me when I entered the morgue could be absorbed at a glance.

Julie was with me. She squeezed my hand, a different squeeze to the grief-stricken clasp that held us together on the flight to New York. This squeeze signalled the need for a different kind of courage but, at first, when I saw the woman standing beside Jeremy's body, I thought she was an official, a liaison officer or even a plain-clothes policewoman. But the face of an official would not be ravaged from weeping. Her hands fluttered slightly when she saw me. Otherwise, she maintained her composure. She was dressed in chic black trousers and a knee-length black coat. I wore jeans and a brown leather jacket. No mistaking the widow. Before walking away, she bent over his body and kissed him. How could she bestow such passion on his rigid mouth? In that gesture, she laid her claim on him, revealed their history.

How is it possible that life and death can be separated by a random decision? If Jeremy had hesitated before leaving her apartment and kissed Anna Kowalski, whose sheets were still warm from his body, he would be alive today. If he had paused to offer alms to a polite but homeless man, or stopped to view the sun between the chinks in the high-reaching glass towers, we would still be married. But he did not pause, nor did he look upwards in time to see his life flash in front of his eyes before it was extinguished.

I wonder, sometimes, what was inside the lunch box that struck my husband's head. Salami on rye, a cream bagel with onion seeds, mayonnaise or mustard? Did it belong to a carpenter, a plasterer, an electrician? I imagine this stranger who killed my husband poised wren-like above the Big Apple, the steel lunch box balanced on the ledge of the scaffold. I imagine the instant he moved and accidentally kicked it over the edge. I imagine it gaining speed, turning into a ballistic missile. I refuse to imagine the instant of impact.

Anna Kowalski was waiting for me in the hotel foyer on the day I flew home. She showed me her ring, a solitaire mounted on a circle of tiny diamonds, and demanded to know why I was so shocked. She had been under the impression that Jeremy had confessed all, was already in the process of obtaining his divorce. She did not explain or apologise for their relationship. When he was unable to meet her in New York, she had flown to join him in far-flung places, and, occasionally, on his home territory. I asked her what she drank. Margaritas, she said. The only time her mask slipped was when she asked me to respect her grief and dispatch a small portion of his ashes to her. To my amazement I agreed and, in time, sent a small casket by special delivery. I did so on the advice of Olive Moran.

Olive visited my sanctuary soon after his cremation. We now maintain a tentative friendship, sharing, as we do, common bonds of betrayal, childlessness, and have, in different ways, lost our husbands. She spoke of Mayan caves and Indian forts and Tibetan monasteries.

'Karma,' she said when I mentioned Anna's request. 'What goes around comes around.'

Where does Anna keep the ashes in her chic New York apartment? I scattered him into Dublin Bay and walked away without looking back.

Olive stayed for lunch, then left. She had a plane to catch. Unlike her successor, she travels light.

54

Nelson

They arrive in Nelson and haul their luggage from the interior of the camper. A young man rushes from the office and lifts Lauren's suitcases into the street. Perhaps, Rebecca thinks, as she surrenders the keys, when they look back over their holiday, all their recollections will be condensed into those three suitcases, always in flagrant disarray as Lauren emptied out their contents in search of the perfect outfit to wear.

They transfer their luggage to a hired car. Havenswalk is only a short drive away.

'No way am I appearing before Cathy looking like a bush woman,' Julie declares when they settle into the car. 'How about it, Lauren, Rebecca? Want to find a friendly hairdresser who'll transform us?'

'Count me out,' replies Rebecca. The thought of sitting in the heated atmosphere of a hair salon is intolerable. 'I'll have a wander round the city and see the sights while you're having your hair done.'

Lauren looks up from the coffee-ringed copy of *Traversing New Zealand*. 'I wouldn't mind some time on my own either. The Queens Gardens looks interesting.'

'Don't you want to be beautified before meeting your husband?' asks Julie.

'Why should I do that?' Lauren's hand moves lightly, almost absently over the contours of her face. Her nails are chipped, the cuticles cracked, and her hair, dried from the sun, needs urgent treatment.

'No reason.' Julie shrugs. 'After living rough for three weeks, I thought you'd be beating down the door to the nearest beauty salon. Steve will — '

'Steve will what?' Lauren's stare challenges her. 'Want his princess in prime condition?'

'Don't go all dramatic on me, Lauren. All I suggested was a blow-dry. Go for your walk. I'll see you both later.'

Rebecca drives Julie to a beauty salon and continues onwards with Lauren to the Queens Gardens.

'Would you like me to keep you company?' She parks the car and turns to her sister, who is staring blankly out the window.

'Would you be offended if I said no?' Lauren rouses herself with an effort.

'Are you sure you're all right?'

'I'm not going to cut myself, if that's what you mean.'

'I didn't — '

'Rebecca, I always know what you're thinking, but you're wrong. I'm not falling apart. I've never felt better.'

She lies with conviction but the strain is tearing at her face.

Rebecca strolls aimlessly through the city. She

is tired of doing touristy things. Wineries and galleries no longer interest her. Her body aches from the numerous activities that have given a focus to her days.

Hardly aware of where she is going, she walks into a shopping mall and enters a fashion boutique. Alien territory and an impulse decision, immediately regretted. Amidst the rustle of chiffon, silk and viscose, she flounders and would have fled if a persistent saleswoman had not waylaid her and ushered her into a fitting room. When she discovers that Rebecca wants something to wear to her sister's wedding, she hands her a succession of dresses, each one more outlandish than the previous one. Finally, having been persuaded to buy a midnight-blue dress with a low neckline and a ruffled hem, Rebecca splurges out on shoes and accessories. She shops with the same grim energy that helped to channel her fear throughout the journey.

Her nephew has an identity, a father, a name, but Rebecca is unable to picture his face, can only imagine it as a blank canvas, his eyes devoid of colour, his features enigmatic, perhaps carrying Cathy's strong wilful mouth, her nose with its cheeky upwards curve. She said he loves animals, as Rebecca does, and so she imagines his skilled hands calming sick animals, using a breathing, silent language that comforts them while he, in apron and gumboots, works by the light of a lantern to deliver a foal or, more likely, it being New Zealand, a lamb.

Who does he resemble, she had asked Cathy and her sister side-stepped the question with platitudes about individualism. But they both know that the answer is all about seed and breed, genetic imprinting, generation upon generation, bending the branches of family trees with the weight of history.

55

Havenswalk, Day One

The wind is strong on the lake this morning. The turbulence increases as Conor steers his kayak between two small islands. He explored them once but, with only stunted trees and bush sprouting on the bare rock, there was nothing there to excite his imagination. But they are tricky to manoeuvre past and sometimes treacherous if he does not concentrate. He passes through the narrow channel, his blades riding the currents, steering him clear of submerged rocks.

The last guests have departed Havenswalk. His mother calls them 'guests', but they pay at the end of their visit, unlike the real guests that have started to arrive. Robbie, Alma's brother, is flying into Christchurch today. She has gone to meet him and they will overnight with friends before arriving in Havenswalk tomorrow. Steve Moran arrived yesterday in a flash rental Jaguar. Conor's aunts will be here by evening time, and Mel . . . he pulls on the blades and increases speed . . . Mel will soon be in the swimming pool and he intends joining her there.

He saw her earlier with his mother. They were sitting at the kitchen table, their heads bent together like they were sharing secrets, unaware that he was watching. He had seen his mother's lips pucker, her face crease as if she was about to weep. Mel had clasped her hand and his mother's shoulders had straightened. She said something quiet and forced a laugh that sounded more like a cry, and Mel, looking up, had seen him. He had moved away, walked quickly from Havenswalk towards the boathouse. Mel caught up with him as he was about to float his kayak. She sat on the jetty, her bare legs dangling, and claimed his mother was suffering from pre-wedding nerves. Every bride, she said, had the right to shed a few tears over her loss of freedom. How does she know? She calls marriage 'bonded slavery', and has loads of lovers, if the hints his mother drops are to be believed.

She was wearing sandals, shorts and a top. Except for her jet-black Cleopatra hair, no one would have guessed she was a Goth. He wonders if she whips her lovers at night and wears high black boots with suspenders. Impossible to look her straight in the face since she became his fantasy. When he thinks about last night . . . the drowning pleasure . . . the stab of excitement almost sickens him. He pulls the blades under his kayak, a mistake that will lose him precious time in the Coast to Coast. Sandy, waiting patiently on the jetty, leaps upwards when Conor returns and licks his hand. He will bring his dog for a walk later but, for now, he wants to swim with Mel.

To his disappointment, she is breakfasting with his uncle on the veranda. She calls Conor's name and beckons him to join them but he keeps going, unwilling to share her with another man, even if he is a geriatric.

'There's one thing for sure,' his uncle declared when he was introduced to Conor, 'your father can never disown you. Put it there, young man.' He offered his hand to Conor and winked as he slyly slipped two fifty-dollar notes into his palm.

When Cathy protested, he said, 'I've always looked after this family and I'm not going to stop now.'

He wants to walk her up the aisle. Giving her away, is what he calls it. Conor imagines his mother gift-wrapped in a box and handed to Kevin at the altar. She must have felt the same way because she flashed that smile on him, the one she uses on difficult guests, and said, 'The only person to escort me to the altar will be my son.'

In the kitchen Ruthie is putting the finishing touches to the wedding cake. She intends icing the tiers in green, white and yellow. Conor wonders what his mother will think of this decision but Ruthie is a law unto herself when it comes to culinary matters.

He fills a glass with water and drinks deeply.

'What do you think, Conor?' Ruthie stands back to examine the cake. 'Will I put a little leprechaun on top?'

'Murder the leprechaun if you want to continue working at Havenswalk,' he advises, knowing the leprechaun will be in place when the cake is finally displayed.

His parents' bedroom door is open. He is

relieved to find the room tidy, their clothes hanging in the wardrobe. It has changed since Kevin's arrival, not so feminine any more. The cushions she used to scatter over the bed are gone and the duvet cover, once white with lace edgings, has been changed to a cream and maroon striped design. Kevin's books are mixed with hers, his shaving lotions on the ensuite shelves beside her creams.

Conor notices a Terry Pratchett book on the floor. His favourite author. Kevin finished reading it last week and has offered to lend it to him. When he stoops to pick it up, he notices the corner of a wicker basket sticking out from under the bed. He recognises it, even though it is years since he last saw it.

When Havenswalk was being built, his mother used to make picnics, which they would eat among the rubble with the builders. He pulls out the basket, lifts the lid. Letters lie inside, divided into bundles and tied together with ribbons. He hesitates, reluctant to open someone's private mail. The notepaper is crumpled and yellow with age. He pulls out a sheet of paper at random and studies a child's handwriting. He can hardly make out the words: 'Dear Mammy, This is Cathy. I hate school but Becks . . . ' His mother had obviously been writing a letter to her own mother.

Intrigued by this glimpse into her childhood, he begins to read the letter. He smiles at her atrocious spelling. Wait until the next time she comments on his school report. Before he can finish it, the back door slams. Sandy barks. His mother orders the dog to hush. She calls Conor's name. He shoves the basket back under the bed and runs to his room. When she taps on his door he yells that he is in the shower. Something about the letter puzzles him. Was his grandmother on holiday when his mother wrote to her? He steps from the shower and dries his hair. The date is wrong. He sees it clearly in his mind. October 1986. His mother must have confused her dates. Or else, he pauses, the towel draped over his shoulders, she was writing to a dead woman.

She stands next to him in the evening when the car carrying his aunts comes through the blue gates. Conor winces when she grips his hand but he does not pull free. She wears a white dress with a red belt and matching shoes. The sun shines through the material and outlines her legs. He decides not to mention this in case it adds to her nervousness. She breathes fast, as if she has been racing towards this moment for a long time. His father stands behind them. His hands rest on their shoulders. Conor's heart thumps as hard as it did on the beach in Sumner when he studied his father's features and settled them like a second skin over his own.

The car reappears from behind a screen of trees and draws nearer. He sees floppy sunhats and dark eyeshades, tanned shoulders, coloured tops, a hand with a turquoise bracelet waving from an open window.

'Cathy!' The first woman to emerge shrieks and flutters her arms. Tears gush down her cheeks. No prizes for guessing her identity. The second woman is slimmer and moves slowly, like a beautiful dark cat uncoiling. His mother whimpers and then she is clinging to his two aunts like they are drowning. All hugging in a circle except for the woman with the square shoulders and long black hair tied high in a ponytail. She makes no effort to leave the driver's seat. Her eyes are dry and unblinking when she looks in his direction. Then she turns her head away as if she cannot bear the sight of him.

56

Cathy named the chalets after native birds. Strange names when she first came here but now they are as familiar to her as swifts and wrens once were: bellbird, kea, tui, kokako, torea, whitehead, fantail, kiwi, weka, silvereye, kaka, kakapo, takahē.

'Takahē!' shrieks Julie when they stop outside the chalet allocated to Rebecca. 'That'll make a cosy nest when Tim arrives.'

Everything about Julie has matured except her giggle, but she is the only one laughing. Lauren and Steve have already entered their chalet and Rebecca, without responding, opens the door and closes it behind her. Cathy walks on with Julie towards the Silvereye. Julie talks about the trip . . . something about elephants and bikers and singing on a stage with Seb Morris, and how her shins will never be the same again . . . and Cathy, nodding, smiling, opens the door of the chalet and escorts Julie inside.

What has she done? What madness possessed her to contact her sisters and believe that the past was a tamed beast? Rebecca knew the truth on the instant she set her eyes on Conor. She stepped from the car gripping the door for support. Her expression almost brought Cathy to her knees. But Rebecca had gathered her strength, as she had done so often in the past, and shook Conor's hand, spoke his name. She

336

embraced Cathy and whispered, 'You asked for closure, Cathy. Is closure for such betrayal that easily achieved?'

Julie is still talking. She wants Conor to come to Ireland as soon as possible and meet his cousins. She stares around the chalet and declares it 'palatial' after the camper van. Her admiration for all Cathy has achieved is genuine.

'The atmosphere is so tranquil,' she says. 'So peaceful and natural.'

Cathy is proud of what she and Alma have achieved. They work hard to create an atmosphere where their guests can relax and find an inner serenity. Rebecca's arrival has knocked it aside as easily as a house of cards.

★ ★ ★

The bathroom fills with steam. Hot water courses down Rebecca's back. She longs to wrap herself in mist and never again emerge into the harsh light of truth. His features are no longer abstract. They are as familiar to her as her own. She stretches her hand towards a towel and takes a step forward, then another. Carefully she dries herself. Her skin feels abrasive, as if some protective coating has been removed. The years since Jeremy died, the reality years when she built a new life for herself, extended the sanctuary, InterRailed through Europe, battled with politicians for funding, attended anti-blood sports and animal-testing protests — everything she has achieved and cherished — no longer has meaning when set against the heartache she feels at this moment.

She sits at the dressing table and opens a jar of non-animal-tested body lotion, rubs it into her skin. Everything in Havenswalk is natural: handmade soaps, eco-friendly shampoos, natural woods and materials, lampshades with the texture of cobwebs, everything contrived to create a harmonious atmosphere. The biggest contrivance of all is Kevin Mulvaney. His handshake was warm when he welcomed her, his eyes defying her to challenge his right to claim paternity on another man's son.

The T-shirt she pulls from her rucksack is limp and smells of airless spaces. Suddenly tired of shorts and casual tops, she flings it on the floor and rummages for a skirt. She locates an iron and presses out the creases. The dress she bought in Nelson hangs from a hanger, mocking her shopping splurge.

★ ★ ★

Cathy has organised a welcome meal in her restaurant. By the time Rebecca enters, the guests are already seated around the table. The only vacant seat is between Kevin Mulvaney and Conor.

'Julie says you're a vegetarian.' Her nephew stands and slides the chair underneath her. 'Do you eat fish? I caught one specially for you this afternoon.'

'Yes, Conor. I eat fish.' She keeps her tone

338

light, opens the white linen napkin and spreads it over her knees.

'Choice!' He sits down again, leans eagerly towards her. 'Mom says your boyfriend's coming to her wedding. I met him last year when he gave a lecture in my school. He knows his stuff.'

'He's a friend, Conor. Nothing more.'

'Whatever. You've got a cool website. I like the advice page on how to look after horses in urban environments.' He flings back his head and laughs. 'I saw *The Commitments*. Do horses really go up in lifts?'

'Poetic licence,' she replies.

'Thought it might be. Is it only horses at your sanctuary or do you take in other animals?'

'We look after injured donkeys as well.'

'Who would hurt a donkey?'

'You'd be surprised at what people do to hurt others.'

'But what if that hurt is unintentional?' Kevin Mulvaney speaks quietly. 'Can such hurt be forgiven?'

'Of course,' Rebecca replies. 'But when the cut is deep enough, it is usually done with malice.'

Cathy's laughter floats towards her. She has developed poise, Rebecca will grant her that. Her face is calm. No stray or nervous glance to disturb the charade.

Occasionally, Rebecca wonders if she is wrong. Her heart leaps at this possibility. But when Conor fixes his eyes on her, a gaze so intimate that it banishes those around them,

Rebecca grips her cutlery in a white-knuckle clasp.

Her thumb throbs, a pain that only manifests itself when she is tired. A bite from a horse. Cruelty breeds cruelty. She never blamed the horse for the ferocious bite it administered. The cuts on its neck were ample evidence of its own suffering. She longs to be alone in her sanctuary. At peace in the silence of a Wicklow night, her head pressed against a horse's belly, Teabag at her ankles, gently purring as she nurses the horse back to health.

To have power in a powerless situation is difficult but she still has self-control. Cathy wants closure, to be shriven and cast free from guilt before she walks to the altar. She must wait until Rebecca decides the time is right for confrontation.

★ ★ ★

Lauren mutters an apology and leaves the table. The bathroom is along the corridor. She reaches it just in time. Afterwards, she grips the edge of the toilet bowl and rises.

In a basket beside the mirror, she removes a small tube of toothpaste and a toothbrush. Her face looks sharper, as if the blood has drained away and still not returned. She rubs hand cream into her hands, pinches her cheeks to restore colour.

Steve is talking to Julie when she returns to the table.

'You look pale, princess.' His concern almost brings on another wave of nausea.

'The night is so warm.' Lauren sits down between them. 'I needed some air.'

He lifts her hand, kisses it. 'I'm relieved the journey is over.'

'Despite your misgivings, we survived,' she says.

'It was arduous, none the less.' He slides his hand across her fingers, rests them on her nails. 'Eat something. I don't want my beautiful wife withering away in front of me.'

Tomorrow morning he will drive her into Nelson. She is due for a maintenance overhaul or, as Steve prefers to call it, some well-deserved pampering.

When dinner is over, they return to their allotted chalet. The downstairs area is comfortable, with armchairs, a bookcase and coffee table, a galley for making snacks. A painting of a bird hangs on the wall, a scarlet dash of colour under its wingspan. 'Kea' is written underneath. The same bird features on a carving attached to the front door. The bedroom is reached by a spiral staircase. Louvre doors open out onto a balcony. Lauren steps outside and leans over the rail. She lights a cigarette, then stubs it out. The sparks scatter and die. One by one the lights in the chalets are switched off. Havenswalk is also in darkness.

Steve steps onto the balcony and rests his arm on her shoulder. 'It's time for bed, princess,' he murmurs into her hair.

He holds the door open for her. She follows

him inside. She opens a tube of night cream, smooths it over her face, her throat. Smile, Lauren, keep smiling, she whispers to her reflection. Dance on your toes if he so requests. The rose he offers you has no thorns.

57

Day Two

A text, arriving from Tim Dawson, startles Rebecca. She sits up in bed and reaches for her phone on the bedside locker. Tim will be with her by tomorrow evening. He wants to know how the reunion went.

'A barrel of laughs,' she is tempted to reply. 'Especially when I met my sister's son, who also happens to be the son of my dead husband. Go figure.' Instead she sent back a brief reply: 'All well. Preps for wed in full swing. Text u later.' Abbreviations and taut phonetics have been the regular means of communication between them since their last meeting in Te Anau.

Heat rushes into the bedroom when she opens the louvre doors and steps onto the balcony. She had dozed throughout the night, waking often, instantly aware of her surroundings and what she must face when daylight comes. Now she sees it: her nephew walking towards the lake. A loose T-shirt and baggy calf-length shorts add to his awkward lankiness. He even walks like his father, she thinks. The sight of him scalds her eyes. A red setter bounds along beside him. Fastening the straps on his life jacket, the boy launches a kayak and glides, across the lake. The dog settles patiently on the jetty to await his return.

Rebecca phones for a taxi. She flings her swimsuit and a towel into her backpack.

Julie knocks and enters. 'I ate like a horse last night and I'm starving again. Are you ready for breakfast?'

'I'm going into Nelson. I'll have breakfast there.'

'But Cathy has set tables on the veranda.'

'I need some space, Julie. I'll be back later.'

'Try and make an effort, Becks.'

'Stop calling me Becks. How many times must I repeat myself?'

'I guess we're all falling back into old habits,' snaps Julie. 'God! I'd forgotten what a nark you can be.'

'I'm just tired.'

'No, you're not. You're still furious with Cathy.'

'Does that surprise you?'

'At least you have the pleasure of knowing you were right all along about Kevin.'

Rebecca nods. Julie's comment has been made without guile. It is easy to fool people. She has been doing it for years.

'I've ordered a taxi. It'll be here soon. I'll text you later.'

'Cathy's organised a barbecue for this evening. I hope you'll be back for it.'

'I'll be there. Now, go. I need to get ready.'

She closes the door on Julie's disapproving gaze. The taxi arrives shortly afterwards.

★ ★ ★

The Pacific Ocean offers a calmer shore than the western seaboard. Rebecca dives into an approaching wave and swims until she is breathless, breaststroke, crawl, butterfly. On shore, she spreads a beach mat and applies factor 30 over her body. A neighbouring sunbather offers his assistance. Unwilling to suffer another dose of sunburn, she allows him to smear lotion across her back. Any hope he has of developing more intimate bodily contact is dashed when she thanks him and moves further down the beach. She runs along the hard-packed sand, jogs until her heart pumps and she is soaked with perspiration. She returns to the ocean, storms the waves again. Nothing helps to ease her anguish. She packs her beach bag and heads to Nelson for lunch.

Hardly aware of where she is going, she stops outside the high grey-stone belfry dominating Christ Church Cathedral. In Bangkok, she entered the temples as a tourist, intrigued by their ancient history, detached from the glittering Buddha statues that rested or reclined in their golden cloisters. Her interest was academic, the surroundings too exotic to move her to anything other than admiration for the long-dead artists who had created such intricate architecture. As an atheist, she clings neither to uncertainties nor ambiguity. Her faith is a donkey with a cross on its back, a bird wing-spanning the sky. But here, outside a different temple, where the childhood rituals of prayer were once familiar to her, she

345

hesitates, reluctant to enter.

Overcoming her resistance, she climbs the granite steps and makes her way to a small chapel on the side of the main altar. She has forgotten the calming atmosphere of prayerful reflection. Under the glow of stained-glass windows, she bows her head and remembers those whom she has loved and lost. Is blood still thicker than water, she wonders. Or has its potency been so diluted that only the pain of kinship remains? She reaches into the pocket of her skirt and touches the locket she once gave Cathy as a present. She jerks her hand away, as if its touch scorches her skin.

★ ★ ★

The locket was in Jeremy's car. Six months had passed since her return from London and Rebecca was searching for a gold, slim-line Cross pen that her father had presented to her on the morning she started university. Its loss had snapped another link in the chain separating her from her parents and she was anxious to find it. After searching the house she tried the car, hoping it had rolled from her bag and was lying under the passenger seat. When she slipped her hand into the groove between the back of the passenger chair and its seat, her fingers touched something cold and solid and curved.

The chain was broken on Cathy's locket. Rebecca had stared at the silver heart for a long time before opening it. The coil of black hair was still springy to her touch, the photographs of her

346

parents as clear as the day she cut them out and inserted them into the heart-shape.

Jeremy shrugged when she showed the locket to him. How many times had he driven Cathy to different places, collected her afterwards. Too numerous to remember. Forgotten journeys and incidents were recalled. Rebecca dredged them to the light and inspected them for flaws. To jeopardise her happiness when she had lost so much was unbearable. She chose to believe her husband. Anything else was too grotesque to contemplate. She allowed him to bury her suspicion under his persuasive words. To silence her doubts under his persuasive mouth.

Years later, when his face was slapped at a Christmas party, the gesture as intimate as the kiss Anna Kowalski would later bestow on his dead mouth, Rebecca remembered the locket and the dread that had clawed through her when she pulled it free from its hidden groove. Yet, even then, she had contained her fear, kept it firmly boxed until the night of Halloween when she lifted the phone and her sister's voice released it.

Chinese lanterns sway above the terrace, tealights gutter on the tables, barbecue grills blaze. The friends Cathy and Alma have made since they came to New Zealand mingle with their Irish friends and family. The buzz of conversation and trill of laughter follows Cathy as she moves among them. She tries not to look towards the Takahé chalet. Rebecca returned earlier but, so far, has not joined the guests.

Steve talks to Alma's brother about cars, offers

to let Robbie drive the Jag. His presence at Havenswalk is impossible to ignore. Cathy hears his voice no matter where she stands. It is not loud but has a definite pitch that carries it above the normal level of conversation. Lauren seems insubstantial beside him. Cathy suspects she is aiming for invisibility. Earlier, she arrived back to Havenswalk fully restored, buffed, massaged and manicured. She was always acknowledged as the family beauty but her beauty has become as glossy as a perfectly executed oil painting — and she is lost behind the brittle layers.

Night has settled when Rebecca emerges from her chalet. Conor, on drinks duty, moves towards her. Rebecca accepts a glass of wine and walks away from him. Something glints at her throat, heart-shaped and once familiar. Cathy stands motionless. Voices fade, faces blur. And the stars look as if they could splinter from the brightness within them.

★   ★   ★

Conor weaves through the terrace with a tray of drinks. He had his hair cut today. It adds a harder, more mature look to his features and diminishes the resemblance until he smiles. He pauses to talk to Melanie Barnes. The Goth from hell turned legal eagle, Rebecca thinks, and wearing a dress designed to cause cardiac arrest on the bench. Occasionally, Rebecca sees her on television, her black gown flapping like the wings of a magisterial raven as she emerges from the

Four Courts with an imposing bundle of files under her arm.

Julie waves and heads in her direction but Rebecca is not willing to endure another blast of Julie's disapproval. She walks past a small, portly man with a thatch of white hair, who is busily turning a rack of ribs on a barbecue grill.

'Try one,' he says. 'Prime New Zealand ribs.'

'No, thanks.' She forces herself to smile at him. 'I'm a vegetarian.'

'There's some veggie stuff over there.' Ignoring her protests, he insists on loading a plate with vegetable kebabs. He is talkative, a retired long-distance truck driver from Dublin called Robbie.

'It's a real eye-opener being here.' Robbie waves a spare rib in the general direction of the South Island. 'Alma had been on at me for years to visit her. I'm only sorry I didn't come when Doris was alive. She'd have loved it here, so she would.' He falls silent, his face scrunched with memory, then smiles broadly. 'Those roads, aren't they something else? What I wouldn't give to try Ramblin' Rosie on the hairpin bends. She'd take them sweetly, so she would.'

Alma Gowan is Cathy's business partner. Doris is Robbie's deceased wife. Who Ramblin' Rosie might be Rebecca has no idea until she realises he is talking about a truck. He nods towards Cathy, who is standing in front of a barbecue pit, talking to Alma.

'Who'd have believed it?' he says. 'The pair of them have turned this place into a right little gold mine.'

Rebecca watches Alma deftly pile a platter with steaks and pass them to the sinewy, silver-haired man who looks after the grounds.

'From what I've heard, they work hard for their success,' she replies.

'Just shows you,' the truck driver nods sagely, 'you never can tell. Cathy was a dead ringer for trouble when I first met her but a lot can happen in a few years.'

'When did you meet Cathy?' Rebecca asks. 'I thought this is your first visit to New Zealand.'

'Not here. In Dublin.'

'You *knew* her in Dublin.'

'Picked her up on the quays and took her over on the ferry, so I did. God knows she was a lost child, if ever I saw one. Thank God I had the wit to get Alma on side.'

'You . . . you took her on the ferry.' Rebecca steps back from him and lays her plate on a table. 'I suppose it never dawned on you that Cathy should have been brought back to her family?'

''Deed it did. What's your name again?'

'*Rebecca*.' Her voice shakes with anger.

'There was no talking to the child, Rebecca. She'd have been off again in the blink of an eye. God knows what could've happened to her then. The best I could do under the circumstances was put a few bob in her pocket and get her on a train to London. I rang Alma and asked her to meet the train, see what she could do for the kid. Cathy is the daughter she never had, that's what she told me once.'

Rebecca glances beyond him to the red-haired

woman with the cropped boyish hairstyle, her long thin neck decorated with a jade choker. A memory flickers but disappears before she can grasp it. The truck driver is still talking. She forces herself to concentrate.

'Quackery, most of it, herbs and potions. I'm not into the stuff myself — prefer the old jab of a needle any day — but they worked like dray horses before they came here.'

This time, recognition is instant. Alma's hair was long then, tossed as tumbleweed, and her bright hard eyes stared Rebecca straight in her face, ignoring her distress, her desperation to find Cathy. Where had Cathy been hiding? Probably in some cubbyhole at the back of the shop, hidden among the incense and aromatic oils, listening to every word they exchanged.

Rebecca leaves her plate on a nearby table and excuses herself. Ignoring Lauren, who calls after her, she walks swiftly into a grove of trees. Her light sandals are unsuitable for the muscular roots that push upwards through carpets of pine needles. She carries on regardless. A signpost signalling 'Glow-worm Grotto' points towards a dense bower of shrubbery. Needless to say, there have to be glow-worms in this garden of contemplation. She moves deeper into the forest. Drooping strands of mistletoe pull at her hair, insects crawl across her face. She finds a wooden bench set among the trees, and brushes leaves from the seat before collapsing into it.

Tomorrow morning she will leave Havenswalk. She will text Tim Dawson and tell him she has changed her mind about the wedding. His disappointment, if any, will be momentary. He is not seeking a long-distance romance and will soon forget their brief encounter. She will spend the rest of the week exploring the inlets at the tip of the island. Cape Farewell seems like an appropriate destination.

Something rustles nearby, a night creature intent on survival. She wonders how Teabag is surviving without her — probably utterly unaware of her absence. If Rebecca wants someone to pine after her, she should keep a dog. Next year she will develop a sanctuary for homeless dogs, the abandoned Christmas presents and tough little mutts no one wants. She has to think about the future. The present is unendurable. So, also, is the past.

Dead leaves rustle. Footsteps approach. She tenses when her name is called.

'A young lad told me I'd find you here.' Tim Dawson pushes aside the tangled branches and peers through the gloom. 'Why are you hiding in the bushes while everyone else is having a bun fight?'

'You're not supposed to be here until tomorrow.'

'Didn't you get my text?'

'No. My battery went down when I was in Nelson. It's still charging.'

He sits beside her and slides his arm across the back of the bench. 'If you'd read my text you'd know I'd an assignment cancelled at the last minute. I decided to hit the gas before I got another call. You haven't answered my question.

352

Why the hidy-hole?'

'Is it a crime to occasionally want to be alone?'

'Not the last time I checked. But that's not the reason you're here. Do you want to tell me what's going on?'

'It's personal, Tim. I'd rather not discuss it.'

'I figured from the beginning that this was more than a family reunion.'

'You're very perceptive.'

'In my job it pays off. I've been worried about you.'

A breeze stirs the leaves. Music from the terrace surges briefly before fading again. She is conscious of his nearness, his arm drawing her closer. His strength consoles her but is a superficial comfort that cannot change anything.

'What do you want me to do, Tim? Pour out my soul?'

'I thought you were a dedicated atheist? Where does your soul come into the equation?'

'I visited the cathedral in Nelson today. After the temples, it seems rather unadorned.'

'We don't go in for too many frills here. We're a simple people.'

'Is there such a species? If there is, it's probably endangered.'

'Why are you changing the subject?'

Reluctantly, she laughs then slumps against him. 'I made an appalling mistake coming here. I thought I could handle it but I'm not strong enough. I'm sorry, Tim. You've already been involved enough in my problems.'

'Do you hear me complaining?'

'If I talk about it, I'll fall apart, I really will.'

Her voice cracks. 'I'm leaving here first thing in the morning.'

'That bad?'

'Yes.'

'We'll go together.'

'Tim, I'm heading home soon. The other side of the world, remember? Is it worth it?'

'Why put a value on it? Let's simply enjoy each other's company.'

He is right. Afterwards no longer matters. She will walk into the dark with him, dance on the grave of Miss Havisham. Rip her cobwebby wedding veil and let it fly like spindrift through the air.

★ ★ ★

After the guests leave, driving home or going to their chalets, Conor helps to clear away the glasses and plates. Rebecca remains on the terrace. She sits there without talking or helping, like she is waiting for everyone to finish and leave her alone in the shadows. He notices leaves in her hair and is tempted to pluck them out. Better not touch. She wraps a man's jumper around her shoulders. Tim Dawson was wearing it when he arrived. Earlier, Conor saw them emerging from the forest. The light is on in Tim's chalet but she makes no attempt to join him or to return to her own place. He wonders if they saw the glow-worms. His father proposed to his mother in the grotto. What words did he use? Probably something like, 'Can I buy you a ring that is brighter than all the glow-worms in the world?'

354

When Conor finishes his chores, he pulls over a chair and sits beside his aunt.

'Can I spend some time with you at your sanctuary when I visit Ireland?' he asks.

'We'll see,' she replies.

He is taken aback by her abruptness. Julie says he can stay with her as long as he likes. Another boy, she jokes, will not endanger the structure of her house or increase the noise decibels that passed maximum volume a long time ago. She is his favourite aunt so far. He has hardly spoken to Lauren, and Rebecca puzzles him. He expected to like her best of all.

'I saw you kayaking this morning.' She interrupts his thoughts. 'You're good.'

'I'm training for the Coast to Coast next year. Have you done any kayaking since you came here?'

'Yes. On some of the lakes. It's fun.'

'We have a tandem kayak in the boathouse. Why don't you and Tim come with me and Lyle tomorrow?'

'Thanks, Conor, but no. We've made other plans.'

'Where are you going?'

'To Abel Tasman Park, then travelling on to Cape Farewell.'

'You should look out for the llamas. You'll find them in the park. When are you coming back?'

'I'm not sure.'

Something in her voice alerts him. 'You will be here for their wedding?'

She bites her lip, then stops as if she is afraid she will cut it with her teeth. Her hesitancy adds to his alarm. Before she speaks, he knows what she is going to say. 'You're not coming back.'

'I'm afraid that's so.' She leans forward and watches his mother pick up a parasol that had toppled over.

'But why? I don't understand.' He doesn't know whether to be amazed or angry. 'Why come all the way from Ireland if you'd no intention of going to her wedding?'

'Weddings are difficult for me, Conor. They remind me too much of my own wedding day.'

'Wasn't it a happy day?'

'I was on Cloud Nine. But my husband is dead and your mother's wedding will stir up too many memories.'

'I'm sorry he's dead.'

She cups his chin, runs her hand along his cheek. 'Did anyone ever tell you that you're a handsome lad?'

Her gaze is like a searchlight. He draws back, embarrassed by her scrutiny. 'Not lately. But thanks for the compliment. Please come back for the wedding. She really wants you to be there.'

'She won't miss me, Conor. And you'll have such a great time, you won't even notice my absence.'

All the time they are talking, his mother moves fast around the terrace, arranging chairs and picking up paper serviettes, blowing out night-lights, sweeping litter and leaves into corners. When there is nothing left to do, she stands in front of his aunt without speaking, the two of them just staring each other out. The silence between them is thick enough to punch.

Then his mother turns to him, as if she has only become aware of his presence, and says, 'Off to bed, honey. Rebecca and I need to talk.'

He opens her bedroom door. The wicker basket is still under the bed. He pulls it out and removes another letter. The slanted childish handwriting has changed to a more legible scrawl. There is no doubt about the date. She wrote all the time to her dead mother. He quickly scans the page. Melancholia's name seems to leap out at him until that is all he sees.

He hears his father returning from his nightly walk with Sandy. Conor shoves the basket back under the bed and takes the letter with him to his own room. 'Dear Mum, Melancholia is truly amazing . . . ' Satanic influences and brainwashing music obviously existed then, just like Oliver's father claims they exist today. This glimpse into her confused world explains so much. No wonder she and Rebecca pass each other as if there is a thorn bush between them.

* * *

'How long was it going on?' Rebecca asks. 'Was it before or after my marriage? Or both? How many times? Give me facts and figures, Cathy. I can handle them. It's better than suspicion, mind games. That's what Jeremy played. Insidious mind games, and I was weak enough to believe him. We made vows to each other, promises. They meant nothing in the end. How could he . . . how could you . . . and now you have the

357

nerve to bring me here to flaunt your son, to hold him like a mirror before me . . . ' Her voice breaks and Cathy quivers, as if the words have stung her flesh.

'Jeremy wasn't worthy of your love.'

Rebecca nods in agreement. 'Obviously, he wasn't worthy. But neither were you, and I loved you even more.'

The chain snaps when she pulls the locket from around her neck and forces it into Cathy's hand. 'Take it . . . take it! I've carried it around with me for too many years.'

Cathy opens it and sees her parents' faces, her mother's hair. She pictures Rebecca carefully removing the black shining strands from the brush and coiling them inside the heart. She clenches the locket and allows her sister to rage at her, assuage her grief.

How can she explain the gravitational lure of seduction and how, so easily, it can turn to rape? How does she know where truth and illusion begin and end? Was Jeremy guilty of doing what she had willed to happen? Her soft-focus fantasy, built around swooning eye contact, gentle hands, violins in the background, heathery moors. She carried no bruises, none that were visible. Rape can be brutal and unexpected, a fist in the dark, pursuing footsteps. It can be a quiet force that creeps insidiously across the flesh and makes it one. Was there a difference? The only music she heard in his car that night was the harsh sigh of the conqueror and the pinned breath of the conquered. In that instant, she lost everything she held dear and gained everything she holds dear.

'You lied to your son. You and Kevin have shamefully deceived him. How could you?'

'It wasn't deliberate — '

'I don't want to know.' Rebecca rises to her feet and stares down at her. 'But I do know this: such deception will turn and flail you to the bone.' Jeremy's face hovers like a death mask between them. Rebecca covers her eyes, as if the sight is unbearable.

'I'm leaving first thing in the morning,' she says. 'I'll meet my sisters at the airport on the return flight.'

She turns and walks away without another word.

Cathy is still sitting on the terrace when Tim Dawson joins her. This burly man, who moves lightly for his bulk, cares for Rebecca.

'Make her stay,' Cathy pleads.

He shakes his head. 'She doesn't like complications. Are you part of those complications?'

'I'm afraid I am.'

'I figured as much. I'm sorry, Cathy.'

The terrace is deserted now. The lights are off in the chalets, except for one window, the Takahē, where Rebecca, like her sister, is keeping a vigil with the past.

58

Day Three

Rebecca finishes packing and sits back on her heels. Tim will be with her shortly. On the wall, the takahē stares stoically from its frame, no doubt reflecting on its rescue from extinction.

A knock on the door startles her. Alma Gowan stands outside.

'We meet again.' Rebecca crosses her arms and leans against the door frame. 'You tell a good lie, Alma.'

Alma meets her gaze without flinching. 'Will it make any difference if I apologise?'

'None whatsoever.' Rebecca is unable to keep the bitterness from her voice.

'Can I come inside for a moment?' Alma glances back towards Havenswalk where the blinds on the windows are still drawn. 'Cathy warned me not to interfere. I'd rather she didn't see us talking.'

Reluctantly, Rebecca moves aside. 'Say what you came to say, Alma, and keep it short. I'm leaving here within the next ten minutes.'

Alma's gaze travels over the closed rucksack and Rebecca's backpack. 'I didn't speak out once before and I've regretted it many times since then.'

'If you think that makes me feel any better,

you're wrong.' Rebecca drags her rucksack to the open doorway. No sign of movement from the Torea chalet where Tim slept last night. Alma sits down and links her fingers into a steeple. For an instant, Rebecca thinks she is going to pray.

'You're a determined woman, Rebecca. You and Cathy are cut from the same cloth.'

'An interesting observation. But you're forgetting something. I'm not the one who deceives.'

'Except yourself, maybe.'

'How dare you try to analyse me — '

'That's not why I'm here, Rebecca. There's too much hurt about as it is. I don't want to add to it by having a row with you.'

'Then why are you delaying me?'

'I came here to apologise. I'm heart sorry I lied that day. It wasn't just for Cathy's sake, but yours also. Sometimes we can make the wrong decision for the right reason.'

'I'm sure that's a profound statement but it makes absolutely no sense to me.'

'More than anything else, Cathy wanted you to have a happy marriage.'

'And she believed a marriage based on such deceit could possibly succeed?' Before Alma can reply, Rebecca holds up her hand. 'Please don't tell me ignorance is bliss.'

'Cathy was only a child, Rebecca. She was out of her depth — '

'I watched her.' Rebecca's self-control is slipping away. 'Dressing up in those ridiculous clothes, always demanding his attention. Putting on her little-girl-lost act . . . laughing with him behind my back, thinking I couldn't hear her

361

. . . but I never . . . never . . . '

To her relief, she hears Tim's voice. His tall frame fills the doorway. He hesitates when he sees Alma. 'Am I disturbing something?'

'Nothing important.' Rebecca lifts her rucksack and hands it to him. 'Sling it into the Jeep, Tim. Alma is leaving now.'

'You're making the wrong decision, Rebecca.' The older woman stands. 'I understand your anger but Cathy was an innocent victim — '

'Was she, Alma? Look into her eyes next time you ask her that question.' Rebecca pauses by the door. 'Just as a matter of interest, do you actually have a daughter called Nadine or was that just another lie?'

'Everybody has their story, Rebecca. I've said what I needed to say and now I'll bid you goodbye.' Without waiting for a reply Alma brushes past her and disappears around the side of the chalet. Tendrils of mist drift across the lawn. The rata trees are in full bloom, clots of red blossom hanging heavy on the branches. Rebecca does not look back as Tim drives from Havenswalk.

★　★　★

Ruthie approaches the veranda where Lauren and Steve are breakfasting. She lays a cafetière of fresh coffee, and croissants, warm from the oven, on the table. In the distance, the faint hum of an engine is heard. Julie, on Hannah's motorbike, flashes into view, a dark shape in black leather

362

before she disappears around the bend of the avenue. The blinds are open in Rebecca's chalet but Lauren cannot see any movement within. Tim's Jeep is missing. She begins to feel the first stirrings of uneasiness. Yesterday, Rebecca also disappeared for the day and offered no explanation. The engine grows louder. Julie is back in view. She parks the bike outside Havenswalk, slings the leather jacket over one shoulder and saunters towards the breakfast table. All she is missing, Lauren thinks, is a beard and ponytail.

'Since when did you join Hell's Angels?' Steve asks.

'That's just a practice run.' Julie sits down and crosses her legs, admires her biker boots. Hannah has obviously made her entire leather wardrobe available to her. 'Paul is checking out Harley prices on the internet. You should have a go, Lauren. It's exhilarating.'

'She'll stick to the Jag,' says Steve.

Lauren smiles and dribbles honey over a croissant. She has already been swimming in the pool and her hair, pulled severely back from her forehead, emphasises the weight she has lost since the start of the trip.

'Did she tell you about the dolphins?' Julie asks.

Lauren sighs, knowing Julie's tendency to exaggerate. She regrets confiding in her sisters but the euphoria she experienced with the dolphin flowed from her when they returned to shore. Rebecca had looked sceptical, obviously believing that if dolphins were going to interact with humans, then she would be their obvious choice. Julie, on the other hand, had been totally credulous and, by now, is convinced she was hanging over the edge of the boat witnessing the scene.

'What about the dolphins?' Steve asks.

'We swam with them in Kaikoura,' says Julie. 'And one of them *actually* carried Lauren on its back.'

'Bareback dolphin riding,' Steve sounds amused. 'I find that an interesting if somewhat incredible concept.'

Lauren does not blame him. She feels the experience diminishing with every word Julie utters. She pours fresh coffee and hands a cup to Julie, who remains oblivious of Lauren's warning glance.

'Not incredible,' Julie replies. 'True. I saw it with my very own eyes.'

'What I find most amazing is that Lauren did not drown.' Steve's amusement is short-lived. 'Lauren was obviously pulled along on a riptide or a dangerous cross-current. It's terrifying to think what could have happened while you were being entertained by a circus of dolphins.'

'Pod of dolphins,' Julie corrects him. 'There was no riptide, Steve. She was never in any danger. You're forgetting she used to be a champion swimmer.' She swirls a spoonful of sugar into her coffee. 'I have all your medals,' she adds in an aside to Lauren.

'Really?' Lauren is suddenly transported back to the noisy swimming pool where their father took them every Saturday morning. 'How many did I win?'

'You won six gold in the under tens and five in the under elevens. I took them with me when I was clearing out Heron Cove.'

'Under tens and elevens — that's not today or yesterday.' Steve cuts an apple into precise pieces, carves cheese from a platter. 'But, thankfully, she survived to tell the story. Where's Rebecca this morning?'

'Having a lie-in, I guess.' Julie shrugs and rises from the table. 'Got to go check my emails. Catch you later.'

Lauren opens Akona's book. Birds fly like arrows through the morning mist and dive into the trees. Akona uses them as her inspiration, the kea, kakapo, kiwi, kaka: such strange staccato names yet the Maori woman's poetry has a melodic cadence, a curious almost rap-like beat, which will, Lauren suspects, imitate the rhythm of various birdsongs if spoken aloud. The poems stir her with a once-familiar excitement. The rhythm of words flowing into poetry. Her introverted phase, Steve called it. Everything is a phase that she can overcome. *Barren moon . . . raging . . . .*

'Put the book down, princess.' Steve leans forward and takes the book from her, lays it on his side of the table. 'We're supposed to be enjoying breakfast together.' Lauren smells perfume, the cheap, cloying perfume that rose from the breasts of the young prostitute in Bangkok. If she breathes any deeper she will throw up. She closes her eyes against the image of the young woman's face, the sunflower tattoo, the dark almond eyes that compared their jewels, fake and genuine, and made no differentiation.

'My name is Lauren,' she says. 'Please call me Lauren in future.'

He shakes his head, bemused. 'If you insist, *Lauren.*'

'It was not a riptide, Steve.'

'I thought we were discussing your identity, not your fantasies.'

'I need you to believe me.'

'What I believe is that you would have drowned under those circumstances.'

A radio can be heard from one of the chalets. The clang of a rake on gravel hurts her head. Even the clink of cutlery is too loud. 'You heard Julie. I was a strong swimmer when I was a child. I've medals — '

'And scars. I don't have to remind you — '

'Yet you always do.'

'When do I refer to your unfortunate tendency to self-harm? All I've ever done is protect you.'

'From myself, you mean?'

'From pain. Is that a crime? Tell me what I should have done differently.'

'Do you believe me . . . about the dolphin?'

'Why should you expect me to believe such a ridiculous story? I'm a realist. As are you, despite your fragility. Forget the dolphins. It's irrelevant to what we're discussing, which is the fact that we are arguing after being separated for almost a month. It's not the welcome I expected from my wife.'

'What do you expect from me, Steve? Apart

from being your precious piece of Dresden?'

'Don't overdo it, Lauren. My tolerance will only stretch so far.'

'Rebecca calls me a trophy wife.'

'Since when has Rebecca's opinion mattered to you?'

'Since I realised she's right.'

'So, live with it.'

His laughter breaks across her face. He is right about realism. Her realism is anger and guilt, a potent mix. And pain also, sharp as ice before it thaws.

★ ★ ★

The note must have been slipped under the chalet door while Julie was sleeping. She had walked past it without noticing, eager to link up with Hannah and borrow her bike. It is only when she returns to the Silvereye that Julie sees the folded piece of paper on the floor. She reads Rebecca's note with a growing sense of disbelief.

Dear Julie and Lauren,

Please forgive my abrupt departure. Remaining at Havenswalk is impossible. Cathy broke my heart when she ran away and I can't forgive her. If that makes me sound like a hard-hearted bitch, then so be it. I'm going away with Tim Dawson for the remainder of the trip and will see you at the airport.

The three of us have travelled a long journey together. Despite our differences, I'd like to believe we've grown closer over that time. For that reason, I hope you'll take my advice in the spirit it's intended. Count your blessings, Julie — and use both hands. Dump your suitcases, Lauren — and all they contain. It will lighten your load.

Until we meet again,
Rebecca

Julie's anger grows when she reads it a second time. How dare Rebecca believe she has a monopoly on pain? Cathy's disappearance affected all of them equally. Why does Rebecca find it so difficult to forgive her? Julie hurries to the veranda, but Steve and Lauren have finished breakfast. She continues on towards Havenswalk. Cathy and Rebecca were together on the terrace last night. Something must have been said, an inadvertent comment shattering the fragile harmony between them.

Two kayaks are on the lake this morning, black squiggles on the mirrored surface. She recognises her nephew and Lyle, the gardener, who, according to Conor, is his trainer for some triathlon. They step onto the jetty and secure their kayaks. Conor removes his helmet and stoops to stroke his red setter. He throws a stick and the dog leaps forward in pursuit. The sun shines on his wheat-yellow hair. Lyle shouts something and Conor tosses his head, laughs. The sound floats faintly towards Julie.

She stands perfectly still and flinches, as if a lost memory has risen and slapped her face. The boy and the man draw nearer. The man nods and passes by without speaking. He has a taciturn manner that does not encourage conversation. Conor stops to talk to her. Yes, he is aware Rebecca left earlier. She hates weddings. Bad memories; he shakes his head. Perhaps she'll change her mind and come back. He grins hopefully and continues walking with her towards Havenswalk.

At the entrance Julie stops. 'I need to go back to the chalet,' she mutters and turns, walks quickly away.

Once inside the chalet, she slumps into a chair. She is too hot; ridiculous weather to wear leather. She kicks off the boots, peels off the leather trousers. She breathes fast, folds over, presses her hands to her stomach. The scene in the forest when she found Rebecca weeping comes vividly to mind. Rebecca never cries, not since their parents' funeral and Nero's death. After Cathy disappeared, after Jeremy's death, no tears. Or if she cried, her tears were shed in private.

Julie runs up the spiral staircase and enters the bathroom. She splashes cold water over her face. The tilt of a boy's head means nothing. His contagious laughter does not evoke a forgotten echo. It is too ridiculous to consider. Rebecca crying . . . the image refuses to go away. Crying as if her heart was breaking.

She stands on the balcony and watches Conor emerge from Havenswalk with Mel Barnes. They head towards the swimming pool. Conor takes her beach bag. Mel tries to take it back but he insists on carrying it. They are laughing together.

Julie cannot hear them but the flirtatious tableau Conor creates is unmistakable.

How could she have missed the resemblance? She saw what she wanted to see. Superficial similarities: Kevin's blond unruly hair, her own bog-brown eyes, Rebecca's sphinx cheekbones, Lauren's delicate fingers, the shape of his face so similar to his mother's. But the truth was obvious to those who sought it.

Has Rebecca always known or has she lived for fifteen years with this suspicion? It would explain so much. In the months following Jeremy's death, Julie waited for Rebecca to condemn Anna Kowalski, rant about her husband's infidelity. She could not understand Rebecca's silence, her remote expression whenever Julie tried to broach the subject. If it was Paul . . . Julie's skin prickles at the thought. If he was unfaithful, she would wade in, boots and fists flying, and separate them with a scythe. Even his ashes would not be safe from her murderous rage. The longing for home is so intense that Julie almost cries out. Home in her husband's arms, away from Lauren's brittle unhappiness, Cathy's enforced calmness and the raw anguish she failed to recognise on Rebecca's face when she was introduced to her nephew and recognised the past staring back at her.

★ ★ ★

The air has a lighter texture since Rebecca left Havenswalk. She can breathe freely again. They speak little as they climb upwards, moving at the same pace, stopping occasionally when Tim points to the distinctive flash of a bellbird or the parrotlike kaka. He is adept at identifying birdsong and naming the alpine plants that flourish on the lower reaches of Mount Arthur. It is a vigorous trek and Rebecca has energy to flail.

Tussocks and forests gradually give way to dramatic limestone structures. Snow is still visible in the chasms, but mainly the track is clear and easy to follow. They stop to eat at the half-way point. Tim unpacks the salads and cheeses, the cold trout and pasta they bought in Motueka. They eat quickly, resting their backs against a slanting slab of limestone, ravenously hungry from the fresh air and exercise.

'What would you like to do after we finish here?' Tim asks. 'Stay a second day or continue on?'

'Continue on.'

'Then I suggest we overnight locally. I know an excellent lodge near Motueka.'

'Sounds perfect.' Rebecca walks to the edge of the plateau and sweeps her binoculars over the curving brows of Abel Tasman Park. A softer landscape lies below her but up here, the buffeting wind and the barren peaks reflect the turbulence of her heart, the emptiness of her womb.

'The wind is deceptive.' Tim joins her. 'It's dangerous to stand so near the edge.'

'I'm being careful.' She hands the binoculars to him. 'It's such a magnificent view from here. Conor says there are llamas in the park. He wanted to show them to me.'

Tim glances through the binoculars, then hands them back to her. 'You travelled a long journey to run from your sister.'

'Cathy talks about closure. It's such a senseless word.' Her voice settles harshly between them.

'What lies behind the word is what counts,' he replies.

'That's the problem.' She touches her stomach, comforting the place where her child should have lain. 'Cathy had an affair with my husband. Conor is their son . . . *not* mine. I knew . . . all the time we were travelling, I knew what I would find when I reached Havenswalk.'

Tim remains silent, absorbing what he has heard, and she is glad he does not try to offer false comfort.

'Why did I come here? Why? Why? Before she rang I had a life. I'd moved on. Why bring all this on myself? How am I supposed to live with the knowledge that she deceived me behind my back and that he . . . I can't stand it . . . what am I doing here?'

'You're setting yourself free,' he says.

'Free? What exactly is that supposed to mean?' She stares angrily at him. 'My suspicions were right all along. The truth doesn't set you free. It traps you.'

She returns to the shelter of the boulder and clears away the remains of the picnic. He kneels down beside her. 'Listen to me, Rebecca. Before you came here, suspicion was all you had. But it's gone now. There're no questions you're afraid to ask because you know the answers. No signs you're afraid to notice, or willing to ignore so that you can continue living the life you choose. The truth is a heavy burden. But you eventually manage to carry it. Suspicion, on the other hand, paralyses you.'

His words penetrate her distress, resonate with his own personal experience. She is aware, for the first time since they met, that behind his easy-going personality, he too has a story to tell. She thinks about Olive Moran. Light footsteps on an open road.

'Are you free, Tim?' She sits back on her heels and stares at him. He nods and takes her into his arms. 'We're on top of the world, Rebecca. It's a safe place to share secrets.'

She looks upwards towards the formidable summit they have yet to reach. 'We're only at the half-way point.'

'Then we'll complete the journey when we're ready.'

Four hours later they descend from the summit and settle into his Jeep.

'Are you still averse to complications?' His tone is noncommittal. 'No problem booking a two-bedroom chalet.'

'One will be fine,' she replies.

'Sure?'

'Yes.'

*　*　*

Rebecca's new dress sways against her knees as she walks towards the balcony where a table for two has been set. She enjoys the feel of the soft fabric against her skin, enjoys the admiration she sees in Tim's eyes. They watch the sea-veined sandbanks glisten like a mosaic on the outgoing tide and talk about books, music, travel, animals. They avoid the subject of deception. Not that she wants to talk about Jeremy or Cathy, or anything that is not related to the present moment.

They leave the bedroom curtains open and undress, their limbs heavy with the foreknowledge of pleasure. In the embrace of this genial man who has entered her life so unexpectedly, Rebecca is surprised by the rush of desire that comes without effort, without pretence. He lies back against the pillows and watches her undress. His strong arms reach out for her. The broad unfamiliar curves of his neck and shoulders block out all she had left behind at Havenswalk. They moved to the same pace throughout the day and now, when she kneels into the hardness of him, their bodies follow another rhythm, tender yet demanding, impatient yet willing to tease and play, to boldly explore and delicately seek out each other's pleasure. She arches back and clasps him deep inside her, his hands holding her steady as they urge each other towards the stormy clash of satisfaction.

'Some complication,' he says when they are sated and resting together. 'What say you now, Rebecca Lambert?'

For once, no words are necessary.

59

Day Four

A lorry turns into the avenue leading to Havenswalk and takes the road to the lake. From the balcony of his bedroom, Conor watches the crew of workmen emerge and begin to unload a marquee. His mother joins them and points towards the site where it will be erected. She looks tiny compared to the burly men in their shorts and singlets, but they will obey her instructions. Conor has seen her in action when jobs are not carried out to her satisfaction. That is why her nervousness around Rebecca was so difficult to figure out.

The balcony rail is hot under his hand. The day promises to be glorious. Lyle is already working in the garden. His white roses are beginning to unfurl. They will form a bower at the entrance to the marquee and decorate the outdoor altar. The wedding rehearsal takes place this evening and his parents will be married in four days' time. Still no word from his aunt, not even a text.

Yesterday, when he mentioned visiting Ireland, his mother nodded dismissively and said, 'We'll discuss it when things have settled back to normal after the wedding.'

The look in her eyes quenched his excitement.

When he was younger and noticed it, the look that told him she had gone somewhere else in her mind, he threw tantrums. Even when she lifted him in her arms and tried to soothe him, he sensed she was still outside his grasp. He found relief in the ferocity of his tantrums and would continue screaming until Alma — who could silence him with stories about ancient warriors with hurley sticks and hounds — appeared and carried him off.

'What's there to discuss?' he asked. 'I've wasted too many years already.'

'Wasted?' Her face flushed. 'Is that how you see our life here?'

'I didn't say that. Trust you to twist it around. I only meant that if things had been different I would have known my relations from the time I was born.'

'Better late than never, don't you agree?'

'But Rebecca's gone. Why did she just bugger off like that?'

'How many times must I repeat myself? I don't *know*.'

'You *must* know.'

'She hates me. OK? Is that answer good enough for you? She hates me and she hates Kevin.'

'Why? That's all I want to know. Why does she hate us?'

'Not us. She doesn't hate you — '

'Yes, she does. I saw it on her face as soon as she saw me.'

Her simplistic explanation insults his intelligence. Conor watches her moving around the marquee. It is taking shape, fluttering and rising like an enormous air balloon. His glamorous aunt appears on her balcony. She leans her arms on the rails, a cigarette between her fingers. He leaves Havenswalk and walks across the lawn towards her. Large sunglasses cover her eyes, a sunhat shades her face. He waves to attract her attention and she beckons at him to come up.

Her bedroom smells of perfume. It clings to her when she walks to the balcony carrying two tall glasses of lemon juice.

'Where's Uncle Steve?' he asks.

'He's taken over Cathy's office.' She taps her fingernail against the glass and smiles. 'I believe you're visiting Ireland. You'll have to stay with us also.'

'Of course,' he replies politely. 'I'm hoping to work in Rebecca's sanctuary as well.'

'Julie's boys often help her in the stables and the clinic.'

'I wonder what she's doing now?'

'Knowing Becks, she's probably chasing geckos through the woods.'

'There are geckos here. And I was going to show her the glow-worm grotto. Have you seen it yet?'

'Not yet. I believe it's beautiful.'

'Yes.' Her dark sunglasses unnerve him. He wants her to take them off so that he can see her eyes. 'Is Rebecca the reason Mom was forced to run away from home?'

'No one forced Cathy to leave — '

'Then why did she leave?'

'I don't know, Conor.' Lauren shakes her

head. 'She left without giving us a reason.'

'Because of me?'

'She was expecting you, yes. But we would have looked after her — '

'Why didn't my father look after her?'

'Kevin was young too.'

'He mustn't have wanted anything to do with me.'

'That's not true either. Cathy was gone before any of us had a chance to help her.'

'I wish she hadn't run away.'

'I ran away too, only in a different way.'

'Where did you run to?'

She touches her chest, her hand resting above the V of her dress. 'In here, Conor.'

He gulps his drink, unsure of what she means. 'I hate secrets.' He blurts out the words before he has a chance to think about them.

'But life would be excruciating if there were no secrets.' Ice tinkles in her glass when she raises it to her lips.

'It would be more honest.'

'Honest, yes. But impossible to bear.' Suddenly, she stands up and says, 'Excuse me, Conor,' before hurrying from the balcony.

He finishes his drink, unsure whether he should leave or stay. The marquee is fully assembled. His mother stands back, her hands on her hips, and surveys it.

He hears the cistern flushing in the bathroom, the door opening and closing. When his aunt comes back, her sunhat is missing and her sunglasses are pushed into her hair. She refills his glass.

'I'm so pleased everything worked out for Cathy. It must have been a wonderful feeling when you met your father.'

'Yes.' He nods vigorously. 'But I'm sorry he missed most of my life.'

'You can always make up for lost time.'

'How?'

She touches her cheek with her index finger and looks thoughtful. 'Now that you ask, I don't believe time is *that* obliging.' She yawns and pulls her sunglasses over her eyes. Her nails are bright red talons. 'I'm going to lie down for a little while,' she says. 'I'm still recovering from the camper and need my beauty sleep.'

'No you don't,' he replies. 'Sleep couldn't make you any more beautiful than you already are.' He offers the compliment with unselfconscious ease. Instead of being pleased, her smile looks pasted on. She taps her cigarette hard with her finger, even though there is no ash to flick and says, 'My goodness, Conor, I never realised you were such a charmer.'

★ ★ ★

Her sisters know. Cathy has sensed the realisation dawning on them, seen it in the quizzing glances they bestow on her son. After the wedding rehearsal, she invites them to the sun room. They listen without interrupting when she tells them about the night everything glistened on a silver stage and how, when she found there was no way back, she could only run forward.

379

Hatred, Jeremy once claimed, was so akin to love that it became a fine line vibrating. Wrong ... wrong. Cathy's hatred towards him never vibrated in any direction. It was a tumour rooted deep in her heart. Thanks to Alma, fostering, nourishing, loving Alma with no degree in psychology, no trained insight into the complexities of conscience and penitence, Cathy's anger was turned into self-awareness and she let him go. Instead of seeing him in Conor's features, she cut the tumour from its stem and gave her son his own unique identity.

Mel phoned her with news of Jeremy's sudden death. The following day, Cathy took to her bed. Psychosomatic symptoms. She knew enough about the subconscious to recognise when her body had to let go. She allowed her temperature to rage and her skin to ache, her lungs to fill with the mucus of grief.

'You fucked someone and I'm the result.' Conor stood above her bed and cast this sullen profanity at her. His school yard language had finally shocked her into his need to understand the other half of his existence. How could she tell him the truth? Rape ... the word too harsh to place on his young shoulders. In that moment of weakness she lied to her son.

She never forgot the night in Kevin's white room. His clumsy attempts to unbutton her dress, his hands trembling on her breasts. It was as near to the truth as she dared to go. In the years following that lie, she began to believe her fantasy, almost. And then it became reality. Everything turned to gold when he came back into her life. But its dazzle had blinded her, delusions and illusions distorting her judgement.

When she falls silent, Julie, dry-eyed for once, rocks her in her arms. Lauren links her fingers, presses her hands against her stomach.

'Rebecca was in London looking after me that night. If anyone is to blame, it's me. I'm to blame for everything.'

'What exactly is everything?' Julie asks.

'For killing them,' Lauren replies. 'And for all that followed.'

For an instant, her expression reminds Cathy of the young secretive girl, with her bleak poetry and slender damaged wrists.

'When are you going to stop punishing yourself?' Cathy asks the question gently. Lauren has bled a river trying to erase the memory of the rainy night that changed their lives. But guilt is a needy bitch, not easily assuaged, and Lauren must find her own peace.

★ ★ ★

Tired from horse trekking on Cape Farewell, they book a cabin and retire early. Rebecca awakens during the night. The cabin door is open. Tim turns when she steps into the star-studded darkness and raises his finger to his lips.

'Listen,' he whispers, and points towards a dense arch of shrubbery. 'That's a kiwi. The male.'

'How do you know?' Whispering also, she strains forward to hear its cry, a high-pitched wheeing call, each note distinctly separate.

'The call is sharper, more defined.' His breath is warm on her neck. 'Shush, his mate is answering.'

The female cry is pitched at a deeper level, as if the effort of calling out demands a hoarse, more laboured response. Rebecca listens to their duet, their unseen manoeuvrings as they scavenge the undergrowth for food. When their cries fade into the night, she and Tim return to bed and to each other's arms.

60

Day Five

A lifetime of stories have been heard and shared. Tim drives slowly, taking the corkscrew bends with assurance. This is his landscape. Rebecca feels no desire to organise, fret, worry, challenge. As her mind relaxes, the anger that drove her from Havenswalk keeps slipping from her grasp. Questions intrude at unexpected moments. Tim does not ask them but she sees them in his quizzing gaze, hears them in his thoughtful silences.

★ ★ ★

Havenswalk is empty. The guests have gone to visit an art gallery in Nelson. His father is working and his mother is still adding ticks to her to-do wedding list. Conor places his hand under his pillow and draws out the letter he took from the wicker basket. He reads it again. 'Dear Mum, Melancholia is truly amazing . . .'

He looks out the window towards the chalets spanning from Havenswalk like the spokes of a wheel. Quickly, before he can change his mind, he enters his parents' bedroom. The basket has disappeared. He checks the wardrobes, pulls open the drawers on her dressing table, shuffles her underwear aside in embarrassment, then her scarves, tops and jumpers. Silently, empty-handed, he returns to his room.

★ ★ ★

After lunch they return to Havenswalk. Lauren lies down. The tiredness she feels is sudden and overwhelming. Steve has emails to send. He draws the blinds before he leaves the room. When she awakens, she feels refreshed, even though she has slept for only twenty minutes. A power nap. She stretches, reluctant to leave the bed, and picks up the copy of the *Southern Eye* she bought in Nelson. She scans the headlines: a murder trial in Christchurch, an investigation into political corruption, the gang rape of a young woman in Wellington. Global news, it never changes. A small item at the bottom of the page attracts her attention. Her hands quiver as she stares at the announcement. In four days' time Niran Gordon will be the guest lecturer at the Christchurch Music Centre. Students from Christ's College, where he once studied, will perform his latest composition.

Lauren folds the paper and lays it on the bedside locker. When Steve returns, she pretends to be asleep. He stands above her for an instant before lifting the paper and walking out to the balcony. When she rises, he is absorbed in the latest news.

★ ★ ★

Ferns waver in the sweep of Conor's torch. Ancient tree trunks leer. When Mel skids on pine needles, she grabs his arm and holds on until the trail to the glow-worm grotto levels off. Her touch sets his blood racing. He found her alone in the sun room, curled into the sofa reading a book.

Her clothes are fantastic, a low-cut black net top with something silky underneath and skin-tight black pants with chains. A tattoo is visible on her right breast. It could be a snake or the branch of a tree, or a long finger, beckoning. She agreed to come with him to the glow-worm grotto. The last time he took her to the grotto, all that concerned him was getting back to his PlayStation as quickly as possible. Not tonight. The air is velvet, quivering with the nearness of her and now, as they penetrate deeper into the trees, he switches off his torch. He loves this moment, the absolute blackness pressing against them before the power of the grotto unfolds.

Faintly at first, then growing clearer, tiny glow-worms become visible. Thousands upon thousands, hanging from twigs, stems, branches, leaves, flowers. Between the branches, he sees stars blazing across the sky. They are too far away, too aloof to interest him. Here in this tiny green haven, he is standing in his own private constellation. Mel's arm is a pale streak in the pool of night, her perfume as musky as crushed orchids, as mysterious as the pulsating light surrounding them.

'It's wonderful, Conor,' she whispers, afraid, perhaps, that a shudder of sound will cause the glow-worms to disappear. 'It's like a scattering of fairy dust.' They sit on a bench and watch the lights flicker and glow.

'Julie tells me you're coming to Ireland.' Her throaty voice reminds him of treacle. 'You'll have to stay with me for a while. We all want a piece of you.'

'I'd like that.'

'I'd like that, also.' Her ear, silver-studded and looped, grazes his cheek when she puts her arm round his shoulder. 'This is even more splendid than I remembered. Thank you for showing it to me again. You're such a sweet, thoughtful boy.'

He turns his face towards her and kisses her before the meaning of her words reaches him. For an instant, a heady, glorious instant, he feels the moist contact of her lips before they settle, resistant against his mouth. Her shock is obvious in the way she sits perfectly still before drawing her arm away from him.

'Wow!' The amusement in her voice is worse than outrage. 'I knew you were maturing into a young man but I didn't realise it was happening so fast.' She speaks loudly but the glow-worms remain undisturbed.

He cringes, stammers an apology.

'Don't be embarrassed, Conor,' she says. 'To be honest, it's flattering that you don't view me as an old harridan.'

'I don't . . . I couldn't! I didn't mean — '

'You don't have to apologise or explain. But can you imagine what your mother would say if she found out?'

'Are you going to tell her?' At last he is able to

utter a coherent sentence.

'Of course not. I haven't forgotten what it was like to be a teenager with all that fire to burn. But not on me, Conor. You're growing up fast and I don't want this to be an issue between us every time we meet. Do you understand?'

'Yes.' The most awful part of the lecture is that she sounds exactly like his mother. He wants to escape but he has to lead her back through the tunnel and escort her to her chalet with the falcon carving on the outside.

'Are you sure you're all right, Conor?' The understanding in her voice adds to his humiliation. Before the night deteriorates any further, he nods and turns towards Havenswalk.

His name is softly called. He turns and sees his glamorous aunt. She looks ghostly with the moonlight shining on her face.

'It's such a beautiful night,' she says. 'I'm going to see the glow-worms.'

'It's that way.' He points towards the arching branches and hurries on. This will be his last visit to the glow-worm grotto, at least until he is old and decrepit enough to forget about tonight. He climbs into bed and pulls his pillow over his face. Melancholia . . . Melancholia . . . he shudders under the power of her wickedly glistening tongue, and her teeth, pearly white against her blood-red lipstick, play sweetly over his throat.

* * *

Lauren has been walking for over twenty minutes before she realises she missed the turning to the

387

grotto. The forest surrounding Havenswalk is a labyrinth of twisting trails and she hesitates, tries to get her bearings. The trees begin to thin. Suddenly, she reaches a low fence of barbed wire. She steps across it and stands on a narrow side road. Once again, she is lost. Bangkok was a neon void and Jackson Bay a jungle. Her mobile phone, state of the art and lying at the bottom of Akona's lake, would be an obvious answer to her dilemma. She mocks herself as she continues walking.

Steve is unaware that she is missing. He drank too much at dinner and, hopefully, will not awaken until morning. She continues walking. Each bend she approaches fills her with hope that the gates of Havenswalk will loom out of the darkness. The trees remain dense and unbroken on either side of the road. Eventually, she reaches a small one-storey shack with a sloping roof and dark windows. The garden has a cared-for appearance and the night is heavy with the scent of flowers.

She knocks but receives no response. Facing back into the trees is not an option and, for the first time since she lost her way, she feels frightened.

She shines her torch on a signpost pointing left. The writing is almost obliterated, a Maori name, unpronounceable, but with the word 'Lake' written below it. Without hesitating any longer, she turns to the left and enters a narrow lane. Shortly afterwards, she hears the muffled wash of the lake over pebbles. Cautiously, she makes her way over the uneven terrain until she reaches a high embankment. Below her, the lake, lit only by the moon, spreads like a dark stain along the shore. Lauren clambers down the embankment. The shore is littered with driftwood, bleached and dry as skeletal bones.

Footsteps crunch on the pebbles. An elongated shadow falls forward into a shaft of moonlight. Lauren is unable to see the person but the footsteps are confident. She remains out of sight, shielded by an outcrop of rocks. The footsteps stop. In the silence that follows, she debates switching on her torch to alert the person to her presence. Before she can move, a disembodied voice rings out. A male voice, the words indistinct yet there is something familiar in the rising and falling cadences. Too embarrassed to interrupt when he is oblivious to her presence, she stays silent. She plays her fingers across the bleached bark and squashes a tiny insect that has unwisely scurried across her hand. She wipes her thumb nail clean on the dead wood. Buddha would not approve. To each its own circle of time.

Shoes are kicked off. She hears them fall against the pebbles, a muddled thud followed by the faint swish of clothes being removed, a grunt of satisfaction as if his body has been freed from all constraints. Still unable to see anyone, she thinks, this must be how a blind person lives, the sense of sound acutely reflecting a world of darkness. Every minute that passes makes it more difficult to declare herself.

He emerges from behind the rocks, a pale diffuse shape heading towards a makeshift jetty.

'Ahhh!' His involuntary cry is lost in the splash of water. He disappears from sight. Still she makes no effort to move. A short while later he emerges from the lake and sits, as she has done, against the trunk of a long-dead tree. He clicks a cigarette lighter. His hands cup the flame. Not that there is any breeze to extinguish it. The smell of smoke wafts towards her.

'Is there another star gazer out there?' he calls out.

She switches on her torch and steps forward into his line of vision. 'I didn't mean to disturb you.'

'No disturbance. The night doesn't belong to me.' A towel is draped over his hips, his chest is bare. Lloyd or Larry . . . something beginning with L, a reclusive man with green fingers, Cathy said. An insomniac, like herself.

'Cigarette?' he asks.

'No thank you. I try to confine my smoking to daylight hours.'

'A worthy aspiration. Why don't you sit down?'

The trunk is smooth against her back, a natural resting place for night wanderers.

'I think I'll have that cigarette after all.'

He lights it for her, his craggy features visible in the flame. Grey hair, lank from the salt water, his profile sharp against the moon's glow. She has assumed he was from New Zealand but his accent is American, a soft Southern drawl.

'You're Lauren?'

'Yes. Do you usually swim at midnight?'

'Usually.'

She draws on the cigarette but the taste of nicotine is too strong. She stubs it out and wonders what Steve would say if he could see her now. 'The grounds in Havenswalk are wonderful. Cathy says you've transformed the place.' She gestures vaguely into the distance behind them. 'Do you live in that house back there? I lost my way when I was trying to find the glow-worm grotto. I'm always losing my way, or so it seems since I came here.'

Perhaps he nods but he makes no other reply. The darkness is absolute. She wraps it around herself, sinks into its silence.

'We've both travelled a long way from home.' His voice startles her from her reverie.

'What part of America are you from?'

'North Carolina.'

'Do you return home often?'

'Not since my parents died.' His voice sinks. He is obviously familiar with her history. 'I lived in Ireland during the eighties.'

'Really? Where?'

'Northern Ireland. A bad scene.'

'It passed me by,' she replies. 'I was too young to care and when I became aware that doorstep shootings and bombing were not part of a natural process, I was too caught up in my own personal tragedy and cared even less.'

'I admire your honesty.'

'I'm not an honest person.'

'Frankness, then.'

'What were you doing there?'

'I was a priest.'

'A priest?'

Amused by her surprise, he slaps his bare chest. 'As you can see, I no longer wear the collar.'

No wonder the earlier words she overheard sounded familiar. Childhood incantations recited when she was a child. Star of the sea. Pray for us. Mother Most Admirable. Pray for us. Blessed Virgin. Pray for us.

'Any regrets?' she asks.

'Every day. Every night. In between I know I made the right decision.'

'So you're happy?'

'Content. For the moment.'

'Before then, what did you do?'

'I served with the US military in Vietnam. After the war ended, I drifted for a few years.'

Alcohol, she thinks, or maybe drugs, probably homelessness. She has no urge to enquire and he does not elaborate.

'I decided I was suited to the religious life,' he says. 'I would save the world through prayer.'

She hears the mockery in his voice and tries to equate the two. A soldier and a priest, each one imposing a particular order on society. Her parents protested against the war, flower power and free love, a heady intoxication. She remembers the photographs taken during the summer when they were students working in San Francisco, her father in a kaftan and beard, her mother with beads and flowers. Iconic images. This man also carries traces, no photographs, just scenes that he can never eradicate.

'And you?' he asks. 'What do you do when you're not star gazing?'

392

'Like you, I run from an ordained life.'

'Don't you ever grow tired?'

'Bone weary at the moment.' She laughs and lifts a pebble, presses its night cold surface against her skin.

'What age were you when your parents died?' The unexpectedness of his question takes her by surprise.

'Twelve. Cathy was eight. It was a long time ago.'

'When we are defined by tragedy, time is meaningless.'

'But we must find the means to pass it,' she replies. 'I seldom think about them.' She senses rather than notices his gaze fastening on her and rushes on. 'Or else they're so embedded in my psyche I can't cut them loose. I'm quite crazy, you see.'

She allows the stone to slip through her fingers, hears the dull thud as it hits the pebbles. Her father used to skim stones across the sea, hop, hop, hop, hop, plop. Echoes everywhere.

The man beside her taps his forehead in a parody of madness.

'In Vietnam, I killed men and never knew their names. I hear their screams. No matter how fast I run or how much silence I seek, they're trapped in my memory.'

She should leave now, flit into the darkness. Forget this mad priest with his hooded eyes and the scent of the lake rising from him.

'You want to run again.' He laughs, understanding her fear. Not a manic cackle but low, sympathetic. 'Go now. I'll direct you back to your chalet. I appreciate the time you've given me.'

'The voices you hear? Are you talking about schizophrenia?'

'The luminous mind? No, I'm not gifted with visions or divine voices. What I hear are reverberations of the suffering I imposed. It deserves to be heard so I listen.'

'Do they ever give you rest?'

'Even in the stillness of prayer, I hear them. But sometimes, yes, I find peace.'

He flicks his cigarette into the dark. She imagines his mind, mauled and stripped of rationality. Yes, she thinks, this is where I would come at night to still the memories, the deprivation in Rebecca's voice, Julie's sobs, Cathy's endless questions about that night. Her fault, all her fault. Sugar plum fairy, selfish, demanding, destructive.

'We cruised Milford Sound during our tour,' she says. 'There are trees growing from moss on the cliffs.'

'I've seen such forests,' he replies.

'I feel like those trees since I came here. My roots waiting to be wrenched free and send me hurtling . . .'

'Where will you land?'

'In a ditch with nettles in my mouth.'

He remains silent. What can he say that will not seem banal, inadequate?

'I used to cut myself,' she continues. 'Make myself bleed. It made no difference. It should have, shouldn't it? Pain? It should bring oblivion but my memories were too dark to penetrate, no matter how deep the cut.' She thrusts the words defiantly towards him. 'I want to bleed again but I'm not . . . I'm not . . .'

'And now you will give life?'

'Yes.' She is unsure if she uttered the word aloud or if it simply swam into her consciousness, embryonic yet fully formed. 'I was told I could never have children. But they were wrong.' She touches her stomach, flat and hard and full.

'To grow from shallow ground and keep reaching towards the light takes courage,' he says. 'You're wondrously brave.'

Wondrously brave. She repeats his words; the unfamiliar nuances . . . wondrously brave. Such foolishness. She is brittle and beautiful but never brave.

'One more swim before I leave.' He flings the towel from him and strides naked towards the lake.

She pulls her dress over her head. The pebbles are sharp against her feet but she runs quickly and feels no pain. The water is silver-streaked and shockingly cold. She screams as she falls forward, swims until she is breathless, moon jewels falling from her fingers. She turns and floats on her back, unconcerned by his nearness when she hears him splashing close by.

They return together to the shore, their nakedness merging into the shadows. She dresses quickly, dragging her clothes over her wet skin. It is time to leave. Their ships have passed. She has no comforting words to scare away his demons and he does not demand them. Scrambled brain . . . tangled . . . mangled . . . she will never know if he is crazy or blessed.

They exchange a brief handshake and an unspoken understanding that the secrets they exchanged belong only to them. Above her the stars move in an unfamiliar sphere. No Plough or North Star to guide her way. And such a moon shining tonight, round and golden as a Buddha's belly.

61

Day Six

In Abel Tasman Park, the llamas peel their thick lips back from their teeth and slit their eyes against the rising flurry of dust and leaves. Apart from their ears, which are laid back inquisitively, their expressions are aloof, almost disdainful as they gaze from behind their fence upon the curious tourists. The wind gusts. Rebecca holds on to her sunhat. The purple dahlias bow into an approaching squall.

'This'll scupper our plan,' says Tim. 'Pity. I hoped to take a kayak out on the lake.'

'Conor wanted me to see the llamas. At least we've had a chance to do that. It's been a wonderful few days, Tim.'

'Yes. It has. And Cathy will be married in two days' time.'

'I'm aware of that.'

'So aware that you're unable to think of anything else.'

'Is it so obvious?'

He smiles and turns her towards the Jeep. 'If we start now, we should be back in Havenswalk by this afternoon.'

★ ★ ★

Mel taps on the door of his room. The guests plan to spend the day touring the wine galleries in Blenheim. His parents are busy with last-minute preparations and need some time on their own. Mel is dressed in jeans and a navy jumper with a high neck. Only for her jet-black earrings with the crystals in the centre, no one would know she was a Goth. Conor shakes his head when she asks if he would like to come with them.

Last night destroyed everything. He can never look at her again without remembering the humiliation. She hesitates at the door. If she tries to discuss what happened, he will sink through the floor.

'I'm meeting Oliver later,' he says.

She nods. 'Enjoy your day.'

A short while later Conor hears car doors slamming. He looks out the window. His uncle's Jag and the car his aunts hired are parked in front of Havenswalk. He watches Julie sit behind the wheel, Alma and Mel settle beside her. Robbie sits in the back of the Jag. As Lauren walks from the Kea chalet, her floppy sunhat is whisked away in a sudden gust of wind. She runs across the lawn and retrieves it. The forecast is for storm conditions later in the day.

★ ★ ★

In the attic Conor shifts broken sun chairs and loungers. He heaves crates of unused crockery to one side, checks boxes of documents, books and magazines. The letters have to be here. Where else would she put them? Havenswalk is an open space for so many people, the attic her only private domain.

An hour later he is covered with dust and still searching. His mother is a hoarder. Has she ever thrown anything out? Next year, when work begins on the attic conversion, she will have some job removing all the junk. He unfastens the leather straps on a large chest and rummages through rows of neatly folded clothes: T-shirts and school uniforms, a pair of 501s he wore until he could no longer breathe in them, parka jackets and anoraks, even baby clothes that smell of mothballs. He finds the picnic basket at the bottom of the chest and removes the bunched sheets of paper. The sun flits in and out of the clouds, slants through the skylight as he crouches among the jumble. A long-dead fly quivers in the centre of an abandoned web. What a dark world she created with her graveyards and fascination with death. What a lost dark world.

She calls his name. Afraid he will sneeze and betray his whereabouts, he stays perfectly still until her voice fades. She always knows where to find him. Wincing from stiffness, he clasps the basket under his arm and clicks the attic door behind him. He descends the staircase to the privacy of his room and continues reading.

She knocks on his door. He checks the bed. The basket is out of sight.

'Lunch is ready.' She crosses the floor and sits on the edge of his bed.

'I'm not hungry.'

'I hope you don't intend going out on the lake.'

'I was out already.'

'What's the matter, Conor?' She always knows when something is wrong. The letter he was reading is under the pillow but he is terrified she will discover it.

'Nothing.' He stiffens when she puts her arms around him.

'I want you always to remember something, Conor. Love expands. You must never be jealous of Kevin. What I feel for him does not take away one iota of the love I have for you. It never will. Do you understand?' He nods, embarrassed by the tears shimmering in her eyes.

'Alma keeps saying Rebecca will be back for your wedding.'

'Perhaps she's right.'

'You don't believe it?'

She shrugs, as if the conversation bores her. 'Who knows?'

'You do. It's your fault that she's gone.'

'Oh, Conor, why do you have to be so difficult?' She rises and walks from the room.

He waits until her footsteps fade before drawing the letter from under his pillow. He hears Sandy barking, the clink and clunk of saucepans from the kitchen, Hannah's shrieking laughter travelling upwards.

He stops reading and walks the length of his room until his heart stops thumping. He does not want to know anything more about her young, troubled life. But moments later he is reading again, devouring the pages.

Oh Mum . . . Mum!

I need to tell you what happened. I can't tell anyone else, never, ever until the day I die. Rebecca will kill me stone dead . . . what have I done?

He lays the letters to one side and listens to the wind rise, the boughs groan. The rata blossom will flutter across the lawn in drifts and Lyle's white roses will scatter.

'Jeremy Anderson.' He speaks his father's name aloud for the first time. Six syllables: Jer-em-y-And-er-son . . . son . . . son . . . son. He should have guessed. Kevin Mulvaney was too neat, too perfect. What happened to his mother was not neat or sweet but something so dreadful she has never been prepared to speak it aloud. Everyone knows. He understands Rebecca's hostility, Kevin's hesitation when they first met. He remembers the feline slant of Lauren's eyes when he told her she was beautiful. Whose voice had she heard prattling? Whose smile had she seen? And Mel in the grotto. The shaky feeling sweeping over him whenever he thinks about her. He wanted to snap her suspenders against her thighs, hitch up her skirt, lift her in his arms and do it to her right there and then. Sick, he is sick like his father, and he can never tell anyone, especially his mother who must have shown Kevin the letters, shared her past with him, left her son in ignorance of the other half of his existence.

She says love conquers everything yet she lived a lie, raped by his father, flash Jeremy Anderson with his flash car and his flash words and his flashing smile. What else can she feel but hatred every time she looks at his son? Her silences make sense now, the way she wrapped herself from him, the photograph she hid, the lost years she denied him, and how she reclaimed them on a lie . . . a lie. Everything he believes has been snatched from him.

Lyle is not in the garden, nor in the walled herbarium. He comes and goes from Havenswalk as he pleases, his timetable known only to himself. He must have returned home. The marquee billows a warning when Conor runs past on his way to the boathouse. Lyle's shack is only five minutes away, longer if he goes by road. With Lyle, Conor can talk about anything. Lyle will just nod and smoke his cigarettes, blowing smoke rings, but he will listen, take in every word. Conor always feels good after talking to him, as if clean water has washed through his brain and he knows exactly what to do.

He slides his kayak into the lake and pulls on the oars, his strong arms straining. He no longer understands love. It's too complicated. He wants hate. It's a tough, gut feeling he can understand. Lyle was once a soldier and soldiers have to hate to survive. His heart is a drum, thoombing . . . thoombing . . . thoombing. The water rears and roars boisterously around him.

★ ★ ★

The wind flattens the ribboned banks of blue hibiscus crowning the coast. Willows swish their green tendrils against the Jeep and the swaying manes of pampas grass bow to the ground. The rain begins to fall as Tim enters Havenswalk. The front door is open. Rain slants into the hall. Rebecca enters, shouts Cathy's name but hears no answering call. Ruthie and Hannah are not in the kitchen. The wedding cake sits on a stand: tricoloured tiers with a leprechaun on top. Rebecca winces, then laughs. She calls Cathy's name again.

'Rebecca!' She turns around. Tim stands in the doorway. Rain soaks his hair, glistens on his beard. 'Conor . . . ' He stops, presses his hand to his chest and gasps.

'What's wrong with Conor?'

'Cathy's worried sick. She found some stuff in his room — '

'Drugs?'

'No. Old letters. He's on the lake.'

She runs to the entrance and stares through the rain. Figures blur and move through the grey haze.

'She checked the boathouse.' Tim grips Rebecca's hand as they run towards the lake. 'His kayak is missing.'

'I've seen him handling a kayak. He's skilled on the water. He's going to be fine. Don't dare think otherwise. *Don't* dare . . . ' She speaks with authority — the situation demands it — but her heart pounds as she draws closer to the lake. A dark shape rises from the jetty and hurls itself against her. The fuggy smell of wet fur rises from

Conor's dog. She steadies herself and hurries on. Sandy, whining, runs beside her.

The turquoise sheen of the lake has been replaced by a metallic grey swell that heaves against the jetty and swirls the pebbles, dragging them against the grain of the shore.

'How long has Conor been missing?' Her feet skid on the pebbles as she hurries towards Cathy.

Her sister's hair blows around her but otherwise she is rigid, her arms clasped across her chest. She seems rooted, her feet submerged in the eddying flow, blind to the rain as she screams her son's name, repeats it like a mantra, defying the wind to toss it back at her.

'Cathy . . . it's Becks. It's all right . . . everything's going to be OK.'

For an instant Cathy seems incapable of seeing her. Then her eyelids flicker, her mouth moves. 'He knows about Jeremy.' Her voice is highly pitched, almost incoherent. 'Oh Jesus . . . if anything's happened to him . . . '

Rebecca tries to hold her but she struggles free and begins to weep. She looks upwards when a helicopter flies low over the lake and struggles for composure.

'Kevin's organised a helicopter. Lyle's taken out the motorboat — '

'Which direction did the motorboat take?' Tim asks.

Her breath rasps as she points to the left. 'I think Conor was going to Lyle's house. There's no other reason he should be on the lake. I warned him . . . '

Tim makes his way to the boathouse and

launches a kayak, whips the paddles against the choppy waters. Rebecca opens an umbrella she grabbed from the hall in Havenswalk. She holds it over Cathy but a gust of wind whips it inside out. Cathy stares at the bent spokes poking through the fabric, then runs along the jetty towards the small boat Conor uses for fishing, It strains at its moorings, bucking the swell and nudging the wooden piles supporting the jetty.

'Don't be crazy.' Rebecca shouts as Cathy wades into the water and attempts to climb aboard.

A helicopter passing overhead distracts Cathy's attention. As it swoops then rises again, she looks upwards and Rebecca, seizing the opportunity, clambers into the boat.

'Keep watch.' She cups her hands to her mouth and forces the words towards her sister. 'Your son needs you here when he returns.'

★ ★ ★

The boat shoots forward when Rebecca releases the throttle and turns starboard. Almost immediately the mountain and forests are obscured. All her attention is focused on penetrating the gloom. Darkness comes quickly here, no lingering twilight leaching light from the sky. It will settle early this evening, aided by the rain and overcast clouds. Icy water washes over her and the turbulence increases as she approaches a cluster of small humped-back islands.

At first, when the paddle floats into view, she

hopes it is a piece of debris or a walking stick, discarded by a trekker. But she recognises its shape, the blades spanning out from the black pole, and knows that this abandoned paddle is the sole clue to his whereabouts. She has to remain calm. He probably had a spare paddle on board. She channels between the hulking islands, instinctively steering from starboard to port, terrified the propeller will catch on submerged rock. She peers into the broiling water and glimpses tree roots. The growth on the islands is sparse and stunted but the roots thrash underwater like the tentacles of a malicious octopus. She recoils from the sight and wipes the rain from her eyes. The lash of wind in the branches is a mournful dirge but, apart from the lone paddle, the lake refuses to offer up its secrets.

She circles the islands, holding the boat on a steady course. She is about to search further along the lake when she spots his kayak. Upside down and sleek as a gliding seal, it floats into view. She draws nearer and leans forward, hoping to find him clinging to the upturned hull. This hope is quickly dashed. She attempts to bring her boat in at a right angle and overturn the kayak but the lake hurls it from her reach.

The rain stops. A saffron hue streams from an opening in the clouds and settles over the water. The washed-out mountain peaks, stippled as a child's painting, swim into view. Dark forests march like a khaki army across the slopes.

A heron flies past, its wings gliding on air

thermals. The wings fold gracefully when the bird lands on the nearest island, white feathers fluttering as it steps over the spiky grass. It poses motionless by the water's edge and balances effortlessly on one leg. Rebecca remembers the lone heron that once maintained the same stoic vigil on the shore of the Broadmeadow Estuary and the memory, pushing its way through her turbulent fears, slows her progress for an instant, swings her closer to the island. The white heron dips its beak, points it like an arrow into the dangling roots. Something is tangled in the black tentacles. Rebecca wants to name it — flotsam, jetsam, a bulky wedge of driftwood. Anything other than the sprawled body of a young man. When she screams his name, the sound is indistinguishable from the anguish she heard earlier in his mother's voice. Her arms ache from the strain of rowing but she is immune to the pain. She turns starboard, her cries melding with the slackening wind. She forces herself to stay silent. Tears and hysterics will not help the situation.

Jesus . . . Jesus . . . Jesus, help me. The familiar refrains of childhood pleas come easily to her as she eases the boat through the churning water. The density of the roots assures her that she will not crash against a submerged reef. A branch, jutting like an elbow from the island, had provided him with a handhold before his legs became entangled. He must have been too exhausted or terrified to drag himself free. She steers closer, using one of the overhanging trees as a handhold, and moors the boat. She clambers up an incline, slipping on decaying leaf and moss. The top half of his body is sprawled between two stunted trees. Their scrawny trunks lean precariously over the water and his fingers still clutch the dangling vines that loop from the branch. The heron waits, impervious to her efforts. She crawls towards her nephew's body. The roots are knotted around the calf of one leg. She leans into the water and forces them loose. His face, tilted to one side, is smeared with a foul-smelling fungus, his skin scratched and bruised. Blood drains from a cut under his eye and seeps darkly from the corner of his mouth. His arm hangs at an awkward angle, broken, she suspects, when he fought to drag himself ashore.

She checks for his pulse, pressing her fingers against his neck, his wrist, leans closer in the hope of feeling his breath on her face. The blood around his mouth, she realises, flows from a deep gash above his lip. When his pulse stirs, such a faint flutter, she is unsure if it is his heartbeat or her own desperation. Her mobile phone was lost in the water, not that it would be any use under these circumstances. Gently, she turns him over and presses her hands firmly against his chest. She begins mouth-to-mouth resuscitation. His waxy face shows no sign of life. The island provides only a primitive shelter and the icy chill seeping from the rocky surface adds to her distress.

She moves from his mouth to his chest and back to his mouth. She shouts at him to stay with her and forces her warm breath into him.

Akona called it the Ha, the breath of life, but this is a one-sided transaction, where time is limited and second chances rarely allowed. Everything has a reason, an explanation, a solution, she tells him. Water dribbles from his lips. His breathing is shallow. Hypothermia has set in. She covers him with ferns, talking all the time about her sanctuary and the things they will do together when he comes to stay. His eyelids open once and close again. Shortly afterwards, she hears the whirring of the helicopter as it glides low over the lake. Kevin leans from the open doorway. She snaps a thick-stemmed fern and waves it like a flag, a Maori signpost. The heron rises. The slender neck curves and the wings soar above the lake as it flies into the saffron evening.

62

Day Seven

It is after midnight when Rebecca leaves the hospital. Her injuries are mainly bruises and cuts, no broken bones. Conor is in an oxygen tent. Drips feed fluid into his arms. Soon he will undergo a CAT scan to see if there are any signs of brain damage or changes in his cerebral blood flow. His arm is badly broken but it will mend in time. The other wounds, the internal ones, will not heal so easily. Cathy will remain overnight in the hospital with him.

Rebecca is thankful for Tim's silence as he drives her back to Havenswalk. She was supposed to remain in hospital for observation but she discharged herself, knowing time would heal her body. They enter the Takahē chalet. It is the same as when she left it yet she senses a difference, which, she realises, is within herself. What had irritated her, the deliberate touches, the blending of textures, colours and materials, now form a harmonious whole. The chalets surrounding them are in darkness. The rescue was over when the others arrived back from Blenheim. They drove straight to the hospital where they stayed until Cathy persuaded them to return to Havenswalk.

Exhausted from the search, Tim is soon asleep

but Rebecca's thoughts race as she lies restlessly beside him. The room is too warm and her body aches all over. She steps gingerly onto the balcony and watches car headlights wavering between the trees. The car brakes outside Havenswalk. A figure approaches the entrance. As the automatic outside light switches on, she recognises Kevin's rangy figure. He is visible for a moment as he opens the door then staggers backwards as Sandy lurches at him. He leaves the dog outside and slams the door. Sandy's bark is outraged and Rebecca, taking pity on the dog, slips on her jeans and jacket. By the time she reaches the house, Sandy has disappeared.

A light shines in an upstairs room. She opens the front door and calls Kevin's name. The silence is oppressive rather than tranquil, as if Havenswalk, which usually resounds with voices and soft background music, has also succumbed to the turmoil of the day. He leans over the banisters, his expression turning from hope to dismay when he recognises her.

'You sound like Cathy,' he says and disappears from view. She hears his footsteps on the wooden floorboards and follows him to the bedroom. A battered suitcase, which looks as if it has accompanied him to many destinations, lies open on the bed. He flings clothes into it, pulls underwear from drawers, drags shoes and a pair of mountain boots from under the bed. He stops packing when he sees her hesitating at the door and beckons her into the room.

'What's going on, Kevin?' She watches the

411

pyramid of clothes in the centre of the case growing higher.

'Cathy's cancelled the wedding. I'll find somewhere to stay in Nelson until I decide what to do.'

'But only for a few days, surely?' She is unable to hide her astonishment. 'It's understandable given the circumstances, and when — '

'It's over, Rebecca.' His harsh expression defies her to argue with him.

She sits on the bed and carefully places the arms of a jumper cross-wise, folds it into a neat square. 'She's distraught at the moment. When Conor is better — '

'Conor is all that matters now.' Again he interrupts, as if he cannot bear to listen to a logical argument. He stops packing and sits beside her. 'You told her that our deception would flail her to the bone. It almost did.'

'Words . . . that's all they were, Kevin. I was angry — '

'And I was as complicit in the deceit as she was.'

'Why on earth did you go along with it?' She had wanted to ask him that question since the night she arrived but her anger would have made his answer irrelevant. Now, she asks it from a genuine need to understand the complexities of their relationship.

He stares at her hands as she smooths the creases on his jumper and tells her how he struggled to come to terms with Conor's belief. His eagerness was palpable, and Kevin, remembering the loss of his own father when he was a

412

boy, became a party to Cathy's deceit. Death pulled them together when they were children. It was the link that drew them together again.

'I've always loved her . . . always,' he says. 'When you accused me of being the father of her child, I wished I was. I met Conor by sheer fluke. But, suddenly, I had a second chance. What seemed miraculous became miraculous. Do you believe in miracles?'

She shakes her head, 'I've never seen any — '

'That's because they don't exist.'

'Until today on the lake.'

'Until today,' he repeats. 'You could easily have missed him. Cathy is not going to tempt fate a second time.'

He takes the jumper and presses it into the suitcase, flattens the pyramid and snaps the locks closed. 'On the night she left, I hung up on her. I was sick with jealousy. If I hadn't . . . who knows . . . she might not have run away.'

'Yes, she would.' Rebecca nods and rises from the bed. 'What other option did I give her? But there are always other options. *Always.* Please, don't give up now.'

'I've tried to change her mind.' He lifts his suitcase, waits for her to leave the room. 'It's what she wants, Rebecca. We lied to Conor. Wilfully, deliberately lied to him. The reasons don't matter — '

'They mattered to Cathy.' She grabs his arms, forces him to listen to her. 'To protect me from the truth, she was prepared to abandon her sisters, her friends, everything familiar and dear to her. But the truth, no matter how heavy, is a burden that can always be borne. Tim has made me realise that truth. Conor should be the one who decides. It's in his remit to forgive you. Allow him that right.'

Kevin shakes his head. His case is closed, his mind decided. He roughly embraces her and strides from the room. She listens to him driving away, Sandy's bark following him down the avenue. She thinks of Heron Cove, two children, their knees hooked into the sturdy boughs of the chestnut tree, Cathy and Kevin, swinging upside down, everything upside down, the two of them filled with the giddy knowledge that their world would be normal again once they returned to earth.

★　★　★

Rebecca stops outside a door with Conor's name written above a 'Do Not Intrude' notice. Cathy's letters are scattered over his bed. She gathers them into a neat pile and sits by the window. The past flickers and comes into focus again, each momentous event viewed through the prism of Cathy's gaze. All the misunderstandings and missed opportunities, the ignored danger signals, their heedless race towards maturity. Rebecca folds the final letter and places them back in the wicker basket. She hopes there is a place where angels read letters at night and bring comfort to a lost child who was not allowed to cry.

A white heron, Lyle said, is a rare bird, seldom seen, and then usually on estuaries. Once upon a time the Maori used their feathers as adornments. If Lauren can swim with dolphins and angels fly at midnight, than a white heron can save her nephew's life. Rebecca returns to the chalet and waits for morning.

★ ★ ★

Conor's condition stabilises overnight. He is off oxygen, his CAT scan clear and he has been transferred from intensive care to a small single bed ward. Rebecca places fruit and chocolate on his bedside locker and sits beside him. He is propped upright, pillows heaped at his back, his arm set in a cast. Already, he looks healthier, rested.

'That was some journey you took, young man,' she says. 'Don't you ever listen to the weather forecast?'

'I can handle a kayak . . . usually.'

'But not in the middle of a storm. And I'm not talking about the weather.'

He breaks off a square of chocolate and chews it. 'She lied to me about my father.'

'Yes, she certainly did.'

He gulps the chocolate down, then immediately gags. Rebecca reaches for the bowl and holds it under his chin.

'Bad choice.' When he recovers, she takes the chocolate from him. 'Perhaps tomorrow.'

'Kevin's *not* my father.'

'You've no idea how much he wishes he was.'

'She lied — '

'Can you accept that she did so for your sake?'

'She had no right to keep the truth from me.'

'Was she right to keep it from me?'

He lies back against the pillows. His freckles are stark against his chalky complexion. 'That's different. She ran away so that you could be happy. She didn't want to hurt you.'

'Nor you. Alma believes people sometimes make the wrong decisions for the right reasons. When the lie your mother told you became reality, it brought happiness into your lives. Would you have wanted her to walk away from that happiness?'

His chest rises and falls, each breath labouring against his desire not to cry. He jerks his arm, winces with shock. 'Tell me about him . . . that fucking lying bastard you married.'

'You can't hurt the dead with words, Conor.'

'But you can hate them . . . and I hate his guts.' He has inherited his mother's defiant tone.

'Yet you want to know about him.'

'Yes.' He blinks furiously as Rebecca talks about a man he will never know. She had air-brushed Jeremy from her life until even his memory seemed insubstantial. But not any more. She hears again his persuasive answers and excuses, his easy words and the whispering murmurs that captured her heart and betrayed Cathy's innocence. She holds Conor's uninjured hand, their thumbs linking. The wound, where the bite of a frightened horse left a pale scar, is almost invisible against her bruised skin. Yes, she replies, when Conor demands to know if he resembles his father. She has recognised many similarities but she sees them as Conor's

416

strengths, not his weaknesses. He drifts asleep, listening to her voice.

★ ★ ★

Outside in the corridor, Cathy holds a Styrofoam cup of cold coffee between her hands, unaware that the liquid is tilting dangerously close to the edge.

'Is Conor alone?' She half rises, her gaze flicking over Rebecca's shoulder towards the ward door. 'I must go back to him.'

'He's sleeping now. Let him rest. You and I need to talk.'

Cathy sinks down again, her shoulders hunched. 'Thank you seems so inadequate. I don't have the words, Rebecca.'

'They're not necessary.'

'I've never been able to explain anything to you — '

'I never gave you the space to do so . . . not then, not the other night.'

'I'm sorry.' Cathy appears to be speaking more to herself than to Rebecca. 'It was a selfish decision to invite you here. But I thought . . . I thought . . . I don't know what I thought. That was always the problem, wasn't it? Not thinking.'

'Kevin loves you. Please, don't turn your back on him.'

'But my son hates me.'

'Jeremy used to say that hate and love — '

'I know what he used to say.'

'A fine wire vibrating. Conor's anger will go. Everything passes, Cathy.' Rebecca touches her

arm. 'Mam told me to look after you but I didn't
. . . not that night and all those other nights. But
Alma did. She did everything I failed to do — '

'That's nonsense.'

'It's my truth, Cathy. I read your letters.'

Cathy bends her head and allows Rebecca to
take the cup from her.

'Do you still write to her?'

'Not for years . . . not since I left home.'

'If you were to write to her now, how would
she reply?'

'She would tell me to look after my son.'

'You already do that, Cathy. Answer my
question.'

'I don't know — '

'She would tell you to stop living with the
past. She would order you, as I'm doing now, to
embrace your future.'

'I hurt the people I love — '

Rebecca leans across the chairs and places her
hand over her sister's mouth. 'Stop talking,
Cathy. Be silent for a little while and listen to our
mother's voice.'

She holds her sister's hands and waits for the
grief to wash over them. When it comes, they
slide into its healing strength.

63

Day Eight

Lauren watches the marquee being disassembled. Lyle speaks to the men, who work efficiently, loading the poles and canvas into the truck. Steve joins her on the balcony.

'Shame about that,' he says. 'It would have been a magnificent setting.'

She nods in agreement. Her view of the lake is clearer since the marquee came down. She returns to the bedroom and removes her dress from the wardrobe. Steve unzips his case and removes his suit. They dress in silence for the wedding.

* * *

The scent of the white roses, forming an arch around the door, fills Conor's ward. Kevin is as nervous as any bridegroom waiting for his bride to arrive. At a signal from Lyle, Julie, accompanying herself on her mandolin, begins to sing an old Irish folk song. Under her breath, Lauren sings the words with her. Her voice will falter if she sings aloud.

My young love said to me,
'My mother won't mind

And my father won't slight you
For your lack of kind.'
And she stepped away from me
And this she did say,
'It will not be long, love,
Till our wedding day.'

Cathy steps through the rose bower. Alma
walks behind her. They approach Lyle, who
stands waiting at the foot of Conor's bed. Two
candles, a vase of flowers and a crucifix have
been placed on a small table. Lyle has given
up his right to dress in consecrated robes but,
even without vestments, even wearing an old
suit that has the creases of decades in its
folds, the simple ceremony he performs has all
the solemnity of a sacred ritual. Rituals are
important. Lauren carried them out in the
silence of her room, her eyes full of
plummeting steel.

Conor is sleeping when they leave him.
Cathy places the roses in a vase beside his
bed. Lauren remembers the red rose she
placed in her hair on the morning of
departure. She remembers the red roses that
filled her ward when Rebecca brought her
home from London. They were delivered in
bouquets, one for each day. At night, unable
to breathe from their scent, she had asked the
nurse on duty to remove them.

In the hospital canteen, a wedding breakfast
has been prepared. What an emotional journey
they took to reach this point, Lauren thinks. All
the planning and decision-making reduced to

this moment in a hospital canteen. The bride and groom cut the wedding cake, which has been transported, complete with the leprechaun, to the hospital. They raise their glasses to happiness. Some of the patients and staff enter and join the celebrations. Rebecca stands to make a speech but Steve is there before her. He wishes the happy couple lots of luck and little ones. The guests clap politely when he finishes. Cathy holds hands with her sisters and when they stand together, they form an unbroken link of memory.

⋆ ⋆ ⋆

Lauren enters the glow-worm grotto. This time there are no missed turns or leafy cul-de-sacs. The splendour of the pulsating light draws her deeper into the clearing. She is standing in a fragile space. She can destroy it with a kick, a flick of her fingers, but destruction seems obscene in this glistening grotto.

Steve calls her name. His feet trample leaves, snap wood. The beam of a torch sweeps across the grotto.

'Turn it off,' she says.

He ignores her request and draws nearer, shines the torch in her face. 'What the hell is going on, Lauren? I've been searching for you for over an hour.'

'You were sleeping when I left.'

'What has that to do with anything? I thought something . . . I've been out of my mind with worry.'

'Why?' She steps back from the beam.

'Why?' he shouts. 'You disappear in the middle of the night. Why shouldn't I worry? You don't even have a mobile that I can contact you on.'

'Turn off the torch and look around you, Steve. It's so beautiful.'

'If you insist.' For an instant the grotto darkens but there is no time to see the clusters of light before he switches the torch on again.

'Come back to the chalet, princess.' He holds her arm, turns her towards the entrance to the grotto. 'It's been a long day. You must be exhausted — '

'Steve, when we stayed with the Maori woman up by the glaciers, I threw my phone into a lake.'

'You what?'

'Yes . . . into Akona's lake.'

'Why on earth did you do that?'

'To stop you controlling me.'

'Control you? Since when did cherish become a form of control?'

'You don't cherish me, Steve. You possess me. I find it difficult to breathe when you stand too close to me.'

'There's nothing wrong with your breathing when you're spending my money.'

'I don't want your money. When we return to Ireland, I'm leaving you.'

A simple statement. Three words that will change her life. Three words that can never be retracted. She feels lightheaded with relief. The consequences will come later.

'You're leaving me?' He sounds indulgent, rather than angry. 'And how, may I ask, do you expect to manage on your own?'

'I will, somehow.'

'Lauren, you have never stood on your own feet since you were born. It's a little late in the day to change. You're over-wrought and not thinking clearly. Do I have to remind you of the times — '

'No reminder is necessary. I understand the risk I'm taking. It's my choice.' She shudders, aware that she is throwing aside the affluence that has cushioned her against guilt.

'You have the nerve to talk about choice.' His anger is as refined as silk. 'It was your choice to marry me. Your choice to be pampered and spoiled. Your choice to take everything I offered you. Your choice to engage in the occasional dalliance, which I tolerated because I knew you were too insecure to cope without me. I desired you, Lauren, but I paid the price, so don't give me any balderdash about control. Being a trophy wife is a hell of a lot safer than opening those delicate veins.'

He tightens his grip on her arm when she tries to walk away. He turns her palm upwards and exposes it to the torch.

'Money, Lauren. Do you really believe you can walk away and expect me to support you?'

'I have some money — '

'Have you really? May I ask what you've been doing? Saving euro in a jar behind my back?'

She pulls free and walks away from him. As she emerges from the grotto she breaks into a run, her footsteps drumming as she passes the Kea chalet and bangs on the door of the Silvereye. Julie answers the door. Without asking questions, she beckons Lauren inside and closes the door.

64

Day Nine

Young people, mainly students, have come to hear his music but older people also crowd the auditorium. Lauren glances at a programme she picked up on the way into the auditorium. His biography is short, written in English and Maori. Six sentences: how easy it is to condense a life and prioritise the essential facts. Niran Gordon, composer, whose latest work is dedicated to his wife, the violinist, Gloria Gordon, who drowned in the tsunami. Her photograph, the ceremonial costume, is instantly recognisable. His own photograph is positioned beside it, a stamp-sized image, Asian eyes and strong Kiwi chin.

The musicians begin to play. His music fills the chambers of her mind. In this requiem to his wife, a beautiful woman in the wrong place at the wrong time, Lauren hears the tsunami rise, the juggernaut roar. Which of them made the decision to take that short Christmas break, she wonders. Did Gloria suggest it? Did he surprise her with air tickets? Did they argue over it, one or the other claiming a too-heavy work schedule then capitulate because they were in love and longed to be together? Cause and effect. A divine hand at work or a chaotic ruthless indifference?

As his lamenting music rises and collapses

425

around her, she closes her eyes until all she hears is the shuddering guilt of survival.

Niran Gordon is a survivor, like herself. A survivor who understands that love, like death, can happen in an instant, between one heartbeat and the next, and be lost in that same blink of time. Was that what she sensed when she first saw him? What stopped her running terrified through the streets of Bangkok? What brought them together with such abandoned passion? She grips the arms of her chair to prevent herself rising and leaving the auditorium.

An instant of silence greets the end of the performance. The audience breathes a collective sigh as if they have been released from an ungovernable force and a solitary clap resounds through the auditorium. The applause rises and sweeps the audience to its feet. He walks on stage and bows in acknowledgement. He is dressed in white, the colour of mourning.

'Your music speaks a terrifying language.' A young woman in the front row asks the first question. 'Who inspired you?'

'My wife, Gloria.' His lips kiss her name. 'She is my inspiration in life and in death.'

He speaks calmly about the tsunami, instructs the students to play various movements that correspond to its destructive power. Lauren shrinks back into her seat. Rage river rage . . . rage towards the night ocean . . . She senses the dedication needed to compose with such controlled abandon. His music is more demanding than any wife or lover.

426

'Did it exorcise your grief?' an elderly man asks.

Niran Gordon shakes his head. 'There are moments when I forget. But that is all they are . . . moments.'

When he has answered all their questions and left the podium, Lauren rises with the audience and makes her way to the foyer. He calls her name as she approaches the exit. She stops and waits until he reaches her. His white trousers are cut just above his ankles and sit snugly against his long brown legs. The high collar of his tunic is decorated with a filigree of gold embroidery. Instinctively, her eyes are drawn to the break on the bridge of his nose. She imagines the crunch of bone and gristle, the blood spurting, his indifference to the pain as he called his wife's name again and again in the throes of the tsunami.

'I sensed your presence in the auditorium,' he says. 'Just as I sensed you in my house. You left your scent behind.'

'It was unforgivable of me to intrude.'

'I wish you'd stayed.'

She shakes her head, holds her arms stiffly by her side. 'You spoke well today. Your music is powerful. I wanted to hear it live.'

'When are you leaving?'

'Tomorrow evening.'

'Can I see you before you go?'

'For how long? A moment . . . two . . . three?'

'Since Gloria died . . . ' he hesitates, aware that people have gathered and are politely waiting for them to finish their conversation.

'There has been no one but you. Those times we spent together . . . they were more than moments. Much more.'

'But not enough,' she says. 'This is not the right time for you . . . or for me.'

She sees the same realisation in his own eyes. His gaze is steadfast when he speaks again. 'Later in the year I'll be in London. Perhaps then?'

'Later in the year . . . who knows? I have to go now.' Unable to say goodbye she turns and walks away. She hails a taxi without difficulty. The driver is silent as he drives towards the airport. Two butterflies dance before the windscreen, twirl around each other, wings fluttering in a giddy, aerial courtship that ends abruptly when they are dashed against the glass. The driver spurts water on the windscreen. The wipers whip into action. The smear disappears. Lauren's throat tightens. Chaos and destruction. Only a breath away from those who dance briefly in sunshine.

Twilight has settled when she returns to Havenswalk. Steve's presence is still in the chalet. She smells his aftershave lotion but the shelf where it stood is empty. He has left a mobile phone on the table. A blue light flashes. She checks the screen, reads his text. 'Phone me when this madness is over. You belong to me and those who lose their way always return to the one who cherishes them.'

Pebbles crunch under her feet as she walks along the shore. Tawny clouds fill the lake with radiance. The turbulence that almost swallowed

428

her nephew is a tranquil mirror with no distortions. All the fire and the fury, rising and dying, transforming, creating new life, restoring memories. Lauren allows the blade to fall from her fingers. A tiny splash, imperceptible ripples spreading outwards but strong enough to shake the order of the world.

Epilogue

Dear Mum,

For fifteen years I never wrote to you. Never yearned to pick up a pen and pour out my heart. But now that my sisters have left, I feel the need to cling to something that was once familiar. It seems strange to write to you on a laptop but you were never to know the miracle of email. The trivial and the terrible relayed around the world in seconds. Communications have improved beyond your wildest imaginings . . . on the technology side, that is. The other kind, the-word-of-mouth, is as cocked up as it ever was.

At the hospital, Rebecca's face was wet with tears when she said goodbye to Conor. Already, he is counting the weeks until September when we plan to visit Ireland. I'll show him familiar places and walk with him along the estuary road where the swans once swam at high tide. The shore is now indented with car parking spaces and the bird sanctuary is straddled by an elevated bypass. But Rebecca says the birds still fly unafraid between the massive pillars and the swans remain unruffled by passing traffic. Yes, she held my hand when I asked, yes, indeed, the heron still stands and guards the water's edge.

I will return from Ireland without my son. He intends spending a year working in Rebecca's sanctuary before applying for a place in Trinity. In the short time she spent with him, I saw the bond between them strengthen and grow. I suspect she will become the best thing in his life. I've tried hard not to be jealous. It's an unworthy emotion but a human one.

Tim will come to Ireland with us. Long-distance romance has the odds stacked against it but they are determined to give it a chance.

Lauren is living with Mel until she finds her own place. She has some money in her bank account, an inheritance from Gramps and the money from the sale of Heron Cove. It's a pittance when weighted against Steve's treasure chest but will tide her over the coming months. Niran Gordon, she claims, was the catalyst, but not her reason for leaving Steve. I know the man, not personally, but through reputation. Alma and I once attended a recital of his music. He is slight and intense and has, I suspect, stolen my sister's heart. She made no further effort to contact him before leaving.

Does a man have the right to know he is to be a father? Will he handle that right, abuse it, discard it, deny it, reject it, trample it into indifference, whitewash it? Jeremy kept the right to remain silent, hoping I was a dark dream that would disappear in the morning. But such dreams do not disappear and Niran Gordon has not been told the truth. Nor has Steve. This pregnancy is a

431

miracle, Lauren said, and she will carry it alone. She will give birth in September.

Steve is convinced she will break against the first wave and wash back to him. Being without him feels like an amputation, she said. She expects to suffer phantom twinges but I believe she'll cope. Even in the bad days, terror shadowing her cat-green eyes, a blade flicking her skin, she had the world at her feet if only she had the courage to look.

Midnight has come and gone. A new dawn is turning and Kevin waits for me. In bed he is a bully, plunging me into pleasure so deep I fear I'll drown. Can you understand this ecstasy? Yes, I believe you can. I wandered into your bedroom one night when you and Daddy were making love. I didn't see much, bedclothes tumbled, your bodies twisted in strange positions. I was young, probably about six years old, yet I understood, or sensed the shivery excitement that sparked the air. Daddy told me to leave the room. His voice was harsh, breathless. It sounded different, not slow and tolerant, as I knew it to be. But he didn't scare me. And you, I remember your face flung back as if you were sunbathing, the languid fall of your limbs. I came into being from such rapture. All of us, four daughters conceived on a sigh, a moan, a deep capitulating surrender. We are women now. Would you recognise us? Would we recognise you? Daddy's face is clear in my mind, young and laughing — but you have aged alongside us, carrying, as you always did, the burden of your wayward girls.

We will never forget you. How can we when

you are the background music to our lives, easy and soothing, until an errant note scrapes against a nerve and we pause, as I do now, to breathe you in even deeper.

Good night, my lost loved ones,
Cathy

X

We do hope that you have enjoyed reading this large print book.

Did you know that all of our titles are available for purchase?

We publish a wide range of high quality large print books including:
Romances, Mysteries, Classics
General Fiction
Non Fiction and Westerns

Special interest titles available in large print are:
The Little Oxford Dictionary
Music Book
Song Book
Hymn Book
Service Book

Also available from us courtesy of Oxford University Press:
Young Readers' Dictionary
(large print edition)
Young Readers' Thesaurus
(large print edition)

For further information or a free brochure, please contact us at:
Ulverscroft Large Print Books Ltd.,
The Green, Bradgate Road, Anstey,
Leicester, LE7 7FU, England.
Tel: (00 44) 0116 236 4325
Fax: (00 44) 0116 234 0205

LOSING CHARLOTTE

Heather Clay

Born and raised at Four Corners, a thoroughbred horse farm in Kentucky, Knox Bolling has grown up within the comforting rhythms of family life and the cycle of growth that transforms the foals into yearlings. Deep ties bind her to her safe, if predictable life, but Knox knows that the world offers more — excitements that her tempestuous older sister, Charlotte, has within her grasp when she marries and moves away to Manhattan's West village. Then disaster strikes. Nothing could have prepared Knox for the loss of her sister. But the powerful bond remains, as her loyalty to Charlotte is profoundly and fatefully tested. Whilst she starts to come to terms with her elusive sister's life, Knox learns deeply moving lessons for her own . . .

CRAZY HEART

Thomas Cobb

At the age of fifty-seven, Bad Blake is on his last legs. His weight, his ticker, his liver, even his pick-up truck are all giving him trouble. A renowned songwriter and 'picker' who hasn't recorded in five years, Bad now travels the countryside on gigs that take him mostly to motels and bowling alleys. Enter Mo. Right. Can Bad stop living the life of a country-western song and tie a rope around his crazy heart?

WHILE MY SISTER SLEEPS

Barbara Delinsky

World-class runner Robin Snow is at the top of her game when her heart inexplicably fails and she sinks into a coma. As hope for her recovery fades, her family is left with a terrible choice — a choice which no-one should ever have to make. Faced with a heartbreaking decision, it is quiet, younger sister Molly who finds herself stepping out of Robin's shadow and into the heart of the family's terrible dilemma. Will they have the courage to do what is right?

IN FOCUS

Anna Jacobs

When a new feature on Pete Newbury's TV programme shows his adult image digitally transformed to that of a young child, Beth is shocked to realise that he's her 'baby' brother, who vanished without trace thirty-eight years ago. Her mother, never having recovered from the loss, desperately needs closure, but Pete is emphatic in not wanting to know his birth family. To further complicate matters, Beth finds herself falling in love with Pete's cousin and manager, Edward. At the same time Beth's runaway daughter reappears, complete with child, and Beth is terrified of losing her again. It's not easy to build bridges and bring families together after so many years and so much heartache, and she may lose the man she loves in the process . . .